THE
NIGHT
FERRY

THE
NIGHT
FERRY

LOTTE AND SØREN
HAMMER

*Translated from the Danish
by Charlotte Barslund*

BLOOMSBURY PUBLISHING
NEW YORK · LONDON · OXFORD · NEW DELHI · SYDNEY

BLOOMSBURY PUBLISHING
Bloomsbury Publishing Inc.
1385 Broadway, New York, NY 10018, USA

BLOOMSBURY, BLOOMSBURY PUBLISHING, and
the Diana logo are trademarks of Bloomsbury Publishing Plc

First published in 2014 in Denmark as *Den Sindssyge Polak* by Gyldenhal
First published in 2018 in Great Britain
First published in the United States 2018

ISBN: HB: 978-1-63557-162-2; EBOOK: 978-1-63557-163-9

Library of Congress Cataloging-in-Publication Data is available

A catalogue record for this book is available from the British Library

2 4 6 8 10 9 7 5 3 1

Typeset by Integra Software Services Pvt. Ltd.
Printed and bound in the U.S.A. by Berryville Graphics Inc., Berryville, Virginia

To find out more about our authors and books visit www.bloomsbury.com
and sign up for our newsletters.

Bloomsbury books may be purchased for business or promotional use.
For information on bulk purchases please contact Macmillan Corporate and
Premium Sales Department at specialmarkets@macmillan.com.

PART I

The Canal Tour Boat

CHAPTER 1

The man on the bridge looked across to the rococo marble church whose gilded cupola and dome reflected the sunlight. It was years since he had visited a city and the setting unnerved him. He liked empty places, preferably forests.

He turned and peered as far up the canal as he could before it turned east. The banks were grassy beneath scattered shrubs. A solitary birch had gained a foothold and was now growing in an unnatural curve. A few children were swimming at least fifty metres away, judging from the sound of their laughter. They wouldn't be able to describe him. He watched them for a while, then turned away.

The next time he looked up the canal, the tour boat had come into view. He took a sharp intake of breath. There were children on board, lots of children. They weren't supposed to be there, he hadn't been told about them. For a brief, heretical moment he considered abandoning his task, before gritting his teeth and clenching his fists. He owed her; it was his turn to help her, that was the deal. Loyalty, solidarity, friendship – nothing else mattered.

The jump wasn't significant and it was much easier than he had expected. He landed smoothly on the roof of a cabin at the back of the tour boat, leaped down onto the deck where he swiftly rolled under two rows of seats. Shortly afterwards he saw the three masts of the *Georg Stage* training ship glide past high above him while the tour boat's female guide explained in English the ship's purpose to the tourists. He wiped sweat from his brow with his forearm and slowly counted to ten as his pulse returned to normal. Then, with some difficulty due to the tight space, he wriggled his arms out of the straps of his rucksack, retrieved his knife and waited patiently as the boat started rocking. It was heading into Bomløbet from where it would change course with a broad sweep to starboard and sail north. The guide continued wearily to talk about the legendary submarine, *The Seal*, visible to their right, now a museum ship but once the Danish Armed Forces' contribution to the conflict in Iraq when Denmark supported the coalition by sending a submarine to a desert war. She repeated the scathing punchline with overemphasis: a submarine to a desert war!

The man lying between the seat rows knew his military history. He was aware that the proud *Seal* was over forty years old and largely junk when it was deployed in 2003. On its way to do battle – or at any rate while en route – the submarine's cooling system had broken down and the crew suffered several claustrophobic days of forty-five-degree heat. As soon as *The Seal* had completed its mission, it had been sent back to Denmark on a German freight ship as cargo. The Danish government, however, was happy and grandiose statements were made: Denmark had done her bit in the war on terror and dictatorship. Bravo. The political rhetoric was in the Premier League, the military hardware in the fourth division. It made him sick.

He pushed these thoughts aside and focused instead on an elongated cloud formation in the sky. When it had rotated by about ninety degrees, he stood and quickly moved up the centre aisle of the boat. He had killed his first two victims before the guide noticed him and started to scream. The captain managed to turn his head before he, too, was murdered, slumping over the wheel as his blood flooded the controls. The attacker then silenced the screaming guide by first gutting her and then stabbing her in the neck as she curled up, stunned, hugging herself inwards. He looked around and caught sight of the only other living adult on board, apart from him. She was Asian, Japanese or Chinese, he couldn't tell, and he didn't know whether to kill her or not. He wasn't going to harm the children, but he was in two minds about hurting her. She solved the problem for him by jumping overboard, but from her flailing arms and incoherent screams she would appear to be unable to swim. He chucked his knife into the water, thinking it was a waste of a good blade and that he had been fond of it.

He returned to his rucksack and quickly undressed, revealing the swimming trunks he had on underneath his clothes. The horrified children stared at him, many clinging to one another, but none of them said anything. He avoided making eye contact, put his clothes and shoes into his waterproof rucksack, swung it onto his back and adjusted the hip straps. He put on the flippers he had taken from the rucksack, popped the snorkel into his mouth and had one last look around before he let himself fall backwards across the gunwale into the canal.

He swam quickly away from the boat. When he reached the southern breakwater at Trekroner Fort, he scaled the rocks, plunged into the water on the other side and swam effortlessly onwards. He had a long haul ahead of him, approximately eight to ten kilometres, but the water was fifteen degrees Celsius so there was no risk of hypothermia. Besides, he had a supply of bananas, energy bars and drinking water, and he loved swimming.

CHAPTER 2

SUNDAY 22 AUGUST 2010, OFF THE PORT OF COPENHAGEN

The captain of the DFDS *Pearl Seaways* was tired. He rubbed his eyes to chase away the dots that danced at the edges of his field of vision, making minor adjustments to the wheel with his other hand to keep the ship on the right course. The ferry would turn before reversing up to the nearby DFDS Terminal quay, a manoeuvre he had executed so often that it had long since become routine. Even so, it was never a task he left to others. He suppressed a yawn and asked the first officer standing behind him, looking across the harbour, for another cup of coffee.

It had been a long night since they left Oslo, and the captain hadn't had enough sleep.

He had been woken at three a.m. One of the passengers, a four-year-old boy, was ill with a fever, headache and suspicious stiffness to his neck. The captain had got dressed in a hurry and rushed down to deck seven to see the child. After a brief conversation with Radio Medical Denmark, he decided to call for a doctor via the ship's public address system. His appeal disturbed the sleep of over one thousand passengers, but it was successful. Four doctors turned up at the Information Point soon afterwards, and one diagnosed the boy as having meningitis and insisted that he be admitted to hospital immediately. A helicopter was dispatched from Gothenburg while the captain stopped the ferry and positioned it so the helipad was in the optimum position for the evacuation. The operation went without a hitch, and although there was nothing more he could do, he had stayed on the bridge until just before five a.m. when he received a message from Gothenburg that the boy was out of danger, but that it had been *touch and go*. When the captain finally returned to his bed, he couldn't sleep; *touch and go* was a distressing thought and hard to dismiss.

He reached for his coffee only to discover that the cup was empty. For a moment he wondered whether he really had asked for more or whether the request had stayed unspoken. Then he glanced over his shoulder and saw the first officer frozen like a statue.

'Are you daydreaming? What's wrong?'

'The canal boat, can't you see it?'

Of course he could. His reply was somewhat sharp: 'What about it?'

'What's it doing out here? It shouldn't be this far out.'

The captain stared at the canal boat. It was coming straight at them and would need to change course soon. Without turning to him, he instructed the first officer: 'Use your binoculars.'

The bridge was five decks up with a semi-circular view out through the sloping panoramic windows. The first officer stepped closer to the windows and took his time with the binoculars.

The captain waited impatiently. The canal boat was approaching quickly; he didn't need binoculars to see that. He blasted five short warning signals on the horn, which even behind the inch-thick glass sounded brutally loud. A couple of stevedores in yellow hard hats and workwear standing on the distant quay turned around, but there was no reaction from the canal boat itself. The captain sounded the horn again, but there was still no response.

The first officer said: 'It looks like the captain is slumped over the wheel and ...' His voice trailed off and he continued to look through his binoculars.

'And what? I want facts.'

'There are children on board.'

'Time, distance, how fast is it approaching?'

'They aren't Danish children, they're Asian.'

The captain was forty-five years old and had reached the pinnacle of his career at an early age. He was in charge of a crew of almost two hundred, responsible for a million-kroner business, but more than anything he was a sailor, an exceptionally talented one – or he would never have been entrusted with this ship.

'Send a bosun with a walkie-talkie down to the front deck, and tell me how far away we are from that boat.'

Later, during the marine accident inquiry, the captain was praised to the skies. In an extremely stressful situation, he had realised that if he turned the wheel to starboard while increasing his ship's speed to the maximum possible, he would gain the few knots and degrees needed to allow the ferry to cut across the canal boat's direction of travel seconds before a collision occurred. In the event, however, things played out differently. The captain hadn't factored in the canal boat's leeway. The current and the waves meant that the boat's random course took the form of a curve rather than a straight line, and furthermore its speed had increased significantly in the last minute. No one could have foreseen that.

The bosun came back to report: *fifty metres to impact*, soon afterwards: *forty metres*, possibly less, and then: *shit, we won't make it!*

The canal boat disappeared below the captain's field of vision and all he could do for the last thirty seconds was wait. Both his hands clutched the wheel and he racked his brains for a prayer.

The bosun's announcement of the disaster was surprisingly subdued at first: *we cut it in half,* then it became hysterical, bordering on unintelligible: *turn off the propellers, for fuck's sake, they're being sucked into the propellers!*

The captain cut off communication. He knew that the two propellers were almost five metres in diameter each, but couldn't remember what they weighed.

There was no way he could comply with the bosun's plea. The laws of nature didn't work like that. For those in the water, it was too late.

CHAPTER 3

Detective Chief Superintendent Konrad Simonsen narrowed his eyes and looked across the harbour. The sea was teeming with activity. Fifteen to twenty vessels were taking part in the rescue operation. Most were RIBs with a crew of between two and four, drawn from organisations such as the Naval Home Guard, Falck Emergency Services, the Maritime Police and the Royal Danish Navy. Two pilot boats from the Port of Copenhagen were hauling major sections of the canal boat to the quay, while the RIBs concentrated on rescuing survivors or bringing bodies ashore.

On the quay half a dozen ambulances were parked, while two helicopters hovered over the harbour basin. One was a Sikorsky from the Coastguard, easily recognisable from its canary yellow entrance section and the oversized rescue symbol above the door. It flew approximately ten metres above the water, monitoring the area. High up above it, towards the Øresund, was the second helicopter, this one from a TV station. A woman from the Port of Copenhagen Authority was coordinating the operation. She was standing near the ambulances and every now and then he would hear her bark orders into her walkie-talkie.

Konrad Simonsen was in his early sixties, tall and broad with a calm demeanour and a direct manner, someone who looked exactly like what he was: a leader used to being obeyed in tense situations. He started towards the head of operations, but stopped a short distance away and waited without disturbing her. A few minutes later she found time to speak to him, her voice hoarse.

'Your forensic technicians and officers will have to wait until we're done. I don't want them going in now and adding to the confusion.'

'How much time are we talking about?'

'An hour, maybe two. I'll let you know.'

'Any survivors?'

'No, not yet.'

'How many fatalities, children and adults?'

'Don't know. The propellers acted like a giant food processor, so we can't tell yet.'

Konrad Simonsen nodded sympathetically, although he knew that it was rare for a ship's propellers to slice bodies into pieces. It had been known to happen, but it was unusual. The woman's exaggeration was a sign of the pressure she was under, he had seen it before.

'When I arrived it was chaos, even worse than it is now, but at least all the bodies or body parts have now been taken to Rigshospitalet. I hope. It's been a while since we last found … found anything. And I'm sorry for not having more time for you. Please join your colleague and wait with him.'

She gestured to the man at the city end of the quay, before she returned to her work.

Arne Pedersen was forty-three years old and had been working as an investigator with Copenhagen Police for the past ten years, and for most of these he had acted as Konrad Simonsen's right-hand man. This role had recently been formalised and he had been appointed Deputy Homicide Chief, which made him feel more proud .than he was willing to admit. He was lost in thought, and didn't immediately notice his boss.

'Oh, hello, Simon. Yes, I know I'm just standing here twiddling my thumbs, but we can't start yet. They were willing to let me in, but only me. Our people are having to wait outside the harbour area until it's been cleared. How about the TV photographer, did you get any more out of him?'

Earlier that day a cameraman had handed in some footage to the Homicide Department. He had been a passenger on the doomed Oslo ferry, and had gone out onto the deck for a cigarette while the ferry docked. From there he had noticed the canal boat and wondered what it was doing out in the harbour basin. Fetching his camera, he had zoomed in on the boat and seen at least three dead adults. He had continued filming roughly up until the collision with the ferry, and once he was ashore, he had gone straight to Police Headquarters. Konrad Simonsen had dispatched his deputy to the port the moment they had watched the film.

'No, he didn't have anything else. It's obviously breaking news on TV, but no one is calling it a crime yet. The Countess is at the Institute of Forensic Medicine, Klavs is coming back early from his course because of what's happened and will be back on duty tomorrow. Pauline is on holiday, as you know, and she isn't answering her mobile.'

These officers made up the inner circle of the Homicide Department and were the staff with whom Konrad Simonsen preferred to work.

The Countess, whose real name was Nathalie von Rosen, was Konrad Simonsen's wife. The marriage was relatively recent, and they had so far managed to combine their work and private lives without any major problems. Klavs Arnold had joined the Homicide Department a few years ago when he moved from Esbjerg to Copenhagen, and was currently away at a seminar in Odense. At barely thirty years old, Pauline Berg was the most youthful member of the inner circle, but her behaviour had been causing problems ever since she had been the victim of an abduction in 2007. There were long periods where she struggled at work or simply didn't work at all.

'Can't we just let Pauline enjoy her holiday?' Arne Pedersen asked. 'I'm sure she needs it.'

It was tactfully put, but his meaning was clear. Konrad Simonsen snapped back: 'If I thought so, I wouldn't have tried phoning her. But enough about her. Do you know if the canal boat has sunk?'

Instead of replying, Arne Pedersen took the few steps towards the water's edge and pointed.

Half the canal boat, its bow section, was swaying against the side of the quay. The boat had been cut through roughly midship, its solid wooden planks looking as if they had been chopped in half by a giant axe. Several of the white plastic passenger seats were missing.

'The other half, the heavy end with the engine, has sunk.'

'If it's at all possible, I want it salvaged today. Make sure our forensic technicians know that, so they can hire divers and any specialist equipment they might need.'

'I've already done it. Everything is in place. All we're waiting for is permission to go in.'

'Good, anything else?'

'No. The RIBs are picking up what's left and it's not much fun to watch, so I'm happy to keep my distance.'

'I believe they're about done.'

'Glad to hear it.'

'Do we know the number of adult fatalities?'

'Only those we both saw on the cameraman's footage, so three, I presume. But I haven't had it confirmed. What's that?'

Arne Pedersen pointed to the northern breakwater on Trekroner Fort, one of two long narrow rocky structures shielding the harbour. Members of the emergency services had been positioned at short intervals along the breakwater, and were scanning the harbour basin. Konrad Simonsen couldn't see anything remarkable; his deputy would appear to have better eyesight.

'Something's happening over there,' he insisted.

Simonsen left him and walked back towards the ambulances. On his way he passed a Falck rescue worker. She said quietly: 'We found a survivor, possibly two. Children.'

CHAPTER 4

It was funny how one thing led to another, it seemed to the man, as he stared through the windscreen and smiled, though there was nothing to smile about. He glanced at the woman driving the car, and remembered that the last time he had done her a favour, things hadn't gone according to plan, which was why they were sitting here now. To his surprise, his memories sharpened and the incident came back vividly to him though it was two years ago now. He hadn't thought about it much recently; in truth he had completely forgotten all about it.

He had shown the young woman the knife, and she and the child had come with him without a fight. They had walked through the dunes while the little girl picked flowers for her mother, pink things that crept meagrely across the sand. When they reached the hollow, he had tied the mother up carefully so she wouldn't bruise if she struggled. He had brought four stakes with him, which he had hammered into the sand. The rope restraining her arms he had slipped through the sleeves of her anorak, he had used her shoelaces to tie her feet to the stakes. And he had a stroke of luck: she had been wearing a skirt, which made everything much easier.

'Open your eyes and pay attention. You've already been warned to stay away from Mads Eggert, so now you have to learn the hard way. Are you listening to me, Juli?'

That was what he had said to her, those very words, and the little girl had sat some distance away, digging in the sand with a yellow shovel. He remembered that clearly, but he didn't want to think about the rest; things had gone wrong, an accident had happened. Something had been impossible to foresee.

He had tidied up after himself and called the emergency services on her mobile, pressing the keys with her thumb. There was nothing else he could do.

He brushed the memory aside.

'Did you have to wait long for me?'

The woman nearly shook her head, but stopped herself in time. She had gone to Rødovre to pick up some things before driving to the beach, but he didn't need to know that.

'I had plenty of time, but I lingered over a cup of coffee at a café, so I was on the beach for less than an hour.'

The man hadn't drunk coffee for years, he barely remembered the taste.

'Are you looking forward to going home to your forest?' she asked.

He said yes, he was looking forward to that.

CHAPTER 5

SUNDAY 22 AUGUST 2010, INSTITUTE OF FORENSIC MEDICINE, UNIVERSITY OF COPENHAGEN

The Countess leaned against the wall in Post-mortem Room B. It was the biggest of the Institute's four post-mortem rooms and normally used for their cases so was generally known as the Homicide Room.

She was a woman in her mid-forties, and everyone regarded her as professional, industrious and pleasant. In addition to her, seven other people were present. There was the pathologist – a young woman the Countess didn't remember meeting before – and two photographers – one from the Institute and one from the police – an orderly, an investigator from her own department, the Institute's departmental head and a Japanese man of indeterminable age who like her was resting his back against the wall, only a metre away from her. Everyone was wearing gowns, sterile white boot covers, hairnets, and masks over their mouths.

The body of a Japanese child lay on a metal table in the middle of the room. The orderly had just opened up the boy, lifted out his organs and placed them on the post-mortem table at the back of the room. Now he was busy cutting away the skin at the neck. When he had done so, he peeled the skin up over the skull, exposing the scalp and forehead, and started sawing through the skull in order to remove the brain. The saw hummed at a low frequency. In the old days it must have sounded shriller, the Countess thought, because in-house the saw was known as the Howling Nun.

The Japanese man cleared his throat. She looked at him, expecting him to be about to say something, but he didn't. He slipped back behind his impenetrable mask, and she couldn't decide if he was closely watching the post-mortem, or if he was deep inside a world of his own.

The child's body was turned over onto its stomach and photographed from several angles and distances. Six deep parallel gashes from the shoulder to the shins were evidence of the boy's encounter with a propeller from the Oslo ferry. The departmental head explained the cause of the lacerations to the pathologist. She nodded, asked a few questions, then walked to her desk over in the corner and mumbled a few sentences into her Dictaphone. Meanwhile the Countess tried and failed to make eye contact with Hans Holgersen, a departmental head at the Institute, a man she knew very well and liked.

He was a consultant forensic pathologist and she had met him often at post-mortems or at crime scenes. For many years he had been the legendary Professor Arthur Elvang's closest colleague. In stark contrast to his former boss, however, Holgersen was easy and uncomplicated to work with.

At the back of the room, the pathologist was taking tissue samples from the boy's organs. These would later be described clinically and the data recorded in a table. This was standard procedure and they never deviated from it. While the pathologist worked with the organs, the orderly applied ink to the boy's fingers with a small roller in order to take his fingerprints.

The Countess finally made eye contact with Hans Holgersen and signalled, could she please have two minutes? He said a few words to the pathologist, who joined them immediately.

The woman took off her mask. She was curvaceous, but seemed strangely androgynous in her white gown, bare shins and boots. Now that the mask no longer covered half her face, her fatigue became obvious. She peeled off her latex gloves with practised ease and threw them in a perfect arc into a bin in the corner.

The Countess began: 'Please give me some information about how the adults in the boat died, even if it's just preliminary. We haven't even had it confirmed yet how many fatalities we're dealing with.'

The woman hesitated and looked reluctant.

'It's not my job to give you that information.'

But she then appeared to have a change of heart or perhaps Hans Holgersen had signalled to her without the Countess seeing. She ushered the Countess out of the room, muttering, 'OK, follow me, but remember it's just preliminary.' Walking quickly, she took them to an office, where she chucked her gown into a laundry basket, changed her shoes and took out a small notebook from a desk drawer.

'The dead children can be divided into four groups: those who died from injuries they sustained when the canal boat collided with the ferry, those who drowned, those who were caught in the ship's propellers, and finally those who bled to death in the water from their injuries.'

The Countess nodded without reiterating that the children weren't her primary concern. The pathologist continued: 'We have fifteen children, all school-age, about eleven, we think, and they're all Asian.'

This didn't match the head count the Homicide Department had carried out when they watched the cameraman's video. Two of the children were missing. The pathologist explained: 'There are two survivors. One has been admitted to Intensive Care and her condition is critical. I don't know where the other one is right now, but he's uninjured.'

This was news to the Countess, and welcome news given the extent of the tragedy.

'What about the adults, what do we know about them?'

'They're in the basement. It might be some time before we get round to working on them.'

'But you've been down to have a look at them?'

She nodded.

'Five adults, an Asian female in her thirties who drowned, two Caucasian men and two Caucasian women, who would all appear to have been stabbed to death. The two women and one of the men are around thirty, the other man in his fifties, and he's … in several pieces.'

The Countess interrupted her.

'Five adults, not four, are you sure?'

Even she could hear the implication behind this, that the pathologist couldn't count, but the Countess had to know.

'Five, yes, and four of them have been identified. Only one woman remains unidentified.'

The pathologist checked her notepad and started reeling off the names. First the captain, then the guide, then the Japanese woman and finally the name of the male passenger.

The Countess felt as though she had been punched in the stomach.

'Please would you repeat that last name?'

'Jonas Ziegler. He had his driver's licence on him.'

'I want to see the victims. Now!'

The pathologist hesitated and the Countess made a beeline for the door, no longer caring about professional courtesy. The pathologist chased after her, then led the way down the corridor to the left, clearly unhappy with the situation. The Countess ignored her lukewarm protests.

It was cold in the basement, barely more than five degrees. The pathologist shivered, but the Countess didn't feel the temperature. She felt as though she was burning up inside.

The room they had entered was large, uninviting and flooded in a sharp neon glare from the ceiling light. The bodies were lined up on wheeled steel trolleys, each one covered with a white sheet.

The Countess marched straight past the first bodies, which were clearly those of children. She stopped at the adults and waited for the pathologist to join her.

'The body of the woman who has yet to be identified. Where is she?'

The pathologist pointed to the second-to-last trolley.

'Would you like me to …?'

'Yes, please.'

The pathologist moved closer and drew back the sheet from the body's face.

The Countess thanked her and told her with forced calm that she was able to identify the dead woman, but that she needed to make a call first. She took out her mobile and rang Konrad, but he didn't answer. Next she contacted the Homicide Department and told them to make sure he called her back immediately. Whatever meeting he was in had to be interrupted, no matter how important it was. He rang her back less than thirty seconds later.

She told him: 'Pauline Berg is dead, stabbed to death. She was on the canal boat.'

CHAPTER 6

MONDAY 23 AUGUST 2010, POLICE HEADQUARTERS

The conference hall was packed. Konrad Simonsen noticed that many of the police officers, some of whom had travelled far – even all the way from Jutland – had to stand. No one had ordered them to be here, no one had organised anything; the officers had come to Police Headquarters this morning out of a shared desire to help if they could. It was very rare for police officers in Denmark to be killed, but when it did happen, the reaction among the force was one of deep solidarity: everyone volunteered to do whatever they could, cancelling holidays, time off, nightshifts, overtime, waiving any kind of employment rights.

Simonsen knew many of the officers who were present in addition to the Homicide Department's regular staff. However, most he hadn't seen before, especially the many young officers who met his gaze, eager to get to work. A few faces surprised him, including that of his own daughter Anna Mia, who was sitting in the middle of the hall with half a dozen young officers from Vestegnens Police.

She was supposed to have gone on holiday today with her boyfriend, ten days in Prague, but must have cancelled it. She smiled at him. He nodded awkwardly in response, feeling uncomfortable. Poul Troulsen had also come. He was a retired officer, ex-Homicide Department, a dry, methodical and efficient man whose qualities Konrad Simonsen had only truly appreciated after his departure. He could certainly use them now.

There was also the senior police management, including the Deputy Commissioner and the National Police Commissioner. They sat in the back row, trying and failing to blend in.

The Countess rose from her chair and joined him. She whispered that he might want to open with a minute's silence to honour the dead. He knew it was the right thing to do, although he was keen to get to work. He had asked his staff to turn up at seven-thirty that morning, in plenty of time for him, or rather for Arne Pedersen, to have officers on the streets lining the canal boat's route exactly twenty-four hours after its departure. Many people had fixed routines, and this was the best way of finding potential witnesses.

The problem was that they now had approximately five times the number of officers they needed, which was ultimately a good thing but meant they took longer to organise. Simonsen solved the problem by rearranging his agenda, then silenced the room by raising his hands. He began by complying with the Countess's suggestion and improvised a few sombre words about yesterday's tragedy and its victims. It wasn't his forte, he thought, as he folded his hands and bowed his head fractionally so that he could still see the large clock on the back wall. Its second hand moved with annoying slowness.

Konrad Simonsen's last twenty-four hours had been tough both professionally and emotionally. The worst part was early last night when he and the Countess had visited Pauline Berg's parents to tell them that their daughter had been killed.

Such visits were invariably one of the most distressing aspects of the job, and the fact that they knew the deceased personally didn't make it any easier. Later there had been press briefings, and it was past midnight before he and the Countess could finally return home to Søllerød. Then he was woken up in the middle of the night by a call from Kurt Melsing, the head of Forensic Services, with information about the dead male passenger. Strictly speaking it wasn't within Melsing's remit to gather such information and he didn't explain how he had obtained it, but given the seriousness of the situation, it didn't matter. The victim was a thirty-four-year-old shop assistant from north-west Copenhagen and his name was Jonas Ziegler. Konrad Simonsen already knew this, but Kurt Melsing could add something more: Jonas Ziegler was a former forestry worker with Halsnæs Forestry Commission and in that capacity he had been in contact with Pauline Berg. This connection was the reason Kurt Melsing had called Simonsen in the middle of the night.

Pauline Berg had been obsessed with a death that everyone else knew was from natural causes, but which she stubbornly insisted on treating as a murder. She had spent most of her spare time, as well as quite a lot of her time at work, investigating it, and this had brought her into contact with Jonas Ziegler. Just as she had pleaded with him – in vain – to do countless times, Konrad Simonsen was now forced to investigate Pauline Berg's non-existent murder case more closely.

The Countess had also been woken up.

'Was it the name Jonas Ziegler that made you suspect Pauline might be among the dead?' he asked her.

'Probably, does it matter?'

His wife sounded sad. He made no reply and they lay for a while in the darkness, neither of them able to sleep. She asked the obvious question.

'What are you thinking about?'

'Whether you, Arne and Klavs are too emotionally involved in this case, and whether I should replace you.'

She jolted upright but it was some time before she said anything.

'What about you? What about your emotions?'

'That won't be a problem.'

She gasped, 'Screw you, Simon!' It was extremely rare for her to swear. She lay down again, this time with her back to him, and hissed: 'Sometimes you can be a real bastard, you know.'

In the hall the second hand completed its sweep and Konrad Simonsen ended the silence with a brief 'thank you'. Then he handed over the organisation of the search for witnesses to Arne Pedersen, and immediately corrected himself: Deputy Homicide Chief Arne Pedersen. Many people smiled, including Pedersen himself.

The Deputy Homicide Chief took over, and Konrad Simonsen seized his chance to drag the Countess, Poul Troulsen and Klavs Arnold out of the room. Arne could easily manage without them. Outside in the corridor, Simonsen didn't waste any time. The Countess was given the biggest task. He handed her a map.

'Take all the officers you need, but leave a handful of the most experienced investigators with me. Make sure you get footage from every single CCTV camera along the streets I've marked in red, and any adjacent streets, if you have enough staff. And do it quickly, preferably today. You need to secure everything: not just our own CCTV, but also footage from petrol stations, industrial areas, shopping centres, schools, cashpoints and foreign exchanges, banks, hotels, restaurants, taxis, buses, train stations, platforms, speed cameras and anything else I may have forgotten. In short, all the footage there is. It's donkey work on a massive scale, but it's crucial. And get hold of Malte and tell him to organise the footage chronologically and upload it so we can watch everything on our own computers.'

The Countess protested half-heartedly.

'Malte is on study leave, his exams are coming up, but I can ask our IT people to make us a GIS application.'

Malte Borup was the Homicide Department's student intern. He had almost completed his computing degree and the time he had had left with them was limited.

'That won't do, IT takes forever to get anything done. If you have to pull strings to get him a special arrangement with the university, then do so, but get him in here. I need him.'

Klavs Arnold interjected: 'And they're crap at hacking in IT.'

The Countess accepted this with a curt: 'OK, anything else?' There wasn't and she returned to the hall.

The next person to be issued with orders was Poul Troulsen. Konrad Simonsen muttered a few half-hearted sentences about how good it was to have him back, then gave him a quick summary of the case.

'It's too soon to say if the killer is among the dead. It's a possibility we can't yet exclude—'

Here Poul Troulsen interrupted him.

'I thought a child had survived?'

'The boy is in shock and can't be interviewed. He's at the Japanese Embassy. They've promised to contact the Danish Foreign Ministry once they know something.'

Poul Troulsen looked unhappy. Simonsen continued: 'If the killer or killers are stowaways, if I can put it like that, then the big question is: how did he or they get on the boat? There's nothing to suggest they embarked at the departure point at Gammel Strand. We know this from several witnesses, including the woman in the ticket office. But that's not your only task. You also need to find out everything you can about that canal boat, including its technical specifications, layout, speed, public address system, rescue procedures in an emergency and so on and so forth. Start by contacting the shipping company. Get yourself a new warrant card if you need one, find yourself a vacant office and take as many officers to help you as you want.'

Poul Troulsen repeated pedantically and with intolerable slowness these instructions, whereupon he declined the warrant card, the office and, initially, the staff. Konrad Simonsen continued to maintain his smile, but heaved a sigh of relief the moment he was free to leave.

The police officers had started pouring out of the hall. Simonsen pulled Klavs Arnold aside a few steps further down the corridor so they could speak undisturbed and told him about Jonas Ziegler and his former employment with Halsnæs Forestry Commission. The Jutlander spotted its relevance immediately. He had accompanied Pauline Berg on a trip to Melby Common where she was due to meet with the forestry worker only for him to fail to show. Klavs had gone with Pauline purely to make her happy, to humour her in her delusion. He didn't recognise the name Jonas Ziegler, but he did remember something else.

'Pauline referred to him as a "forestry worker" not a "forester". I'm sure of it.'

'Forester, forest worker, ranger, who cares? But if you think it might be significant, then look into it.'

Klavs Arnold made no reply. Then he suddenly appeared to grasp the implication of his task.

'So do you think that Pauline, in spite of everything … that she somehow …?'

The words got stuck in his throat, and Simonsen dismissed him brusquely. It was too early to say.

'This is going to cause a shit storm, Simon!' he protested.

Konrad Simonsen ignored this outburst.

'Start by searching Pauline's flat and, most importantly, get hold of her telephone records. And see if she made any notes on her … investigation. She probably did, so find them. When you discover something, report back to me. And one other thing: please would you take Anna Mia and maybe a few colleagues from her station with you? I'm not happy that she's here, but if she's with you, then at least I know what she's doing.'

Klavs Arnold frowned.

'Surely your daughter is entitled to volunteer? After all, she knew Pauline well.'

Simonsen jabbed a finger at him.

'Didn't you understand what I just said?'

The Jutlander nodded.

'Then get a move on.'

CHAPTER 7

Konrad Simonsen's day passed relatively smoothly. He was consulted only on critical developments. Malte Borup turned up about nine, not minding much about having to put his studies on hold in order to help the investigation. Simonsen brought him up to speed – it didn't take long – after which the student intern got to work.

They had soon compiled preliminary CVs for the four adults who, in addition to Pauline Berg, had been on the canal boat. The Japanese schoolteacher's was straightforward. She and three other teachers had travelled to Copenhagen with a group of Year Five students as a part of a cultural exchange programme between Japan and Denmark. The visiting children and their teachers came from the town of Sendai, north of Tokyo, near the Pacific Ocean, and they had been in Copenhagen for nine days, since Thursday the previous week.

Several witnesses had seen the teacher jump overboard near Søndre Toldbod, and shortly afterwards the canal boat had turned ninety degrees and sailed towards Yderhavnen. This confirmed their theory that the teacher had been so terrified of the killer she had chosen to jump into the sea. Three witnesses had tried swimming to her rescue, but none had reached her before she disappeared under the surface. That evidence, taken along with the other witness statements, established that everything seemed normal on the boat when it sailed along Stadsgraven, and allowed the location of the killings to be determined with considerable accuracy.

Pauline Berg, Jonas Ziegler, the captain and the tourist guide had all been killed near Søndre Toldbod, at about nine-thirty. The Japanese teacher's body was found at Langelinie just after eleven o'clock, one and a half hours after she had jumped overboard.

Neither the tourist guide nor the captain appeared to be of interest to the investigation. The captain was fifty-two years old and lived with his family just outside the capital. The tourist guide was a twenty-three-year-old woman who studied English at the University of Copenhagen and lived alone in a shared ownership flat in the city centre. Neither had a criminal record and Konrad Simonsen found it hard to see them as anything other than collateral damage. Nevertheless their lives would still be scrutinised in the coming days, and things might well change – it had happened before – but his conclusion so far was that if the killer had any kind of meaningful motive, his target was Pauline Berg and/or Jonas Ziegler.

Ziegler was born in 1977 and had grown up near Halsnæs. After leaving school, he began an apprenticeship with Frederiksværk Steelworks in 1992. He qualified as a blacksmith and worked at the steelworks until 2002, when he went on long-term sick leave due to back problems. In January 2003 Jonas Ziegler started working as a landscape gardener for the Works Department of Frederiksværk Council. Two years later he changed employer, but not profession, and started working for Halsnæs Forestry Commission. He stayed with them until the autumn of 2009, when he changed career again and became a shop assistant with the Tune branch of the supermarket chain Dagligkæden, where he was still employed at the time of his death. Except for a drink-driving conviction in 1998, Ziegler had no criminal record. In November 2009 he had moved from Halsnæs to north-west Copenhagen.

Simonsen read the information about Jonas Ziegler twice before skimming a series of appendices, which didn't add anything significant. Just as he finished, Klavs Arnold called. He was in Pauline's flat in Rødovre where he had been updated by the other investigators. There had been three telephone conversations in the last two weeks between Pauline Berg and Jonas Ziegler. The first two times she had called him, the last he had called her. On Sunday 22 August they had arrived together at Gammel Strand and got on the canal boat. They had sat down next to each other about halfway down the ship.

Konrad Simonsen thanked him and had barely rung off before Kurt Melsing called with preliminary post-mortem reports. Based on DNA tests of the stab wounds inflicted on the four bodies, it was possible to determine the sequence of the killings, as the knife had transferred blood from each victim to the next. Jonas Ziegler had been killed first by a single stab wound to his throat. The angle of the wound showed it had been inflicted while he was sitting down and the killer standing up.

Pauline Berg had then been stabbed in the back twice, with one cut penetrating her heart. She had had time to stand up before she died, but had then collapsed and fallen between the seats, which explained why she hadn't been visible on the TV cameraman's footage. The next victim was the captain, whose throat had been cut. He had been sitting down and the killer had attacked him from behind. Finally the tour guide had been killed while standing up, as she had been gutted before being stabbed in the neck. The knife was likely to be an Army combat knife, but they wouldn't be able to say for sure until later.

Kurt Melsing's information proved that the killer wasn't one of the four victims, a conclusion that was confirmed when Konrad Simonsen received a brief report informing him that the surviving Japanese boy had described a man who had stabbed the Danish adults with a knife and had left the boat after the teacher had jumped overboard. The report made it clear that the Danish Police would be able to interview the boy at some point, but not immediately, and that it would have to be in Japan.

As he always did when he wanted a break, Simonsen took up position by the window in his office and looked down at the street without taking in anything. His mind was elsewhere.

Pauline and the other victims wouldn't benefit from his grief or regret, and it was his right to structure his investigation so that unhelpful feelings didn't interfere. He expected his closest colleagues to show commitment and passion, and if they couldn't do that, he had no use for them. It was as simple as that.

He bore his own pep talk in mind when, shortly afterwards, he began writing his report on Pauline Berg's obsession with Juli Denissen, whose death Pauline had regarded as murder. It was a case he had frequently wished would go to hell, only for it now to become relevant; it might well prove to be the vital clue to solving the canal boat murders. He remembered most of the facts and only occasionally had to look up any information, which eased his work-load considerably.

Pauline Berg had started working for the Homicide Department in 2006 at the age of twenty-seven. At that point she had been industrious, talented, willing to learn and incredibly ambitious. This lasted for about a year until she was abducted and held in a bunker in Nordsjælland by a man who was a suspect in a police investigation. She was freed eventually, barely alive, but mentally had paid a high price for her survival. After an extended period of sick leave, she had returned to the Homicide Department. Physically she had recovered, but her personality had changed. She would do exactly what she wanted, taking orders only when it suited her, and had acquired a pronounced anti-authoritarian attitude. She had attempted suicide at least once.

She had been deeply committed to investigating and solving this one death, possibly the only case she really cared about after her return to work. During Pauline Berg's abduction, a young woman had contacted the Homicide Department with information that proved pivotal for the investigation. That woman was Juli Denissen and she lived in Frederiksværk. Barely one year later, on 10 July 2008, she died on Melby Common, a picturesque area overlooking the waters of the Kattegat. She was found by Jonas Ziegler, who had been working in the forest a little deeper into the countryside and had heard the cries of the woman's child. He had called the emergency services, as presumably had Juli Denissen herself, as her prints were found on her mobile, but by the time the ambulance arrived, she was dead.

There was nothing suspicious about the cause of Juli Denissen's death: she had died from a brain haemorrhage, something the post-mortem at Hillerød Hospital subsequently revealed she was predisposed to. A brain haemorrhage provoked by a massive panic attack, true, but in all likelihood this was something that would have killed her sooner or later.

Subsequently the Homicide Department had been contacted by a handful of Juli Denissen's friends and relatives who were convinced that she had been the victim of a crime. It was pure chance that Simonsen had asked Pauline to deal with them, the intention being to make them realise they were barking up the wrong tree and then get rid of them. It was possibly the biggest mistake of his career.

Pauline had swallowed the conspiracy theory hook, line and sinker and stubbornly insisted on investigating the case, even after Simonsen had persuaded the other members of the self-appointed pressure group that Juli Denissen's death was from natural causes. He had achieved this mainly by persuading a retired professor of forensic medicine and former head of the Institute of Forensics, Arthur Elvang, to review the woman's post-mortem report with them. Only Pauline Berg refused to be convinced. She had become obsessed with the case to the enormous irritation of the Homicide Department, especially Simonsen who hadn't been able to get his junior officer to abandon her delusion by using either stick or carrot.

Finally everyone, himself included, had given up and learned to accept Pauline Berg's fixation on the death of Juli Denissen. The only alternative was to sack her, but senior police management had made it clear that wasn't an option, and Simonsen had never seriously considered doing so in any case. Instead he and his closest colleagues would take turns, in their own time, to 'help' Pauline in her futile efforts to solve the phantom case. That way at least they knew what she was doing. In the Homicide Department the case was known as the 'Juli-non-case' – usually followed by an ironic smile.

Konrad Simonsen folded his hands under his chin. He was having second thoughts about the 'non-case' now, of course, but as he wrote his review, he had the oddest feeling that these doubts had briefly surfaced in him once before. Only, to his frustration, he couldn't remember when or where.

He finished his report, allocated it a case number and circulated it to a handful of colleagues.

Fifteen minutes later there was a cautious knock on his door. He barked, 'Enter.'

A young woman, tall and square-built with black hair and strong features, appeared in the doorway.

'Please may I sit down?' she asked in a deep, accented voice.

Simonsen furrowed his brow.

'That very much depends on who you are and what you want.'

To his surprise, she gave a disarming smile and sat down without permission. The change of expression transformed her appearance, making her almost pretty.

'I'm sorry, but my feet are killing me. My name is Anica Buch and I've recently joined Glostrup Police Violent Crimes Unit. Today I've volunteered to look for witnesses as have many of my colleagues. One day I hope to work for you, but don't worry about that now. I promise to leave soon.'

'I'm not worried. What do you want?'

She told him. He had just circulated his report on Pauline Berg and she had read it on her boss's computer – entirely above board, she stressed. She had come to see him now, in her break, because her superior had banned her from emailing the Chief of the Homicide Department, explaining it wasn't the done thing, certainly not for an officer as junior as she was.

Simonsen interjected with a small smile: 'But he didn't ban you from coming here in person?'

'That's right, he never said anything about that.'

'So what have you come to tell me?'

'That there are no autopsy facilities at Hillerød Hospital, so when you write about the young woman who died on Melby Common ... Juli Denissen ... saying that her post-mortem was carried out there, then that's wrong. It's probably irrelevant, but at least now you know.'

Konrad Simonsen was disappointed. She had stirred his curiosity and he had nurtured a faint hope that her contribution would be game-changing. But she was mistaken. During busy periods Hillerød Hospital was used as back-up for Rigshospitalet and he knew that from the most authoritative source you could find: Professor Arthur Elvang himself. He told Anica Buch this and expected her to back down, possibly a little shame-faced. She didn't.

'Whoever told you that was wrong. What busy periods? The summer of 2008 when Juli Denissen died? The post-mortem capacity is limited solely by available rooms, not pathologists. At Rigshospitalet they can perform up to fourteen post-mortems a day. Surely even you can see that it doesn't make sense to use another hospital?'

He stood up without concealing his sense of rising irritation. He had a copy of Juli Denissen's post-mortem report somewhere. It took him five minutes to find it. Anica Buch remained fixed in her chair throughout. With a mixture of annoyance at the interruption and satisfaction at being right, he slammed down the post-mortem report in front of her. The logo for Hillerød Hospital was clearly visible in the top corner.

And still Anica Buch refused to back down.

'That only proves the post-mortem never took place or that the report was written on the wrong letterhead. Because it would have to have been done in Copenhagen, Odense, Aarhus or abroad. That's it, the end – there are no other options.'

Simonsen sat down again.

'The end!?'

She nodded somewhat hesitantly, but confirmed it. 'Yes, *the end*. Even though he was the Homicide Chief, and she was just—'

Here he interrupted her.

'OK, you sort it out then. Contact the pathologist, his name is on the report, and find out what happened. You can work in there.' He pointed to a room adjacent to his office that had been adapted for him a few years ago when he had returned to work after heart surgery. She got up, moved towards the annexe, then turned around.

'My boss will go mental if I'm not back in fifteen minutes, and he'll be even angrier if he finds out that I'm here.'

Konrad Simonsen reassured her that there was no need to worry. No one would go mental.

She came back twenty minutes later and sat down without interrupting his reading. He looked up from his papers with a brief, 'Well?'

Her summary was short, precise and with a total absence of bragging proved that she had been right. The name of the pathologist concerned was Hans Arne Tholstrup. He and his wife, who was also a pathologist, had been working at the Institute of Forensic Medicine in Copenhagen until the spring of 2008, when she left him for her lover. For that reason he was granted a year's leave during which time he was employed by Hillerød Hospital, where on 10 July 2008 he received the body of Juli Denissen and declared her dead.

Nordsjællands Police, however, insisted that a post-mortem be carried out on the young woman, partly because of her age and partly because of the circumstances of her death. At that point Hans Arne Tholstrup's wife had left her lover, and he was now very much interested in seeing his wife again. He contacted his former workplace, and was permitted to carry out the post-mortem at Rigshospitalet rather than at Hillerød. He did so the following day, and the day after that he wrote his post-mortem report, but by then he had returned to his office in Hillerød, which explained why he had used that hospital's letterhead.

'Two student pathologists also attended. I've spoken to one of them, and she remembers the post-mortem clearly because the circumstances were unique.'

'You didn't speak to Tholstrup himself?'

'He's dead. Killed himself last January when his new girlfriend left him.'

Konrad Simonsen said nothing. He was having second thoughts again. His earlier nagging doubts could have been prompted by the post-mortem that Anica Buch had just looked into. It made sense if that discrepancy had been lurking at the back of his mind, but nevertheless he felt there was something else, something more important. He got up to show her out.

She said: 'The divers working in the Port of Copenhagen on raising the other half of the canal boat ...'

'What about them?'

'Have you made sure they also check the seabed?'

'What for?'

'The children's mobiles. Perhaps they filmed something we ... you can use.'

He looked at her. She came across as a busybody, verging on the offensive with her know-it-all manner and her suggestion of measures that were obviously already in hand. It was almost as if she wanted him to slap her down. At length he said: 'You have an irritating manner. Perhaps you should work on your attitude.'

'You're not the first person to tell me that.'

'And you've ignored them?'

'No, I try. I try every day.'

30

She smiled and seemed sincere.

'Send me an email with your personal information, and thank you for your help,' Simonsen said.

He closed the door behind her and his thoughts returned to Arthur Elvang. Why had the professor tricked him into believing a lie?

CHAPTER 8

MONDAY 23 AUGUST 2010, POLICE HEADQUARTERS

The second Japanese child – a girl of eleven – who had been pulled from the wreckage died late that afternoon, bringing the total number of victims to twenty-one.

Konrad Simonsen received the news of the child's death without betraying much emotion. He broke off his phone conversation and shared the information with Arne Pedersen, who was sitting at the other side of his desk. Simonsen checked his watch. It was almost five o'clock.

'Poul Troulsen is on his way here. You'll review his results with him. I'll be back in an hour and by then he really must have finished, even if you have to throw him out.'

Arne Pedersen didn't complain about this task though they both knew it would take a great deal of patience and that Simonsen's reasons for skipping the review were unlikely to be purely professional. As indeed they were not.

'I'm going out for an early dinner and some time to myself. Make sure Troulsen comes back in early tomorrow morning, I'll need him. Also you yourself should expect to work late tonight. I'll come in tomorrow to liaise with Troulsen. Any questions?'

Pedersen shook his head; the proposal sounded fair.

Poul Troulsen had carried out a first-class piece of investigation: detailed, systematic, bordering on obsessive, and his presentation was as pedantic as Arne Pedersen had feared.

The shipping company had made a canal boat and skipper available to the retired police officer, and on four occasions the two of them had sailed the route taken by the ill-fated tour boat: the first two in order for Poul Troulsen to form initial impressions and calculate timings, the last two to work out whether the attacker could have jumped onto the boat while it was in motion, and if so where that could have happened.

Troulsen had brought along a naval chart of the Port of Copenhagen and had marked the canal boat's route in red pen, ending in a cross on the water between Søndre Toldbod and Nyholm, while a blue line indicated the rest of the voyage the boat should have completed.

After this briefing Arne Pedersen dismissed him for the day, but kept hold of the naval chart in order to repeat the essence of his investigation to Simonsen and the Countess when they returned from dinner an hour later.

'The only way the killer could have boarded the canal boat is by jumping onto it from a bridge. Unless he was already on board when the trip began, and I have multiple witnesses saying that he wasn't.'

He explained that the canal boat had sailed under six bridges on its red route, four on the mainland side and two on the Amager Island side, but the first four bridges were in central Copenhagen and so busy that there was no chance of anyone jumping on board a canal boat unnoticed.

A Belgian photojournalist had taken a series of pictures of the canal boat going under the last bridge on the mainland side. He was in Denmark to write an article for his magazine about the Danes and their bicycling habits and had photographed a group of cyclists crossing the bridge with Christiansborg Parliament and the Stock Exchange in the background, and the canal boat going under the bridge in the foreground. There were no jumping men in his pictures. That left two bridges, one spanning the water between Arsenaløen and Frederiksholm, which had no name, and then

Battery Bridge between Frederiksholm and Nyholm. A road called Danneskjold-Samsøes Allé crossed both bridges. Pedersen placed his finger on the map.

'He jumped on board from Battery Bridge, Troulsen and I are sure of it. I don't have a lot of witnesses yet, only two so far. But it's a quiet area and the location is the obvious choice for him. The killer wanted to reach open water so he couldn't easily be seen from land as he carried out his attack, and by jumping into the boat at that point, he would only be visible to onlookers for a few minutes.'

The Countess asked with some incredulity: 'And it's possible to do that?'

'Absolutely. Poul got an officer to try it four times, and it's much easier than you would think. The distance from the bridge to the deck is about three metres, but if you hold on to the railings and dangle from the bridge at the right time, you can practically step straight onto the roof of a small storage locker for life jackets at the back of the boat. The only thing you need to remember, if you choose the eastern side, is that you must jump off the roof as soon as you land, or you'll hit your head against the bridge. Even so, it's still the better option because at that point the passengers will be going under the bridge themselves and will almost instinctively look ahead. And more importantly: at that point the guide is also sitting down. Normally she stands with her back to the direction of travel in order to address her audience.'

Simonsen asked: 'I'm assuming Poul called in a team of forensic technicians to examine the railings before he used one of my officers as a guinea pig?'

Pedersen confirmed he had done so.

'Has Poul discovered anything else?'

'Yes, indeed. Plenty. For instance, the canal boat was built in 2001 at Gilleleje Shipyard, and its capacity was one hundred and sixty-seven passengers, excluding the skipper and the guide. It was powered by two Leroy Somer electric motors, it was twenty metres long and five point two metres wide and weighed ... all right, so that escapes me, but the reason that it's made from wood rather than fibreglass is that a wooden boat fits in better with the canal boat image: it's more appropriate when you're showcasing a mediaeval city. Also it had one hundred and eighty rechargeable lithium-ion batteries, and they were charged for eight—'

Here Konrad Simonsen cut his deputy off.

'Anything else *relevant*, Arne?'

Pedersen shook his head.

'No, but you should go on TV tonight, Simon, and ask any witnesses who were on Battery Bridge at just before nine-thirty yesterday morning to contact us.'

Simonsen felt a surge of irritation. He loathed going on television, but could see the value of the suggestion.

The Countess had been studying the chart for a while.

'There are three islands, Arsenaløen, Frederiksholm and Nyholm, and four bridges, of which one is closed to regular traffic and open only to buses. I think that if we use the surveillance footage my team has gathered, we stand a good chance of mapping the road traffic on the islands. However, it's complex work. Please may I hire a couple of statisticians or mathematicians from the University of Copenhagen?'

Simonsen gave her the go-ahead. He didn't think he had to worry about the budget, given the seriousness of the crime. Arne Pedersen and the Countess exchanged secret smiles: their boss never worried about his budget anyway.

Simonsen said tentatively: 'We know one more important thing. Unless the killer is a psychopath, we must presume that his target was Pauline and/or Ziegler, in which case at least one of them must have known and possibly feared him.'

His junior officers agreed. It would have been much simpler for the killer to board the boat at the Gammel Strand departure point like all the other tourists. He could easily have avoided witnesses from the ticket office and the camera opposite on Højbro Plads by wearing sunglasses, a cap, and averting his head at the right times.

Arne added sadly: 'Which brings us back to Pauline.'

CHAPTER 9

Klavs Arnold and Anna Mia arrived at the home of Konrad Simonsen and the Countess in Søllerød at around ten o'clock that evening. Simonsen had decided that they would meet privately rather than at Police Headquarters in an attempt to keep his daughter out of the Homicide Department.

Anna Mia hugged the Countess and planted a big kiss on her father's forehead. She was in high spirits and bursting with energy despite having worked for over fourteen hours that day. Klavs, however, had rings under his eyes on what was only the second day of the investigation.

He began by sharing the limited results of the search of Pauline's flat and her office at Police Headquarters. In her basement storage room, they had found six removal crates containing some of the late Juli Denissen's belongings, mostly books and magazines, but also her iPad, her diaries, her mobile phone and her personal papers. There were also several pictures of Juli's flat in Frederiksværk as it had looked at the time of her death. The self-appointed group investigating her death on the grounds that it was suspicious had taken the pictures, and Juli's family had passed on her belongings to Pauline. At this point in his account Anna Mia interrupted Klavs.

'We'll come back to the photographs, Dad, because they're interesting. Oh, sorry, I mean, Dad and Countess.'

The girl's eyes shone with excitement and the Countess couldn't remember ever seeing her display such eagerness before. Perhaps, in becoming a police officer like her father, she had found her vocation in life, no matter how hackneyed that sounded. Klavs Arnold stoically accepted the interruption and the Countess thought it unlikely this was the first time today that Anna Mia had failed to curb her enthusiasm. He even smiled in response or else at her – it was hard to tell which. Then he continued his presentation.

'We know that Pauline used paper diaries, but we haven't found any. We also know that she owned a laptop, but we haven't found that either. And we're convinced that Pauline kept two files on the "Juli-non-case" … which, incidentally, I think we should rename … but again, we haven't found them. We believe someone removed these items from her flat, and that they did so yesterday morning because her neighbour swears that he heard the door to Pauline's flat slam and footsteps on the stairs after the time we now know she was murdered.'

The theory had been corroborated by Pauline's sister, who had been asked to check the flat. She had quickly pointed out that two files were missing from the bookcase in the living room. She could even remember their colour – they were red – and that they were labelled on the spine as *Juli I* and *Juli II*. But more importantly: she had seen them only four days ago when she'd last visited Pauline.

The Countess said pensively: 'When Pauline moved into the flat, she had her front door fitted with a new, high-security lock. It made her feel safer – after her kidnapping, I mean. I helped her buy the lock, and I know she had only two keys cut, which she kept in a safe place.'

She looked at Klavs Arnold. The Jutlander nodded. One key had been found in Pauline's flat, well hidden at the back of a drawer, and the other in her bag, which had been salvaged from the sea. The Countess concluded glumly: 'It takes specialist tools and a fair amount of practice to pick that lock. As I'm sure you discovered for yourselves when Forensics let you in?'

They both confirmed it. Klavs Arnold said, 'Yes, I called in Forensics, of course, and I've also secured any CCTV footage from the area; her apartment block is monitored, but the cameras are positioned in plain sight and they're easy to evade. So all in all, I'm not getting my hopes up. What I'm saying is … she wasn't burgled by some random junkie.'

Konrad Simonsen grunted in agreement and silence followed until Anna Mia realised it was her turn to speak. She started with a quick review of Juli Denissen's life, or what little they knew of it.

Juli was born in 1985 in Frederiksværk, the younger of two sisters. Her home life had been difficult, both her parents drank, yet she did reasonably well at school and went on to complete a further education course at Frederiksværk Gymnasium. She was married in 2004, and the couple had bought the flat where she was still living at the time of her death. She had a daughter in 2005 and divorced later that same year. She had a handful of temporary jobs, including as a teaching assistant, nursery school assistant and waitress. At various points she had been unemployed and on benefits. In 2008 her caseworker had pretty much forced her to start training as a catering assistant at a technical college in Frederiksværk. Her dream was one day to become an architect.

Anna Mia continued eagerly: 'So nothing suspicious, nothing that jumps out at you, an ordinary, somewhat dull life. Or so you would think ... but you'd be wrong. Please would you move your cups?'

She took four pictures from her bag, unfolded them and spread them across the coffee table. They were A3-size and of reasonable quality, each depicting Juli Denissen's flat.

'I discovered something when I studied these pictures, something that kept coming up and puzzling me. What do you think it is?'

Simonsen hadn't said much during either Klavs Arnold's or Anna Mia's presentations. Now he straightened up, automatically attracting everyone's attention. He asked for silence; there was clearly something he wanted to think through. When he had done so, he turned to his daughter.

'If you've discovered something of interest, then you share it without the theatricals. And if you're part of a team, you say *we* discovered, not *I* discovered.'

A shocked Anna Mia looked at her father and then at the Countess, whose expression made it quite clear that she agreed with her husband. An embarrassing pause ensued until Klavs saved his new partner by first addressing her and then his boss.

'Your father's right, you've got a lot to learn. Now don't get upset, you're part of a murder investigation and we don't have time for that sort of thing. But, Simon, please listen to what we've discovered, and then give us a pat on the back because we deserve it.'

Anna Mia pulled herself together and explained as she pointed at the pictures: 'The lamp on Juli Denissen's desk was a PH 3/2 desk lamp, a design classic costing six thousand kroner. On her window-sill was a rare flowerpot holder from Royal Copenhagen Porcelain, worth approximately four thousand kroner, and on the bookcase was a French Empire carriage clock, costing at least ten thousand kroner. In her hallway was a Persian Luri-Baktiari runner, which wouldn't sell for less than eight thousand kroner. And then, the crown jewel in the collection ...' Anna Mia found the picture on her mobile phone and raised her voice: 'Ta-dah! Hans Christian Andersen's *Fairy Tales*, a first edition, which includes "The Princess and the Pea" and "The Emperor's New Clothes". It's in perfect condition, as you can see, and signed by the author. The guy I spoke to at Bruun Rasmussen's Art Auctioneers gave me a very conserv-ative sale estimate of no less than one hundred thousand kroner.'

The Countess asked her: 'You visited Bruun Rasmussen for the evaluation?'

No, of course not, the valuation had been carried out using a photograph taken on her mobile. The Countess felt like a relic. What a stupid question to ask.

Anna Mia concluded: 'We know that Juli Denissen worked cash in hand for a local cheesemonger in addition to various private cleaning jobs, but her income can't possibly have allowed her to buy such items. You may question her taste, but that doesn't change the objects' value. There are bound to be more such valuable items too. It took us a long time to examine the photos from her home and we're not done yet, but we found the Hans Christian Andersen book in Pauline's basement, so that was easy.'

The Countess asked: 'What about her clothes? You can spend a fortune on those, I'll have you know.'

But no, Anna Mia dismissed this: as far as they knew Juli Denissen's clothes had been cheap and bought mainly at the local supermarket, as were her daughter's. She added: 'But we would like to go to Frederiksværk and talk to her bank manager. Could we do that tomorrow, Dad?'

Simonsen was intrigued by this new information. He had met Juli Denissen when she contacted the police during Pauline's abduction.

She had owned an unreliable mobile phone and told him that she couldn't afford a new one. That didn't tie up with a Persian rug costing thousands of kroner, and he wanted to know why. Nevertheless he said to his daughter: 'I thought you were meant to be going to Prague. What does Oliver say?'

'Oliver says what he's supposed to say if he loves me, which is that if it means that much to me to be a part of this, then we can go on holiday some other time.'

Klavs Arnold made a quip about how lucky he was not to be a young man these days. Simonsen asked: 'Is there any point in you spending more time on Juli Denissen, Klavs? I could get the local police to do it, wouldn't that be better?'

Klavs Arnold had his doubts, which he frankly admitted. Nor did the Countess have an answer, and Anna Mia wasn't asked. Simonsen thought it through carefully before making up his mind.

'Find a handful of officers tomorrow and tell them to go systematically through Juli Denissen's life. I'm talking about finances, telephone records, emails, her diaries, her iPad, Facebook, friends, schoolmates, teachers, boyfriends, lovers, ex-husband, family ... you know, the full works. If you can use Anna Mia then do, if you can't—'

Here Klavs interrupted him.

'I can.'

'That's fine. However, if you come across any witnesses you think might be central to our investigation, then take a more experienced partner with you. And you, my girl, report to Klavs and only to him, and stay away from the Homicide Department because if you don't, it could easily be misinterpreted. That said, what you've achieved so far is excellent. As I would expect it to be when you're working for me.'

Klavs Arnold grinned. What he had achieved today was neither better nor worse than on any other day, but Anna Mia beamed. This was exactly what she so desperately craved: professional recognition from her father. Konrad Simonsen thought that praise was indeed due, and that his daughter had helped him more than she knew. He finally had the answer to the question that had been nagging him all day.

A few years ago somebody else had also had second thoughts about Juli Denissen, or more precisely about her post-mortem report, which would otherwise appear to be as simple and straight-forward as her life had been. For one brief moment Professor Arthur Elvang had shaken his head in irritation at something in the report when reviewing it at the Institute of Forensic Medicine. A sure sign that someone had screwed up. Back then Simonsen hadn't followed up his hunch by questioning the expert pathologist, but now he was going to.

CHAPTER 10

When Konrad Simonsen appeared on TV asking for witnesses from Sunday morning at Battery Bridge to come forward, the Danes rushed to their phones and swamped the Homicide Department with calls. They were eager to help the police and vituperative in their hatred of the child killer, whom everyone wanted caught as quickly as possible. The vast majority of calls were worthless, many rang purely to say they had seen nothing or had been too far away from Battery Bridge to see anything. Some offered the officers well-meaning but useless advice, while others reported their neigh-bour, son-in-law or postman as being the killer.

One and a half day's work resulted in two promising leads. A handful of people had, independently of one another, called to report an ambulance, which was odd because it wouldn't appear to have anything to do with the man on the bridge. Konrad Simonsen got Anica Buch, the young police officer who had contacted him two days previously, to find out where the ambulance had come from and what the emergency was.

He had made enquiries about her, and liked what he heard. According to her fellow officers and superiors, she was industrious, intelligent and bright, but had very sharp elbows. The last bit didn't bother him, Simonsen liked ambitious officers. She wasn't a native Dane. She and her mother had fled the former Yugoslavia in 1990; her mother had been a senior official in the security police there until she fell from political grace. In Denmark Anica's mother married and her new husband adopted the girl, who was then eleven years old. At the same time she changed her name from Danica to Anica and took her new father's surname. The following year she became a Danish citizen.

The second lead was more promising: an old woman had been out walking her dog about two hundred metres from Battery Bridge. At about nine, nine-fifteen, she couldn't be sure, she had noticed a car driving from Frederiksholm to Nyholm. The car had stopped on the bridge and dropped off a man, while another car had overtaken it. The woman knew nothing about cars and couldn't identify the make, she hadn't even noticed its colour, but the car that had overtaken the first had a large sticker on its side, some kind of advertisement, although for what she didn't know. Nor could she give a detailed description of the man on the bridge, except that he was tall and had definitely been wearing a small hiking rucksack on his back. In itself it wasn't much to go on, but added to the work of the car team it paid off.

The car team had set itself the ambitious target of identifying every vehicle that had driven to or from Nyholm in the period between seven a.m. and eleven a.m. on Sunday 22 August. It was no small task, and they couldn't expect to achieve complete accuracy as it was possible to access and leave Nyholm without being caught on camera if you chose a winding and illogical route. Their work was further complicated by several of the more crucial cameras being of such poor quality that it was impossible to make out fine details, including one on a cashpoint machine where they could distinguish the colour and shape of the vehicles but only guess at the model.

Finding a car with a large vinyl sticker on its side, however, was a much simpler task. Soon Konrad Simonsen had pictures of three vehicles that had accessed or left Nyholm and had advertising visible on their bodywork. One was a public bus, which he could immediately eliminate. The other two were a company car from a timber supplier, which quickly proved to be of no interest, and the third a silver Ford S-Max, with a poster on its side for a parliamentary candidate in an election which, according to the Constitution, was due to be held next year, but which everyone expected to be called at any moment. The witness was shown the picture of the car with the election advert, and immediately confirmed that it was the one she had seen. The police then called the political candidate, who informed them that the owner of the car was his brother and gave them his name and address. The next call was to the owner of the car. The man confirmed he was indeed the owner of a silver Ford S-Max with a political poster on its side, but adamantly denied having been on Nyholm at the time in question, insisting the police must have made a mistake. To them, it didn't smell right.

When Simonsen was told of the conversation with the Ford's owner, he took out the photograph again. There was someone in the passenger seat blocking the driver's face, someone who was unfortunately also turning their own face away from the camera. Going by the haircut it was a woman, and she was holding up her hand as if discussing something with the driver. He wrote the man's name and address on the back of the picture, folded it and went to Arne Pedersen's office.

He looked happy and Simonsen had barely sat down before the Deputy Homicide Chief started talking. Forensic technicians had managed to match DNA material found on the Battery Bridge railings with samples taken from a seat at the back of the canal boat. Unfortunately it wasn't with the usual, extremely high probability – the DNA sample from the boat was only partial – but it was enough for it to be presented as circumstantial evidence in a subsequent trial. And there was even better news: on the bottom railing they had found ten top-quality prints, presumably the result of the killer hanging from it before jumping onto the boat. Unfortunately, the prints didn't match any on record.

And that wasn't all: divers in the harbour had retrieved two mobile phones so far. Theirs was a difficult job. The water was ten metres deep and the seabed made up of sand and mud, so the divers literally had to feel their way through the detritus and were only halfway through their search. However, technicians were expected to have unlocked the two mobiles by later that night.

Pedersen continued: 'And there's more. We've established that the killer used a close combat knife. Kurt Melsing contacted the FBI in Washington and SKL in Sweden as both laboratories have specialist knowledge of combat knives, and they quickly came back to us.'

He explained that normally this kind of investigation would produce a long list of possible knives, but not in this case. The Swedes and the Americans had both suggested the NR-40, a Soviet combat knife from the Second World War, because its design was unique. Between the handle and the blade it had an S-shaped guard, which curved towards the blade rather than bending away from it. The imprint of this guard could be clearly seen on two of the victims, as the killer had plunged the blade in right up to the hilt. Given the blade's dimensions as measured from the stab wounds, it was possible to identify the knife beyond reasonable doubt. It was made at the Zik factory in Zlatoust in the Urals. Here Arne Pedersen launched into an explanation of the inverted guard, the Soviet soldier's standard grip on a knife was ...

Simonsen stopped him with a shake of the head and summarised: 'So the knife is unusual?'

'It certainly is. According to Melsing's report, it's a rarity today, a top-class weapon, a knife for connoisseurs. But I've been wondering about something, Simon. He's a skilled swimmer, he owns a rare combat knife, he's fit and has knowledge of close combat. He could be a professional soldier.'

Simonsen didn't comment on the theory, but instead asked: 'What about the Japanese boy?'

'He's back in Tokyo. I'll follow it up tomorrow, but I gather that you have something for me?'

He gestured to the paper in Simonsen's hands. He explained and then asked, 'Please would you go and see him tonight?'

Arne Pedersen agreed that he would.

CHAPTER 11

On a quiet, residential road in a Copenhagen suburb, Arne Pedersen tried to convince the owner of the silver Ford S-Max of the benefits of helping the police. The man was around forty and clearly uncomfortable with the situation. The two of them were sitting on the terrace outside the potential witness's house as Pedersen showed him a still from the CCTV footage.

'Would you please tell me the name of the woman sitting next to you?'

He had already guessed that this was yet another version of the extramarital affair that so often made sensible people disregard their civic duty. The man's reaction lent weight to Arne Pedersen's theory. He barely glanced at the picture but looked nervously inside the house, clearly worried that his wife might come out. He turned over the picture. Pedersen said in a placatory tone: 'We can be very discreet. It's not our business to pry into private matters. I'm only seeking information, then I'll go.'

The man shook his head.

'It's not my car and I've nothing to say.'

He gestured half-heartedly with one hand. Pedersen faked surprise.

'So are you also telling me that you never had a political poster on your car? I saw in the garage that you've taken it off.'

The man launched into a lengthy explanation: he had removed the poster, that was correct, but it was pure coincidence, and he had an alibi for Sunday, a watertight one. He was a chiropractor and had been to a weekend conference in another part of Denmark, so couldn't possibly have been in Copenhagen at the time in question. Arne Pedersen let him talk. When the man finally stopped, the Homicide investigator was brutal in his response.

'I'm tired and now I'm also angry. I'm investigating the murder of sixteen children, and I've more important things to do than waste my time unpicking your lies. It's true that you attended a chiro-practors' conference at Trelleborg conference centre from one p.m. last Friday, but you left the centre on Saturday afternoon around four and didn't return home until the following day, that is Sunday, around lunchtime.'

He had told three officers to investigate the man's alibi. It was probably only ever meant for his wife and not the police. Besides, the car team had passed Pedersen a clear photograph of the vehicle from the front. Admittedly it was taken some distance from Battery Bridge, on the motorway, but that didn't matter. In the passenger seat next to the driver sat a pretty young woman, or rather teenager. It wasn't difficult to work out the rest. Arne Pedersen had dispatched a couple of officers to the Galion Hotel, the only hotel on Nyholm, and it had paid off. They had also obtained more pictures.

'This is you and the girl – whose name I want to know – driving down the motorway towards Copenhagen on Sunday at ten-fifteen in the morning. You had spent the night together at the Galion Hotel, in room sixty-four, and registered as father and daughter, calling yourselves Ole and Pia Jensen and giving a false address. Here you are photographed in the hotel lobby on arrival on Saturday the twenty-first of August, and here a good hour later on your way to dinner. You seem very fond of your "daughter", I must say, and not in a good way, but then again that's none of my business. You checked out from the hotel at nine o'clock on Sunday morning and you paid one thousand six hundred and fifty-five kroner with your credit card, partly for the room, partly for frequent use of the minibar, but you returned ten minutes later because the young lady had left her bag behind. Here we have a photograph of you filling up your car at a nearby petrol station. It's just a black-and-white picture, but the registration plate on your car is perfectly clear.'

The man slumped; his eyes grew shiny. Even so he didn't give up.

'Those pictures are fake, you made it all up. I don't want to talk to you, go away!'

Arne Pedersen paused meaningfully. It made no difference to the man. The detective then shouted in a barely controlled voice: 'Bloody well stop it! Do you think this is a game? If you don't give me the girl's name right now and tell me what you saw on Battery Bridge,

I'll issue a wanted notice for her on the morning news and I'll plaster your ugly mug all over the media.'

At last the man cracked. Arne Pedersen could see it coming long before he started talking, but the man carried on squirming a little longer.

'We saw nothing important on the bridge. A car pulled over to drop off a man, I overtook it, but we don't remember the car or the man. Otherwise we would have come forward, of course we would.'

'The girl's name, address and mobile number. Now!'

The man sniffled and struggled to speak.

'Emilie … Emilie Damgaard.'

He stuttered his way through her telephone number. Arne Pedersen carried on without mercy.

'And how old is Emilie?'

'Sixteen.'

'Lucky for you. And her address?'

It was the final hurdle; the man covered his eyes with his hands and rested his elbows on the table:

'She's my next-door neighbour's daughter. Now please will you leave me alone?'

Arne Pedersen would not. He continued his questions until he was absolutely sure that the witness had nothing more to say.

CHAPTER 12

THURSDAY 26 AUGUST 2010, HALSNÆS

These were glory days for Anna Mia. She blossomed in her debut as a detective and her good mood rubbed off on Klavs Arnold. She had a natural talent for investigation, but also for management. The colleagues working for Klavs Arnold uncovering Juli Denissen's life … well, it took less than half a day before they were also working for Anna Mia. And one thing was certain: the officers' willingness to listen to her wasn't because her father was their boss. This wasn't how the informal, internal mechanisms of the police force worked; quite the opposite. Of course she made some rookie mistakes, but she absorbed information like a sponge whenever Klavs guided or corrected her, and she never made the same mistake twice.

They had spent the last three days at Frederiksværk Hotel where a small but perfectly adequate conference room had been made available to them. It made sense to work from there because most of the people they needed to talk to lived in and around Halsnæs. Besides it was free, so no one could accuse them of wasting taxpayers' money. When the owner of the hotel heard what they were investigating, she absolutely refused to take their money, and she made sure that they had plenty of coffee, cold drinks and fruit at their disposal, as long as they promised to catch the bastard who had killed all those poor Japanese children.

And they got results. They had soon built up a picture of Juli Denissen's life, and two things stood out. The first was that she had been a very impulsive character. She would get excited about an idea or a thought and pursue it to the exclusion of all other things for days, weeks and, on rare occasions, months until another passion came along – often for something completely different – whereupon the old project was dropped and the new one consumed her.

She would often throw herself into ventures she lacked any hope of realising, without it seeming to bother her in the slightest. In some cases her infectious enthusiasm would draw people to her, only for her to lose interest and leave them behind. In one way she inspired those around her, friends as well as lovers – she was always burning with enthusiasm for something – but for her personally, this pattern of behaviour was destructive. She never saw anything through to the end. Abandoned projects and burned bridges trailed in her wake. Anna Mia concluded: 'That's how many people describe her. The only fixed point in her life, as far as I can see, was her daughter.'

Klavs nodded, busy munching a hotel apple. Anna Mia continued speaking.

'One month she and a friend decided to write a four-hundred-page children's book, the next she wanted to make fizzy drinks as a side business to Halsnæs Brewery, a local microbrewery, then two months after that she wanted to map pollution in Lake Arresø. What a life ... and it's a similar pattern with the sugar daddies.'

This was the second aspect of her life where Juli Denissen fell outside the norm. She had dated many men, all considerably older than she was, aged from forty-five to sixty. They were all fairly affluent, and at least two of them could be described as rich. It hadn't been particularly difficult to uncover details of these men in the last two days once Malte Borup had found the address and password of Juli Denissen's email account on her iPad. The legality of this project was dubious at best, but Anna Mia had had no great difficulty in talking Malte into doing it. When they gained access to Juli Denissen's emails for almost four years leading up to her death, she and Klavs Arnold kept this information to themselves. Once they had the men's first names and email addresses, it was easy to find their physical addresses, and more information on them.

Between her divorce in the autumn of 2005 and her death in the summer of 2008, Juli Denissen had seen eleven men. A relationship would usually last between two to three months, then she would end it and quickly find a new man. The cashier in her local bank could tell all sorts of stories about those men, but not here in the bank, oh, no, she announced in a loud voice so her closest colleagues couldn't help but hear. She would never reveal confidential information about her customers, living or dead. Such requests must always go through the manager. But later, when she had finished work, she put on her sunglasses, pulled up her collar and came to the hotel where she revealed herself to be a gossip of the worst kind and a goldmine of information for the police:

'I don't wish to speak ill of the dead, but really ... she slept with half the town! Anyone could see that, a new man every week. And they paid her bills if she wanted them to, and more. You didn't hear this from me, but that restaurateur from Melby paid off her mortgage, though she was on benefits at the time – she had no shame. Same thing happened with her car loan about a year later.

It was the estate agent in the centre who paid that off, and he has a wife and children, and – you won't believe this, but he's also a member of ...'

She wouldn't shut up and Anna Mia kept her talking with prompts such as *you don't say* or *oh, God, no, please tell me it's not true*. Indignation was painted all over Anna Mia's face, and all the while Klavs Arnold was making notes.

An hour later they had summarised their information.

'A timber supplier, a radiologist, a restaurateur, a police lawyer, an estate agent, a first violinist, a scrap metal dealer and more ... a motley crew in other words, but they all have fat wallets. I think we should send an officer round to each of them to get their side of the story. We might learn something interesting. But it needs to be a man, preferably a mature one – they're easier for another man to confide in. And the officer needs to come prepared with a cover story for the men who are married, perhaps something about problems with their car insurance, that should work. And you should be the one to brief them.'

Klavs replied: 'The scrap metal dealer from Ølsted has a record, so we'll deal with him, and as for the last man on the list, or rather his widow, then I want a more experienced colleague than you to approach her.'

Anna Mia swallowed her disappointment:

'Because Juli Denissen was having an affair with him when she died? Is that what you're saying?'

'Yes, that's why. And also because I don't quite know what I'm looking for, or if there's anything there at all. So I want more professional backup than you can provide. But you and I have pretty much answered our most important questions, which were how Juli Denissen could afford such expensive things, and whether she had any links to Jonas Ziegler who found her body, and there's nothing to suggest that she had. So we're almost at the point where we can write our report.'

It was plenty, Anna Mia agreed. They drove to the harbour to eat lunch.

On their way in the car, Klavs said casually: 'The scrap metal dealer, what do you know about him?'

She didn't hesitate for a second.

'Two convictions for embezzlement and insurance fraud in 1998 and 2004 respectively, one for assault in 2008, where he served eighteen months. He's also suspected of extensively handling stolen goods.'

'And you would have sent an older officer to him without backup?' Anna Mia practically quivered with irritation at herself.

'Yes, I would have. D'oh!'

'Idiot.'

She said nothing in response. A little later he added more kindly: 'You've been a detective for three days. Do you think you could lower your expectations for yourself to the level of merely realistic? You're talented, and you know it, but even you can't work miracles.'

CHAPTER 13

THURSDAY 26 AUGUST 2010, NYHOLM, COPENHAGEN

There is an excellent view of Battery Bridge from number 2 Kongebrovej, which was the place where, on Sunday 22 August, at just before nine-thirty in the morning, the killer had jumped onto the canal boat. The building consisted of four wings surrounding a courtyard containing six parking spaces reserved for the three businesses housed in the property, and a sandpit and climbing frame for the residents' children.

Anica Buch was standing outside the gate leading to the courtyard, which had formed the original mid-nineteenth-century entrance when the building housed administrative offices for the Danish Navy, and had been known as Peter Willemoes Palæ. Yesterday, when Konrad Simonsen had tasked her with investigating the ambulance, she had been overjoyed and her work was going well, possibly for the investigation in general, but especially for her in particular, which was Anica Buch's top priority.

As expected the ambulance had proved easy to track down. The emergency services had received a call at 9.48 a.m. on the Sunday morning, and an ambulance had been dispatched to the property where she now was. A man had been found lying injured in the courtyard. The timing meant that this incident had taken place *after* the killer had jumped onto the canal boat, which initially annoyed Anica Buch enormously. Nevertheless she followed it up and it was just as well she did.

When the ambulance had arrived at 9.55, paramedics found a groaning man lying in the sandpit while the caretaker, who had called the ambulance, tended to him. The injured man's name was Kim Steensen and he was the owner of a small telemarketing firm with offices on the second floor of the south wing. But although Kim Steensen was in a bad way – he had been given a severe beating – he refused to get into the ambulance, which ended up driving off without the patient. Nor did he want to report the matter to the police, so the caretaker had helped him up the stairs to the man's office. Soon afterwards one of his employees helped him back down again, and he was picked up by a friend.

Anica Buch tried to work out the sequence of events. The caretaker told her that shortly after getting out of his car, Kim Steensen had been beaten up by a man looking like a member of a biker gang, who had appeared out of nowhere. The caretaker had witnessed the attack from a basement window and called for an ambulance. As he was hitting him, the attacker had shouted to Kim Steensen something about girls who needed their wages paid within the hour.

The next step was to take a closer look at Kim Steensen, and there was much to ponder there, as it turned out. The man made his living from a series of frauds, con tricks and scams. Currently it was telemarketing, where he had nine young people making cold calls to flog energy-saving light bulbs whose specifications were wildly exaggerated. It was mostly old people who fell for the pitch.

Anica's theory was that the attacker had lain in wait for Kim Steensen. He could have hidden himself either in the courtyard or in the street near the gate, where he would have had six seconds to slip in after Steensen had remotely opened the electronic gate after arriving in his car. The problem was that there were no good hiding places in the street, unless you gained access to the stairwell of number 2b, which lay to the left of the gate. This, however, would require either a key or a reason to enter, as an intercom was mounted outside the front door. She started checking the residents and got lucky with the third floor. A retired teacher remembered that some idiot of a newspaper boy had woken him up on Sunday morning.

It all made sense. On the first floor of number 2b, the stairwell window offered a perfect view down Danneskjold-Samsøes Allé from where Kim Steensen's dark blue Skoda Octavia would arrive, which gave the attacker plenty of time to walk down the stairs, hide in the doorway, wait until the car had driven through the gate before slipping in after it. However, what was more interesting was that the attacker would also have been overlooking Battery Bridge at the critical time. It was impossible for him not to.

Anica Buch realised at this point that she should stop working alone, so she called Police Headquarters, asked to be transferred to Konrad Simonsen and was put through without delay to the Deputy Homicide Chief.

Arne Pedersen tried focusing on Anica Buch's news. He had just been bickering with Simonsen, who was annoyed because he had been forced to postpone his visit to the nursing home where Professor Arthur Elvang now lived. More important matters had arisen, matters which had nothing to do with Pedersen, and yet his boss had taken out his irritation on him.

When Anica Buch had finished her account, Arne Pedersen decided to drive to Nyholm to join her.

She was standing outside the entrance to the building when he arrived twenty minutes later. She told him again what she had discovered. They ended up on the first floor in the stairwell of number 2b where the attacker, according to Anica Buch's theory, had been waiting for Kim Steensen. Arne Pedersen looked out of the window for a long time. Battery Bridge was directly in his field of vision, so the young officer had made a good call. Anica Buch stood behind him without saying anything.

'Have you checked the windowsill for fingerprints?'

She had, but only for fingerprints and DNA evidence, not for footprints, nor had she called in Forensic Services; her rank didn't allow her to do that.

'And what did you discover?'

'Several clear fingerprints, which could belong to the same person, but I haven't had time to study them more closely.'

Pedersen nodded as she spoke. She had done everything by the book. On their way down the stairs, he said: 'I want those prints checked, so I'll call in Forensics and get someone to come over right away.'

When he had finished the call, they visited Kim Steensen's company. The owner wasn't there, but they quickly learned that he had returned to his office later that Sunday morning looking bruised and battered and had given orders for the immediate payment of wages outstanding to twin girls who had been employed by his company up until June. The detectives got the twins' address and were in and out of there in less than five minutes.

The girls proved less co-operative. They were students and lived in a flat half a kilometre from Peter Willemoes Palæ. One had the flu – she was lying on a sofa looking ill – and the other had skipped today's lectures so she could stay at home and look after her sister. Neither of them was particularly accommodating.

Anica Buch read them the Riot Act.

'The biker who beat up Kim Steensen so that you could get your money knew when his victim would turn up for work – information he got from you. That makes you accessories to grievous bodily harm and blackmail, enough for a suspended sentence and a criminal record, so you're both well and truly screwed unless we decide to overlook your involvement. In order for us to do that, you need to cooperate.'

Arne Pedersen rose and heaped on the pressure.

'Come, Anica, we're leaving. I'm not wasting my time arguing with two spoiled brats who don't get that this is about sixteen dead children. We'll call a patrol car and some officers who can take them to Police Headquarters; that'll make our lives much easier.'

It was the flu-stricken twin who spoke: in a croaking voice she said that they hadn't been paid as promised for telemarketing work and had complained about this to their uncle, who had links to Hell's Angels. He had assured them he would fix their problem, how he didn't say, but couldn't have carried out the attack personally because he had been in wheelchair since a car accident in 2003. Anica Buch took out her notepad and pen.

'And your uncle's name is?'

On his way back to the car, Pedersen received a text message. The fingerprints from the stairwell had been checked against the fingerprint register and there was a match. Now they had two names. They got into the car, but Pedersen didn't start the engine.

Anica Buch asked: 'Now what?'

'We'll ask Karlslunde Police for assistance.'

'Task Force East?'

Pedersen confirmed it. Task Force East was a specialist unit set up to fight gang-related crime in east Denmark. The unit had extensive knowledge of the biker-gang scene.

The last pieces of the jigsaw fell into place: the attacker was a wannabe who desperately wanted to become a Hell's Angel. The twins' uncle had once been a member of a chapter and still visited the clubhouse on Svanevej in north-west Copenhagen. The rest was easy to figure out.

Anica Buch asked again: 'Now what?'

Arne Pedersen took his time thinking about it before he replied.

'The attacker will cooperate if the Hell's Angels tell him to, and they probably will. Many of them have children of their own. But otherwise, nothing that concerns you. Except that we won't forget you. Simon and I will remember your contribution to this investigation.'

CHAPTER 14

It was the Countess who would interview Emilie Damgaard, daughter of the neighbour of the chiropractor from Ballerup. In view of the situation the Countess, a mature woman, was the obvious choice, and neither she nor Arne Pedersen had involved Simonsen in the decision-making. She had arranged with Emilie Damgaard – who had just started Sixth Form – that she would come to Police Headquarters. Afterwards the Countess had called Emilie Damgaard's mother, who by law must be informed either before or immediately after her daughter was interviewed as a witness. The Countess had opted to tell the mother herself rather than involve a social worker. However, she hadn't divulged any specific details to the mother, and hoped that the girl would turn up at Police Headquarters alone.

Emilie Damgaard's witness statement could prove crucial, and the Countess was well prepared for their meeting. The energy she had lacked at the start of the investigation had returned, thanks to her husband. Simon's leadership had set everyone a good example, and after a few days where she had struggled to shake off her grief at Pauline's death, the Countess was now able to concentrate on her work. And as far as she could see, the same applied to Arne and Klavs, who had initially been glum and despondent. Like her, they probably felt guilty for not taking Pauline's investigation into the death of Juli Denissen seriously.

The Countess had located a Ford S-Max, the make of car owned by the chiropractor, and hired a cameraman to produce a brief film recorded from inside the car from the passenger's point of view. The film began in the Galion Hotel car park, and stopped two minutes and twelve seconds later, when the car drove past Peter Willemoes Palæ after having passed Battery Bridge for the third time, because Emilie Damgaard had left her bag behind. It was the second trip that was crucial and here the Countess had been helped by two different sources: one was the car team looking for the vehicle that had dropped off a passenger on Battery Bridge at five minutes past nine, the car the chiropractor and Emilie Damgaard had overtaken. The team reckoned it must be either a dark blue or black four-door recent model saloon and produced a long list of possibilities, which didn't really help the Countess.

The other finding that gave the Countess new hope had come from the divers whose search for mobile phones and cameras at the bottom of the sea had finally produced useful information. After several days' hard work, they had found three more mobile phones belonging to Japanese children, and one contained a video sequence recorded as the canal boat rounded Frederiksholm and headed for the mainland. On Battery Bridge, approximately one hundred metres away, they could see a figure leaning against the railings. At first it faced the camera, but two seconds later it crossed to the other side and was obscured by the road. Judging from the images it was possible to estimate that person's height – he was about one hundred and eighty-eight centimetres – but apart from that the technician could deduce nothing else, and could only offer guesses as to the colour of the person's clothing.

The Countess had chosen randomly from the list of cars that the Ford had overtaken and so she had it overtake a black Toyota Yaris on Battery Bridge, while an officer of the right height and wearing neutral clothing got out.

The final piece of information the Countess received had come from Arne Pedersen's interview with the chiropractor. He could remember nothing from the bridge, but was certain that the car radio had been on and tuned to Radio 80, a commercial station playing non-stop popular music, news and commercials. The Countess obtained a sound recording from the radio station and using video surveillance tape from the Galion Hotel car park, synchronised the music with her short footage. At least that was the theory. Now she was hoping that her efforts would prompt Emilie Damgaard's memory. Film footage was often better than a re-enactment on location as it gave the witness more time to think. If, however, the footage proved ineffective, then Plan B was a trip to Battery Bridge with the girl.

The Countess's hope that Emilie Damgaard would arrive without her mother was fulfilled; the girl turned up unaccompanied.

The Countess took them to her husband's office, which she had borrowed in order to show Emilie the footage on the large flat-screen in the annexe. The girl smiled and was charming, seemingly natural and without any sign of nerves. The Countess thought her a ray of sunshine.

'Please would you start by telling me a little about yourself?'

The girl did so and talked about her affair with her neighbour. The Countess was satisfied, feeling there was no need to pry into further details, so they proceeded to the footage.

After Emilie Damgaard had seen the film once, she asked to see it again. There was something … something she couldn't put her finger on, but … something. The penny dropped on the second viewing.

'The song is wrong! I love it, but it starts too early. It began as we headed back and turned the corner before the bridge, I'm sure of it. Can you change it?'

The Countess could. She had several images and sound clips because although she knew when the film started, she didn't know how fast the car had been travelling. Malte Borup had identified this potential problem and had shown her how to change the timing of the song to correspond with different car speeds. They made four attempts before Emilie Damgaard was satisfied. Then it was as if the girl went into a trance. 'Yes, yes, that's right!' She hummed along to the song, before she exclaimed: 'I turned up the volume as we crossed the bridge, and she started the chorus, or whatever it's called … Céline Dion, I mean … and I sang along, but Casper turned down the volume – that's why he was late seeing the car in front pull over and the man getting out. He swore at them: "Stupid cow, look where you're going!" Can we try again and louder as we reach the bridge, and then turn the volume down, but only a little, before we overtake?'

The Countess did as the girl had asked. Emilie Damgaard sang along, her voice surprisingly powerful and her pitch perfect. The girl's voice merged beautifully with Céline Dion's lyric soprano, as she swayed to the violin accompaniment softly pining in the back-ground. She raised her arms as if she were conducting an orchestra and let rip before stopping halfway through a note. She said in a stunned voice: 'He looked at me. I mean, we looked at each other,

I remember it now. He had a ponytail, dark hair, and he wasn't young, forty at least, tall, very tall … and slim, strong too, he had a rucksack. I've got him! I can see his face clearly.'

In her mind the Countess jumped for joy.

'Do you think you can keep the man's image in your head until tomorrow?' she said calmly.

'I'm sure I can. I can really picture him now.'

'Are you able to come back and work with another witness and a sketch artist, so we can produce an image of this man?'

The girl smiled.

'Do I have a choice?'

'Not really, but we can pick you up and drive you home afterwards. And we can speak to your college about you getting time off.'

They agreed on ten o'clock the next morning. On her way out the girl asked: 'So Casper didn't want to tell you about me even though he knew that I might be a witness?'

She caught the Countess's eye. The Countess tried to deflect the question:

'It doesn't work like that. Casper's statement is irrelevant to yours, as yours is to his.'

Emilie Damgaard's eyes hardened and she hissed angrily, 'What a bastard!'

The Countess couldn't agree more.

CHAPTER 15

FRIDAY 27 AUGUST 2010, THE NURSING HOME

Konrad Simonsen chose to send the Countess and an officer from Glostrup Police Force to Japan to interview the boy who had survived Sunday's tragedy. It might seem a little strange that he picked his wife – after all, there was no shortage of volunteers for a trip to Japan at the taxpayers' expense – but people could think what they liked. How he managed his staff was up to him. She had left for the airport this morning, he hadn't even had time to take her there himself, and he was missing her already, which irritated him. As if he couldn't manage without her.

The nursing home, White Swan, bordered the beautiful Deer Park north of Copenhagen. It was a noble old house with whitewashed walls and glazed black roof tiles that shone even in dull weather. Two-storey extensions had been added to either side of the house, and kept in the same style as the main building. The garden had well-trimmed lawns, gravel paths and plenty of benches. Konrad Simonsen thought that a place here didn't come cheap, but also that Arthur Elvang deserved it; for years he had worked harder and longer hours than anyone else Simonsen knew.

The manager's office was in the main building and a member of staff took Simonsen from there to the retired professor's room where she knocked hard twice before she entered and announced in a loud voice that he had a visitor: 'It's a police officer.' The old man in the armchair by the window jumped, and Konrad Simonsen wondered if their arrival had woken him. The staff member marched off with a patronising remark about the professor's sight being poor. Konrad Simonsen stepped inside the room, placed his inappropriate bouquet of flowers on the chest of drawers and couldn't work out whether he should sit down before he had introduced himself or not. He chose to remain standing.

Arthur Elvang had never in the course of his long life tried to be a people pleaser; on the contrary, at work he had been notorious for his brusque and rude manner, especially towards people in positions of power. It was only because of his indisputable expertise in forensics, which had earned him an international reputation, that those around him had tolerated his eccentric behaviour. Konrad Simonsen could certainly vouch for that.

The professor was now nearly blind and nothing but skin and bone. It seemed a miracle he was still alive. Simonsen introduced himself without receiving any reaction. He added: 'I have some important questions for you.'

This finally got through to him and the old man replied, in a feeble but clear voice: 'And I have one for you. When they put me in my coffin shortly, will you promise to leave me alone?'

Simonsen took a seat on a chair opposite him, unsure as to how he should proceed. He began tentatively.

'Nice place this, isn't it?'

The old man looked irritably in the direction of his voice.

'It's fantastic. My personal favourite is every time that brain-damaged cow you've just met shouts at me because she thinks that if you can't see, then you can't hear either. She nearly gave me a heart attack.'

He insisted that they went out to the garden. Simonsen agreed that was an excellent idea. What else could he do or say? He assisted the old man down the corridor.

'If you'll remand that wailing banshee in custody for a few months, then I'll help you with anything you want.'

Simonsen laughed without knowing if the offer had been made purely in jest.

They sat down on a bench with its back set against the wall of the house. The sun had partly broken through the clouds and it was mild. The professor had talked himself warm. The only thing about him still working perfectly was his brain, and Simonsen felt his old insecurity in this man's company return. He had always struggled to deal with Arthur Elvang, and his only consolation was that he was far from being the only one. Cautiously, he asked his first question, mostly to satisfy his own curiosity.

'When you helped me a few years ago, you told me there was something called the Department of Forensic Pathology at Hillerød Hospital.'

He had been worried that the professor might not remember the incident, but he could.

'Was it that business with young Berg and her foolish fellow conspiracy theorists you'd managed to get yourself involved in? And the dead woman from Nordsjælland?'

Konrad Simonsen confirmed this was a pretty apt description.

'They had a list of ten items, which they believed the police had deliberately kept from the public, or some similar nonsense, and the location of the post-mortem was one of them.'

It was pretty much as Konrad Simonsen had worked out for himself: the professor had invented a non-existent forensic pathology department, rather than launch into a lengthy explanation about the pathologist Hans Arne Tholstrup and his complicated love life. It was easier and more credible, though it was still wrong. The fact that the old man had known the truth about the tragic pathologist all along was another matter.

'Else was giving it away to anyone and everyone, and Hans Arne was the only one at the Institute of Forensic Medicine who didn't know. Nevertheless she was a much better forensic pathologist than he ever was, poor man. Tell me, can you see if there's anyone looking out of the first-floor window in the building to our left?'

Konrad Simonsen checked. There was no one there.

'Then go to that tree and get me a handful of plums. I can't believe you fell for that Hillerød story! Are there no limits to people's naivety?'

Konrad Simonsen picked five plums, all he could reach, while glancing nervously up at the window and feeling like a schoolboy. The plums were Opals, and they looked delicious.

When he returned with his catch, the professor sank his teeth into the first plum. The dark yellow juice trickled down his chin as he greedily scoffed the soft fruit, smacking his lips. The next plum went the same way after he had wiped his mouth on his sleeve. Konrad Simonsen took the opportunity to explain the real reason for his visit. Back when Arthur Elvang had done him a favour and reviewed Juli Denissen's post-mortem report in front of the conspiracy group, he had paused at something he'd seen in it. He hadn't commented, but there had definitely been something he had regarded as strange. Konrad Simonsen had dreaded this moment, but to his enormous surprise the professor remembered the episode vividly. He was munching his third plum and his words weren't entirely clear, so Simonsen had to ask him again.

Arthur Elvang repeated: 'I said, there were notes from two student pathologists in the report. They claimed to have found arinoasis and arinosine in the woman's vagina. That seemed bizarre, to put it mildly.'

'Please would you elaborate?'

Arthur Elvang explained. It wasn't unusual for pathology students to take samples, often semen samples from the anus, vagina and oral cavity; it wasn't directly relevant to the post-mortem report, and it was a clear error that the students' report was attached to the post-mortem, but an error the professor had seen before. It happened during busy periods. One of them had probably wondered at the look of the cells when they had studied scrapings from the dead woman and requested a chemical analysis. But someone must have made a mistake, because those two particular substances seemed highly unlikely. That was why Elvang had paused.

'What is arinosine and … the other substance you mentioned?'

'Arinoasis is an enzyme, and arinosine is a protein. Both are trace elements of snail slime.'

Konrad Simonsen was confused. 'A snail?'

'No, a moose. Seriously, of course a snail.'

'Are you saying that someone put a snail inside her vagina?'

'Yes, or she did it to herself. I highly doubt the snail crawled in there of its own free will.'

'Does that explain her fear? Her high adrenaline level or whatever the term is? And thus her brain haemorrhage?'

'How would I know? I'm not clairvoyant. Ask me some real questions or get out of here.'

Konrad Simonsen helped himself to one of the remaining plums, then got up and walked away so Elvang couldn't hear him.

He called Klavs Arnold's mobile, and asked him if Juli Denissen had had any phobias. The Jutlander didn't know the answer, but it was easy to check and he promised to call him straight back. Before Arnold hung up, he gave his boss the good news: after several days of searching the divers had finally found the murder weapon at the bottom of Bomløbet, and it was indeed a Russian combat knife from the Second World War. It had been passed on to Forensics and final confirmation that it was the murder weapon would be available within twenty-four hours.

Konrad Simonsen ate his plum, which was delicious, then he walked back to the professor at a leisurely pace and had barely sat down before he received a text message. It was from Anna Mia:

*JD had a mortal fear of snails. According to a female friend, she would
scream at even the sight of one.*

'Oh, I thought you had left,' Arthur Elvang said. 'Where's my
last plum?'

CHAPTER 16

'There are three possible scenarios. One of her lovers took revenge
when she dumped him. The wife of one of her boyfriends wanted
to hurt or frighten her. Or a third option—'

Anna Mia was on a roll and refused to be put off her stride by
Klavs Arnold's sarcastic quip about him agreeing totally with her
third option. Arne Pedersen, who had joined them at Klavs Arnold's
request, laughed.

They were walking down the pavement on their way to interview
their last witness in Frederiksværk, the widow of the man who had
been having an affair with Juli Denissen when she died.

Pedersen said: 'So Pauline was right about Juli Denissen's death
being suspicious. It's a hard one to swallow when I think of all the
times we used to make fun of her.'

Konrad Simonsen had updated them on his meeting with
Arthur Elvang, and the information had been confirmed by the
Institute of Forensic Medicine, where the samples taken from the
young woman's vagina were stored and had been analysed again as
a matter of urgency. It was the final proof that Pauline's hunch that
a crime had been committed on 10 July 2008 on Melby Common
had been right all along.

Klavs Arnold commented: 'That only makes this interview more
important. After all, we can't change the past.'

No one said anything and Anna Mia changed the subject.

'Which one of you convinced my father that I could come along today?'

Klavs Arnold replied: 'You're not coming along, you're here to watch and learn, and your father didn't need convincing. But after today you're going on your holiday. And don't call him and pester him to ...'

Here Anna Mia cut him off belligerently.

'What I discuss with my father is none of your business.'

Klavs Arnold continued unperturbed.

'... to allow you to take part. You've done well, but it ends today.'

Anna Mia surrendered with an *OK, OK*. Arne Pedersen asked her:

'As you're reading law, why don't you tell me how many years the man or woman who attacked Juli Denissen might get?'

She was clearly surprised by the turn the conversation had taken, but having thought about it, replied: 'The death of Juli Denissen was an accident. Her attacker can't have foreseen it, so it's not murder. That requires premeditation. Say, a conviction for unlawful force, which gets you up to two years, plus presumably unlawful imprisonment, which is punishable by up to four years in jail, but as we all know sentences don't run consecutively in Denmark, so I reckon between three and four years, and closer to four than three. Intrusion and the assault on her in the presence of the child are clearly aggravating circumstances.'

'Four years. That's not long. He'll be out in three maximum.'

'Yes, I can see why you might think so. But there is a silver lining: we can now apply for a warrant to access Juli Denissen's emails so they become official and can be used in evidence.'

Arne Pedersen knew that the Homicide Department was already working on that, but he said: 'What a good idea.'

The man's widow led them into her living room. She was in her mid-forties and had been left well off by her late husband. Her home showed signs of her wealth. Provincial ostentation, showy and vulgar, Anna Mia thought as she sat down on the richly carved Neo-Renaissance chair to which she was shown, as hideous as it was undoubtedly expensive. The woman's name was Ella von Eggert.

She had added the 'von' soon after her husband Mads Eggert's death less than twelve months ago.

He had been an exceedingly successful architect and talented businessman, the sole owner of an architectural practice employing over forty staff and providing him with an annual income, according to his most recent tax return, of over five million kroner, depending on how much money he could be bothered to take out of his business. The couple had married in 1998. Prior to that she had briefly worked as his secretary.

After the wedding, she had moved into her husband's house in Frederiksværk, the town where, except for his time at university, he had lived his whole life. They had no children. In July 2009 Mads Eggert had died in a car crash on his way to work. While taking a sharp bend he had lost control of his car, a Maserati GranCabrio Convertible, his pride and joy, which he had imported directly from Italy before it was available to the general public. The car skidded and rolled over, and he was crushed beneath it.

Klavs Arnold explained the reason for their visit to Ella von Eggert. With the necessary tact, but also without beating about the bush, he informed the woman that her husband had been seeing Juli Denissen in the period leading up to her death in July 2008, and that the police wanted to know if Ella could tell them anything about the affair. She couldn't. She didn't dispute her late husband's infidelity, but claimed to know nothing more.

Klavs Arnold said: 'You don't seem terribly surprised that your husband was having an affair?'

Ella von Eggert let out a theatrical sigh: no, she wasn't, it had happened a few times before, but it was never anything serious and they had come through it.

'A few times. Is that twice?'

'Three that I know of, but they were a long time ago, in 2001 and a few years after that to be more precise. But surely they don't matter? Like I said, we had come through it, the women didn't matter.'

Klavs Arnold thought that she had a fair point. Ella von Eggert added:

'Mads was a very passionate, free-spirited man and that wasn't something anyone could change.'

'We know that in May 2008 your husband gave his mistress a very expensive book – a conservative estimate values it at over one hundred thousand kroner. Do you know anything about that?'

Ella von Eggert thought about this before dismissing it almost apologetically.

'No. Like I said, I didn't know the girl, and if Mads chose to spend a little of his money on her, then it was his business.'

Arne Pedersen showed the woman a picture of Juli Denissen. She shook her head, *I'm sorry, I've never seen her before*, and gave the same reaction when shown a picture of Jonas Ziegler.

'The three mistresses you know about, the women from … was it 2001 and 2003?'

Ella von Eggert nodded.

'How old were they?'

'My age, I would think, or my age at the time, I mean. Perhaps one of them was slightly younger. Why do you ask?'

Klavs Arnold was equally curious. Nevertheless he said automatically: 'We ask the questions and you answer them, not the other way around.'

The two men interviewed the widow for another half-hour, without eliciting anything of interest. Finally they ran out questions.

The moment they had stepped outside the front door, Anna Mia exclaimed in triumph.

'She's lying, she knows Juli Denissen! She called her "the girl", did you notice? Why would she say "girl" if she didn't know that Juli Denissen was much younger than the other women her husband had been having affairs with? She referred to the other two as women, not girls.'

Arne Pedersen praised her. That was well spotted. They walked on, then Anna Mia said: 'You heard it too, that's why you phrased the question the way you did, am I right, Arne?'

Klavs Arnold said: 'You did really well, Anna Mia.'

PART II

The Man in the Wood

CHAPTER 17

Arne Pedersen, Klavs Arnold and Konrad Simonsen began the day by reviewing the death of Juli Denissen.

On the floor they had spread out the large map that Malte Borup had made for them from Google Earth printouts. The map showed Melby Common, and the three men had sat down to study it.

Jonas Ziegler had originally claimed to be working in the forest when he heard a child's cries. He had walked towards the sound and eventually discovered the dead woman – a claim Pauline had often argued couldn't be true because of the distance involved. Now it seemed more likely that Jonas Ziegler had heard the woman scream rather than the child cry.

'Unless Ziegler took part in the attack because Juli Denissen was either restrained somehow or there was more than one attacker,' Arne Pedersen said.

One of the many unanswered questions concerned Juli Denissen's jacket. The fact that she had brought one along in the middle of July suggested that she intended to walk along the shoreline where it was windy and could be chilly, in contrast to the common itself, which was sheltered by the dunes.

'So it's reasonable to assume that she and the child were overpowered the moment they got out of their car. The child made her vulnerable,' commented Klavs Arnold.

Pedersen nodded vaguely; Simonsen grunted. They were going round in circles. What was the relevance of this to their current investigation, if any?

Simonsen said: 'Jonas Ziegler isn't our only link to the kill-ings – there's also the break-in to Pauline's flat last Sunday when her files were stolen. But we're not getting anywhere.'

He ordered an even more thorough background check of Juli Denissen's acquaintances, focusing on her various lovers, and assigned Arne and Klavs to the task even though Klavs and Anna Mia had researched much of this already.

Simonsen instructed: 'Try to get more information out of that widow. She wasn't terribly helpful when she was first interviewed.' He added a tad ironically: 'We can now legitimately access Juli Denissen's emails, but whether that gets us anywhere, I can't say. However, there are a lot of emails, more than seven hundred, and I need someone to read and organise them. Perhaps someone like Anica Buch would be the right person for this job?'

It was a rhetorical question and it annoyed Arne Pedersen, who could see where this was going. He had always objected to the boss's habit – despite the years of service and documented skills of existing staff – of bringing in people his intuition told him would do well in Homicide. And although Klavs Arnold had been one of those people, and it had turned out well, Pedersen said: 'For God's sake, Simon, why can't you pick one of our own people?'

Klavs Arnold said nothing, which was understandable given the situation, and Simonsen cut through the strained atmosphere.

'Just give her a chance, Arne. And if it doesn't work out, then get rid of her.'

The next task required another large map and they spent almost more time reviewing this than on their discussion. This concerned two pieces of information the Countess had got from the Japanese boy.

First, the man who had carried out the killings on the canal boat had let himself fall backwards into the water. Secondly, he had waited much longer before abandoning the boat than they had first assumed. In the Japanese boy's own words, it was long after his teacher had jumped overboard and long before the collision with the ferry, which made it likely that the killer had jumped overboard at the point where the canal merged with the harbour basin. This information suggested that he must be a strong swimmer, but then again so were many people. A more interesting question was where he might have swum ashore. The police had received expert help from divers and frogmen from the Navy, but there were still too many options for them to regard the lead as worth prioritising.

Klavs put away the map and Arne said: 'So all we have is the artist's sketch, though I'm sure that will pay off.'

All Sunday Emilie Damgaard and the wannabe biker-gang member, who had beaten up Kim Steensen, had worked hard with a sketch artist, and after much discussion and hundreds of tiny adjustments, the result was eminently usable and lifelike. Konrad Simonsen had pinned up the sketch on his noticeboard, and the three of them looked at it.

Judging by the drawing the killer was about fifty years old. He had an imposing face with a prominent bone structure and a broad, flat nose like a boxer's. His eyes were dark and deep-set, his gaze steady, calm – not aggressive. His hair was black and gathered in a ponytail, which reached to his shoulders; his hairline was receding and the wrinkles on his forehead and around his mouth showed that he was no longer young. His legs were muscular and his jawline and upper lip showed signs of stubble. The overall impression reminded them of a Stone Age chief.

Klavs Arnold asked: 'When do we release it?'

'The sketch artist has made pictures of another seven random men. All eight are currently being shown to the Japanese boy. We haven't heard back yet, but are expecting to do so soon.'

Another two hours went by, then they heard from Japan. The boy had picked out the right sketch.

CHAPTER 18

THURSDAY 2 SEPTEMBER 2010, KIRKEGAARD SCHOOL

'Your brother is a cop, isn't he?'

The teacher at Kirkegaard School stopped in front of the father of a pupil, and confirmed that, yes, her brother was a police officer.

'I know who killed those people on the canal boat. And the knife used was either a KA-BAR or an NR-40. Not many people know that.'

The teacher was speechless. For a moment she thought she was the butt of a tasteless joke, but when she realised that the man was serious, she was furious.

'If you know anything, I strongly recommend that you contact the police.'

'No! I don't want to go on record. Call your brother, say KA-BAR or NR-40 and tell them that I know the killer, but don't mention my name. I'll be in the library, they can find me there.'

'What is a KA-BAR or an NR-40?'

'KA-BAR is a contraction of Kill a Bear, an American knife brand. The NR-40 is a Soviet combat knife, which was first produced in 1940. NR is short for *nozh razvedchika*, which means scout knife. Not that it matters, just say KA-BAR or NR-40, that's all you need.'

It took less than two hours after the father spoke to the teacher for the Countess to arrive at the school. When Arne Pedersen received the call from his sister, he was in Frederiksværk, so he contacted his boss. Konrad Simonsen, too, was intrigued by this information. Perhaps it was their much-needed breakthrough.

Releasing the sketch had produced nothing like the response the Homicide Department had hoped for. The number of calls from the public had been so small that the police were starting to think the murderer must be a foreigner who could only have been in Denmark for a short time. This was disastrous because the investigation didn't have much more than the sketch to work with. Arne Pedersen and Klavs Arnold's efforts in Frederiksværk to find Juli Denissen's killer were going nowhere, nor could the Countess's work with the car team be said to have borne fruit. Reducing the list of car models, which matched the vehicle that had dropped off the killer on the bridge, was going extremely slowly, and that was the polite version. The real truth was that this part of the investigation was also stalling.

The Countess spoke to the father in the school library. His explanation was straightforward. He was a veteran of Afghanistan and a frequent visitor to an ex-servicemen's club on Vesterbro in Copenhagen, where he also volunteered. There he had heard two

Balkan veterans discussing how the sketch shown on TV bore some resemblance to an old friend of theirs as he might look today.

'And they mentioned two knives that their friend used to carry, and reckoned that if he were the man in the sketch, he would undoubtedly have used one of them for the killing.'

The father pushed a note across the table to the Countess.

'Here are the names of the two men. But I'm warning you, they don't give a toss about the authorities, they've been let down too many times for that. And I would appreciate it if you don't tell them that you got this from me.'

The Countess was disappointed, she had been expecting more.

'Why do you insist on anonymity?'

'I don't trust the government.'

'You could have sent an email or called us without leaving your name.'

'I did, it got me nowhere. Now I just have to hope that you don't put my name on record.'

The Countess made no promises, but she thought she wouldn't need to identify him at this stage. She asked: 'Did your friends mention the man's name?'

The father said no, not directly, but: 'They called him "The Pole" three times. They referred to him as "The Pole".'

'Because he was from Poland?'

'I don't know. Poles usually are, but … like I said, I don't know.'

The Countess repeated the name as if tasting it. The Pole. Maybe she was making progress after all.

CHAPTER 19

TUESDAY 7 SEPTEMBER 2010, THE EX-SERVICEMEN'S CLUB

There was a new man at the lunch table. He wasn't tall, 1.65 metres would be Konrad Simonsen's guess, but he was broad-chested, strong and sinewy. The new guy didn't say much. Even so Simonsen sensed that he wanted to tell him something, and that he was struggling to overcome his distrust of strangers. Whenever Simonsen looked at him, he would avoid eye contact and stare at the table, yet he would study the Homicide chief whenever Simonsen pretended to ignore him.

It was Konrad Simonsen's fourth day at the ex-servicemen's club, and he didn't like being there. Not because the men who frequented it were unpleasant, they were not, and their initial reserve had long since evaporated, but the many stories he had heard, an endless list of betrayals and double standards, saddened him and ... yes, he had to admit it ... made him ashamed of being a Dane.

The club, which had no official name, consisted of two ground-floor apartments that had been knocked together, with stairs leading down to a basement with nine rooms that stretched under most of the apartment block. In the basement there was a range of different activities: a lounge where they showed films, an area for pool and darts, a gym with various exercise machines, a room for private conversation and one with computers used mainly for gaming. The place was privately funded, which explained its popularity. Many of the veterans preferred it to the publicly funded and better-organised clubs run by the Ministry of Defence or the local council.

There were no externally appointed managers. Instead a small handful of veterans acted informally as de facto leaders. Financially the club survived because the rent, water and utility bills were paid by the woman who owned the property. She had a son who had been injured in Afghanistan, and the veterans were the only people with whom he felt comfortable. Two local hotels supplied the club with surplus food from their restaurants, and a handful of volunteers from different backgrounds would turn up and help out when needed. They included a psychiatrist from Glostrup Hospital, a wealthy art dealer who owned four major galleries, several social workers and a retired police officer, whom Konrad Simonsen knew very well. The club was open 24/7, all ex-servicemen welcome.

After the Countess came back from Kirkegaard School with information about the man known as 'The Pole', Simonsen had found the two veterans at the club and interviewed them both. They, however, had shaken their heads and in monosyllables both denied ever hearing about a Pole, let alone having spoken about one. They recognised the sketch artist's picture, which Konrad Simonsen showed them, from the television, but said they had no idea who the man might be. They would co-operate eventually, but Simonsen had already decided not to browbeat them; he had carried out enough interviews to know that it wouldn't get him anywhere. These weren't people he could pressurise. However, the profile of the killer being a former soldier made sense, and their knowledge of the murder weapon was a convincing argument that somebody at the centre knew something they weren't prepared to say yet. Konrad Simonsen was sure that the two reluctant witnesses weren't telling the truth.

The next step would have been to have the sketch artist draw a younger version of the man and take the picture to the TDA, the Total Defence Archive in Ballerup, which stored paper-based records for ex-service personnel, but Simonsen was reluctant to do this. It would require a lot of resources and he couldn't guarantee a result. His only real option was to persuade someone at the club to share their knowledge with him, and the best way of doing that was to make himself accessible, visiting regularly as a constant reminder. He had put up a copy of the sketch on the wall and no one had taken it down. He took that as a positive sign.

On the second day he had spoken to the psychiatrist and asked with genuine surprise why none of the veterans were willing to help him. He was convinced that some of them could, if they wanted to. The psychiatrist had smiled, a small, tight smile, while exhaling through his nose. There was so much that Konrad Simonsen didn't understand. Only later that afternoon over a cup of coffee had he explained, as he pointed out three veterans in the room.

'That's Jens. As you can see, he lost his legs and one arm to a roadside bomb in Helmand. He has been fighting for years for decent prosthetics. He has finally been successful and, when he's well enough, he'll start rehabilitation at Rigshospitalet. If he's lucky, the council might at some point pay for electrically oper-ated curtains for him, and special cutlery to make it easier for him to eat ... we can always hope, though I doubt it will ever happen.

But all in all, he's one of our success stories, though he also has his bad days, when the feet that he no longer has start to itch unbearably. He struggles to cope with that and on those days he stays at home.'

What could he say to that? Simonsen tried to look sympathetic.

'Then there's Steven over there. His big dream is to go back to Afghanistan, get himself some sort of job with his mates. It's where he feels he belongs. His leg stayed behind, and he has only a stump now. He has battled the Army and the council for three years to be given a prosthetic limb he can run on, but they say they can't afford that kind of luxury. He'll never see Afghanistan again and everyone except him knows it. Sometimes when he talks no sound comes out, and if anyone laughs he is depressed for days afterwards. Oh, and his girlfriend dumped him a few months after he came back. He can't cope on his own, so he rarely goes home. He spends most of his time here, including the nights.'

This time Simonsen only nodded to indicate his sympathy. The psychiatrist continued talking unperturbed.

'Evil, death, betrayal and broken promises are recurrent themes here, and remember that what you see is only the tip of the iceberg. In that context your Japanese children are just ... another incident, let's call it, on top of everything else.'

'OK, I think I understand.'

'No, you just don't like what you're hearing. That guy over there, his name is also Jens. He's a Balkan veteran and since returning to Denmark fifteen years ago, his life hasn't been worth living, if you ask him. He suffers from aggression and anxiety. You probably don't care about his diagnosis, but I can tell you that he's terrified of going to the loo. At times he will drink or take cocaine, and when his daughter comes to visit him – they always meet here – he spends weeks getting all excited about it and usually breaks down when she leaves. He feels that he has let her down, but he hasn't, it's his country that let *him* down, but he can't see that, sadly.

'He has repeatedly tried to kill himself, and who knows? One day he might well succeed. He wouldn't be the first. And that would suit the State just fine because then he won't qualify for the disability living allowance he's currently applying for. We have two thick files of paperwork. His payment is still being processed and has yet to be authorised.'

Konrad Simonsen tried another angle.

'I'm investigating a mass killing. Surely everyone here would care about that?'

The psychiatrist ignored him.

'Most people here believe in Denmark, in the flag, in honour and friendship, old sayings about a man's bond being his word, and that you always help your friends if you can. What they don't believe in are our bureaucrats, desk generals, politicians – in short their fellow Danes, the people they fought for, but who turned their backs on them when they came home and needed help. Take a look at this.'

The man pulled a newspaper from a pile on a table behind him. On the front page was a small piece about the death of a Danish soldier in Afghanistan, below it an article double the size: *Your guide to fighting dust mites.*

'That's hard to look at if you've lost a friend. Nor did it go down all that well here when the Defence Minister was caught using the same eulogy at different soldiers' funerals. Cut and paste, why create unnecessary work for yourself? If the enemy dies, he gets virgins; when our soldiers die, they get recycled eulogies.'

By then Konrad Simonsen had needed some fresh air and had gone for a walk. On his way back he bumped into the psychiatrist.

'Are you telling me that I'm wasting my time?'

The man lit a cigarette before he replied.

'No, you'll probably get what you want in the end, but it'll take time. When you're not here, they discuss you at length. But you should continue to drop by whenever you can. Also, when you've got your information, there might be something you can do for them. Don't forget, they also fought for you.'

Simonsen cringed, he didn't like the suggestion. It hit home because more than anything he wanted to leave this place and forget all about it, forget the men's wretched fates, forget that his country was at war, forget everything … just like most other Danes had done.

He chose the easy way out and gave a non-committal reply.

'I might just do that. So you're sure someone here knows something?'

The psychiatrist turned and walked away from him without a word. Then he changed his mind and came back. 'Yes, somebody here knows something.'Then he left.

The breakthrough came when Simonsen was in the kitchen making coffee. The new man he had seen at lunch came in and as usual avoided making eye contact, but this time he spoke.

'Bjørn Lauritzen. He was deployed in Bosnia in 'ninety-five. He's the man in your sketch.'

'Bjørn Lauritzen is The Pole?'

The nickname had become so familiar to him that Konrad Simonsen failed to realise its irrelevance until he had asked the question.

'Yes, The Pole, if you like. But you have a problem.'

'Which is what?'

'Bjørn is dead.'

CHAPTER 20

'Gone? How can it be gone?'

Konrad Simonsen challenged the Countess as if she were personally responsible for the disappearance of Bjørn Lauritzen's personnel file from the Total Defence Archive. The Countess repeated calmly what she herself had been told, which was that several personnel files were lost in 2001 when the Army's Personnel Service had decided to scan its paper records in order to digitise them in a grandiose IT project that had later had to be abandoned. Bjørn Lauritzen's data was among the lost files.

Simonsen asked angrily: 'So as far as the Army is concerned, he might as well never have existed?'

'Not entirely. They have payroll information on him for the whole period. He was in the Army from 1983 until he was declared dead in 2000, since when his widow has received a pension. However, we have no information on what he did during his time in the Army or where he was based. We can find this out, of course, it'll just take time and more resources.'

'I don't think he's dead.'

The Countess had already realised this and yet she struggled to see why her husband and boss was proposing to devote more time and resources to discovering Bjørn Lauritzen's life history before they could even be sure that the man was still alive. Even so she had spent most of the day piecing together information about the soldier; work that might so easily turn out to be a complete waste of time. Simon's explanation – that he wanted to be well-prepared when they visited Bjørn Lauritzen's widow tomorrow – hadn't convinced her, and she was left with a disloyal feeling that her husband simply wanted the man not to be dead and was behaving accordingly. Whatever the truth was, at least they now had a basic CV to work from.

'He was born in 1961 in a small village in Vestjylland. He attained excellent A-levels in 1979. He married ten years later. His widow is a shop assistant and they have two sons. However, I found something on him at Kongsøre Torpedo Station—'

Konrad Simonsen exclaimed: 'He was a frogman?'

'As good as. He began the frogman's course in 1982, by which time he must have completed his National Service or he wouldn't have been eligible. He passed the course with flying colours, undoubtedly the best member of his team. As you know, the training is gruelling, bordering on inhumane, and only one in ten trainees qualifies, so it's fair to say that he was the best of the best. However, shortly before his graduation, he dropped out. No one knows why, he kept that to himself. I've spoken to several officers who remember him very well, and they described him as a man of few words, somewhat introverted, extremely focused, a leader, and here I quote from his old close combat instructor: the last person on earth you would want as your enemy.'

Simonsen asked for more information; the Countess had none. She wanted to go home. Tomorrow would be another long day and they weren't getting anywhere.

Her husband started speculating out loud: it was all too convenient, Bjørn Lauritzen wasn't dead, it had to be a mistake.

The information they had stated that one night in October 1998, a man had sneaked past the Storebæltsbroen Bridge toll booths on the Sjælland side, and not been spotted on the surveillance cameras by a sleepy security guard until he was close to the first pylon on the suspension-bridge section. The guard had dispatched a security car, but before it caught up with the man, he had committed suicide by jumping over the railings and into the water. This happened from time to time, though it wasn't something that the bridge management tended to publicise. And indeed the death passed more or less unnoticed, except that the local newspaper, *Korsør Posten*, ran a brief article on the incident. The man's body was never found, but that wasn't unusual. Bodies from such suicides could drift ashore in one of numerous locations for a long period afterwards, often at a considerable distance from the bridge.

However, six months later a woman happened to spot the newspaper notice. She knew Bjørn Lauritzen from his time in the military, and the very night he jumped, she had been driving past in her car and seen a man walking along the bridge. She had slowed down and opened her window to ask if anything was wrong, at which point she had recognised him. Bjørn Lauritzen. He, however, had told her to get lost, and she drove on when she saw the yellow light from an approaching security vehicle, thinking that they could deal with the problem. Based on events surrounding the suicide and the woman's witness statement, Bjørn Lauritzen was declared legally dead by a court in May 2001.

Simonsen let the Countess off the hook. He could sense her eagerness to get home, and promised to follow in the next hour. He spent that hour staring into the air and thinking.

He had found a handful of pictures on the Internet of Bjørn Lauritzen in Bosnia in 1994 and 1995. They had been uploaded by veterans who maintained ex-servicemen websites and Facebook groups about their postings in former Yugoslavia.

One showed three soldiers in camouflage uniform standing under the barrel of a white-painted Leopard tank, with the blue UN flag blowing in the wind and the Danish flag painted on the back. None of the three was identifiable, the picture had been taken from too great a distance for that, but the caption listed the middle soldier as Captain Bjørn Lauritzen. The picture's background was bordering on picture postcard: beautiful green mountains in the distance and a well-tended vegetable garden to the right. But there was no mistaking the firepower of the tank – the Danish peace-keeping soldiers in Bosnia had been heavily armed.

Another picture showed a white Jeep with three Danish soldiers in camouflage uniform sitting inside it. The Jeep was struggling to get past a horse-drawn cart carrying a family of five, their belongings piled high, driving in the opposite direction, away from massacres, ethnic cleansings and night-time attacks on defenceless families, a living hell he could see in the reproachful eyes of the man of the refugee family. Simonsen could also see Bjørn Lauritzen's face clearly; he looked exhausted, and initially there were few similarities between the 1994 photograph and the sketch made sixteen years later.

However, what was interesting was that once Konrad Simonsen knew the name Bjørn Lauritzen, some of the Balkan veterans from the ex-servicemen's club in Vesterbrogade became willing to talk about him. They insisted that they had met their old captain at the funeral of a mutual friend who had killed himself. Bjørn Lauritzen hadn't come inside the church, only appeared in the cemetery when the coffin was lowered into the ground, and he had kept away from the other mourners. But they had nodded to him and definitely recognised him, though his appearance had changed a great deal since Bosnia. He had looked like the embodiment of a Stone Age man, but in good physical shape, and his eyes exuded the same calm they remembered so well. They also said that his appearance was a close match to the police sketch. The odd thing was that particular funeral had taken place in 2006, but the two witnesses were adamant: the man they had seen was Bjørn Lauritzen, no matter how dead he had been declared.

It was this paradox that was on Konrad Simonsen's mind as he sat in his office, staring into thin air. And it wasn't his only concern after what the Countess had reported back to him.

The Army had accidentally deleted Bjørn Lauritzen's personnel file – all right, these things happened. Then a woman, an ex-Army employee, had recognised Bjørn Lauritzen on the Storebæltsbroen Bridge, and her statement had resulted in his being declared dead. Again, people make mistakes, including mistaking their old acquaintances, so that too could be dismissed as a coincidence.

But to Konrad Simonsen it was one coincidence too many.

CHAPTER 21

THURSDAY 9 SEPTEMBER 2010, SKØRPING

It had been some time since Konrad Simonsen and the Countess last visited Jutland, and they had both been looking forward to the trip.

It represented a break from work, a chance to talk, enjoy the Danish autumn landscape and see the harvest gathered in. At least that was the plan, but the reality proved otherwise. The weather was drab, oppressive, grey with intermittent showers, and Simonsen was sleep-deprived. He nodded off several times in the car and tried in vain to keep their conversation going, until the Countess pulled over and ordered him into the back. Better a proper sleep than a series of naps, better for both of them. He didn't protest and proved impossible to wake when she later stopped at a motorway service station for lunch and a cup of coffee. She let him sleep and listened to an audiobook as a substitute for his company. He didn't wake up until they were less than ten kilometres from their destination, the village of Skørping.

The two officers from Copenhagen were met by Rikke Lauritzen, Bjørn Lauritzen's widow, and her elder son. She was a plain-looking woman of medium height with dyed blonde hair, tired features and a somewhat sallow complexion, but that might be because of the weather, the Countess thought, as their hostess showed her guests into the kitchen-diner where she had set out coffee and cake. From the moment they had shaken hands in the driveway, Rikke Lauritzen had insisted that she wanted her son present during the conversation. He was tall, eighteen years old, with an open face and a calm manner most often found in older people. He sat down next to his mother and would at times pat her forearm discreetly. Though she was clearly apprehensive about the conversation, he wasn't.

It was the Countess who, after small talk about the weather and their drive from Copenhagen, opened the interview. They had actually agreed the opposite, but it was clear that Rikke Lauritzen was much more comfortable with her than with Konrad Simonsen.

The Countess explained the situation: the police were starting to doubt whether her husband really was dead, and they suspected that he might be responsible for the mass killings in Copenhagen on Sunday 22 August. Rikke Lauritzen started crying and apologised immediately, she vowed to pull herself together, but this was awful, please could she have a break? She was aware that they had only just started, but …

Her son was the first to reply: she could have all the breaks she needed. The Countess followed this up, speaking in a soft voice.

'Perhaps we should start elsewhere. The Army has lost most of the information about your late husband, so his CV is full of holes. If you could fill in some of them, that would be a great help.'

Again it was the son who spoke up.

'My mother can and will do that, but what's the point if my father is dead? Shouldn't you find out for sure first?'

The Countess thought it was like hearing herself yesterday when she had raised the exact same objection to Simon. She tried half-heartedly to cobble together an explanation, which she didn't believe either, and the son openly shook his head at her. Rikke Lauritzen interrupted, almost inaudibly:

'Bjørn isn't dead.'

Simonsen wanted to know more, but Rikke Lauritzen ignored his question and pressed herself against her son while she held up her palms as though she were being physically attacked. Simonsen looked quizzically at the Countess, who nodded imperceptibly. It sometimes happened that a witness feared one officer and trusted another, a situation that could sometimes be exploited to the police's advantage, while at other times, like now, it got in the way of the interview. The Countess turned to her husband.

'I think I can take it from here, so if you want a car to be sent from Aalborg to drive you there, that's all right with me.'

When he had left, the three of them agreed to start with Bjørn Lauritzen's Army years before going on to more difficult subjects. Rikke Lauritzen fetched a file and during the next half-hour, they documented her husband's career, piece by piece. It was real work, fact-based, not up for discussion, and it eased Rikke Lauritzen's anxiety. Or perhaps she was just more relaxed now Simonsen had gone. Whatever it was, she worked constructively, without emotional outbursts. Her son and the Countess kept track of the chronology.

1981	*Nine months of National Service with the Royal Horseguards*
1982 – 85	*Frogman training at Kongsøre Torpedo Station. Abandons his training shortly before graduation*
1985 – 88	*Joins the Scout squadron of the Royal Horseguards*
1988 – 90	*Selected for Officer School and trained at Farum Barracks. Appointed Second Lieutenant, qualifies as a close-combat instructor and tank driver*
1990 – 92	*Tank commander at Camp Oksbøl*
1992	*First deployment to Bosnia, six months*
	Field appointment to First Lieutenant during deployment, commission confirmed on return. Works as platoon commander for three to five tanks
	Awarded the Armed Forces Bravery Medal on his return for great personal courage
1992 – 95	*First Lieutenant at Camp Oksbøl, occasional postings to the Frogman Corps as a close-combat instructor*

1995	*Second deployment to Bosnia, six months.*
	Acts as Company Commander, often takes part in tank patrols
	Field appointment to Captain, commission confirmed on return
July 1995	*Sent home early from Bosnia, reason unknown*
Other:	*Winner of the Danish Military Pentathlon in 1998, 1990, 1991 and 1994; Nordic champion in 1993 and Silver Medallist at the World Championship in Brazil in 1994*

'So you've no idea why Bjørn was sent home before his deployment had finished?' queried the Countess.

Rikke Lauritzen shook her head. He hadn't said and she had only asked a few times before she gave up when it was obvious that he didn't want to talk about it. Like so many other things from Bosnia, which he also kept to himself.

'Please would you stop referring to him as Bjørn? It's not as if you knew my father,' put in the boy.

The Countess apologised and resumed: 'We know that your husband continued to receive his Army salary as though he were still deployed in Bosnia for almost two years after his return home. Do you know why?'

Rikke Lauritzen apologised, sorry, she had no idea. Nor could she answer the Countess's next question about why her husband continued to be paid up until the time he was declared dead. She had merely received the money and never asked any questions.

'Please would you tell me what happened when Bjørn Lauritzen came home in the summer of 1995?'

Rikke Lauritzen sat for a while, staring at nothing, then she said miserably: 'Things went from bad to worse. I already had Victor here, who was three years old then, and I was about to give birth to Emil. I mean ... I had enough on my plate, but Bjørn didn't lift a finger. He was wrapped up in himself and hardly ever said anything. He only really talked to me at night when he woke up after a nightmare, and I would comfort him. This would happen a couple of times every night, more often if it was really bad. He spent most of his days sitting on the terrace, when he didn't go running in the forest. He was in a bad way, really bad, and it got worse rather than better. He ignored Victor all the time and most of the time he also ignored me.'

'Didn't you ask for help?'

'Yes, I contacted Social Services and the Army, and they were very nice, but nothing ever happened except they sent me a couple of useless letters. I also tried getting Bjørn to meet a psychologist, but I failed. Bjørn would ignore me, it was like talking to a wall. And he didn't want me to touch him, only at night when he needed comforting. Then he would be like a child.'

'Alcohol, drugs, anything like that?'

She shook her head.

'Eventually his trips to the forest became longer and longer. In September 1995, he would only come home to sleep, and some nights he would stay away altogether. I was sick with worry for him, for our marriage, but mostly for my children, for Victor and the baby I was pregnant with. Not being able to reach my husband was frightening. He was also scared of himself, he told me one day. He was scared that he might kill us, that was what he said, that he *might kill us* – so of course I was terrified. It's difficult to explain, but it was as if he had lost the ability to value life, not just his own but everyone's. Something inside him had broken in Bosnia.'

She came to a halt, and the Countess prompted her.

'So where did he live?'

'In the woods, I think. After I'd had Emil, he mostly stayed away. To begin with I would leave bags with food on the terrace for him, and often the bags would be gone without me having spoken to him. I would also leave money, but he would usually ignore it.'

'Did you ever talk?'

'Yes, sometimes, and he seemed a bit better. He told me that he couldn't stand being indoors, I remember. Or being with other people.'

'So he kept to himself?'

'I believe so.'

'Do you remember what, if anything, he took with him?'

Rikke Lauritzen tried. Slowly and hesitantly, she listed several items, everyday things: toothbrush, shaving kit, boots, sleeping bag … there was more, she thought, but most of it she wasn't sure about now and had to guess at. The Countess let her finish, making some notes meanwhile. Finally she put the one really crucial question she had been waiting to ask.

'Was he armed?'

Rikke Lauritzen's eyes flitted away, and her son uttered an urgent *Mum*, nothing more, but it did the trick.

'Two knives, Army combat knives, as far as I know.'

The Countess showed Rikke a picture. She nodded miserably. Yes, that was Bjørn's knife. The Countess skipped the obvious follow-up question: then why hadn't Rikke Lauritzen already contacted the police? Instead she asked, 'And you have known for some time that your husband isn't dead?'

She had. Six months after he had been officially declared dead, he had turned up out of the blue. She had driven Victor to his Boy Scout meeting and come back to find her husband sitting on the terrace. She had hugged him, held him tight for a long time without either of them saying anything. Afterwards he had told her that he was OK, but that he was only rarely in Jutland. He lived elsewhere in Denmark and sometimes in Sweden. He didn't say precisely where, but it was obviously in the woods. He had just come to show her that he wasn't dead. Then he had left, and there was nothing more to say except that he had looked strong and muscular, and that he had drunk a glass of water and asked for a packet of rye bread, that was all he had wanted, nothing more. He hadn't asked about his children.

The Countess prodded carefully, but Rikke Lauritzen was right – there was nothing more to tell. Rikke would be interviewed again later, but the Countess didn't tell her so. She had only two questions left and was given time to consider them while Rikke Lauritzen fetched some letters that her husband had written to her from Bosnia that she said the police were allowed to borrow. The Countess thanked her and put the letters in her bag, then she showed Rikke the artist's sketch, but was met with a dismissive gesture. She already knew the drawing. *Please would you put it away?* The Countess folded the drawing as Rikke Lauritzen practically whispered: 'It does look like him, not completely, but yes, that's

Bjørn, I'm sorry to say. Someone should have helped him when he needed it.'

The Countess couldn't agree more. Someone really should have.

'Bjørn Lauritzen dropped out of his frogman training in 1982, shortly before completing his course. Do you know why?'

Rikke nodded; she did. He loathed the initiation rites that invariably followed the end of the course, yet he had wanted to show that he was capable of completing his training. His departure had been an act of protest. The Countess accepted this explanation; it was what the Homicide Department had surmised. She produced some cotton-wool buds and two small plastic bags.

'I need a DNA sample from each of you. I hope you'll co-operate.'

The boy asked: 'And if we won't?'

'Then I'll get a warrant, but I prefer to avoid that.'

The boy shook his head. What a load of tosh! They had done nothing illegal, how could a judge demand a DNA sample? Besides it was only his DNA that was of interest to them, not his mother's. How stupid did she think he was?

The Countess said quietly: 'I have with me a great many photographs of children who hadn't done anything wrong either, and who died far too young.'

'Because my father didn't get the help he needed and was entitled to?'

'Yes.'

Rikke Lauritzen was the first to open her mouth for the swab to be taken, then her son followed suit.

CHAPTER 22

THURSDAY 9 SEPTEMBER 2010, LISELEJE

'Mum, it's the man in the wood.'

The child pointed triumphantly at the television so his mother could see that he hadn't been making it up and that the man in the wood was real. He was five years old and when the sketch of the man disappeared from the TV screen, he lost interest and turned his attention back to his Lego helicopter. It was about to fly a Lego figure to the hospital from the washing-up bowl where it was drowning and that was much more important. However, something made his mother feel uneasy.

'What makes you say that?'

Her voice was a little sharp, and the boy reacted to it immediately. He replied in a surly tone: 'Because I saw him.'

It wasn't the first time the man in the wood had been mentioned. At home the boys would tell stories of a mysterious man they met in the forest from time to time, a man who looked like a troll, but who was nice and had showed them how to build a proper den and follow animal tracks. These had been dismissed by their parents as nonsense. Whenever they spoke about him, their father would tell them off: *stop talking about him, you know your mum doesn't like it.* If they couldn't tell the difference between fantasy and reality, they were too young to play in the wood on their own. This was a serious threat: the children loved the wood, it was their favourite playground, and so they had stopped mentioning the man they saw there unless they were alone. Yet from time to time the younger boy would forget his father's warning.

The family's home was a former gamekeeper's cottage about one kilometre from the town of Liseleje, and it lay deep inside Liseleje Plantation. The children were used to playing among the trees that surrounded the cottage on all sides. Today, however, rain had forced them to stay indoors. The family car was at the garage for an oil change, and their mother had kept the boys home from school, a rare occurrence, but she had a day off and rather than cycle back and forth with the kids, had granted them a duvet day, which her husband had decided to join in and was working from home. She had been doing the ironing while half-heartedly watching the television, a repeat of yesterday's summary of police efforts in the canal boat case. As part of this, they had showed the artist's sketch of the presumed killer. Now she switched off the iron, put it on its end and turned on a computer behind her. She looked up the sketch and left it on the screen. Her younger son watched her carefully, wondering if he was in trouble. She stroked his head while she called his older brother and her husband.

The older boy was ten and thus more observant than his younger brother, and he backed him up. Yes, that was the man in the wood, but they weren't supposed to talk about him. The parents exchanged looks; on the contrary, they very much wanted to hear more about the man in the wood, as much as the boys could remember. The boys started talking.

They met him while they were playing on their own, but only rarely. He would hide in the forest and whenever they looked for him, they never found him. They could only be with him when he allowed it. He was mostly in the forest during the winter; in the summer there were too many people, and he didn't like strangers. He'd also kept a rabbit and that had been during the winter – the big brother corrected the little brother: it was a baby hare – they were allowed to stroke it, and the man in the wood had promised them that he wouldn't eat it, but mostly he only lived there in the winter.

Their mother asked, forcing herself to stay calm: 'When you go off with the man in the wood, where do you go?'

'Nowhere. Around the wood. He sets traps, or we sit down and he tells us stuff from when he was a boy or things about the forest or the animals, he knows loads about animals, and about the trees.'

Their father asked them gravely: 'Does he touch you?'

The boys' baffled expression provided him with the best possible answer. Touched them how? Then the younger boy, keen to make a positive contribution, said: 'He carried me across the brook when I was little.'

Their mother asked: 'Have you visited his house?'

'He sleeps in the old bunker, the one down by the beach, but he doesn't want us to go there, so we don't. We only ever see him in the wood.'

'If you've never been inside his bunker, then how do you know that's where he lives?'

The older boy shook his head, he had no answer to that. The younger boy said: 'Because he says so.'

The boys were sent to their rooms while the adults discussed the situation. Their mother wanted to call the police, their father thought her reaction excessive; it could be childish make-believe and that would be embarrassing to report. The outcome was that he cycled to the bunker, a former munitions depot for Camp Melby, a military training ground up until its decommission in 2003, to seek confirmation of the children's story. After struggling with a padlock, which he broke apart with a rock, he opened the rusty steel door to the bunker and found in the remotest corner of the room clear evidence to support his sons' story: a pile of neatly folded blankets, a rubbish bag containing mostly empty food tins as far as he could see, a plastic water canister, books, apparently second-hand, and a picture of a woman he didn't recognise, stuck to the wall. He took a few pictures on his mobile phone, then stepped outside and called the police.

Two hours later Klavs Arnold was searching the bunker while the man who had made the call was standing behind him. Klavs called for a team of forensic technicians, drove the man home where he interviewed the two boys and got pretty much the same story as the one told to their parents four hours earlier. Except for one aspect: Klavs Arnold was particularly interested in what the boys meant when they said that the man in the wood was *mostly* there during the winter. Did that mean they had also seen him in the summer? And which summer was it? The older boy wavered. Not this summer, but possibly the last one or the one before that, it was hard to remember. But the man had given him a present on his birthday and he still had it. He darted upstairs to his room and soon returned. It was a wood carving that must have taken some time to make, a finely chiselled Midgard Serpent coiling around itself and the world, carved in oak possibly – the density of the wood and its pale colour would suggest it, Klavs Arnold thought. Two crossed flags and the text *Per 8 years* were carved into the back.

He asked the boy: 'How old are you?'

'I'm ten.'

'When is your birthday?'

His mother replied: 'The sixth of July.'

Klavs Arnold thought it all added up: Bjørn Lauritzen, because Arnold had no doubt that it was he, had been in Liseleje on 6 July 2008. Four days later Juli Denissen was attacked less than two kilometres from where they were now. He asked the boy in a friendly manner: 'Please may I borrow your present if I promise to give it back?'

The boy thought about it and replied: 'No, it's mine.'

CHAPTER 23

FRIDAY 10 SEPTEMBER 2010, POLICE HEADQUARTERS

The killing was inconvenient, as killings invariably are. Konrad Simonsen was forced to comply with his own rule that either he or Arne Pedersen must turn up at any crime scene when a murder had been committed, as it had been last night in Bellahøj.

For the past twelve months a young single mother had been plagued by a stalker, who had made her life a living hell. Unluckily for the stalker, his victim was an electrician and out of sheer desperation she had taken matters into her own hands: she had run a cable from her cooker to her letterbox, which she would connect at night when she disabled the flat's fuses and circuit breakers. Unfortunately it worked only too well. When the stalker turned up to deliver more hate mail, three hundred and eighty volts were sent through him, and he was killed. When the woman discovered what she had done the next morning, she had left her daughter with the downstairs neighbour and gone on the run.

Konrad Simonsen checked his watch. He had agreed to meet Arne Pedersen and review the canal boat killings. He resisted the urge to call him and instead went through the case in his mind.

On Monday he would learn whether the DNA sample from Bjørn Lauritzen's son was a familial match to the DNA gathered from the railings on Battery Bridge, but he regarded the matter as a formality. He had no real doubts that there would be a match as fingerprints on tins found in the old bunker had already been found to match fingerprints taken from the bridge. Bjørn Lauritzen was his killer, he was sure of it.

People who knew about these things had told him that an estimated thirty to fifty hermits lived in the Danish woods. They survived by setting traps, foraging and, in the winter months, visiting supermarket skips at night. They were rarely addicts, that simply wasn't compatible with the daily struggle to live in and off the forest. Many of the hermits were said to be war veterans, who were suffering from PTSD and didn't feel comfortable indoors. And to make matters even more complicated, Simonsen thought, it wasn't unusual for these hermits to change location, usually in accordance with the seasons. The bottom line was that his chances of finding Bjørn Lauritzen were minuscule, unless he could obtain more information about the killer's possible whereabouts, and he had no idea how to do that.

However, his prospects of solving the attack on Juli Denissen looked more promising. He believed that the young woman's death was somehow central to the canal boat killings, and was now able to place Bjørn Lauritzen at a nearby location during the same timeframe.

In addition Anica Buch had submitted her report on Juli Denissen's emails. In two emails written during the winter of 2006, the young woman had described her snail phobia to her then lover, a doctor. Other witnesses had mentioned her phobia, so no further corroboration was needed, but the observation was interesting in relation to Anica Buch's second point: someone had gained access to or hacked Juli Denissen's email account and deleted emails to and from her last lover, Mads Eggert. Despite Anica Buch's two-page speculation about this claim, it didn't seem entirely convincing. Even so Konrad Simonsen decided to re-interview Ella von Eggert, the widow from Frederiksværk, but this time he would do it himself.

That left the letters Bjørn Lauritzen had sent to his wife from Bosnia. In conjunction with the information Simonsen had found on the Internet and with the help of veterans from the club in Vesterbrogade, he now had a reasonable idea of which men Bjørn Lauritzen had spent the most time with in Bosnia, especially the soldiers from the DANSQN squadron, which formed part of the joint Nordic NORDBAT 2 battalion, to which Lauritzen was posted for the last few months before he was returned to Denmark. And that had to be Konrad Simonsen's next move. He was determined to find out what had happened in Bosnia, why Bjørn Lauritzen had been sent home early, and why, after returning home, he continued for almost two years to be paid as though he were still deployed abroad, and was paid the then basic salary of a captain. The Army payroll listed him as a consultant during the first period, but no one could tell Simonsen what the man had been consulting on – and the job title belied Rikke Lauritzen's account of her husband's behaviour at the time in question.

Arne Pedersen entered the office noisily and interrupted Simonsen's thoughts.

'Sorry, Simon, that took longer than expected, but we've got her now. She was with a girlfriend on Funen, and we persuaded her to turn herself in to our colleagues over there. Crazy woman. Couldn't she have found a less permanent solution?'

Konrad Simonsen wasn't terribly interested, so he muttered something vague, but Arne Pedersen continued: 'I hope that the government gets its act together soon and increases penalties for brain-dead, heartless stalkers when they breach their injunctions. They make life hell for so many people.'

'Yes, but let's also pray that one woman's solution doesn't inspire her fellow sufferers to copy her.'

They didn't disagree about that. Then they discussed Bjørn Lauritzen, mostly their chances of finding him. It wouldn't be easy. Simonsen said tentatively: 'I'm not sure that we can hold him accountable for anything. He could have been irreparably damaged in Bosnia, we must bear that in mind.'

Arne Pedersen was shocked. First, because this wasn't relevant to the investigation; the judicial system would have to deal with that issue when or if the time came. Secondly, it was out of character for Konrad Simonsen to excuse serious crimes because of the killer's past. Pedersen avoided his boss's gaze and mumbled that he might be right about that.

Konrad Simonsen returned to practical matters.

'Go to your office and clear your diary. I want you and Klavs to visit the people on this list and find out how Bjørn Lauritzen behaved when he was in Bosnia.'

He handed Pedersen a piece of paper, and got up to go to lunch. If he hurried, he would have time to eat at the ex-servicemen's club.

CHAPTER 24

'I had a brother. We both tagged around Copenhagen, you know, street art on walls, trains, anything. It was in the late 1980s and we were young. One night he fell, it was only two metres, all that should have happened was a broken leg, but he died right in front of me and there was nothing I could do. We were twins and it was like losing myself. In the years that followed, I drifted around feeling like shit, I drank, smoked dope, partied ...'

The man's life story before Bosnia was irrelevant, but it was how he had chosen to start and the most important thing was to keep him talking.

They were in a meeting room on the third floor of A. P. Møller Mærsk's head office in Copenhagen, where today the former soldier worked as a business development manager. Who would have thought it? Arne Pedersen mused to himself. His witness's story was in sharp contrast to his stylish appearance in a dark grey suit, which fitted him perfectly and which had undoubtedly cost a fortune, and the room, which was functional and beautiful at the same time, but all the effortless efficiency that surrounded them evaporated when he spoke. He talked about joining the Army, how it gave his life structure and how he later volunteered for Bosnia. That was in the spring of 1995.

'I don't know where to begin with Bjørn, it's hard, but perhaps by telling you that he was a born leader. Every one of his men looked up to him, they trusted his decisions and followed his orders when he gave them, although mostly we talked about how things should be done. But there's no doubt that apart from being the appointed leader, he would also have been our elected leader, getting every single vote, if we'd had a choice. He was considerate towards us rookies without being overly familiar, a thoroughly decent human being in everyday situations, but he could also be the most effective and ruthless warrior I have ever met, should the situation require it. Soft and hard, day and night, if you like. When he had to, he could speak that macho language, which was the only language anyone in that shithole respected or understood.

'You only had to spend a few days down there to realise that the mandate the politicians back in Copenhagen, yes, across all of Europe, had cobbled together at their desks, was horseshit. Peacekeeping, peace-building, you can call it whatever the hell you like, there was no peace, there was only war, so what good was it that we pretty much needed written permission from the Ministry of Defence before we could even point our guns at a Bosnian?

'I'm telling you that Rules of Engagement manual was almost one thousand pages long, they had rules for *everything*, especially all the things we *weren't* allowed to do. The only people who really knew what was going on were the Americans. They controlled the airspace with fighter planes from their aircraft carriers and their drones, of course, which you never saw, but you knew were there. Even the Americans were cautious to begin with ... civilised, I guess you could say. They also hoped for and believed in a negotiated settlement. Except when they discovered the location of a SAM system, those fucking surface-to-air missiles, a Russian abomination that the Serbs had got their hands on, hellishly effective, unfortunately. The Americans would go mental and bomb them to high heaven if they even suspected their presence. It can't have been much fun being a Serbian SAM commander. If anyone lived on borrowed time, it would be them. You've seen an ethnic map of the Balkans at that time?'

Yes, Arne Pedersen had, but …

'Croats, Serbs, Muslims, it looked like a patchwork quilt with the three groups mixed up left, right and centre, a complete nightmare. And we were stationed in one of the worst hellholes, Ljubicevac, a cluster of ten or twenty dilapidated houses in the woods near the border of the Dutch zone that included Srebrenica, where things went seriously pear-shaped in the summer of 1995. We had built ourselves an observation post, a small house made from sandbags. We called it Little Denmark – not very original, but it was where we spent most of our time when we weren't on patrol or had business in Tuzla or one of the other towns. We also frequently slept there.

'Bjørn Lauritzen was our commanding officer and we were lucky to have him. His rank entitled him to a comfortable office at headquarters in Tuzla, but he insisted on coming out where he could make a difference, and his superiors were probably only too pleased to see the back of him – he was known for his plain speaking, which didn't always make him popular. When he was with us, Bjørn would cut through all the crap. He dished out his own brand of peace or rather justice. I witnessed several examples of that, problems he solved in his own inimitable way. Do you want to hear about them?'

Arne Pedersen nodded. Yes, please. The man pulled off his tie, tossed it on his desk and unbuttoned a few buttons on his shirt, then he continued talking.

'In a town some kilometres away there was a market. I don't remember the name of the town, all those Bosnian names are completely impossible to pronounce, but we tended to visit the market to keep an eye on things, especially on Wednesdays and Saturdays, when it was at its busiest. They sold mostly fruit and vegetables, but also the sort of tat most Danes would have thrown straight in the bin, but the population was quite poor. Anyway, there was often trouble at the market, the Muslim women couldn't do their shopping in peace. They were harassed. People would shout at them, Serbian women would push them, and sometimes young Serbian louts would throw stones at them. And not for fun, I'm telling you, they would throw stones the size of a fist. Once I saw a little girl, just a toddler, get hit in the head, and to be frank, I don't think she survived.

'Eventually we found out that it was all masterminded by an old Serbian crone who would sit in a corner of the square where she had a good view of everything and then order her henchmen around. Bjørn tried talking to her and telling her to stop, but it made no difference. So one Saturday he brought along a stick and beat her until her vicious old bones ached. But it worked. There was never any trouble after that. We only had to show up, even just one of us, and everyone behaved as if they were at Sunday School. Now Bjørn's problem, of course, was that rumours started flying around that he had beaten up a poor old woman and so on and so forth, and everyone knew that he would get into trouble for it eventually.

'Then there was that business with the petrol, and I admit that was brutal. I was there myself so I know the story is true. It was the Serbian Army … this would happen quite a lot … they would stop our trucks and steal our supplies. On this occasion the Serbs had nicked a truckload of petrol on its way to us. We knew exactly who had done it and where our petrol canisters were, but when we spoke to the Serbian soldiers, they would just laugh in our faces or make all sort of promises that were never fulfilled. Bjørn was furious, almost as if he personally had been robbed, and he got into the tank and drove it over to where the Serbian bandits were. I went along. It was a Leopard tank – you've probably seen pictures of them? Big khaki bastards, you definitely don't want to pick a fight with one of those, and Bjørn had tarted up ours.

'Do you remember crazy Colonel Kilgore from *Apocalypse Now*? How he had mounted speakers on his Apache helicopters so they blasted out "The Ride of the Valkyries" while they were mounting an attack? Bjørn had copied that stunt by mounting two giant speakers at the front of his tank and playing the Copenhagen Town Hall bells on a loop. It sounded like hell had erupted on earth. You wouldn't believe how terrifying it was. So we drove with this music blasting into the local Serbian headquarters, headed for the officers' barracks, rammed the muzzle of the gun through the window and fired a shell straight through the room and out the wooden wall on the other side, scaring the shit out of the handful of officers who were inside. They staggered outside, stunned, deafened by the blast, several of them bleeding from the nose. Bjørn collared the highest-ranking guy and forced him to read a note that we'd brought along: *Petrol one hour* – there was no mistaking the meaning and less than twenty minutes later the Serbs returned the goods they had stolen, with many apologies. After that, whenever they met Bjørn, the Serbs would salute him, and they carried on doing so even though he ignored them. It was on that occasion that he got his nickname, I believe.'

'The Pole?'

'No, that was just among the Danes, and not many called him that, most people just called him Bjørn. But locally he was known as The Crazy Pole and the business about him being Polish was because the locals couldn't tell the difference between the Danish and the Polish flag, but Crazy was a sign of respect, partly because he did things no one else dared, and partly because the locals were terrified of him, especially the Serbs. When we returned to Little Denmark, Bjørn called Army HQ and complained that they had short-changed us a shell and he wasn't going to take responsibility for them not being able to count. You see, we had to report everything, account for absolutely everything, but he got out of that by blaming their inefficiency. And would you believe it? A few days later they sent us the missing shell, after which the books balanced.'

A pause ensued.

'Was it due to those incidents that he was recalled?' Pedersen asked after a while.

'Yes and no. I mean, there were things that happened that were worse, much worse. But when they pulled him out, I was on leave so I don't know exactly what the reason was.'

'And the worse things were?'

Again it took some time before the man began talking.

'In the area where we were supposed to be peace-keeping, there were some Serbian gangs, irregular troops with ridiculous names but all of them psychos. They slaughtered Muslim families systematically, one household after another. The things they did to them were vile … beggar belief. Men, women, old people, young people,

99

children – they didn't draw the line anywhere. Sometimes we would hear their victims scream at night, if they took them out into the forest, and I've seen … the results of their savagery afterwards. I prefer not to go into details and I guess there's no need to, but I've often wondered how I got through it without any mental scars, while some of my friends cracked when they came back. Is it because I'm more callous than other people that I don't have nightmares?'

'Your mind is your mind, you can't blame yourself for the way it works.'

'You may be right. Well, anyway, one night after three families had been burned alive in their own homes, Bjørn disappeared and didn't return until the morning. He had blood on his clothes. Several people saw him. A few days later we heard that six members of one of those psycho gangs had been killed, including their leader. They had had their throats slit while they were asleep. We never talked to Bjørn about it, but everybody knew that he had done it, and everyone privately agreed that the dead men had got what they deserved. Later on there was a particularly vicious major from the regular Serbian Army. They found him in a ditch, also stabbed to death. But no one could prove that Bjørn did it.'

'But you think he did it?'

'Of course he bloody did! And as rumours reached headquarters, his position became untenable. Everyone, except the Americans, was terrified of upsetting the Serbs. So they decided to dispatch a judge advocate from Copenhagen, a goody two-shoes with a spotless career both with us and with the Americans, to evaluate his conduct and make a recommendation. I think she might even have had a degree in psychology.'

'Because his reactions were excessively violent?'

'Yes, you could say that, but our superiors in Tuzla, and indeed those in Copenhagen, only had rumours to go on. They had nothing concrete they could pin on him. Besides I want to stress, like I already said, Bjørn wasn't always violent. For him violence was the last resort, never the first. I've seen a Norwegian soldier beat the crap out of him for no reason. The man was clearly unstable and Bjørn could have beaten him to a pulp or reported him, but he did neither, just walked away with blood running from his ear.'

'OK, so he wasn't sent home initially?'

'No. I mean, we were all expecting that he would be summoned to Tuzla to meet some tight-lipped bitch who'd interview him, but we couldn't have been more wrong. The lawyer turned out to be a gorgeous woman with no airs or graces. When she got to Tuzla, she borrowed a Jeep and drove out to see us, no escort or anything. And in no time she was utterly under Bjørn's spell. You could tell from looking at her that she was totally smitten, anyone could see it. There were all sorts of rumours, of course, such as him screwing her on top of the tank – they would often go driving in the Leopard – but I think it was mostly talk. I don't think that Bjørn was the unfaithful type; he had a wife and child back in Denmark. Some people said that he had known her in the past. But that was none of our business and the upshot was that she went back to Copenhagen and filed a report that totally exonerated him from every accusation and rumour.'

'But she came back?'

'Some months later. Yes, we couldn't work it out either. We assumed she simply wanted to see him again because he hadn't done anything wrong in the meantime ... I mean nothing worse than usual. But I went on leave on the day she arrived, so I don't know much about it.'

'What was her name, do you remember?'

'Of course. Her name was Irene Gallagher.'

CHAPTER 25

MONDAY 13 SEPTEMBER 2010, LORUP FOREST NEAR SLAGELSE

The hut was right on the edge of the clearing, and it was difficult to spot unless you were very close to it, so although Arne Pedersen had had its location described in detail, it still took him a while to find it. The man who lived there was called Ole Nysted and he had barely any contact with the outside world. That no longer surprised Pedersen, after recently speaking to several veterans from Bosnia, who also wanted to isolate themselves as much as possible. Nevertheless, he was shocked to learn that Ole Nysted didn't even know about the canal boat killings, nor did he show the faintest interest when told about them.

The hut consisted of one big room with a primitive kitchen at one end, a sofa that doubled as a bed at the other, and in the middle of the room a wood-burning stove, whose flue led straight out through the plain wooden wall, and definitely didn't comply with fire-safety regulations. Cupboards had been put up wherever there was room for them. Empty bottles of various alcoholic drinks, on the table in front of the sofa and on the sill in front of the only window in the room, bore witness that the man drank heavily, but though he clearly wasn't sober, he wasn't as drunk as you would expect. To Arne Pedersen's astonishment, Ole Nysted was surprisingly well groomed. His clothes were old, but not filthy, he had a crewcut, his beard was neatly trimmed and his nails clean. Arne Pedersen was tempted to ask how he got water to wash, but decided against it. They had more important things to talk about.

After some initial reluctance, Ole Nysted quietly related his experiences in Bosnia. At the start he told the investigator nothing new, nothing the police weren't already aware of, his account merely supporting the impression they had formed of Bjørn Lauritzen. Even so Arne Pedersen listened patiently, only prompting him from time to time. Otherwise he let his witness speak without interruption. It wasn't until an hour later that Pedersen asked his first real question.

'Thirteenth of July, 1995. I want to hear more about that day, please.'

Nysted shook his head. It wasn't clear whether he couldn't remember the day or he didn't want to talk about it. Arne Pedersen hoped it was the former and quickly summarised events for him.

'That morning you and nine other men were at the sandbag house you called Little Denmark. It was one of the three days of the

Srebrenica massacre that took place mostly in the woods around the city. Thousands of men were slaughtered when they tried to flee through the mountainous terrain to Tuzla. You had an excellent view of some of those woods. I know that you monitored the area through your binoculars, but otherwise you didn't take part except for driving to safety the handful of refugees who managed to reach you. At some point Bjørn Lauritzen received a message that a female advocate called Irene Gallagher was heading his way from Tuzla in a Jeep. You and Lauritzen immediately drove off in your Leopard tank. Those facts are confirmed by witnesses. I don't know why you drove off or where you went. But I know that you entered the Dutch zone where you had no business to be, to put it mildly.'

Ole Nysted replied in a whisper that was difficult to hear although Arne Pedersen was sitting right next to him.

'It wasn't a good day. I don't want to think about it.'

'You have to.'

'No, you're wrong, I don't. No matter what you threaten me with, it doesn't matter compared to … compared to that.'

'Did you drive off because Irene Gallagher was on her way? Was Bjørn Lauritzen scared of her?'

It took a few seconds before Nysted understood the question. Then he howled with laughter.

'Bjørn wasn't scared of her. He wasn't scared of anything.'

'So that wasn't why you left?'

'No.'

'What did she want, do you know?'

'No. Why don't you ask her yourself? Everyone said they were having an affair, so perhaps she just wanted to see him. It didn't matter.'

'So what did matter?'

Nysted tilted his head and stared emptily into space. Arne Pedersen told him that he knew from one of the other soldiers that Lauritzen and Nysted had driven to some house, and that when Irene Gallagher arrived later, she had driven after them. Nysted didn't react to this information, but neither did he deny it. Pedersen tried again.

'Did she catch up with you?'

Ole Nysted shook his head. No, she didn't. In fact, he had never met her in Bosnia, on that day or any other, he had only heard about her.

'The remaining soldiers were summoned to Tuzla an hour after you had left. Why?'

Nysted's response was a vague gesture as if to say that too no longer mattered. He abruptly got up, and Arne Pedersen was momentarily taken aback by the man's speed. From a cupboard at the other end of the hut, he produced a full bottle of schnapps and two beer glasses. He twisted the cap off with a small squeak, then sat down, half-filled both glasses and shoved one towards his guest. Pedersen made his excuses, he was on duty and he was driving, but his protests were ignored and something told him that if he wanted more out of this man, he would have to drink with him.

Ole Nysted drained his glass as if it were water; Arne Pedersen took a small but respectable sip and wondered how he would explain to the Homicide Department that he had been forced to drink himself into a stupor in order to carry out a simple witness interview. Ole Nysted picked up the bottle again, but refilled only his own glass, then quietly began to speak:

'It was a farm, not a house. It was only one or two kilometres away, I think. Afterwards we drove around inside the forest, up and down a brook, or a river – if you like, it wasn't very deep, ten to twenty centimetres that's all, but wider than the Leopard. We brought five people back with us, three men and two boys. I'm sure we saved their lives.'

It was clear the man was taking a run-up to the heart of the matter, which he emphasised by taking a proper swig of his schnapps after first raising his glass in a toast. Arne Pedersen joined in, know-ing full well he was no longer safe to drive. Finally it came out, in fits and starts to begin with, then interspersed with lengthy pauses, then more fluently.

'Bjørn asked me if I would go with him in the tank, and of course I said I would. We drove down to the farm, which lay below us in a valley ... or perhaps the exact opposite, perhaps it was up the mountain, I don't remember, only that we could see it through our binoculars. Bjørn didn't tell me what we were doing, but it was obvious that he was angry and keen to get going. When we drove the tank into the yard in front of the two buildings that made up the farm, Bjørn jumped out and raced inside one of the houses.' The veteran stopped only to make inroads on his schnapps and demand that Pedersen keep up with him.

'He came out some time later behind a group of men. Eight filthy guys in random uniforms, ugly as sin they were. The two oldest were around fifty, the youngest probably only eighteen. An irregular mob the Serbs used to do their dirty work, a danger to women and children, disorganised and useless in combat. One of them – a beanpole with glasses – had had his nose broken by Bjørn, I think. He was clutching his face and whining like a little kid. Bjørn herded them along the front of the building and checked each of them carefully for weapons. They obeyed without protest, and afterwards he left them for me to guard. I was told to shoot them if they moved, or if I just felt like it; those were his words and he was serious. Then he returned to the house.

'I made myself comfortable on the tank and pointed a machine gun at the men without knowing what was really going on. The sun was baking hot, the men scowled and there were cicadas – crackling, invisible, creepy crawlies – I can't stand that sound. It gets inside your mind and stays stuck behind your eyes so you can't see or think. Fucking summer ... fucking country.'

His voice had dropped an octave.

'Soon afterwards a girl appeared in the farmyard. She staggered slowly towards me on stiff legs like an old woman without her walking stick. She stopped in front of the tank, looked up at me and said, "*Taj blesav Poljak*". That was all she said, nothing more.'

'The Crazy Pole ... that was Bjørn Lauritzen, right?'

'Yes, that was Bjørn. At first I thought she might be referring to me. But she wasn't. She said it twice, loud and clear – then she fell silent, like a clockwork toy that had stopped working.'

He straightened up and gripped the armrest of the sofa with both hands.

'That war was insane. We were well trained and armed to the teeth, but we were allowed to do fuck all. Those paramilitary gangs ... there was a handful of them, all with childish names. The members were nothing but a bunch of perverts We could have taken them out in an afternoon if we had been given permission. And, by God, we should have been! Because they had it coming, every single one of them. But everything was topsy-turvy. All those fine, international words about safe zones while people were being murdered in the forests, our ridiculous mandate about keeping the peace in the middle of genocide, chains of command where no one dared take responsibility for anything, and now this girl was just standing there in front of me, her dress torn and blood running down the inside of her legs. For fuck's sake, she couldn't have been more than thirteen years old. It wasn't meant to be like this. She shouldn't ...'

He stopped and stared at nothing with empty eyes. Arne Pedersen offered him his hand. He took it, and sat in silence for some time before he continued.

'I came as close to shooting those eight pieces of vermin as you can get without actually doing it. And they knew it. I could see it in their eyes: they were terrified. A brief salvo from left to right across their bellies, and they would have curled up, screaming their way to hell, while they tried to keep their guts inside them. I'll regret not shooting them for the rest of my life, but I was too well-trained, too disciplined, too civilised. And all for nothing.'

He stopped talking. Pedersen said gently: 'Do you need a break? Another drink before you go on?'

Nysted shook his head. Even so he didn't continue until he had had more schnapps and Pedersen had prompted him.

'What happened next?'

'Nothing. It was a Mexican stand-off. The girl was scared of the men, the men were scared of me, and I was scared of the girl. Scared because I didn't have a clue what to do with her although I was the adult and I bloody well ought to have known. And worse than that – I'd been sent all the way from Denmark to this hellhole and my mission was to protect her, only I didn't know what to do other than wait for Bjørn. I was petrified. When I looked at her, my hands would shake so badly I could barely hold my gun, and when I looked at the men ... Well, you already know.'

He took another swig as did Arne Pedersen. Strictly speaking he didn't have to, but he felt the need and besides, he was now so drunk that one more wouldn't make any difference.

'To this day I still don't know if it took two minutes or one hour before Bjørn came back outside, only that it felt like forever. First he beat up one of prisoners before he let him go, he was just a boy, then he got started on the men. He began by fixing their hands behind their backs with cable ties. Then he forced them to sit on the cobblestones up against the wall. At that point a handful of women were starting to come out from the farmhouse, but they went back inside and he couldn't make them come out again. Perhaps they were scared of him just like the men were. Everyone was terrified of Bjørn. All the men did as they were told, me included, I have to admit. After he had forced the men to sit down, he tied their legs together with a rope he had found inside the house. He tied each man's legs to the legs of the guys sitting either side of him, solid knots so they could only stand up if they did it together. Finally he forced their eyes open before rubbing gravel into them. When he had finished, none of them could do much other than stay where they were, which was the point. Afterwards we drove around the forest and up and down the brook, playing the Copenhagen Town Hall bells at full pelt. We saved some refugees, but saw no Serbian soldiers, and they can count themselves lucky that we didn't. I think Bjørn would have shot them, he was in that sort of mood.'

Arne Pedersen took his Dictaphone from the narrow coffee table in front of them. By now he was very drunk and struggled to press Stop; the small buttons eluded him and he tried several times before he succeeded. He had many follow-up questions, but they would have to wait for another day because there was no doubt that he would be interviewing this man again. Pedersen slurred his words as he explained that he would be back, and the veteran confirmed that was quite all right, he was welcome. Then he added:

'I'm sorry I made fun of Irene. She's all right.'

'Irene Galga?'

Even Pedersen could hear that he'd mispronounced the surname, but he gave up correcting himself. Nevertheless Nysted replied with a brief 'yes'.

'You refer to her by her first name?'

'She helps me from time to time, her and Bjørn.'

Arne Pedersen was painfully aware that what Ole Nysted was telling him now was important, but he was unable to pay proper attention to the information. His concentration was gone and he was in desperate need of fresh air. Even so he made a half-hearted attempt.

'You claimed earlier that you'd never met her, so how is that possible?'

'I said I'd never met her in Bosnia. I didn't meet her until after I came back. Bjørn brought her along one day when he visited me.'

'She and Bjørn Lauritzen visit you?'

'Mostly they come on their own. And rarely, once a year at most. I prefer to be alone.'

Pedersen stumbled to his feet. He told Ole Nysted for the second time that he intended to come back very soon.

'You can come back on Friday, is that soon enough?'

Pedersen agreed, it was a deal. As he was leaving, Nysted asked him: 'Tell me, has Bjørn done something wrong?'

CHAPTER 26

TUESDAY 14 SEPTEMBER 2010, LORUP FOREST NEAR SLAGELSE

The two young lovers were destined to be together. They would whisper tenderly to each other while they strolled through the woods along deserted paths, hand in hand, as if words could change their fate, and when they reached the deepest part of the forest where they were sure to be unseen, they would kiss, but always chastely, almost cautiously. They couldn't allow themselves to get carried away, it would only make matters worse. They both agreed on that, though it was mostly she who kept saying it.

They had met two years ago at Sørbymagle School in the village of the same name, not far from the town of Slagelse. The boy was an assistant caretaker at the school, and although she was an able student, the girl had been taken out of Slagelse Sixth-form College so she could act as a teaching assistant to her younger brother, who was in Year Two and had special educational needs. She was a Roma and her younger brother was the only boy among her four siblings so the family invested everything in him – and not her – receiving an education. She had been beyond boredom sitting next to her brother lesson after lesson, making sure he paid attention to the teacher, behaved himself and learned what he should, but had never complained to her father. She knew it would do no good. She only had a little time to herself during break while her brother played with his friends. And that was when she had met the boy.

If love at first sight exists, it had happened for them. Soon the young man would arrange his work so he always had something to do in or near the playground for the youngest pupils during break time, and the caretaker – a kind old man who had eyes in his head – helped his love-struck assistant: please would he shovel the sand back into the sandpit, check the climbing frame or pick up litter from the area behind the Year One and Two terrace? For the few months it lasted, these were happy times for the lovers, but at home the girl's little brother told tales about his big sister's interest in the young man, adding that she had started showing up late for his lessons. She had been removed from her teaching assistant role immediately, and three months later was married off to a forty-three year old, a family friend, a decent man – her father had told her so when he had picked him. Now she lived with her husband in Helsingør and was expected to produce her first child soon, although as yet there was no sign of pregnancy.

Once a month she would visit her parents and her siblings, and that was when the lovers met. Only for a few hours, never more, when she could persuade her mother to let her go for a walk while her father was at work. She and her young man would meet in a secret location and spend a little time together, preferably where the forest was at its densest and they could hide away. Which was what they were doing on this beautiful day when the leaves were turning yellow or piling up on the paths, rustling beneath their feet.

'Will I see you next month?'

They had agreed not to waste time discussing sad things while they were together. Why meet only to weep? They had plenty of time to do that while they apart, but that particular question had to be asked, and he always did, though he dreaded the answer. He breathed a sigh of relief when she confirmed that he would, and promised as usual to text him with a date. Suddenly she stopped fearfully and said: 'Someone's coming.'

He protested that no one came here, who could it possibly be? There was no need for her to be worried – he interrupted himself when he too heard footsteps ahead of them in the forest. She was right. He pulled her behind the root of an upended tree, which would hide them until the stranger had passed.

It was a middle-aged woman, of medium height, slim, almost skinny, and it was clear from the effortless way she moved that she was fit. Her face was pretty with regular features and her wavy blonde hair reached almost to her shoulders. She wore a red soft-shell jacket and a pair of pale blue Bridgewater work trousers, and if you didn't know any better, you would think she was on her way to work in the woods. Her gait was purposeful, which seemed odd. In one hand she carried a toolbox; two grey-painted boards were tucked under the other arm.

When the woman had passed and was at a safe distance, the boy filmed her from behind with his mobile.

'Why did you do that?' the girl asked.

'Running around the forest with a toolbox is weird, don't you think? What's she doing here?'

The girl replied anxiously: 'We don't want to get mixed up in anything. Perhaps she's looking for mushrooms, though I'm sure she's rich enough to buy them rather than pick them herself.'

'You know her?'

'Not really, but she's married to the man who owns Dagligkæden – the supermarket chain, you know – and there's one opposite the petrol station. When I used to clean there, she would sometimes turn up to collect her husband, if he was in working in that branch.'

CHAPTER 27

Arne Pedersen had a hangover.

The morning had been awful. He had struggled to think straight. Even though it was the first time in his career that he had got drunk while at work he felt unprofessional. But the situation had demanded it. At least that was what he had told himself at the time, only it was tricky to justify afterwards. Besides he was hacked off by the way the twins and his wife had treated him when he came home, as frosty as if he were an alcoholic, a reaction completely out of proportion and entirely undeserved, he thought. As if he drank himself into a stupor at work every day, when the truth was that it had never happened before and would probably never happen again.

His sons' hurtful withdrawal from him was distressing. They ought to be old enough to think for themselves and not always side with their mother's surly self-righteousness. When something didn't go according to plan, she would, as sure as eggs is eggs, turn sour as vinegar, if for no other reason than to make a point. At least that was how Arne Pedersen interpreted it.

His boss had been the only mitigating factor in the whole sorry situation. Yesterday when Arne Pedersen had returned to his car, he'd had sufficient sense not to start it, but had called Konrad Simonsen instead and slurred out an explanation. He had been met with unexpected sympathy and was picked up by two police officers and driven home in his own car by one of them as far as he could recall, but that detail wasn't entirely clear to him as he had been asleep most of the way. And this morning at work Simon practically babysat him, which was very much out of character for him. Nevertheless Arne Pedersen wished the situation had been reversed, that he had experienced sympathy on the home front and the opposite at work — and these thoughts opened a door in his mind to memories of Pauline. They had once had an affair, which later turned into a deep friendship until he had begun to distance himself from her.

He pulled himself together and staggered, still on wobbly legs, to Simonsen's office, where he collapsed on a spare chair and made a huge effort to suppress his nausea. He was meant to report on yesterday's interview. Klavs and the Countess had already arrived, and both of them looked irritatingly well rested and ready to listen to his update.

His account of Bjørn Lauritzen's tank trip to the farmhouse in the valley, and Irene Gallagher arriving at the observation post only to drive straight after the captain, went better than anticipated. He also told them about the veteran in the hut. No one interrupted him. Not even when he stopped for much-needed sips of water from a bottle he had brought along. He concluded: 'I'm going back to see him on Friday. There were quite a few things I didn't manage to cover.'

Klavs smirked. *Still thirsty, are you?* The story had clearly done the rounds of Police Headquarters, put about no doubt by the officers who had picked him up because Simonsen hadn't said anything to anyone. However, the Jutlander's smile was soon wiped off his face. Simonsen barked at him: 'No one in my department makes fun of veterans or laughs at Arne for drinking with a witness. It was necessary for him to keep up with Nysted in order to secure that statement, and I would be only too happy to buy a few bottles at the taxpayers' expense for Arne's next meeting on Friday, if that's what it takes. Is that clear to you, Klavs?'

It was only too clear, the otherwise excellent mood was ruined and the subsequent silence strained. It was Simonsen himself who, after glancing at the Countess, salvaged the situation.

'I'm sorry, I didn't mean to sound quite so angry. But recently I have seen and heard of so many cases where our former soldiers have been betrayed that ... well, it makes me angry. I had no idea they were being treated this badly. Do you have anything else, Arne, details you haven't shared yet – impressions even?'

There was no point in Arne Pedersen trying to put on a brave face. He heaved a deep sigh and clutched his head. The other three laughed.

'The crystal-clear impressions become rather blurred when your blood alcohol level goes that high, but there was one thing. Before I got him to talk coherently, he uttered random sentences mostly about the girl from the farmyard, the one who had been raped, though I guess the women inside the house had been raped too.'

He looked around for a moment, thinking before he continued.

'He was mostly upset about her, there's no doubt about it, so what he told me at the start was a kind of run-up, you could say, but later he told me that she spoke Danish or, more accurately, she also spoke Danish – Danish and Serbian.'

The Countess was taken aback.

'The girl was Danish?'

'He said she spoke Danish. I don't know if she was a Danish citizen, he didn't say. But like I said, he was erratic to begin with, so I don't know if it was his imagination or rather his nightmare doing the talking. On the other hand, it's worth looking into.'

They all agreed that it was, but no one had any idea how. Klavs Arnold summed up what they knew.

'Judge Advocate Irene Gallagher convinces Copenhagen to send her to Bosnia on 13 July 1995, apparently using some feeble excuse about wanting to follow up a conversation with Bjørn Lauritzen. Other witnesses claim it's purely a private trip taken during her holiday. At that point Bjørn Lauritzen is a member of the Nordic battalion, NORDBAT 2, meant to safeguard the UN safe zone around the town of Tuzla and protect Bosnian Muslims. However, he isn't based in Tuzla, but at an observation post in Ljubicevac, popularly known as Little Denmark. The post lies about thirty kilometres south-east of Tuzla towards the Dutch-protected safe zone in Srebrenica. Here he commands twelve men – some say ten – and two, sometimes three, tanks. Are you with me?'

The Countess replied for all of them. *Completely.* Klavs Arnold continued.

'Everything suggests that the meeting between Irene Gallagher and Bjørn Lauritzen was of a personal nature, and the judge advocate may or may not have used her work as a cover. She was in love, plain and simple, and the feeling might have been mutual, we don't know.'

Simonsen asked: 'Can we be sure that it isn't just gossip? I mean about her being in love.'

Klavs nodded to show that that was still an option, and went on.

'In Tuzla, Irene Gallagher borrows a Jeep and drives to Little Denmark. She just so happens to arrive at the time the massacre is being carried out in the mountains and forests around Srebrenica. The Bosnian Serbs, led by General Ratko Mladić, have seized the Dutch headquarters in Potocari after which thousands of Muslims, mostly men or boys, flee into the woods in order to reach Tuzla. Many don't survive and seven thousand people are murdered in the worst war crime in European history since the Second World War. However, the full extent of the massacre doesn't become clear until much later. Many Muslims are captured by the Serbs and later executed; others are killed by gunfire or shelling. From the observation post, the Danish soldiers can hear what's going on inside the forest in front of them, the thundering and exploding of live fire from handguns as well as from heavier weapons.'

Klavs stopped and looked around as if to say, *that's pretty much the situation*. Simonsen told him, 'Excellent, please continue, you're doing well.'

Klavs continued mainly by repeating what Arne Pedersen had already explained, without anyone minding. When he had finished, Simonsen said: 'We don't currently believe that Irene Gallagher and Bjørn Lauritzen met during her second trip to Bosnia. She drove back to Tuzla long before Lauritzen returned to the observation post with his tank and the handful of refugees he had picked up. His men were waiting for him in the other two tanks. They had been given orders to retreat to Tuzla, but had delayed doing so until Lauritzen returned.'

The Countess asked: 'So why didn't Irene Gallagher wait for him as well? It would be the obvious thing to do given that she had moved heaven and earth to see him.'

No one knew. Simonsen continued his summary.

'The next day or possibly the day after, it's a little unclear, Bjørn Lauritzen is summoned by his superiors after which he's flown back to Denmark, but without being charged with anything so far as we know. He continues to be paid for several years after he was sent home without the Army demanding anything from him in return. Except possibly for him to keep a low profile. The veteran from the hut – he has a name, I must start calling him Ole Nysted – is also sent home, but he won't give us any further details, which raises the question: why? What happened that summer's day in Bosnia between the two of them?'

The Countess added pensively, 'Whatever it was, it must have been something major because Bjørn Lauritzen was returned to Denmark immediately, and it seems to have created a strong bond between him and Irene Gallagher. So far as we know, she's the only one who has stayed in contact with him since then. But what do you think, Simon?'

He remained silent for so long it began to get embarrassing, then he said slowly, 'I think Irene Gallagher is in up to her neck in the canal boat killings. I think she was the driver who dropped off Bjørn Lauritzen on Battery Bridge, but I have my doubts about whether it has anything to do with Bosnia. However, I do think she knows where he is.'

'Will you be bringing her in? Or rather: when will you be bringing her in?'

Simonsen tilted his head from side to side to indicate that had yet to be decided, then he said:

'Later. First, I want to see her CV, and I'll work on getting that myself. If I need help, I'll ask. Secondly, I would appreciate it if you kept our interest in Irene Gallagher just between us. Appreciate it as in that's an order.'

Klavs Arnold asked cautiously: 'You're thinking security services?'

'Yes, everything points to them. Possibly our own and others.'

'You're not seriously suggesting that Danish Army Intelligence or our security services are behind the canal boat killings? Or other countries' intelligence services, for that matter?'

'Of course not, I'm not paranoid. But I fear that Irene Gallagher could prove very difficult to investigate, that's all I'm saying.'

The Countess had a worrying thought. She asked anxiously, 'You're not taking advantage of Malte, are you, Simon? I mean, we all know that he can … work his magic with various databases and not always entirely in accordance with a strict interpretation of the letter of the law. And sometimes on his own initiative. But some databases you definitely shouldn't—'

Simonsen interrupted her. He had yet to involve Malte in researching Irene Gallagher, but agreed that it would be a good idea to stress the legal position and the department's inviolable ethical guidelines to the student intern.

The Countess said, 'I'll have a word with him when we're done here, but without giving too much away.'

Everyone thought that sounded sensible. Working his magic with the wrong databases might prove seriously dangerous to a young man's health.

CHAPTER 28

WEDNESDAY 15 SEPTEMBER 2010, FREDERIKSVÆRK

'This is harassment, it can't be legal!'

Ella von Eggert was furious. Her clenched fists were planted on her hips and she was blocking the front door, clearly unwilling to let in Simonsen and the Countess. She snarled at the two officers: 'This is the third time you've interrogated me, but I keep telling you that I didn't know the little slag Mads was having it off with. How many times do I have to say it before you understand?'

Simonsen retorted without hiding his anger.

'The woman you refer to as a slag was called Juli Denissen. She's dead and she left behind a three-year-old daughter, so perhaps you could show some respect.'

The Countess added in a more conciliatory tone of voice: 'Please may we come inside and discuss this quietly?'

But it was no use, Ella von Eggert wasn't tempted by the prospect of a quiet discussion. The situation was at an impasse until

Simonsen forced his way past and grabbed her roughly by the arm The woman's protests were ignored. Once inside the living room, he pushed her down on a chair by the dining table and took the seat opposite. The Countess closed the front door and followed tentatively, concerned about her husband's conduct. They really ought to have taken Ella von Eggert to Police Headquarters, but what was done could not be undone. The Countess sat down at the end of the table.

Ella von Eggert had tears of rage in her eyes.

'You're not allowed to do that, this much I do know, and trust me, I'll make a complaint. It's not fair to force me to sit here without anyone to represent my interests while the two of you interrogate me.'

The Countess rushed to reply before her husband could.

'Then call your lawyer, I'm sure you've got one. You have the right to legal representation. We'll wait for him to arrive.'

Simonsen scowled at the Countess. There was no lawyer in his script. She, however, believed that they could exploit the waiting time. But the question became irrelevant when Ella von Eggert turned down the offer with an air of resignation.

'No, let's get it over with. I don't know anything, so I'm hoping you'll be done soon.'

Both the officers were astonished. They had been convinced that she would want legal representation.

Interviewing Ella von Eggert had gone from being one of those jobs the investigators would get round to when they found the time to absolute top priority. And this was down to Simonsen.

He had been trying to piece together Irene Gallagher's CV – a task that proved more complex even than he had feared – when he noticed the name of her younger sister as listed in the 1965 National Register of People, in the Copenhagen suburb of Vangede where the girls' parents lived and where Irene Gallagher had spent some of her childhood. Her sister's name was Ella, not a very common name and unusual for her generation, but a name he had already come across in connection to his current murder investigation. Where he couldn't remember, but Malte Borup could and soon confirmed it: Ella von Eggert and Irene Gallagher were sisters. Their maiden name was Egeskov until the older sister married her New Zealand husband, James Gallagher, and the younger sister the successful architect, Mads Eggert.

The information about the two sisters was the missing piece of the puzzle that Konrad Simon had been looking for: Juli Denissen becomes Mads Eggert's mistress, Ella von Eggert discovers the affair and goes to Irene Gallagher for help. Irene Gallagher persuades Bjørn Lauritzen to frighten the girl, which he does very successfully, unfortunately so successfully that it kills Juli Denissen. Later Pauline Berg insists on investigating the death as a crime and practically stalks the forester, Jonas Ziegler, who must have seen and heard more than he had originally admitted to. Bjørn Lauritzen and presumably Irene Gallagher decide to get rid of both of them, and Lauritzen kills them on the canal boat.

There were plenty of blank spaces to fill in, the most important of which was that killing twenty-one people was an insane and illogical overreaction to the death of Juli Denissen, which after all wasn't premeditated. But that must have been what had happened. And that in turn placed Ella von Eggert's witness statement in a much more central position than had previously been assumed.

Sadly there was little to suggest that she was willing to help the police with their enquiries. The first hour of the interview dragged on. The widow merely repeated the statements she had already made, which were that she knew nothing about anything. Konrad Simonsen threatened her. First with macabre pictures of dead Japanese children, which didn't affect her much. *Terrible, terrible, but what does that have to do with me? I didn't kill those children.* The tone of her voice contradicted her sympathetic words. It was cold and distant, she didn't care one jot about the children, but the point about her own lack of involvement was irrefutable.

Then Simonsen fell back on an old trick: the Homicide Department could paint her as a true enemy of the people, someone who was withholding important information needed by the police to crack a deeply tragic case that the whole country wanted solved: what would her neighbours say then? That didn't work either, she wasn't worried in the least about what people said. She practically spat this out, the words brimming with contempt, and sounded as if she meant it. All that was left was threatening her with being an accessory to the death of Juli Denissen. She would pay a high price for that, she was looking at at least eight years behind bars. Konrad Simonsen would have no choice but to take her to Police Headquarters and have her remanded in custody, initially for four weeks. Perhaps they should stop now so she could pack a suitcase with essentials before they departed, yes, she should do that, given her refusal to cooperate. She pretty much laughed at him then, and he realised he had totally underestimated her.

She said calmly: 'I like your interpretation of the law. If I co-operate, as you put it, you're willing to let me off eight years in prison. I would call that legal horse-trading. Even you don't believe that nonsense. Besides, I am co-operating: I know nothing more than I've already told you.'

Simonsen looked at the Countess in despair. He had nothing more. The Countess, however, did have something up her sleeve. She had had plenty of time to study Ella von Eggert while Simon had tried in vain to intimidate her, and she was struck by the woman's unexpected refusal of a lawyer. She looked Ella von Eggert straight in the eye.

'Your lawyer, because I'm sure you have one, isn't the kind who knows about police procedures and the penal code, is he? He's more knowledgeable about corporate law, finance, offshore accounts and tax, am I right?' It was a shot in the dark, but it clearly hit a nerve.

One of Ella von Eggert's eyelids began to twitch uncontrollably. She looked down and hissed: 'What's my lawyer got to do with you?'

The Countess continued unabashed.

'Nothing, except that you clearly don't want us to meet him. The police and your lawyer would be a bad mix, and I've been wondering why. Perhaps you and your late husband saved for a rainy day beyond the reach of the Danish Revenue? San Marino, the Cayman Islands, the Isle of Man, or possibly good old Switzerland ... there are so many to choose between. And I'm guessing that your lawyer has been helping you do so in return for a sizeable fee, given what I know of how such people operate.'

Ella von Eggert went bright red. She didn't say anything, but was obviously uncomfortable with the change of topic.

'Listen, I'll give you five minutes to have a good think,' the Countess went on, 'and if you reach the wrong conclusion, I'll contact the Revenue on my way back and tell them to get three senior accountants to go over you and your lawyer with a fine-tooth comb. They'll check every *krone* you've ever looked at and if there are any irregularities, they'll find them, trust me. The problem is, or rather *your* problem is, that once the Revenue starts its investigation, I can't stop it. That's not how the system works. So, over to you.'

The Countess looked at her watch, but Ella von Eggert didn't need five minutes, only five seconds.

'I know nothing about the killings on the boat, nothing at all, and you have to believe me because it's the truth,' she said wearily.

'So what *do* you know?'

She sighed, got up and went to a sideboard where, with her back to them, she poured herself a glass of white wine. Simonsen seized the chance to turn on his Dictaphone and leave it on the table. When Ella von Eggert returned, she said sadly: 'I had long suspected Mads and Juli of having an affair, but I had no proof. So I downloaded a spy program from the Internet and installed it on Mads's laptop. Three weeks later, I knew the passwords to Juli's and his email accounts. Once I read their emails, I became really scared. He was totally smitten by her … wrote that she made him feel young. It was nauseating. The bottom line was that Mads might well leave me, and then what would I do? And for some little cu—'

Konrad Simonsen slammed his hand against the table.

'There's no need for that, stick to the facts.'

'OK, so I spoke to my big sister about it. Her name is Irene, and she has always been there for me. First she called the … Juli a few times to persuade her to end the affair, but the girl couldn't have cared less. I think that she might genuinely have been in love with Mads, but Irene didn't buy that. She said someone would have to have a word with Juli in person and convince her to stay away from other people's husbands.'

'You mean frighten her?'

'Yes, frighten her, and I thought it sounded like a good idea. I'm afraid I helped. From their emails, I knew that Juli and her daughter were meeting Mads to go for a walk along Melby Beach, so on the morning of that walk I sent an email to Mads in Juli's name saying she had to cancel because her daughter was ill. That was Irene's idea and it gave her a chance to speak to the girl alone. That night Irene called to tell me that the problem was solved, but that we shouldn't talk about it again, not on the phone or anywhere else. It wasn't until later that I realised the girl was dead. There was a notice in the local paper, but I must admit I already had an inkling because Mads was really upset in the days that followed, much more than if, say, she had dumped him, even though … Well, I couldn't be sure and I couldn't very well ask him.'

Konrad Simonsen asked darkly, 'Aren't you missing something? You had a very good idea about how to persuade Juli, didn't you?'

Ella von Eggert bowed her head, clearly embarrassed.

'Will I get into trouble because of this?'

'You're already in trouble. How would they frighten Juli?'

'I really hated her …'

'How, dammit! Out with it.'

'Snails. She was afraid of them, had a phobia or whatever you call it. I had read that in one of her emails, not one to do with Mads. And I told Irene.'

'So you used this knowledge to terrorise her?'

Konrad Simonsen was angry. The Countess could hear that it went beyond a professional level. She hastily interjected: 'Did your sister attack Juli Denissen herself?'

'I don't know, we've never spoken about it, but I can't imagine that she would have done it herself. She would have got someone to help her, she knows people.'

'People willing to scare young women to death? Literally.'

Simonsen was trying to regain control of the conversation, but Ella von Eggert ignored him when the Countess asked, 'Do you know who helped her?'

'No, I didn't want to know.'

'Could you make a good guess?'

She shook her head.

The Countess changed the subject.

'Does your sister ever borrow your car?'

Ella von Eggert denied this. Her sister had her own car, so why would she need to?

'So your sister didn't borrow your car on Sunday the twenty-second of August this year? You're sure about that?'

'I was in Berlin that weekend. I took the train and didn't come home until Tuesday, so … well, I don't think so, but I can't be sure.'

She let the doubt hang in the air. The Countess wanted to know if Irene Gallagher had a key to her sister's house and thus access to her car keys. Ella von Eggert reluctantly confirmed this. Simonsen concluded: 'So your sister could have used your car that weekend?'

'Yes, I guess she could. But I'm sure she didn't.'

'We would like to bring in your car for a forensic examination. You don't mind, do you?'

'No, I wouldn't mind, but it was stolen the other day, so you'll have to wait until it's found.'

She launched into a lengthy story about how she had left her car unattended for ten seconds to post a letter, whereupon two young louts had spied a chance to drive off in it. It was hard to tell whether or not she was lying.

The Countess asked: 'Have you reported it?'

'Yes, of course I have.'

Konrad Simonsen made a mental note to contact Frederiksværk Police and tell them to prioritise the alleged vehicle theft. There was nothing else he could do.

They spent most of the next hour trying to extract further information from her, but everything indicated that the woman had nothing further to tell them. Eventually they gave up. As they left, Ella von Eggert said hesitantly:

'Do you think Irene is involved in the canal boat killings?'

Neither of them answered her. Then she asked, almost pleading with them: 'What's going to happen to me now?'

Again the two officers remained silent. The truth was that nothing very much would happen to her, though neither of them wanted to tell her that.

CHAPTER 29

The evening was warm and Konrad Simonsen was sitting on the terrace with his papers, a laptop and a well-deserved glass of beer. The Countess was in the living room watching television. The blue-ish glow from the screen reflected in the French doors in an irritating way every time the picture changed, and he considered closing the curtains, but abandoned the idea as it might be interpreted as a wish to be alone when the opposite was the truth. He was tired and as he read his head would nod involuntarily and he would doze off for a few seconds. At other times what he read made no sense, but mingled with irrelevant information and turned into an absurd mix of dream and reality. He had been going back over it with steely determination since early that morning to piece together a basic CV for Irene Gallagher, but his efforts weren't reflected in the result. Sadly what he had managed to uncover was extremely patchy.

Irene Gallagher, née Egeskov, was born in 1962 and lived with her parents until leaving home at the age of eighteen to study law at the University of Copenhagen. Both her parents were highly educated: her mother lectured in thermodynamics and her father was a successful diplomat with a career that peaked with four years spent as Denmark's Ambassador to NATO, followed immediately afterwards by six years as Danish Ambassador to the United States. The family was wealthy. In addition to her parents' excellent salaries, her grandfather owned a large carpentry and timber business, where Irene Gallagher would often work to earn pocket money while still at school. She graduated with a first. In 1985 she did her National Service after which she was employed by Defence Command Denmark, the country's supreme military command authority.

In 1996, at the age of thirty-four, Irene Egeskov married James Gallagher, a New Zealand national with permanent leave to remain in Denmark. Her husband was the sole owner of Dagligkæden, a handful of village stores on Sjælland. The shops were all located in sparsely populated areas and were run with admirable financial and stock control. James Gallagher had built up his successful chain based on a business model from New Zealand where his family owned several hundred of this type of small store. The couple lived in Næstved and they had no children. Irene Gallagher left the Army in 2007 and had for the last three years filed a nil income tax return. Konrad Simonsen had also learned that she owned a red Audi Locus, but her younger sister had a black Opel Corsa, which could easily match the car that had dropped off Bjørn Lauritzen on Battery Bridge, but unfortunately so could many other car models. In any case, her Opel would still be sent to Forensic Services for examination as soon as it was found.

He rubbed his tired eyes and discovered that the Countess had joined him when he looked up again. She was in mother-hen mode and stroked his head affectionately.

'Don't you think you ought to go to bed soon and get a good night's sleep?'

He took her hand and held it for a while before letting it go.

'Sadly I can't. I'm expecting a visitor shortly.'

'Who would turn up this late? Is Irene Gallagher troubling you?'

This was the perfect opportunity for a moan. He had worked his socks off all day, and yet there was still a big hole in Irene's Gallagher's CV from 1986 to 2007.

'The Army refuses point-blank to co-operate. Her files are classified, and when I eventually managed to convince the National Police Commissioner to try, he got exactly the same response.'

'But surely you have your own sources? You know a handful of extremely senior civil servants.'

He had tried them too and got nowhere: the files were hermetically sealed. Irene Gallagher's Army activities were, and would remain, secret. He was starting to think that he might be the victim of a conspiracy.

'I'm not getting anywhere. In fact, everyone strongly advises me to drop it.'

'Well, perhaps that might be the best thing to do.'

That certainly was an option, for no other reason than he didn't have the faintest idea what to do next. Apart from inviting over the man who would arrive shortly, but Simonsen was starting to doubt that even he would help the investigation make progress.

However, there was one glimmer of light. Konrad Simonsen changed the subject to that.

'Malte found an interesting link we haven't been aware of so far. It concerns Jonas Ziegler, the man killed along with Pauline, remember him?'

'I do, you're the not the only one working on this case. What about him?'

'He worked at the Dagligkæden store in Tune, so he was employed by Irene Gallagher and her husband. He got the job two months after the attack on Juli Denissen, and without having any experience or qualifications as a shop assistant. And his salary was higher than that paid to the business's other shop assistants, approximately two thousand kroner more per month.'

'Irene Gallagher hired Jonas Ziegler in return for him keeping quiet about the attack. It meant she could also keep an eye on him. But Pauline kept hounding him and at some point must have worked out Irene Gallagher's role. So Irene Gallagher got Jonas Ziegler to arrange a meeting with Pauline, who must have suggested the canal trip where they were both killed. Is that what you're thinking, Simon?'

Konrad Simonsen confirmed it; this had to be how things had happened. Someone should take a closer look at Jonas Ziegler's telephone records to see if he had been in contact with Irene Gallagher. But there was a big problem with this hypothesis: why solve a relatively modest problem – an affair – only to create an even bigger one in the form of at least two murders? It made no sense and could surely only backfire. He went on: 'There must be another motive for the killings, and I'm sure it has to do with Bosnia, but I'm getting nowhere with Irene Gallagher's Army career, let alone her exploits in the former Yugoslavia.'

The Countess said optimistically, 'Let's hope your secret friend can help us. Where do you want to meet?'

He thought the summerhouse might be a suitable venue. He would often hold meetings there when working from home. He had painted it himself a few years ago as a form of occupational therapy following his surgery.

'Fine, I'll make some fresh tea and coffee and leave it there, but make sure it doesn't get too late or I'll turn off your alarm clock and let you have a lie in tomorrow. You have been warned.'

She kissed him and went back inside.

———

The head of PET, the Danish security service, was a man of about Konrad Simonsen's age. He had a bulky physique and the fleshy features of a man who lives well, but his main characteristic was his almost total lack of facial expression. He was an introverted man who rarely smiled, and when he did, it was usually with a hint of *schadenfreude*. Over the years he and Konrad Simonsen had occasionally worked together, at times closely, but mostly at a distance. They had no relationship outside work, but as they had both grown older and were approaching the end of their respective careers, an unspoken solidarity had developed between them, as if by joining forces they could keep the young upstarts at bay, resist the tide of progress a little longer before it inevitably swept them away.

The PET chief greeted Simonsen on the terrace. His handshake was soft and clammy, best avoided. Konrad Simonsen hadn't heard a car, so the man had presumably parked several streets away. How typical of him to take precautions. Together they walked to the summerhouse. The PET chief poured himself a cup of coffee and lit a cigarette without asking permission. His host pushed his own saucer closer, for use as an ashtray, and then they went straight to business. As Konrad Simonsen told him about his troubles with Irene Gallagher, what he had learned, but more importantly what he hadn't, the PET chief listened without interruption. He sat with his eyes half-closed, as if he were dozing off, but Simonsen knew that appearances were usually deceiving. When he had finished his summary, the PET chief said: 'You say she was in Bosnia as a judge advocate? Tell me more about that.'

'Do you know her?'

'No, but I knew her father very well, Adam Egeskov. He was a stuck-up, arrogant bastard, but cleverer than most. I'm sure he could open plenty of useful doors for his daughter.'

'Any doors in particular?'

The PET chief dismissed the question with a wave. 'Be patient. Bosnia, Simon.' He made it sound like an order. Konrad Simonsen swallowed his irritation, accepted the situation and told him how Irene Gallagher had, for the second time in her role of judge advocate, sought out Bjørn Lauritzen in the summer of 1995, immediately after which he had been sent home. His visitor asked for more details, which Simonsen mostly didn't know. When the PET chief had run out of questions, he sat for a while mulling things over, then he said resolutely: 'I'll help you from the sidelines if I can, give you a few pointers and tips. But I'm not going to do anything directly operational; your case is too far away from my remit for me to be able to do that. Let's start with your Bosnia story. It doesn't add up at all. I spent some time down there myself, and judge advocates don't behave like this, far from it, but … but …'

He began muttering to himself while wringing his fat hands and staring into the air as if Konrad Simonsen weren't there.

'… so the Americans are the obvious suspects, it could hardly be anyone else, but the summer of 1995? That doesn't make sense. It was under UNPROFOR, a UN operation the Americans supported, but they were on the outside of it and would never have allowed a non-American … never, ever, it's out of the question … it wasn't until later, towards the end of 1995 and in 1996, that it becomes a NATO operation, IFOR and later SFOR, but not at that time … under no circumstances.'

Then his face suddenly lit up and relaxed into its normal inscrutable expression. He took his Smartphone from his inside pocket, and asked, as if he already knew the answer: 'Have you checked where Adam … her father, I mean … was posted when she was born? He began his career early, and it's common for …'

He let the sentence hang in the air. Konrad Simonsen said no, he hadn't looked into that, without quite understanding where this was going. The PET chief checked his phone and thought out loud again.

'I can probably find this out from the official homepage of the Danish Foreign Ministry. In my experience people like him love nothing more than to boast of their ... hang on ... here we go. Yes, I knew it! From 1960 to 1962, posted to the General Consulate in New York. I'll just get a secure line and cross-reference this with her passport or maybe see if she has an old driver's licence. Not even the Army can keep police records secret, and if you can't think of anything else, you can always check church records in the parish where she was born.'

There was barely room for his fat fingers on the screen, yet he handled his mobile with virtuosity, sliding it in front of Konrad Simonsen as he said:

'Place of birth: New York, where her passport was also renewed in 1988.'

'Which means that she's an American citizen?'

'Exactly. Every child born on American soil automatically acquires American citizenship, and Americans don't give a toss about whether they hold other citizenships as well. As far as the USA is concerned, they're Americans unless they officially renounce their citizenship to the American authorities. There are a few exceptions for children of high-ranking diplomats, but her father wasn't one of those at the time, he was pretty much a student intern.'

'So Irene Gallagher worked for the Americans as ... an intelligence officer?'

'Call it what you like, her title doesn't matter. But, yes, I'm sure she worked for our great ally, and probably also for Denmark. There is no conflict of interest between the Danish Army Intelligence Agency, FE, and the US Defense Intelligence Agency. We've always worked closely with the Americans, mainly because they're very interested in any ships passing through our waters – or rather *under* them. This gives you an excellent way in because she's likely to have supplemented her Danish law degree with a Masters from an American university, preferably one of the more prestigious ones,

Harvard or Yale, say, or possibly Princeton or Chicago ... but let's return to that later. Before we do I need you to understand and accept two things.'

First, Konrad Simonsen had to abandon any hope of accessing FE archives in order to investigate Irene Gallagher. He would never succeed, no matter what he did or whomever he tried to nudge. All he would succeed in doing was to ruffle a lot of feathers, which the PET chief could do without. Secondly, if he came up with some ridiculous conspiracy theory claiming that either American intelligence or its Danish equivalent was behind his canal boat killing, the PET chief would walk out right now because Simonsen would simply be wasting his time.

'FE might cover for her and possibly obstruct you, if they have sufficient reason to do so, but that's as far as they'll go. They wouldn't dream of killing Danish citizens, things simply don't work like that here, and if it really had to happen, it would certainly never be done so clumsily. If Irene Gallagher is involved in your killings, she acted on her own and in her own interest.'

Konrad Simonsen accepted this at face value: the man sounded as if he knew what he was talking about and it all seemed reasonable.

'But then what?' he asked. 'You mentioned pointers.'

'Which I've already given you, but OK. I know a ... someone who's very good at getting information about people in the USA, and she has the essential quality of knowing what to stay away from and when to back off. I'll talk to her tomorrow, find out if she's interested. If she is, I'll put you in touch with her, but she's expensive ... about twenty thousand kroner, I would think ... and you don't get a receipt. There's no guarantee what and how much she'll find. Sometimes her findings are minimal, others more comprehensive, but the price is the same. Are you interested?'

Konrad Simonsen nodded. The PET chief glanced at his watch, preparing to leave, but there was one more outstanding matter.

'Tell me, why are you really helping me?' Simonsen asked him. 'I contacted you pretty much out of desperation and deep down I didn't believe you would be willing to talk.'

The PET chief reluctantly grunted an acknowledgement of this.

'I hear you treat our veterans with respect.'

Simonsen struggled to hide his astonishment.

'Is that why? Because I've been a good boy?'

Initially there was no reply. The PET chief merely flapped one fat hand as if getting rid of an insect. Then his eyes flashed with a bitter light.

'Gedsted, Fårdrup, Spjald, Frøbjerg, Sprove, Stillebæk – villages at the back of beyond, no one's ever heard of. That's where they come from: the young men who couldn't keep up at school, who can't find manual jobs in our new globalised world. They're the ones we deploy to uphold Denmark's alleged international obligations.

'But let me tell you something: it's never the young who speak fluent English and drink flat whites in trendy cafés in big cities who join up – oh, no, they know to stay the hell away! And what do we do with the others when they come back, our brave soldiers from Denmark's forgotten villages, broken because the fairy tale crippled them? What does Denmark do about her national obligations then? Sweet FA. Because these things cost money. Meanwhile the broken men are more than welcome to go home and cry about it in their backward villages, so the rest of us don't have to listen to them ... the top brass, the pen-pushers, politicians from every party.'

The PET chief stood up and rounded off this diatribe angrily.

'Arseholes, the lot of them!'

CHAPTER 30

On the morning of Arne Pedersen's return visit to Ole Nysted in Lorup Forest, the sun had just come out after a burst of fine rain and the whole area was teeming with life: birds, hares, mice and insects. Half-hidden by the bramble thicket skirting the path from the village of Kirkerup, he saw two deer grazing shyly. This was a rare sight and he stood very still to watch them for a few minutes, until a noise startled them and they disappeared deep into the undergrowth in a series of elegant leaps.

When he walked on, he felt his previously pessimistic mood lift, even though he had been dreading today. There was a tacit understanding in the Homicide Department that if he had to drink with the veteran again to get him talking, he should do so, but the last thing Arne wanted was another massive hangover only a few days after recovering from the last one. Still, he had made preparations: he had told his family that he might not be back until the following day, and booked a hotel room at the Homicide Department's expense, just in case things went wrong. He hadn't given his wife an explanation, nor had she asked for one but had merely taken his information on board and carried on with her morning routine as if nothing had happened. He had discovered that he missed Pauline Berg desperately and wished he could go back and relive the last four years of his life over again. Only this time his courage wouldn't fail him.

Ole Nysted was sitting on the same filthy sofa where Pedersen had left him, and he looked unwell. He was pale, his eyes shiny and slightly protruding from too much alcohol and not enough sleep. There were two bottles of strong beer on the table in front of him, one empty, the other half-full. On the table next to the bottles Nysted was resting his right foot, which was wrapped in a big bandage made from newspapers with a pink plastic bag wrapped around it. Arne Pedersen, who had knocked politely before entering when no one replied, greeted his witness when the man looked up.

Ole Nysted said: 'Is it Friday already? I didn't think you were coming until tomorrow, but you could have saved yourself the trip. It's best that I keep quiet, no point in ripping open old wounds.'

Pedersen ignored this and asked about his foot, which seemed the easier option.

'What happened? Did you fall?'

'I was chopping firewood, but it doesn't matter, it'll be better in a few weeks.'

'How about water and food, can I get you anything?'

The veteran said no, thanks, he had everything he needed, but it was kind of Pedersen to ask. Then he added: 'I prefer to be alone. You make me remember all the things I'm trying to forget, all the things I want to bundle up and throw away.'

Arne Pedersen sat down at the other end of the sofa. He felt he was intruding. He started thinking about Pauline, which helped. He said in a placatory tone: 'I only have a few additional questions, so we'll be done soon.' That was a lie. In contrast to the last time, he had numerous questions and a clearly structured interview plan.

Nysted drank the rest of his beer and heaved a sigh, then he pointed and said: 'Go to that cupboard, open the right-hand door, and fetch me a glass and the bottle of whisky that is in there. If you really want to help me, you can start by bringing in some logs, the woodpile is behind the house. You won't want to get your shoes muddy so you can borrow my clogs, they're by the door. Afterwards I'll give you fifteen minutes, no more.'

Arne Pedersen began by fetching the firewood, but didn't put on the hermit's clogs; he could handle a little mud on his shoes. Then he went over to the cupboard concealed behind orange curtains, which he drew back. The doors behind it were home-made with a roughly ten-centimetre circular hole in the cupboard door itself behind which a metal pipe had been fitted horizontally on the inside and acted as a handle, clearly a temporary arrangement. He pulled the door to no avail.

'It's locked.'

Ole Nysted looked confused, then he pointed.

'I meant the left side, sorry.'

That worked. Arne Pedersen fetched the bottle and the glass, and closed the curtain again while politely declining to participate in the drinking, something his host fortunately accepted this time without any comment. The man poured himself a generous measure and took a deep glug. *All right then, get on with it, seeing as I can't get rid of you.*

'The young girl you met in the farmyard, the one who had been raped ...'

The veteran cut him off.

'She was nothing but a kid, but what about her?'

'You told me last time that she spoke Danish. Did you speak to each other in Danish?'

'We didn't talk at all. She just said a few words to me, and they were in Serbian.'

'So what made you think she was Danish?'

'It's not something I think, it's something I know.'

'All right, all right. So how do you know that?'

'Because she spoke Danish to Bjørn when he came out from the house.'

'Bjørn Lauritzen?'

'Yes, Bjørn Lauritzen! Who the fuck else?'

Suddenly Ole Nysted began shaking uncontrollably, as if he had a fever. Pedersen offered him the glass of whisky. Nysted clutched it with both hands as he swallowed the contents. The alcohol eased his tremors.

'The world doesn't care about me, and I don't care about the world.'

He didn't sound self-pitying, it was more a statement of fact, and in his own way, he was right, Arne Pedersen thought.

'It's fine, I'm not complaining … it's just the screaming, I can't bear the screaming. Do you understand? I can't bear it.'

'Was the girl screaming? Is it her screaming you hear?'

Looking perplexed, the veteran denied this. No, the girl didn't scream, her ordeal was over, she was just standing there, anyone could see that. Then, without warning and with astonishing speed, he lunged at Pedersen and bit him on the shoulder. The pain was excruciating. He jumped up smartly, his self-defence training kicking in. Nysted smashed a beer bottle against the table, and swung the jagged end at him viciously. The bottle was nowhere near its target, but Pedersen took another step backwards.

'Get out of here, you bastard, and scream your way to hell with all the others!'

Pedersen took Nysted up on his suggestion and got out of there fast. What else he could do? It was the biggest failure of any interview he had ever undertaken, he thought, and now he would have to stop off at A&E for a tetanus injection. He clutched his shoulder and swore.

CHAPTER 31

Pauline Berg's funeral took place in Grundtvigs church in the Bispebjerg area of Copenhagen, not far from where she was born, grew up, went to school and played as a child.

Almost a month had passed since the canal boat killings and the four Danish families affected, including that of Pauline Berg, had contacted the police with increasing levels of impatience in order to have the bodies of the victims released. They wanted to bury their loved ones, so that they could start to move on. Their requests had been passed on to the Deputy Commissioner, who had willingly agreed to pretend that it was her call, though in truth it was Konrad Simonsen who made the decision. He was usually reluctant to release the bodies of murder victims too soon; you never knew what might come out during the investigation. Once in his career he had been forced to exhume a body for further forensic tests. He was desperate to avoid that ever happening again, especially with Pauline. But it was hard to imagine that it might become necessary in his current investigation, and after three weeks the Deputy Commissioner – rather than go to Simonsen from whom she risked receiving a point-blank refusal plus a complaint that she had interfered in his work – discreetly asked the Countess whether it wasn't about time. Two days later the bodies were released.

Simonsen, the Countess, Arne Pedersen and Anna Mia, who had just returned from her holiday, drove to the church in the Countess's car. Anna Mia and Arne Pedersen were in the back. The Countess was driving. She would deliver the eulogy and she was in uniform which no one, except for Simonsen, remembered having seen her wear before. Pedersen took the opportunity to brief their boss on yesterday's interview.

Simonsen seemed uninterested, as if he were only half-listening, but when they had driven in silence for some time, he announced that he intended to borrow Anica Buch for a couple of weeks, possibly longer, ask her to find the girl from the farmyard. If the girl spoke Danish, it must be possible to track her down.

'Was that everything, Arne?'

It was, except for one potentially interesting detail.

'I noticed that many of the groceries Nysted kept in his cupboards came from Dagligkæden, that chain of village stores owned by Irene Gallagher's husband. And there's a branch less than four kilometres from his hut. I wonder if Irene helps him out.'

It was Anna Mia who responded.

'And maybe she also helps Bjørn Lauritzen. If she does, then we know ... then *you* know which locations to investigate because I don't believe there are very many branches. What do you think, Dad?'

Simonsen had no time to reply before the Countess interjected sharply: 'And that's the last we'll talk about the investigation until we're back at Police Headquarters. At least so long as we're in my car.'

None of the other three dared challenge her. She was right, of course, but it was a relief to talk of something other than the imminent funeral.

The church was packed to the rafters. Many fellow police officers were there, and Pauline's family and her other friends made up a considerable number, though they were definitely a minority compared to the officers. It was a big church, but even so people had to stand in the porch and several outside the entrance. Seats were reserved for Konrad Simonsen and the Countess, but Arne Pedersen and Anna Mia had to stand. Pedersen made sure to get away from her as quickly as possible and mingle with a handful of strangers in the porch. He was scared that he might start to cry: not just shed a few tears, which would be OK, but sob uncontrollably. He gritted his teeth and reminded himself that it would all be over in an hour.

He spent most of the service clenching his jaw and making a partially successful attempt to force his mind elsewhere. Only during the single hymn he knew did he join in, and during the Countess's eulogy, which echoed in a strange, flat way off the stone walls of the porch, he reeled off lists inside his head: months of the year, planets, Danish towns on Funen and Bornholm, German adjectives taking the accusative – or were they adverbs? Who the hell cared – and afterwards those taking dative, as he had been taught a long time ago, without ever managing to make use of this knowledge on the rare occasions he'd had to speak German. When they finally carried the coffin past him, he bowed his head and looked the other way.

The church emptied slowly and people followed the hearse, which drove the few hundred metres from the church to the crematorium at a snail's pace. Arne Pedersen fell into line at the end of a stream of mourners. In front of the crematorium, but still at a suitable distance, he folded his hands briefly to say his goodbye, while unknown voices that irritated him beyond belief spoke quietly around him: *what a lot of police officers there are here today ... and have you seen? It's called the Dancing Chapel ... how appropriate – she loved to dance.* He was filled with rage, which suited him fine. It was an easier emotion to control than grief.

He felt a hand hesitantly touch his shoulder and turned around. It was Klavs.

'We'll get him,' Arne Pedersen vowed to the Jutlander, 'and that Gallagher bitch, just you wait and see. We'll nail them. I don't care how.'

People turned around in alarm. Pedersen had spoken much more loudly than he had intended. Klavs Arnold calmed him down.

'Perhaps you should adjust the volume? There are journalists here – though it's a bit late for that.'

The mourners were lining up to leave the cemetery. At the gate Pauline's family were waiting to shake hands and say goodbye. The mourners expressed their condolences and stuttered inadequate words of comfort. The queue moved slowly. It took almost half an hour before Arne Pedersen reached the front and he was lost in his own dark thoughts when he happened to look up.

The shock hit him like a physical blow, and for a moment his legs shook so badly that he could barely stand. Dazed, he staggered to one side and managed to get himself to the very back of the queue in order to gain a little time. He peered towards the front. And there she was! Standing next to her parents, Pauline

Berg was shaking hands, sombre and burdened, clearly, but so beautiful, just as vibrant and alive as the very first time he had met her.

No matter how forbidden and absurd the thought was, he couldn't help but think it. He was being given a second chance, a gift, an opportunity to do the right thing. He decided to join the family for the reception afterwards, something he had previously decided against. The others would have to drive to back Police Headquarters without him.

He was the last person to shake the family's hands, first her father, *I'm sorry for your loss*, then her mother, where he repeated the same stupid words, then finally her. Her handshake was still firm, though she must have said goodbye to hundreds of people. She put her other hand on top of his, held it for a while. Softly, but firmly.

'Are you Arne Pedersen?'

He said yes, and noticed that the voice was also Pauline's when it said: 'My big sister often talked about you. You meant a great deal to her.'

CHAPTER 32

MONDAY 20 SEPTEMBER 2010, NÆSTVED

The house was a former village school that had been completely renovated. It lay in the northern part of Næstved, not far from the city centre, but it also bordered Rådmandshaven, a conservation area through which the River Susåen runs. Arne Pedersen studied the house as he and Konrad Simonsen got out of the car. It stood two storeys high with a front porch and casement windows. The red-tiled roof looked recently refurbished and was in good condition. Red and yellow roses climbed up the front wall and in between the windows. It was a lovely home.

It was Irene Gallagher herself who opened the door and welcomed them in with a genuine smile.

'Detective Chief Superintendent Konrad Simonsen and Detective Superintendent Arne Pedersen. The Homicide Chief *and* his Deputy, I am impressed. Do come in.'

She spoke slowly, deliberately, as if weighing every word. The two officers followed her as she led the way down a passage and into a study where she herself sat down behind an adjustable desk and invited her guests to take a seat. Before the two officers had sat down, a man popped his head around the door and asked her how long she thought she would be and if she could be ready in an hour. He was in his mid-forties and spoke accented Danish. She didn't reply immediately.

'May I offer you something – tea, coffee, a cold drink?'

The two officers shook their heads, no, that wasn't necessary.

'Do you think an hour is enough? We have an appointment we would rather not have to cancel.'

Arne Pedersen stated that an hour would be fine, which Irene Gallagher repeated to her husband. Simonsen wondered whether the question had been prearranged; it felt like it. He took out his Dictaphone, pressed Start and placed it on the desk in front of him. Then he looked at Arne Pedersen to signal that he could begin.

'We noticed from the sign outside that your house is for sale. Do you mind telling us where you're moving to?'

Irene Gallagher didn't reply, but reached calmly across the desk and took Konrad Simonsen's Dictaphone. She turned it off and said: 'I'm really sorry, but no recordings. I've seen too much manipulation of that sort of thing, though not by the police. Please leave it there. That way I know you won't turn it on again.' She paused, apologised a second time, and then answered Arne's question.

'We're selling our house and our two holiday homes because we're moving to New Zealand where my husband has family. He has also put his business up for sale and we think we've found a buyer. You're welcome to ask me, of course, but my husband knows the details far better than I do. Would you like me to fetch him?'

Simonsen shook his head.

'Where were you on Sunday the twenty-second of August in the morning?' he asked.

'Here, and the answer to your next question is yes – my husband can confirm it. We slept late. I did some gardening. Later we cooked lunch together, warm liver pâté with bacon, smoked eel and scrambled eggs, mini veal meatballs – we like spoiling ourselves on Sundays, when we have the time.'

'Can anyone else confirm that you were here?'

'No, unfortunately. Or maybe they can. I used my mobile to call my sister, who was in Berlin at the time, but she didn't pick up. But perhaps you can trace it? I give you permission to obtain my telephone records.'

'That would only prove that your mobile was here, not that you were.'

She turned up the palms of her hands and flung out her arms.

'Yes, of course. But that's the best I can do.'

Arne Pedersen took over:

'Talking about your sister, she owns a black Opel Corsa, do you ever use it?'

Not so far as Irene could remember, but she might have done so on the odd occasion.

'And yet your sister told us that you borrowed her car the weekend of Friday the twentieth to Monday the twenty-third of August. How do you explain that?'

That was a lie. Ella von Eggert had never said this to the police. Irene Gallagher frowned and narrowed her eyes. Quite convincingly, Konrad Simonsen would have to admit. Then she said softly, as if she could provide a better explanation: 'Ella is wrong. Why would I borrow her car when I have my own? I prefer mine to an Opel Corsa.'

Arne Pedersen laughed. It was dry, fake laughter. He shook his head and said: 'I would have expected you to be more ... how can I put it? ... convincing. I mean, given your excellent education, your social status and being the daughter of a top diplomat. You really disappoint me, I must say.'

It was obvious to all three of them that he was trying to provoke her, but his timing was poor and his remark merely sounded rude rather than a demonstration of superior interview technique. Simonsen looked at him with a frown. Perhaps Arne was allowing his feelings to get the better of him. To their surprise Irene Gallagher smiled a winning smile.

'I'm sorry to hear that. It's probably because I'm a little nervous. After all, it's not every day I'm interviewed by the police.'

She wasn't nervous in the slightest. She knew that perfectly well, as did the officers, so it seemed entirely natural when she then said: 'I know you're only saying that to rattle me, and also that you're just doing your job.'

Konrad Simonsen placed a photograph in front of her.

'You were photographed in Copenhagen on the morning of Sunday the twenty-second of August at nine-thirty-six opposite the Orlogs Museum. You're driving in a south-westerly direction towards Torvegade where you can turn off either towards Amager or the city centre. As you can see, you're driving your sister's car. What do you have to say to that?'

Irene Gallagher snatched up the picture and studied it closely. It was grainy and blurred, and it seemed to the officers that she heaved a sigh of relief when she took a closer look.

'I can see that it resembles my sister's car and that could be my hair and my nose, but as I was here in Næstved, then it couldn't have been me in the car.'

She was right. The image was too vague to prove anything. She slid it across the table to Konrad Simonsen. Arne Pedersen changed the subject.

'Do you know a man called Bjørn Lauritzen?'

She nodded, yes, she did.

'Did you meet him in 1992 during his first deployment to Bosnia? And did you meet him again in 1995 during his second deployment?'

She sat for a long time without replying. Finally, she said: 'I'm sorry, because I know it might easily seem as if I've done something wrong, but everything I did when I was working for the government is without exception classified information, which I can't confirm or deny or comment on in general.

'I'm simply not allowed to. If you want me to give evidence, I can only do so in an Army setting, probably at Kastellet in Copenhagen, and even then I'll only be permitted to do so once I receive written permission from someone with the necessary authority in the Army as well as any other employers I may have had during the period in question.'

'You mean the Americans?'

'No comment.'

To his irritation Konrad Simonsen conceded that at least her answer was clear. He also had no doubt that Irene Gallagher had the law on her side, and unfortunately there wasn't a great deal he could do about that.

'In April 1999 you contacted the police and told them that you had met Bjørn Lauritzen on the Storebæltsbroen Bridge roughly two years earlier. On the basis of your statement, he was later declared dead. However, Bjørn Lauritzen has been seen by witnesses on several occasions since then.'

'I could have been mistaken, of course; it was dark, so it's always possible. But I was fairly certain that it was Bjørn.'

The landline on her desk rang with a loud, old-fashioned ring tone. She answered it, listened and paled while she looked at Konrad Simonsen.

'Yes, he is, and yes, I will.'

She rang off and said in a trembling voice: 'I've been told to tell you to turn on your mobile.'

Konrad Simonsen did so and soon afterwards it started ring-ing. He answered, was asked to identify himself, which he did. He was then asked the name of his daughter, which he stated with rising panic – '*Tell me, who is this?*' – and received the worst possible answer: it was the trauma unit at Rigshospitalet. If he would please wait on the line the consultant would be there to talk to him in a moment. Simonsen stumbled out of the room, down the passage and out of the house, with a pounding heart and trembling hands.

In shock he braced himself for the worst news, but no consultant came, not even when he shouted down the phone. At length – he had no idea how much time had passed – he had no choice but to hang up. Out of sheer desperation he called his daughter's mobile, and when he heard her carefree voice – '*Hi, Dad, can we speak later? I'm just going to a lecture*' – he collapsed onto the doorstep with relief. When he had regained his composure, he tried to get through to the number that had called him earlier, without success, then he contacted Rigshospitalet, which informed him that none of their staff had called him. Then he called the Countess, told her about the incident, ignored her concern and ordered her to get his mobile provider to triangulate the fake call immediately and find the owner of the following number. He dictated it to her twice, then hung up.

The mood had changed completely when Simonsen returned to the study. Irene Gallagher had put a bottle of brandy and a glass on her desk in front of Simonsen's vacated chair, but she was clearly angry.

'I heard that it was Rigshospitalet calling. I hope nothing bad has happened, and do help yourself to a glass of brandy if you need it. But frankly, I'm starting to wonder if your urgent call wasn't just a stunt to enable you to snoop around my home. I don't want you running around on your own again.'

Simonsen declined the brandy and apologised, after which Arne Pedersen brought him up to speed on what had been said in his absence. Irene Gallagher didn't know Pauline Berg, nor had she any information about Jonas Ziegler and she had nothing to do with his employment with Dagligkæden. Arne Pedersen managed to present his summary while at the same time making it quite clear that he didn't believe her for a second.

Irene Gallagher sneered: 'I can do without your sarcasm.'

He ignored her and carried on speaking: Irene Gallagher had been made aware of her sister Ella's admission to the police that she had persuaded Irene to frighten Juli Denissen into breaking up with her sister's now late husband Mads. Addressing Simonsen, he said: 'Mrs Gallagher has confirmed that conversations took place between her and her sister, as Ella von Eggert has testified, but claims that she never took any action regarding the matter and was merely telling her sister what she wanted to hear.'

Simonsen asked his deputy: 'Have you also told Mrs Gallagher what happened to Juli Denissen?'

Arne Pedersen said no, not yet. Simonsen announced icily: 'Juli Denissen died as a result of a violent attack suffered on Melby Common in the summer of 2008.'

Irene Gallagher was unperturbed.

'Then the problem ultimately solved itself, which is probably why my sister hasn't mentioned it since. Incidentally, your time is almost up. Do you have a final question?'

Arne Pedersen leaned across the desk and caught her eye.

'It's only been forty minutes. We agreed an hour.'

'I'm cutting our conversation short. I'd like you to leave now. Or rather, I'd like *you* to leave.'

'We could take you with us to Copenhagen.'

'By all means. You'll just be wasting your time and mine.'

'Has anyone ever told you that you're a real bitch?'

Irene smiled frostily.

'Lots of people, and many with much more power than you have.'

The two investigators had left Næstved and reached the motor-way back to Copenhagen before Arne remarked: 'She won't play ball, the stupid cow.'

Simonsen asked him: 'What the hell happened while I was gone? Did you provoke her? You already knew that wouldn't work.'

'No, I didn't provoke her, not in the least, but the moment you'd gone, her manner changed completely. It was utterly absurd, there was no reason for it at all. So what was going on with the call you got?'

'That'll have to wait, but I will tell you at some point. I need a little time to work it out. So you didn't provoke Gallagher?'

'No, dammit, I keep telling you.'

It was not until they had passed Køge that Konrad Simonsen explained what had just happened. Shortly afterwards he received a text message from the Countess. He opened it and shook his head in despair, before reading it aloud to his deputy.

'*The number that called you belongs to a burner phone. The number has only been used twice: to call Gallagher and then you. TDC triangulated it: both calls appear to have been made from Police Headquarters.*'

CHAPTER 33

Bjørn Lauritzen spent the autumn and often the winter in the south-eastern part of Store Hestehave Forest on the Stege Bay side, where the forest ends and the broad meadow that borders the shore begins. There was an old drystone wall just inside the forest and up against it, right where it rounded a big boulder, he had built his home. It was well hidden from curious passers-by, should any ever stray into this remote place.

The walls of his modest hut were of turf held together by birch saplings, which he had rooted deep into the ground. The roof was made from layers of willow interwoven with plastic bags. All the joints were held together with bicycle inner tubes that would stretch in stormy weather, but not break. He had lined his den with newspapers and Army waterproof groundsheets. This was where he lived. He spent his days carrying out his ritual of physical activities, which included long swims in the bay when the water temperature allowed it, or on other occasions just sitting without a thought in his head, letting the little wonders of the forest unfold around him: a beetle going about its business, a beautiful flower, a hedgehog with her babies. Sometimes a startled cock pheasant would take flight between the spruces. It was a good life, he thought, an honest and quiet life, exactly as a life should be. On his better days he would carve quaint little figures, often trolls, which he would hide around the forest and be pleased when – sometimes years later – he rediscovered them. He got his food from his traps or night-time trips to the Dagligkæden village store near Præstø. He had a key for the gate to the backyard and would fill his backpack from the skip where all the groceries whose best-before date had expired or had been damaged were discarded. He got water from the lake, and he had a mirror, a pair of scissors, a knife and a whetstone, an Arctic sleeping bag and fleeces stitched together for when the winter was truly fierce. He lacked for nothing.

He rarely saw other people and only spoke to two at regular intervals. Irene Gallagher was one of them. He knew her from the old days and they helped each other. He didn't want to think about how, but that was what they did: they helped each other out. He had long since suppressed any memory of the canal boat killings. They had sunk into oblivion along with so many of his other bad experiences.

The only other person who would occasionally visit him was Gry. Like Bjørn, Gry could sit still and silent for a long time while watching him curiously, as if she discovered something new about him with every visit. Until her dog woke up, that is, hungry and wanting to go home, and dragged her off. Gry was a joy, and if too many days had passed since her last visit, he would listen out for her footsteps or the rattling of her dog's collar.

On this very autumn day Gry had come to visit her friend, but Bjørn Lauritzen didn't hear her approach. When she saw him, she grunted with displeasure and kneeled down to nudge him without that changing anything. He only stared idiotically at her. Tentatively she poked her finger into the small hole in his forehead, but that didn't make any difference either. Eventually she gave up and started picking blades of grass, which she threw into the wind, laughing when they were blown back in her face.

When she got home, her mother wanted to know about the blood on her clothes, and so Gry had to show her where her friend was hiding. She grunted angrily as they headed towards the forest together.

About the same time, a pensioner on his butcher's bike cycled out to deliver groceries to the war veteran living in Lorup Forest. The pensioner worked as an odd job man for Dagligkæden, to supplement his pension and to give him something to do. He had no official employment contract; the owner paid him cash in hand every Monday, but never exploited him. The pensioner worked his own hours and was always paid according to that figure. It was a matter of trust. His jobs were many and varied: he swept the pavement in front of the shop or cleared snow in the winter, cleaned the big front window when necessary, washed the shop floor thoroughly every Saturday, took care of minor repairs and would sometimes stack shelves in the evening, if the day had been busy and the regular staff hadn't had time to do it. He also took groceries to Ole Nysted on his bicycle; indeed as a young lad he had delivered milk to local families on the very same bike. Ole Nysted's essentials, mostly beer, wine and spirits, were delivered once a fortnight. Nysted paid cash on delivery, but if it was the end of the month and he didn't have enough money, the pensioner had been told to ignore it. The debt was simply forgotten and never carried forward to when the veteran next got his pension because that was a vicious circle, as the owner of Dagligkæden had explained in his funny, broken Danish.

It was a magnanimous gesture, which the pensioner valued. He was an old Guardsman himself, and had guarded Amalienborg Palace for the previous monarch, a popular king who wasn't too high and mighty to stop for a chat with a sentry. Since then the pensioner had felt a certain kinship with other ex-soldiers: the veteran might be an alcoholic wreck, but he wouldn't hurt a fly and would often offer the pensioner a beer when he brought the groceries.

The pensioner parked his bicycle and lugged the first crate of beer behind the hut. He put it down next to the woodpile and discovered that a plastic bag had been stretched across the mouth of the flue that provided ventilation for the wood-burning stove inside. A strong elastic band held the bag in place. It wasn't until then that he noticed the nauseating smell of smoke and soot. The smell was stronger inside, though there was no longer any smoke visible in the hut or fire in the wood-burning stove. Ole Nysted was lying on his sofa with two empty bottles of alcohol on the coffee table beside him, one a cheap whisky, the other a bottle of Aalborg Jubilæums Akvavit. His face was red and his eyes stared blindly at the ceiling. The pensioner thought it might be a case of carbon monoxide poisoning. He had seen something similar before.

CHAPTER 34

The National Police Commissioner was sweating. The tiny beads of moisture that had formed around his nostrils and his hairline revealed, even before the meeting had started, that he was ill at ease with the situation. The representative from the Ministry of Justice sitting at the conference table, however, wasn't uncomfortable in the least.

He was young, brazenly so, Konrad Simonsen thought, not a day over thirty-five, and he waited confidently in his expensive suit while checking his iPhone with a bored expression. He had just about deigned to look up and say hello when Simonsen arrived, but hadn't offered to shake his hand. Again, this was in contrast to the National Police Commissioner, who was profusely hearty in his welcome to the point of embarrassment. He had offered his Homicide Chief a chair, and announced that there was coffee, tea and soft drinks, which Simonsen would have to have been blind not to see: four Thermos flasks, two white and two red, were on the table right in front of him along with a selection of soft drinks. Simonsen thanked him.

The National Police Commissioner checked his watch and said: 'We've also invited the Public Prosecutor, the new one. Her name escapes me, but she'll be here in a moment.'

'Kirsten Hansen.'

The young man from the Ministry of Justice subtly managed to convey his horror that the holder of such an important office could have so common a surname.

It took more than ten long minutes before the Public Prosecutor arrived. She greeted the others politely but formally, and sat down without apologising for her lateness. She declined anything to drink.

She was close to forty, pretty and stylish though she tried hard to signal gravitas with her conservative outfit: a dark green pencil skirt, a white shirt, black blazer and a silk scarf in muted colours.

The National Police Commissioner said: 'Right then, I might as well get started.'

Which was as far as he got before Kirsten Hansen interrupted him by addressing the man from the Ministry.

'Sorry, I didn't catch which department in the Ministry of Justice you're in charge of.'

It was hatred at first sight, Konrad Simonsen thought. The representative said, reluctantly and as carefully as possible: 'Criminal Law.'

'Ah, you mean the Office for Criminal Law that reports to the Department for Police and Criminal Law? Why thank you, I'm glad we got that cleared up.'

She ignored his tersely uttered 'Quite' and turned expectantly to the Commissioner. He stammered and stuttered as he explained that the Homicide Department had identified the canal boat killer – a poor, deranged war veteran, who had unfortunately been found shot dead, but that his death, which probably had nothing to do with the other killings, could easily be handled by local officers from Sydsjællands Police.

The Commissioner was aware that not every aspect of the veteran's death had been accounted for as yet, but that was not uncommon, and all in all it was probably in everyone's best interests if the investigation was brought to an end as quickly as possible, so there could be closure on the dreadful canal-boat incident.

Konrad Simonsen could barely believe his own ears. He asked incredulously: 'Tell me, are you closing down my investigation? Is that what you're saying?'

The Commissioner tried to explain.

'Sometimes you have to look at the bigger picture ...'

'So are you ordering me to close my investigation?'

'No, no, of course not, you misunderstand. It's not an order ... I mean, you'll do it of your own accord. Only you need to do so in the next few days.'

Simonsen weighed up the situation, then said with forced calm: 'All right then. In that case I'd better call Steffen and ask him to join us immediately.'

His boss didn't follow: Steffen? Steffen who? Surely everyone who needed to be here was already present?

Simonsen explained, 'He's the leader of the Police Officers' Union. When Denmark's rank-and-file officers hear about this, they'll be furious and we need to discuss how we'll deal with the situation because, God knows, they won't take this lying down.'

The National Police Commissioner considered the issue in all seriousness. So long as the parties could agree to talk the matter over, show restraint, the situation should be containable. He didn't like the sound of angry officers.

Konrad Simonsen launched his next attack.

'Will you be contacting the Foreign Ministry yourself to handle the Japanese reaction?'

The Commissioner paled and clutched his head. The pressure he was already under was bad enough, but pressure from two directions was even worse, the sort of thing that gave you stress. He should have called in sick that morning, as his wife had suggested, and dumped this meeting on someone else.

The man from the Ministry of Justice intervened and addressed Konrad Simonsen directly.

'Let's cut the crap. You suspect that former Army Judge Advocate Irene Gallagher is somehow involved in your case. But I gather that you're nowhere near charging her.'

Simonsen protested feebly: 'We have some evidence, including photographs from surveillance cameras, and I'm sure we'll get more.'

The civil servant snorted derisively and pulled out two pictures from a plastic folder ready in front of him. One was of Irene Gallagher taken on Christiansbro where she was driving her sister's car. The other was a picture of Irene with a new short haircut where she looked nothing like the profile in the car. The haircut made all the difference.

'I believe it's only in your imagination that this blurred picture is of Irene Gallagher.'

'How did you get that?'

'From your own investigation. Not all officers in your department are as – how shall I put it? – over-optimistic as you. I had hoped we could resolve this matter in a more civilised manner, I won't deny that, but you don't even have enough evidence for a search warrant, am I right?'

Simonsen had to concede he was. The civil servant continued: 'It just so happens that your investigation into Irene Gallagher involves classified information which, if it becomes public, threatens national security. This was made clear to you as long as three months ago, and yet you went ahead and contacted the Army again. You even persuaded your Deputy Commissioner to get involved ... and that despite procedures clearly stating that as a minimum requirement you must inform my Ministry, and preferably go via them.'

'What do you mean, three months ago? Three months ago I didn't even know the existence of ... wait! Who contacted you?'

The civil servant had to search for the file in his folder; he hadn't memorised the name. It took some time before he found what he was looking for. Eventually he said: 'Sergeant Berg from the Homicide Department contacted the Army three – I repeat three – times, the first time in the middle of May this year. And not only that, Sergeant Berg also contacted Irene Gallagher directly to make her reveal military secrets. It's utterly intolerable, but I realise from your reaction that you didn't know anything about it, so perhaps you should try to find out what's going on in your own department!

'But enough about that. The bottom line is that the two of you have from now until close of business on Tuesday next week, and if you haven't charged anyone by that point, you'll close down the investigation. End of discussion.'

'No!'

This was Kirsten Hansen's first proper contribution to the meeting. It was, however, a forceful one. The civil servant looked at her, somewhat taken aback.

'What do you mean, no? Who do you think you are?'

Kirsten Hansen replied in a neutral tone, but her eyes revealed exactly what she thought of him.

'I'm the woman who's going back to her office to write detailed minutes of this meeting, after which I'll submit a formal complaint about your abuse of power to the Director of Public Prosecutions. And I'm perfectly aware that the DDP reports to the Ministry of Justice, so to be on the safe side, I'll send a copy to the President of the Supreme Court to make sure he's informed. Your conduct is completely unacceptable – there's a reason we've divided power in this country into three independent branches, and it's to stop people like you serving your own interests.

'So far as the national security argument goes, you can tell them back in your Ministry that I don't give a damn about your cloak-and-dagger games. Our nation is safest if killers are investigated, charged, prosecuted and convicted. And besides that, while I'm in the process of making announcements, you can also tell them the next time your Ministry wants to talk to me about my charging policy, this will happen at Permanent Secretary level or higher.'

While the civil servant struggled to get the redness in his cheeks under control, Konrad Simonsen was quick to show his co-operative side.

'I'd be happy to assist you with the minutes, it's important that they're as accurate as possible. And we must take great care that they're not leaked to the press because if this gets out, public outrage could very easily lead to the reassignment of a minor civil servant from the Ministry of Justice to a Health and Safety inspector's job on Greenland.'

Kirsten Hansen got up.

'Right, Simon, we're leaving. You don't mind me calling you Simon, do you? After all, everyone else does.'

Konrad Simonsen played along: *of course I don't*. She smiled at him and did so again as he gallantly opened the door for her. The civil servant called out after them like a petulant child: 'You'll pay for this!'

The National Police Commissioner, who couldn't quite decide whether to get up or stay sitting down, chose an awkward half-way position for a few seconds before he finally opted for slumping down. He said: 'Well, I'm delighted we reached consensus.'

CHAPTER 35

Kirsten Hansen and Konrad Simonsen went to see the judge them-selves. This was highly unusual; normally the Public Prosecutor would never turn up in person, and Simonsen had no business being there at all as a representative of the executive branch of govern-ment. The judge, however, made no comment. He looked bored, but livened up when they made their entrance.

Kirsten Hansen argued to the best of her ability for a search warrant for Irene Gallagher's house, her two holiday homes and her sister Ella von Eggert's car, which had just been found in a car park in Hillerød, but which had been returned to her and not – as Konrad Simonsen had expressly requested – sent to Forensic Services for examination. A clear and irritating error. After Kirsten Hansen had presented the rather weak reasons for requesting the search warrants, she expressed outrage at the hidden powers trying to protect the suspect from prosecution.

The judge listened with interest and then concluded that at times the law should be interpreted from the standpoint of public inter-est, after which he signed the search warrants.

Konrad Simonsen divided up the work between his closest colleagues. Arne Pedersen got the suspect's home in Næstved, which he had already visited. The Countess got Irene Gallagher's holiday home in Gilleleje and Ella von Eggert's Opel Corsa. Klavs Arnold was allocated the second holiday home, which lay on the island of Falster.

Simonsen was unable to take part himself, though he desperately wanted to go to Næstved. That, however, wasn't possible: he was the operational head not only for the searches, but also for the two teams from Sydsjællands Police who were busy investigating the possible murder of Ole Nysted and the murder of Bjørn Lauritzen. The decision to appoint Konrad Simonsen as head of these two investigations was approved by the National Police Commissioner himself. He made no objections, possibly because his Homicide Chief had presented the situation to him as a sensible measure. Simonsen's many hats meant that he couldn't very well leave Police Headquarters during the day, so he stayed where he was and instead started to read the contents of a brown envelope a messenger had delivered earlier that morning.

There was no sender's name on the envelope and Simonsen's name was written in neat capital letters on the front. The contents consisted of three A4 pages listing information about Irene Gallagher in chronological order, although it didn't cover her whole career. There were still gaps. The report was interesting nevertheless and painted a picture of an intelligence officer who had worked for the Armies of the USA and Denmark.

The report began by stating that Irene Gallagher had had two careers and relevant training for each of them: one as legal adviser to the Army and one as an intelligence operative – a rare but not unique situation. From the late 1980s she had studied at the National Intelligence University in Washington DC. There she had graduated in Intelligence Studies, specialising in the Baltic States, and in addition to strategic military topics, was also taught classic intelligence skills such as surveillance, breaking and entering, weapons use and close-combat training, handling agents and so on. She had been deployed on missions in at least two countries, one to Poland under President Jaruzelski in 1990, and then in Bosnia in 1992, 1994 and 1995, but had presumably been to many other places. From 1992 to 1994 she sailed for two years with one of the eleven US aircraft carriers as legal adviser to the commander. She had served with the Sixth Fleet based in Gaeta in Italy, which had the Mediterranean as its area of operation. She served in the same capacity in 2001 and 2002, this time with the Second Fleet based in Norfolk, Virginia, and with the Atlantic as its area of operation.

From the summer of 2002 she was reported to be the primary intelligence link between the USA and Denmark. In terms of languages spoken, in addition to Danish and English, she was also fluent in French, Mandarin, Polish and Russian, and she had a working knowledge of Finnish.

It was difficult to know how to react, Konrad Simonsen thought. It was easier to deal with the three snippets of information at the end of the report, which the writer stressed originated from a single source. The first was that Irene Gallagher was alleged to have a personal interest in Bjørn Lauritzen because her trip to Bosnia in July 1995 had taken place during her holiday and on her own initiative, though it couldn't be ruled out that she could also have pursued professional interests at the same time. Whatever the reason, she had flown to Tuzla and driven on from there with the stated intention of meeting the Danish captain.

The second piece of information was more substantial: in the spring of 2006, Irene Gallagher had formally renounced her American citizenship at the American Embassy in Copenhagen – something the report could verify, in contrast to the third and last piece of information it gave, which was that during the last four years of her employment with the Army, Irene Gallagher had consistently refused to travel to the USA, something that had proved a major obstacle to her work and ultimately led to her leaving the Army by mutual agreement.

Konrad Simonsen read the information, went to lunch and read it again when he came back. Then he summoned Anica Buch, who was working two offices down at Pauline's old desk trying to trace the girl from the farmyard who had apparently spoken Danish. Anica had no new developments to report, and was sufficiently honest to say to her temporary boss that it might be a while before she could present him with anything. She continued, with youthful hubris: 'But I promise you that if the girl exists and is Danish, then I'll find her.'

Konrad Simonsen decided that there was something strangely child-like about Anica that was an odd fit with her intelligence and obvious work ethic. He responded to her optimism with an *of course you will*, and made it clear that she could leave.

When she had done so, Simonsen could do little else for the investigation except wait – wait and hope for good news from the searches or from the two homicide investigations he was heading up. He felt edgy and struggled to concentrate on other tasks, though he had plenty of them. The department's accounts, for example, as he was always hopelessly behind with them.

Towards five o'clock he received the first bit of good news. It came from Forensic Services: they had examined Ella von Eggert's car and discovered that it had been cleaned meticulously, but they had found a hair that definitely belonged to Bjørn Lauritzen caught under an Unbrako nut in the passenger-seat lever. Konrad Simonsen had barely stopped cheering before the next two breakthroughs occurred. It was Arne Pedersen who, in a state of telephonic euphoria, informed his boss that not only had the sleeve of one of Irene Gallagher's jackets tested positive for gunpowder residue, but that the officers who had searched her home had also found a pistol in a plastic bag, hidden in a bucket of road grit – a Ruger Mark I 22LR, which could easily be the weapon that had killed Bjørn Lauritzen. The pistol had been sent off for tests, which would involve a ballistic comparison with the bullet pathologists had removed from Lauritzen's head. Arne Pedersen estimated that it would take three to four hours before the result would be available.

At a quarter-past ten that evening Simonsen received a call from Kurt Melsing. At that point there were two of them in his office, as the Homicide Chief had asked Public Prosecutor Kirsten Hansen to wait along with him, so that they could discuss their next move, depending on the news from Forensic Services.

Simonsen listened carefully to Melsing. It had now been scientifically established that Bjørn Lauritzen had been shot and killed with the pistol the police had found in Irene Gallagher's garage, but there was more: on the pistol, technicians had found two sets of prints. The first set, found on the barrel, was unknown; the second, lifted from the grip, belonged to Irene Gallagher. Additional forensic tests also proved that she had held the weapon.

Konrad Simonsen and Kirsten Hansen celebrated. A brief discussion followed and they concluded they were in agreement. An hour and a half later, former Army Judge Advocate Irene Gallagher was arrested in her home in Næstved, charged with the murder of former Captain Bjørn Lauritzen on 22 September 2010 in Store Hestehave Forest; and accessory to the murder of Sergeant Pauline Berg, shop assistant Jonas Ziegler, student Carina Hastrup and skipper Theis Lund Mikkelsen on 22 August 2010, in Copenhagen, along with the manslaughter of schoolteacher Yuuma Kawahara and her pupils – here Public Prosecutor Kirsten Hansen insisted that every single child be named as a question of ethics – and, finally, accessory to GBH against student Juli Denissen on 10 July 2008 on Melby Common.

The defendant didn't comment on the charges, and she accompanied the arresting officers without a struggle.

PART III

The Trial

CHAPTER 36

Christoffer Brinch's life was nothing but a complete success. He excelled at school and, after a brilliant set of exam results, read law at the University of Copenhagen. In 1973 he graduated with a first-class degree, and spent the next three years in his hometown of Holbæk working for the town's leading law firm. In 1979 he borrowed some money from his parents and moved back to Copenhagen, where he rented a small office in the desirable location of Højbro Plads. Here he set up his own firm specialising in corporation and tax law. It flourished. He was a naturally amiable character who loathed showing off, and there was something awkward about his big, clumsy gestures, as though God had been a little careless when creating him. People who didn't know him tended to discover too late in the conversation that he had an incredibly sharp mind. His potential clients – often a managing director or a captain of industry – would narrow their eyes and wonder whether the young man might not prove to be useful. Perhaps he was worth hiring for a minor case, just to check him out.

By 1980 he had bought the whole floor containing his original office, and in 1985, the entire building. At that point he had a staff of more than thirty, including four law students whom he had cherry-picked from the university. His firm gave them time and office space for their studies while quietly training them in corporate law. The idea of the student placements was his own; he thought long-term and was sure that in the future highly qualified and loyal staff would emerge from the arrangement, which proved to be the case. There was one exception, and he married her.

The marriage was happy: they had three children, and they never stopped loving one another. He worshipped her and she looked after him. When he took on too much work, she didn't shy away from turning up at the office to drag him home, no matter how important a meeting was. She would complain vociferously: it wasn't right that Christoffer did everything, he was no longer a young man, others would have to take over because her husband wouldn't be back until Monday morning at the earliest. Once home he would be given a good talking to: she didn't want to lose him to a stroke, and he could stop arguing with her – did he really think he was immortal? Christoffer Brinch took her point and brought partners into his business and shared out the management responsibility, a process that succeeded without Brinch & Partners losing its standing as one of Copenhagen's leading corporate law firms.

In 2001 Christoffer Brinch turned fifty and had a long talk with his wife. He wanted to devote the last part of his career to his first love, criminal law. He knew perfectly well there wasn't much money in it, but he could afford to ignore that. His wife backed him. His partners also proved sympathetic, though privately they had strong doubts about the project. After all, the man hadn't had any experience of criminal law since he was a student. However, they forgot to factor in his brilliant legal mind, and in a remarkably short space of time, Christoffer Brinch managed to become a highly sought-after defence lawyer, especially within the legal community. Other lawyers would contact him if they themselves had got into trouble.

He had a reputation for being the best. These were good years, possibly the finest of his career. He took on only the cases he wanted to, and never too many, which gave him time to stroll through the offices and help others whenever he got the chance. He was never happier than when one of the student interns, who were still trained and hired according to his original concept, asked for his help with a university assignment. He would move heaven and earth, work for hours in his office, to ensure every detail was correct, often sending a taxi to the university library if he thought one of his old textbooks might be useful, and would hand his efforts to the student the next day, as if it was nothing at all, dear Lord, no, just a few little scribbles that might come in handy. The result was always the same: the student would have to return to their tutor and ask for a new assignment, as they couldn't in all honesty pass off the brilliant work as their own. Brinch & Partners had eventually introduced a strict ban on students showing any university assignments to him.

Irene Gallagher's request to Christoffer Brinch for representation came in a roundabout way. It was sent via one of her old Army colleagues and then on to a retired judge, who had once tutored the star lawyer. This judge turned up in person at Højbro Plads and, having outlined the main points of the case while Christoffer Brinch sat nodding his head and weighing up the pros and cons, Irene Gallagher got her defence lawyer. It sounded like an exciting case. Brinch agreed to take it on.

He first met his client in Vestre Prison, where she had been remanded in custody for four weeks in isolation.

She got up when the prison officer let him in, and they shook hands. They both sat down on the bed. The cell was small and furnished austerely: the bed on which they were currently sitting, a table and chair, a wardrobe, a bookcase above the table, with one barred window set high up in the wall. A doorway led to a bathroom with a lavatory. The walls in both the small rooms were bare and painted a muted yellow.

Christoffer Brinch said: 'Perhaps we could start by telling each other a little about ourselves. I'm happy to go first.'

Irene Gallagher interrupted before he had a chance to begin.

'That won't be necessary. I know exactly who you are. That's why I requested you as my lawyer.'

'Why, thank you. However, I don't know very much about you.'

She took him up on his invitation and told him briefly about her life. When she had finished, she spent some time explaining why she couldn't be more specific in terms of her past employment. She finished by saying: 'It'll be the same in court. The judge will almost certainly be informed that there will be matters he can't allow anyone to bring up and … Listen, please can you stop nodding your head? You look like an idiot.'

'It's a habit of mine, you'll have to get used to it. Are you always so blunt?'

'Not always, but usually.'

'I like that. I'll try to be the same. As for not being able to discuss your work, is that something you think might harm your defence?'

Irene Gallagher said that no, it wouldn't.

'You intrigue me. When I meet other clients who have been remanded in custody, they always start by asking me when they'll be released, and they try hard to convince me of their innocence – whether or not they actually are. But you seem to be taking it all in your stride even though the charges against you are very grave indeed.'

'I'm staying calm because getting worked up won't do me any good. Besides, I'm trained not to panic. Also, as I told you, I'm a lawyer myself, and I know that not much will happen until we get my indictment, and that may not be for some time. The probability that I'll be remanded in custody for another four weeks is very strong. We both know that.'

Christoffer Brinch agreed. It was how the system worked.

'Have you thought about your line of defence?'

'Yes, I have. And it's important that we agree ground rules. I need you to act as my mouthpiece during the trial whether or not you agree with me.'

'Of course, that's the whole point of having a defence lawyer. However, I was thinking more of what you have to say to the charges in general.'

'That the evidence against me is trumped up, and we'll prove that in court. Because that's the truth, though it's hard to believe.'

Now it was Christoffer Brinch's turn to mull things over. When he had done so, he said: 'Right, then, we'll have to try that. The charges of manslaughter of the children will definitely be dropped. Even Bjørn Lauritzen wouldn't be charged with those, if he were still alive. There's no causal link or reasonable expectation that you could have foreseen those deaths, in my opinion. The same may apply to the Japanese teacher, but that's debatable. And the charge of being an accomplice to the attack on the young woman in Nordsjælland will go too. I simply can't imagine how the prosecution can prove that beyond all reasonable doubt. With regards to the other charges, we'll have to wait and see, as you say. I'm presuming you already know that the line of defence you're suggesting is pretty much the worst you could pick.'

'Yes, I'm aware of it, but … but … I can't imagine that you'll bother listening to me if I try to convince you that I didn't do the things they're charging me with.'

'I'm willing to listen.'

'I'm afraid I lied to the police during an interview, but I had no choice. I'll explain that to you later, in as much as I'm able to explain it to you.'

'Fine, we'll deal with it when that time comes.'

'Have you any experience of representing a client who maintained their innocence even though it flew in the face of all logic?'

'Yes, plenty.'

'What happened to them?'

'They were convicted.'

'Fairly, in your opinion?'

'Yes, I would say so.'

'Then I'm the exception because if I'm convicted, it'll be a miscarriage of justice. The evidence against me really has been fabricated. I'm hoping I can convince you of that along the way because it's the truth. And we must go with the line of defence I'm suggesting.'

'Of course, if that's what you want, we must.'

Privately Christoffer Brinch was convinced that Irene Gallagher would be given a whole life sentence.

CHAPTER 37

SATURDAY 2 OCTOBER 2010, ISRAELS PLADS, COPENHAGEN

She reached her hand across the table and placed it on top of his. It lasted only a moment, a second's enthusiasm to stress her point, then she withdrew it. He thought that it was the first time they had touched except for a few handshakes, which didn't count. He felt happy, he could think of no other word for it, and drank the rest of his weak, cold coffee that had tasted awful, even when it was hot. She leaned forward, placed her elbows on the table, interlaced her fingers and rested her head on them. She had asked him a question, and perhaps he might be persuaded to give her an answer. She looked seriously attractive.

Arne Pedersen said: 'Please would you say that again? It sounds suspicious.'

Louise Berg smiled, her pretty eyes sparkling with a hint of mischief.

'I said, I know a place nearby where we can get a lot of food for free, if we play our cards right. It's a bit of a gamble, of course, but are you up for it?'

It was impossible for him to say no. They paid for the coffee, forty kroner each ... ridiculous, what a rip-off, even five kroner would have been too much. She insisted on going Dutch and made up her contribution from coins in her purse, which she lined up in front of her as she counted them out. She explained that it was a principle she had, given that she didn't know him yet. That little word *yet* sent an unfamiliar warmth from the pit of his stomach right down his legs, and he realised then that he was crazy about her. He pulled himself together before he made a fool of himself. He was old enough to be her father, and anyway, what did he have to offer her?

The Torvehallerne Market on Israels Plads was still under construction. The billboard in front of the building site promised a foodie heaven of speciality shops, a veritable cornucopia of good, fresh ingredients. The stallholders, however, were keen to get a head start and every Saturday from May to October would erect their stalls among the construction mess that covered most of the square.

Louise grabbed him by the arm and explained: 'We're not going to buy anything. Although the food here is delicious, it's incredibly expensive. The trick is to convince yourself that you *might* buy something. Take your time. Ask questions. The vendors are proud of their produce so they're easy to talk to.'

She dragged him off to a stall selling sausages, looked at the products with interest, then took a sample from one of the small plates that had been put out. She evaluated as she ate.

'It's good ... lovely and smoked and not too strong. You should try it.'

He tasted while she chatted to the stallholder about the provenance of the sausage and whether it was organic.

They wandered around for half an hour, talking mostly about food, a safe subject: what was the most delicious thing to eat each season? She had never tried truffles or caviar – had he? A bright sun high in the sky warmed them despite the season, and when they laughed and she momentarily pressed herself against him while resting her forehead on his shoulder, their shadows would merge. He liked watching this.

They finished off with a glass of red wine at a café in Vendersgade, and as they sat there – suddenly a little awkward with one another – she grew serious.

'The woman you've arrested, will she be convicted?'

His answer was as genuine as he could make it.

'It's hard to say right now, but my best guess is that some of the charges will have to be dropped. She can't be convicted of the death of the children and the Japanese teacher, or of Juli Denissen ... Do you know who that is?'

'You bet. Pauline spoke of little else during the last two years of her life.'

'OK, again I think it's highly doubtful we can get her for that. Then there are the stabbings of your sister and the other three victims, and here I also have strong doubts. We need more concrete and forensic evidence, and I think we'll get there in the end, but what we are badly in need of is a motive, and I'm not sure that we can come up with one. Then there's the murder of Bjørn Lauritzen, the man who murdered your sister. Gallagher will be convicted of that, that's not up for discussion, even if we did lose one possible piece of evidence yesterday. After we arrested her, she tested positive for gunshot residue on her clothing, but she claimed that she had been in Næstved Gun Club practising with her pistol, and sadly that turned out to be true, even though it's just too convenient.'

Tears welled up in Louise's eyes. Arne sensed that it was best to let her be, so he waited silently until she had composed herself. When she had, she surprised him by saying: 'When Pauline lived in Reersø, she was genuinely in love with you. You could have moved in with her, if you had wanted to. Did you know that?'

He replied that he knew it, but that the needs of his children had weighed more heavily, which was the truth.

'Of course I know that it's worse for you,' he told Louise, 'but I miss her terribly. Since her death, I'm remembering her like she was before she got … ill. I made the wrong choice back then, but I've only just realised that. And now it's your turn to speak. I don't even know what you do.'

She was a receptionist and worked for First Hotel Østerport. She lived in a small flat with a friend, a situation she wanted to change only it was terribly difficult to find somewhere affordable in Copenhagen. Perhaps she should move into Pauline's flat in Rødovre, but she wasn't sure that she could afford the mortgage or that she wanted to live there.

'When Pauline became mentally unstable, she dated a lot of men. A new one every weekend, at least, and I'm not exaggerating. Were you one of them?'

'No.'

'And what about the Jutlander? I don't remember his name.'

'His name is Klavs Arnold, and no, I don't think he was either.'

Louise nodded somewhat wistfully.

'I'm glad to hear that. You get to ask one last question, then I must go.'

He had to ask, there was no other option, and she could interpret it as she wanted.

'Do you have a boyfriend?'

He could see that she had been expecting the question. She said in a neutral tone: 'Now you're getting too personal.'

It was a bad ending, but he knew he was in a hole and should stop digging. He made eye contact with the waiter, and they shared the bill as they had done earlier. Then Louise got up to go. 'I'll call you,' she said.

CHAPTER 38

The two men studied the statue together. After a while Helmer Hammer turned to Konrad Simonsen.

'What do you see?'

Simonsen's disparaging grin revealed his lack of interest. Opera, ballet, painting, sculpture, classical music, poetry ... the list was endless ... these highbrow activities were not for him. He preferred watching cycle racing on TV or a good American movie. Not to mention a game of chess.

'I see a naked man wearing a Roman helmet. He has flayed a sheep and is leaning against a pile of laundry.'

Helmer Hammer rolled his eyes theatrically. Visiting the museum had been his idea. Konrad Simonsen would have suggested a walk or a visit to a restaurant.

'This is a major work of European neoclassicism you're ridiculing, you pleb! It represents our belief in the freedom of mankind, our hope for Western democracy, no less. Besides, it's a ram, not a sheep, but I won't waste my time telling you the story behind it because I'm sure you don't care.'

Konrad Simonsen gave the statue a second glance, but could see no sign of democracy at work.

'Its genitals are disproportionately small,' he observed.

'Right, that's the final straw! You clearly have no interest in receiving a classical education. Let's go to the museum café. I'll enjoy the collections on my own some other day.'

Helmer Hammer held an important post in the Prime Minister's office, reporting directly to the Permanent Secretary. His work gave him a unique insight into the workings of the Central Administration and he always kept a finger on the political pulse. His official title was Special Adviser.

Over the years the two men had developed a kind of friendship, and, though they rarely met in person, they would do each other favours from time to time. Yesterday Hammer had called Konrad Simonsen. He had heard on the grapevine that the Homicide Chief could do with a little friendly advice.

They found a table in the farthest corner of the café. There were hardly any other visitors so they could speak undisturbed. Konrad Simonsen remarked: 'You look unusually relaxed. Are you on holiday or has the activity in the Prime Minister's office been brought down to a more humane level?'

Helmer Hammer shook his head. It was for neither reason. He had quit his job, but it wasn't official yet. Konrad Simonsen was taken aback. Hammer explained that he had long sought an ambassadorial posting to somewhere warm and pleasant, but his family was reluctant to travel and he didn't want any of the other jobs he had discreetly been offered.

'So what on earth will you do with yourself?'

'Have you ever heard of the Oracle?'

Konrad Simonsen had. The Oracle had enjoyed a promising career in the Ministry of Finance before the stress of it became too much for him. When he had recovered, he was given a sinecure with the Royal Mint in a small office in Købmagergade, where he could twiddle his thumbs until his retirement. However, the man had managed to create a new job for himself, acting as a consultant to anyone in government administration, from the highest to the lowest, in need of good advice. And given his extensive knowledge of the bureaucracy in ministries and committees, his advice was very good indeed. The Countess had used him once.

Helmer Hammer elaborated.

'He and I have set up a small consultancy firm together. We've found offices in Bredgade.'

'Consulting for whom?'

Hammer smiled.

'Anyone who needs us and can pay.'

Konrad Simonsen thought that the new venture was bound to succeed. There were undoubtedly many people – not least lobbyists – who could benefit from the two men's knowledge.

'Then I'm glad you're still working for the State right now because you won't be getting any of my money.'

That was their cue. They both sat upright and their expressions grew serious.

Simonsen asked: 'Do you want an outline of my investigation?'

'That won't be necessary, Simon. I've had a few words with a mutual friend who visited you the other night, and I think I know everything I need to know. However, I want to tell you something. You believe that Irene Gallagher's and Bjørn Lauritzen's activities in Bosnia in the mid-1990s are relevant to your investigation, but when you ask the Army, more specifically FE, for help you hit a wall. Not only do they not want to help you, they're positively obstructive. But I'll return to that later.

'Their lack of corporation is likely to be rooted in some defence secret – big or small – that somehow involves Irene Gallagher. Let's assume so, it sounds about right: there's something they don't want to come out. So you need to bear in mind two things: first, if that is the case, then only a few people know what the secret is, probably just two or three, and they all work for the Army. Secondly, the only people who can force the Army to co-operate with you are the Minister for Defence, the Minister for Justice and the Prime Minister, but none of them would want to – or not voluntarily at least. They don't want to know anything about the case. Their respective ministries are perfectly aware of that and their civil servants are working very hard to make sure things stay that way.'

Here Simonsen couldn't stop himself from interrupting.

'But that's intolerable. Thank God that statue can't hear us talking or he would crumble in shame.'

'Yes, he probably would. It's a fact that Denmark is undoubtedly the Western democracy with the least political control of its intelligence services, but there's nothing we can do about that today.'

Konrad Simonsen rubbed his forehead. He didn't like what he was hearing. On the other hand he was grateful that someone was telling him the truth.

'You said "Not only do they not want to help you" – what did you mean by that?'

'That FE will actively be working against you. That might be because the Army prefers Irene Gallagher to be acquitted and shipped off to New Zealand. Or it might be that you and your Public Prosecutor friend – Kirsten Hansen, that's her name, isn't it? – have upset FE big time, along with major parts of the Ministry for Justice, and what we're talking about here is purely a power struggle, a turf war. We've seen that sort of thing before. And finally it could be a combination of the two, which is what I personally believe.'

'And how are they obstructing me?'

'Currently by spreading rumours. That sounds harmless enough, but it isn't. Remember, FE are experts in that type of work.

'They've let it be known among police officers that anyone helping them with this case won't be forgotten, and that there are great career opportunities in military intelligence and the security services. The latter has hacked off our mutual friend considerably, because it affects his own staff and because he has no wish to be caught in the crossfire between the Homicide Department and FE. Not that there's a lot he can do to stop it.'

Simonsen's face grew red from suppressed rage.

'Why the hell haven't I heard about this before?'

'Give it a rest, Simon. Sometimes you're too busy being the boss. Imagine if you were young and ambitious and you heard a rumour that it would be a good long-term investment to make friends with FE, would you run to your immediate superior or all the way up to you, for that matter – if you know what I mean – and say that you've just heard a whisper in the canteen? Of course you wouldn't. And nor would anybody else.'

Simonsen realised that Hammer had a point. He calmed down.

'So what do I do now? Any ideas?'

'Haven't I always? Attack them, Simon. Put as much pressure on FE as you can and then some. It's the only way. Not that that's going to make them grant you access to their files, of course, but it'll show them that thwarting you comes at a price, and they might be better off backing down a little. They'll be hopping mad and probably also aggressive – at least for a while – but ... well, they already are. And they never forget. Sooner or later they'll come gunning for you. You must realise that.'

'Gunning for me?'

'To retire you, possibly also intimidate you … but nothing more than that. No one would dare to harm you physically. You don't have to worry about that.'

'I'm not worried and I like the idea of attacking them, as you put it.'

'Excellent. Now listen to me. You need to draft a request, which you know will be rejected, and which consists of …'

Helmer Hammer gestured eagerly as he began to explain his plan.

CHAPTER 39

MONDAY 4 OCTOBER 2010, FORENSIC SERVICES

The Countess always felt welcome when she visited Forensic Services in Vanløse. She especially liked the head of the department, Kurt Melsing, and she wasn't alone in this respect.

Melsing knew that the Countess was coming, but not why. She explained she had video footage for him; only a short clip, barely a second's duration. However, it was of interest because it showed Irene Gallagher and possibly also Bjørn Lauritzen on the afternoon of Sunday 22 August. Kurt Melsing dragged her towards his computer while he said, 'Very, very good.' These were big words coming from him, she knew, and she agreed that it probably was very, very good.

The Countess had received the video footage only the other day. An unemployed man had called Police Headquarters and explained that he had an ultra-short film clip of Irene Gallagher with a man on Charlottenlund Beach taken on the day all those children were killed. The duty officer in the Homicide Department had been less than enthusiastic, thinking it was a hoax. After the arrest of Irene Gallagher media interest in the case had flared up again, leading to a corresponding surge in calls from the public. An extra police officer had been temporarily assigned to the main switchboard and told to deal with anyone calling with information for the Homicide Department. Internally this job was known as being a gatekeeper and at peak times this role could be assumed by three or four officers before being dropped entirely once the number of calls subsided.

The vast majority of calls picked up by the gatekeepers were useless, and this man had sounded like just another time waster, the gatekeeper had thought. However, he had arranged for the man to email his video to the police, who would get back to him if his information turned out to be of interest. Which, as became clear the moment the Homicide Department had viewed the film, it very much was. Simonsen was informed and he called the Countess, who was due in later that day, and asked her to drive to work via Ryvangs Allé where the man lived.

At his flat the man explained the circumstances of the recording to the Countess. He was divorced and saw his three children every other weekend, which had included Sunday 22 August. On that day he and the kids had caught the bus to Charlottenlund Beach, where they loved to play. It hadn't been a very hot day and there were few people on the beach, but a middle-aged woman had settled down not far from him and the children. She had a big wicker bag next to her and was scanning the sea with her binoculars. She did nothing else apart from wave to his children from time to time. He didn't know exactly how long she had sat there, but estimated it to be about an hour, or just under. Then a man of around fifty had emerged from the sea. The moment the woman spotted him, she had kicked off her shoes and socks and run down to the water's edge with two big towels under her arm and her bag over her shoulder. She had handed the swimmer one of her towels and he had started drying his hair. She draped the other towel around his shoulders as he was doing this and in this way, hiding his face, she led him away. She picked up her other things on the way past, after which the couple followed the path up towards the car park.

'It all happened in a flash, much more quickly than the time it has taken me to tell you, so I don't think anyone but me noticed anything. And besides, there was nothing unusual about it. The man would appear to have been out for a long swim, and so what?'

The Countess agreed and the witness continued talking.

Around the same time he had used his camera to film his two older children next to the sandcastle they had built on the beach. Afterwards, the boys wanted to do some filming themselves, and each was allowed to record a short sequence. They did well until the youngest one, who was two years old, also wanted to have a go, only her skill didn't match her ambition and she held the camera without understanding the need to point it at her subject.

A few days ago he had viewed the children's and especially his daughter's footage on his computer. It was mostly of sand or sky, but there was also a second's worth of Irene Gallagher at the water's edge as she met the swimmer. According to the camera's time code, this had happened at 12.22. The witness had recognised the woman from pictures on the Internet, although the court had issued a ban on publishing her name and picture. However, surely that injunction didn't apply to him, did it? He and his kids had only filmed her by accident. The Countess assured him that what they had done wasn't a crime. In fact, it was brilliant.

Kurt Melsing viewed the footage a few times; it didn't take him long. Then he went through it one frame at a time, which didn't take long either. One of his staff watched it with them and Melsing said to the technician: 'Perhaps we can measure his body and paste him into the footage, to see if he fits. That new girl, Elise, she can do it.'

The other forensic technician, used to his boss, translated for the Countess.

'We could attempt to calculate the height of the man in the video and compare it to Bjørn Lauritzen's actual height. We can also see if we can add him to the footage based on pictures taken of him during the autopsy. Or we could possibly take more pictures of him from the right angle – his body is still in storage. The identification is never going to be one hundred per cent accurate, but then again it's also possible that the man in the video isn't Bjørn Lauritzen, something we might also be able to prove. We'll assign this work to our new colleague, she's highly skilled in picture processing. She worked as an animator for Disney for two years, and they don't hire people who don't know what they're doing.'

CHAPTER 40

The duty officer on reception at Police Headquarters said harshly: 'Stop bawling. You won't get to see Detective Chief Superintendent Konrad Simonsen and that's that. You can't just walk in off the street and demand to talk to a senior officer.'

The young man tried to pull himself together. He cried easily, he had always been like that, even a sentimental film would make him well up, but he felt strongly about this – what had happened was all wrong. He wiped his nose on his shirtsleeve and tried again.

'Why would he be so mean? Call her a gypsy slag and accuse her of being a criminal? We were only trying to help, and we didn't know the video was illegal. Now she's terrified that he'll tell tales to her husband.'

The duty officer shook his head in despair.

'Just a moment.'

Klavs Arnold's voice was calm, measured and brilliant at defusing any situation. He walked up to the duty officer. 'This man's coming with me, I want to hear what he has to say.' The officer went back behind his counter and Klavs Arnold led the young man into the colonnaded courtyard, which lay just behind the building's entrance, saying, 'Sit down and take your time, I'm in no hurry.' The young man sat down, leaned against a column and composed himself.

Slowly Klavs Arnold dragged the story out of him. He was from Slagelse and would appear to be having a secret romance with a Roma girl. They would sometimes go walking together. On one of these strolls, the young couple had seen Irene Gallagher walking through Lorup Forest, but she hadn't noticed them. She had been carrying a toolbox and some boards under her arm. The young man, curious, had recorded a short video of her. The two young people had now learned that Irene Gallagher had been charged with involvement in the canal boat killings and other crimes, and had decided to contact Police Headquarters and tell them about the video. They had called from the young man's home and put it on speakerphone, both wondering if their call was relevant. After explaining themselves to the gatekeeper, they had been transferred to Konrad Simonsen. He, however, had been exceptionally rude.

He had accused the girl of terrible things, and claimed that she and her family made their living from crime and were parasites, a burden on the Danish taxpayer. Worst of all, he had threatened to tell the girl's husband that she was sleeping around, even though they had specifically asked the police not to involve her husband. He had told the young man that photographing other people was a criminal offence and insisted he delete the video from his phone. After the telephone conversation and obeying the police officer's order, the young people were very upset and didn't know what to do. Eventually the young man had caught the train to Copenhagen to speak to Simonsen in person.

Still somewhat suspicious of the story, Klavs Arnold asked: 'How do you know that the defendant in the canal boat trial is Irene Gallagher?'

The boy sounded incredulous.

'The whole of Denmark knows that. It's all over the Internet. People talk of little else.'

Klavs Arnold took him to his office. On the way he popped his head round the door to his boss's office, pushing the young man in front of him like a suitcase.

'Have you spoken to two young people, a young man and a young woman, who told you about seeing Irene Gallagher in a forest?'

Simonsen looked up at them with a frown.

'No, I haven't, have you?'

Klavs Arnold asked the young man: 'Is that the man you spoke to?'

He shook his head. No, it wasn't, the voice was completely different. Then he was dragged further along the corridor, put on a chair in Klavs Arnold's office and told to wait. Shortly afterwards Klavs Arnold returned with Malte Borup.

'Give Malte your mobile.'

The young man did as he was told.

'Have you recorded any other videos since deleting the one from the forest?'

The young man had not. Klavs Arnold sounded tense.

'Recover that video, Malte, then come back and show it to me. On your way get hold of Arne and tell him to come here now, no matter what he's doing. And get a move on!'

It took less than five minutes before Malte Borup returned with Arne Pedersen. Everyone watched the video. There was no doubt that it showed Irene Gallagher. Klavs Arnold produced four hundred kroner from his wallet and said to the young man: 'We'll have to keep your mobile and I'm afraid that you have to leave now because a situation has arisen that is … very important to us. We'll lend you another phone and I'll call you on it tonight. Tell your girlfriend that we need to speak to both of you as soon as possible, but that we won't involve anyone but you and her. And please accept my sincere apologies. What happened was a very regrettable error. The money is for your train fare and some food on your way home. Malte, please escort the young man out and come back here as quickly as you can.'

Klavs Arnold updated Arne Pedersen, who realised the seriousness of the situation immediately.

'I've known the officer who is on gatekeeper duty today for more than eight years, and I am absolutely sure that he wouldn't deliberately transfer the call to the wrong person. So we can disregard that possibility. The gatekeepers listen to all incoming calls and then follow up any they deem relevant.'

As soon as Malte Borup came back, the two officers practically fell on him.

'How do you manipulate a switchboard?'

The student intern thought about it for a few seconds.

'In terms of technology a switchboard consists of two parts. An IVR, that's the server that undertakes the transfers, and then a front-end application, which the people who operate the switchboard work using a computer or a Smartphone. The employee controls the application, the application controls the IVR, and the IVR controls the calls. So if you want to tamper with it, you can hack it and change the application or the IVR. The former is easier, all it takes is a reasonably competent programmer, the latter much harder, you need to be a real pro. However, if you can do that, it's nearly impossible to discover the physical location of the phone to which the call has been maliciously transferred.'

'So you need experts to pull off something like that?' Klavs Arnold asked.

'Definitely, but if we're at war with FE, then don't forget that they have some of Denmark's best hackers at the Centre for Cyber Security.'

Arne Pedersen went down to instruct the gatekeeper, Malte Borup fetched two headsets, found a spare mobile phone and Klavs Arnold started rehearsing. Fifteen minutes later they were good to go. Arne Pedersen locked the door to his office before Klavs Arnold made the call. It was answered by the switchboard, then taken over by a gatekeeper. Arnold told the gatekeeper his story, after which the officer transferred him to Konrad Simonsen. The three men waited in suspense before a voice, definitely not that of their boss, introduced itself gruffly as *Simonsen*. Klavs Arnold asked: 'Are you the Homicide Chief?'

'Speaking. Who is this?'

'My name is Kaj and I live in Bønsvig, and this is the fifth time I've called the cops … the police, I mean … and sod all happens.'

'Please state your name, address and telephone number.'

'You can get that from the two morons I had to speak to before being put through to you. This is the last time I bother calling. After all, I'm doing you a favour.'

'What favour? And I must have your personal details.'

'The favour is telling you where that Gallagher bitch parked her husband's car when she eliminated that bastard who killed all those children. There are still tyre tracks, I've just been down to check again, but it's a miracle they haven't been rained off while you sit at Police Headquarters counting your paperclips.'

A lengthy pause ensued, then the voice said: 'Where are the tyre tracks?'

'If you drive down Bønsvigvej towards the sea and then shortly after ... put out two orange cones ... arrghh, shit ... bloody battery! Listen ... charging cable ... in an hour.'

When the conversation had ended, Arne Pedersen was impressed.

'That was brilliant! Where on earth did you learn to do that?'

The piece of paper that Klavs Arnold had been crunching in front of his mobile during the last sentence landed elegantly in the wastepaper basket. He got up and put on his jacket.

'It's a long story. I had a bet with some friends, but let's save that for another time. Better get going so we'll have a head start. We can call Sydsjællands Police on the way. Malte, in one hour you need to have fixed that IVR so it works properly, then make sure it's monitored from now on – or whatever you call it in cyberspace.'

'How about we brief Simon first?' Arne Pedersen suggested.

Klavs Arnold shot down his suggestion.

'He's in a meeting with the Director of Public Prosecutions. We'll call him from the car once he gets back to his office. Let's break for the border.'

CHAPTER 41

THURSDAY 7 OCTOBER 2010, STORE HESTEHAVE FOREST

'You do know we're being watched, don't you?'

Klavs Arnold said it casually and couldn't help laughing when he saw how Arne Pedersen froze and started looking suspiciously around the forest. He couldn't see anyone. The Jutlander pointed to a maple tree in front of them where someone had placed a small, carved wooden troll in a hollow left by a fallen branch. Arne Pedersen breathed a sigh of relief and told him: 'You're an idiot.' Klavs Arnold laughed again.

The two officers were sitting on the trunk of a toppled beech tree. They were well concealed, but had a good view of a forest track twenty metres in front of them. The track was narrow, only just wide enough for two cars to pass each other. On their arrival they had found a suitable place in which to leave fine tyre tracks in the soft soil extending from their car into the forest. They marked the location with two orange cones, which they had borrowed from the local police, before driving a further five hundred metres to park their car. Then they had walked back and found the hiding place where they were now sitting.

'You don't like the outdoors very much, do you, Arne?'

He denied it vehemently, while thinking that his colleague was right. Arne was always bored to tears whenever he was too far away from … well, anything. Once you had seen one beautiful autumnal tree, it was hard to swoon at the sight of the next one. He changed the subject, but the Jutlander cut him off.

'I think we're on.'

Klavs Arnold turned his head and listened. Soon afterwards, Arne Pedersen could hear it too. A little later they could see it: a silver Mercedes-Benz with two men in the front. The car stopped, and one man got out and knocked away the cones. Then the other drove the Mercedes-Benz over the tyre tracks Arne Pedersen and Klavs Arnold had made earlier, after which the pedestrian used a stick to scratch out both new and old tracks. FE didn't do things by halves.

Klavs Arnold stepped out onto the path and laid on his Jutland dialect thick. 'Hello to you,' he greeted them as he strode towards the car. Meanwhile Arne Pedersen picked up his mobile.

Both FE officers reacted swiftly, without panicking. The driver reached across the passenger seat and opened the car door for his partner, who quickly got into his seat. The driver hastily reversed for about fifty metres before turning the car around expertly, until he was forced to stop. Two police cars were approaching and they stopped along-side one another, blocking the track. Then the same thing happened behind the Mercedes-Benz, and a small army of uniformed police officers got out. As did the man who had covered the tyre tracks, only now without his stick. Arne Pedersen walked up to him.

'I think they brought the dogs as well, in case you fancy a run through the forest.'

The FE officer glared at them both and snarled: 'What the hell do you think you're doing?'

'Vehicle inspection check, no drivers in this area are exempt.'

As Arne spoke, he raised his palms to stop the police officers approaching them from both sides. They were as close as they needed to be. He continued: 'I want to see a driver's licence from both of you and we'll also take some nice pictures of you and your car. The only question is: are we doing this the easy way or would you rather come along with me to Præstø police station? It's your choice. Though I think I should warn you: they're terribly busy today, and it wouldn't surprise me if they don't release you until tomorrow morning. So why don't you be good little spooks and do as you are told?'

CHAPTER 42

FRIDAY 8 OCTOBER 2010, HELSINGØR POLICE STATION

It wasn't the first time the Countess had summoned a witness to a police station using the pretence that he or she had witnessed a non-existent traffic accident in order that the witness's spouse or lover never learned the true reason for the visit.

People kept secrets from one another, it was the way of the world, and it wasn't the job of the police to interfere in people's white lies, if they could avoid it. However, the reverse also happened: such information could be used by the police to pressure a witness into saying more than they wanted to. Those were the rules of the game, though the threat was rarely carried out.

The Countess had borrowed an office at Helsingør police station where she was now sitting with two young people: the boy from Slagelse who had come to Police Headquarters yesterday, and the Roma girl.

The Countess opened the interview by reassuring the girl that there was currently no risk that she would be exposed, or whatever she would call it. The young man, however, was on his guard immediately. He was much brighter than the girl, the Countess thought.

'What do you mean by *currently?*'

The Countess had no choice but to explain, though she would have preferred not to. There was no reason to frighten the young people with a scenario that was unlikely ever to happen.

She looked at the girl and explained in a professorial tone: 'If you, collectively or individually, are called as a witness to give evidence in the forthcoming trial, you have a duty to tell the truth, as do I. But the defence, the prosecution or the judge won't care what you would like your husband to know or not to know. That's how it is, and you have to accept that.'

The young woman, who had had the last twenty-four hours to review the situation, said in a sad but steady voice: 'It's not that my husband beats me up or forbids me to leave the house, like you read about in the papers. He wouldn't do that, he's not like that. He's a decent man, hard-working, and I'm very fond of him, but I should never have married him.'

She wiped away a single tear with her knuckle and continued to address the Countess. Perhaps because it was important to her that the other woman understood.

'I can get a divorce or I can simply leave him. No one will punish me – physically, I mean – but I would lose my family if I did and I couldn't bear that. But that's enough about me. Let's get this over with so I can go home.'

The interview took less than ten minutes. The young man repeated the explanation he had already given to Klavs Arnold, and the girl backed him up in every respect, without being able to add any further details. The incident the two young people described was quite straightforward: on 14 September at 15.22, they had seen Irene Gallagher on a path in Lorup Forest, carrying two grey boards and a toolbox. The boy had filmed her for about ten seconds from behind after she had passed them. That was all there was to it. Yet the Countess kept going, it was her job, although in this situation it seemed as though she was trying to get blood out of a stone.

'Do you have any idea what Irene Gallagher was doing with the toolbox? A guess, an assumption, a hunch, anything, no matter how crazy it might sound.'

They shook their heads, and did so again when asked about the two grey boards.

The Countess racked her brains to come up with a brilliant question, especially about the boards, but in vain. The Homicide Department had already discussed the purpose of the boards at length, and they couldn't come up with a sensible suggestion – or a far-fetched one for that matter. No one had the faintest idea.

They all agreed that Irene Gallagher was on her way to visit Ole Nysted who lived nearby, but they had found no trace of the two grey boards inside or outside the hut. The Countess herself had visited Slagelse that morning to check, and her conclusion was unequivocal: no boards. At the same time, Konrad Simonsen had ordered a second search of Irene Gallagher's home, but that too revealed nothing. When the Countess later returned to Police Headquarters, she and the others had discussed the case, and at one point had seriously contemplated ordering a search of the whole of Lorup Forest, but it was huge undertaking, and ultimately seemed over the top for the sake of two grey boards.

The Countess made one last attempt. Based on the young man's video, she had requested a close up of Irene Gallagher's left arm and the two boards she was carrying. The forensic technician had worked on the prints, so they were in better focus than on the video, and he had been very proud of his work. Even so she had forgotten about them until now. She made her voice as optimistic as she could when she addressed the young couple.

'Take a look at this. It's an enlarged close up from your video where you can see the boards more clearly. Irene Gallagher did bring those boards with her, so there's no doubt that they're important.'

She turned the print over and slid it across to the young people without reflecting on her own nonsensical logic.

'Take a good look at it. I'm sure it will help you to remember … something.'

The two young people both stared dutifully and tried their best to extract a secret from the picture, which it didn't possess. Eventually the boy said: 'It was just a couple of boards. How are we supposed to know what use she was going to make of them?'

The Countess had no answer to that.

CHAPTER 43

MONDAY 11 OCTOBER 2010, POLICE HEADQUARTERS

Over the years Konrad Simonsen had grown to respect his immediate superior personally as well as professionally. She was loyal to her staff and she didn't interfere unduly in his work. In addition she had a refreshingly unique style, which more than made up for her, at times, rather trying naïveté.

The Chief of the Homicide Department had been summoned to a morning meeting. The Deputy Commissioner wanted a summary of the investigation into the canal boat killings, and Konrad Simonsen had also brought along his deputy. Arne Pedersen got on well with the Deputy Commissioner; in fact, they were on first-name terms, Arne and Gurli, a throwback to the time Simonsen had been on sick leave following heart surgery. Arne Pedersen and the Deputy Commissioner shared a familiarity she had with no one else at work, not even her two secretaries.

In the reception area, the Deputy Commissioner welcomed Konrad Simonsen and Arne Pedersen almost heartily. Then she showed them into her office where a table had been laid with her home-baked bread; she had got up early to make it for them especially. It was touching and so very like her. During breakfast they had, as if by tacit agreement, not talked shop, but the two men had exchanged glances. There was something different about their boss today, that much was clear, though neither of them knew much about fashion.

This morning the Deputy Commissioner was dressed exactly as one would expect a woman in her position and of her age to be, which was a total turnaround for her. She would normally light up the department with her eye-watering colour combinations and penchant for embarrassingly juvenile outfits, which set people gossiping in every corridor at Police Headquarters. Sadly the Press Office had recently held internal courses in management and media skills, and there she had been moulded into normality, made boring and safe, which was how PR consultants thought senior management ought to come across. It was a crying shame.

After breakfast the Deputy Commissioner came straight to the point.

'I hear that the Homicide Department is engaged in open warfare with FE. Please would you tell me what has been going on?'

Arne Pedersen thought that was nothing compared to what was coming next. Fifteen minutes before the meeting he had been briefed by his boss about the plan that Helmer Hammer had recommended to Simonsen at Thorvaldsens Museum, but which so far he had been reluctant to initiate. Despite FE's tampering with the Homicide Department's switchboard and their willingness to wreck what they believed to be important evidence in a homicide case, Simonsen had wanted to think things through over the weekend before escalating the feud.

However, even the Countess found the FE's behaviour intolerable, and Simonsen realised that he no longer had a choice unless he was prepared to let his department be bullied by an organisation which, to all intents and purposes, was beyond democratic control, and which would appear to have developed its own set of ethics that were in direct contrast to how a society governed by the rule of law ought to work.

He began: 'I've drafted a request to the Justice Minister, which I'll give to you shortly and ask you to pass on to the National Police Commissioner, possibly with a few of your own comments attached. But first I need to inform you about a couple of incidents that happened on Thursday and some organised rumour-spreading that has been going on for a couple of weeks. I should possibly have spoken to you sooner, but I've been dealing with three investigations, so it has had to wait until now.'

The Deputy Commissioner listened without interruption as Konrad Simonsen and Arne Pedersen explained. When they were done, she said sadly:

'If you had told me those stories five years ago, I would have accused you of making them up. But after the string of Defence scandals in recent years, I'm not surprised, not at all. Let me see your request, Simon.'

Simonsen had taken great care over drafting it, ably aided by Kirsten Hansen. The first two pages of his letter to the Justice Minister argued convincingly that the investigation into the canal boat killings should be informed of Irene Gallagher's activities in Bosnia in 1995, which the Homicide Department presumed the FE was aware of but refused to release. Furthermore the Homicide Department would like a list of all the defence staff who had either worked with Irene Gallagher back then or, through their positions, might have known what she had been doing. However, the Army wouldn't even compile, let alone issue them with, such a list. The police were therefore asking the Justice Minister to use his influence and order the Army to comply with these two requests.

The Deputy Commissioner read the request twice, then asked Simonsen: 'Did anyone help you with this?'

'Don't I normally express myself well?'

'Yes, but not to this high standard. Who wrote it?'

'Kirsten Hansen, the new Public Prosecutor. She wrote most of it.'

'Hmm, I had a suspicion. However, if you think the National Police Commissioner will forward this to the Justice Minister, you're out of your mind. It'll never happen, not in a month of Sundays. Besides, he and his wife are on a fortnight's holiday in a mountain cabin in Courmayeur in the Italian Alps. It's said to be a very beautiful place, but sadly there's no mobile coverage. And I guarantee you that his deputy will sit on your request until the Alpine traveller returns. That is assuming I even send it, which frankly I struggle to see why I would. Arne, what do you think? Why would we start a war we can't ... unless ... Oh, damn you, Simon.'

The penny dropped. She gulped and then concluded: 'You're going to leak it to the press.'

Arne Pedersen gazed out of the window. *Shit happens, Gurli.* Simonsen didn't comment on her allegation, but instead said: 'Tomorrow I'll summon the Chief of Defence, the Deputy Chief of Defence and the Head of FE here for interviews. We'll talk to them until we learn the identities of the more junior staff who worked with Irene Gallagher.'

The Deputy Commissioner asked, not unreasonably: 'What are you really trying to achieve here? Apart from irritating the hell out of the Army. I can perfectly well understand why you would want to do that, but in terms of your investigation, what do you hope to gain?'

It was Arne Pedersen who explained.

'We don't yet have a motive for Irene Gallagher's actions, which may well prove damaging once her trial begins. But we're convinced that the motive is connected to her time in Bosnia, and our only hope of discovering it is to persuade someone in the Army to talk, just give us a few hints perhaps, a crack we can chip away at. Right now we're stuck. Our hope is that if we interview the lot of them, whoever they are, there might be just one person willing to help us. Anonymously, if that's what it takes.'

Simonsen backed him up.

'It's a slim hope, we admit that, but it's all we've got. Unless you can come up with something better.'

The Deputy Commissioner couldn't. She remarked dryly: 'The Justice Minister is going to tear strips off us.'

Simonsen replied: 'And the media will tear strips off the Justice Minister.'

A pause ensued. The two men waited while the Deputy Commissioner stared into the air. Then she reread the request one final time, shook her head in despair and said to her Homicide Chief: 'Tell the Countess I'll be eating dinner in your house three times a week once I lose my job and can no longer afford to feed myself.'

CHAPTER 44

TUESDAY 12 OCTOBER 2010, POLICE HEADQUARTERS

Anica Buch began with a summary.

'On the thirteenth of July 1995, Captain Bjørn Lauritzen and nine other Danish soldiers are in Bosnia manning an observation post just outside the village of Ljubicevac. Through his binoculars, Bjørn Lauritzen sees that a handful of Serbian militia soldiers are keeping some Bosnian Muslim women captive in a house in the valley below. He and Ole Nysted drive down there in a tank. When they arrive, Lauritzen herds the soldiers out of the farmhouse. He forces them to sit down, ties their hands behind their backs and their legs to the man sitting next to them so they are on the ground in a row. He smears gravel into their eyes. Then he drives the tank along a brook into the forest, where the genocide later known as the Srebrenica massacre is in full flow. Serbian soldiers are murdering Muslim men and boys. A few hours later Bjørn Lauritzen returns to the observation post, together with a few refugees he has managed to save.

'Meanwhile, a liaison officer – or possibly a judge advocate – named Irene Gallagher arrives at the observation post from Tuzla and drives on immediately after Bjørn Lauritzen to the farmhouse but doesn't find him, at which point she returns to the observation post.

'At the farm Lauritzen had met a young girl who speaks Danish and Serbian. She has been raped, as have the other women. My task was to establish the identity of that girl.'

Anica Buch was nervous, but her introduction was going well. Last Friday she had submitted her report and informed Simonsen that she now knew the identity of the girl from the farm, sadly now dead. But the young police officer had still been asked to present her research in Simonsen's annexe. He, the Countess, Arne Pedersen and Klavs Arnold were her audience. Malte Borup managed her slides on the flat-screen.

Anica Buch took a sip of water and then pointed to a map indicating the location of the observation post and the farm.

'Today, fifteen years after these events, this place is in Bosnia-Herzegovina. The observation post is long gone, of course, and the house or the farm or whatever you want to call it, is gone too. Perhaps it was destroyed by the Serbian Army, who used heavy artillery and shells to terrorise the refugees, but it's more likely that the Serbian militia Bjørn Lauritzen tied up, burned it down once they were freed or managed to free themselves. Many houses in the region were destroyed when the Serbians torched them.'

She nodded to Malte Borup, who changed the slide to a photograph of a girl. She had black hair and brown eyes, wore braces on her teeth and had dimpled cheeks. A typical school photograph: dull but professional.

'That's Jelena Khrobic, and it's the only picture I've been able to find of her. Here she's in Year Five, and she's ten years old. The picture is from 1993. Her family lived in Randers and had permanent leave to stay in Denmark. Her father worked in a warehouse, her mother was a cleaner, and Jelena's older brother was at Sixth-form College. In the summer of 1995 the family travelled to Bosnia to visit the children's maternal grandparents, who lived in the town of Bratunac ten kilometres north of Srebrenica. None of them survived the trip.'

She went on to tell them how the family had been caught up in the war when the Serbian Army invaded the Dutch safe zone. Jelena's father and brother were shot in the forests around the town. The girl and her mother were taken prisoner by Serbian militia soldiers, along with some other women. In the house near the village of Ljubicevac, close to the Danish observation post, they were raped until Bjørn Lauritzen arrived with his tank and freed them. Afterwards they fled, as did so many other people, on foot to Tuzla, where the UN was operating another safe zone.

Along the way more refugees joined them and eventually their number had reached fifty, including several boys too young for the Serbs to bother killing. But that evening, south of the town of Cerska, it went wrong. Two trucks carrying Serbian soldiers had overtaken the column of refugees and, out of sheer malice, some of the soldiers machine-gunned the refugees. Twenty-two people were killed, including Jelena Khrobic's mother. Jelena herself was badly injured, and some other women attempted to carry her to safety, but she bled to death from her injuries within an hour.

Anica Buch continued: 'The tragedy has been described by eyewitnesses in the newspaper *Dnevni Avaz* – that translates as *Voice of Today* – in its edition of Sunday the twenty-first of May 2000. I'm attaching a copy in my report, together with the translation. It says the following about Jelena Khrobic: "Of the seven who were injured, four later died. These included a young girl who lived in Denmark but who had come on holiday to visit her family."'

Anica Buch had finished her briefing. Malte Borup turned off the screen. Simonsen said: 'No, we're not letting you go yet. We also want to hear how you discovered the things you've just told us. Including the dead ends you came across along the way. But do sit down. I'll stand up and stretch my legs for a moment.'

Anica Buch protested after which she sat down, since a chair had become available. She explained that she had got nowhere with the National Register of Persons or other official databases. So she had called and emailed the many clubs for former Yugoslavs in and around Denmark, but that hadn't paid off either.

Then she had read various reports on the Internet: from the International Criminal Tribunal in The Hague, the Dutch government's investigation into what happened in Srebrenica in 1995, official papers from DUTCHBAT, the Dutch UN force and also other reports, but still she got nowhere.

Eventually she had resorted to using Facebook to ask for help from anyone with even the faintest connection to the former Yugoslavia. She hadn't asked people if they knew the girl, but just if they had any idea how to trace her. And one person did. He suggested that if the girl was in Bosnia with her family, and the family was desperate to return to Denmark, they might well have contacted the Danish Embassy in Beograd.

'I wish I could boast of having thought of it myself, but I didn't. At that point there was no longer an embassy in Belgrade. That responsibility had been transferred to our embassy in Vienna. The Ambassador has now retired and lives in Hellerup, so I went to see him. It turned out that he did remember a family wanting the embassy's help to get out of Bosnia in the summer of 1995. But as no one in the family had Danish citizenship, and because the embassy was rushed off its feet with other consular matters in Bosnia, with extremely limited abilities to help, I'm afraid it looks like their plea ended up at the bottom of the pile.

'The embassy never registered the request in any way, and he couldn't remember the name of the family, but he did remember where they lived in Denmark because it was where he had been born, in Randers. So I called all the local schools, and asked if anyone remembered a Bosnian student going missing at the start of the 1995 August school year. One of them did, and so I got the girl's name, and then learned the whole family had died. I called Randers Council because they must have dealt with the estate at some point, so would probably have checked whether the family had relatives in Bosnia. This was how I found Jelena Khrobic's maternal grandmother, and she told me the story and also sent me the newspaper article.'

Anica stopped talking. Simonsen praised her as he made eye contact with the others. Anica Buch asked hesitantly: 'So where do I go tomorrow morning?'

The Countess replied: 'You turn up for work here.'

CHAPTER 45

Christoffer Brinch was warming to his client.

Irene Gallagher was a woman who improved on closer acquaintance. In the beginning she had seemed controlling, and at times arrogant as well as calculating. But first impressions can be deceptive. As he got to know her better, he realised that her haughty manner was a cover for her insecurity, and that she was vulnerable in many ways. Besides he was genuinely starting to wonder whether the evidence against her had in fact been fabricated by the police, as she claimed. What had at first seemed unthinkable to him was now an option he was seriously considering, no matter how far-fetched it might sound.

It was the fourth time he'd visited her in prison. On the last three occasions he had brought her books, dense tomes all in English, biographies or historical works about warfare from the 1943 Battle of Kursk to Hannibal's defeat of the Romans at Cannae a few hundred years before the birth of Christ. Her appetite for reading material was voracious, and he had calculated from the speed with which her books needed replacing that she must read in excess of five hundred pages per day unless she skimmed through them, which seemed unlikely as she would often tell him about something she had read since his last visit, and when he asked for more details, she would reply promptly. It was her way of making small talk.

When the prison officer let Christoffer Brinch into the cell, Irene Gallagher was, as usual, lying on her bed absorbed in a book. She looked up, smiled, happy to see him.

'Is it all right if I just finish this paragraph or are you in a hurry?'
'No, do continue.'

He put the new books on the small table in her cell: a biography of Robespierre, a military history review of the Battle of Gettysburg and finally a novel in two volumes about the Wars of the Roses. When she had finished her paragraph, she thanked him for her new books, then gestured to the eight-hundred-page book on Stalin she had just put down.

'In the late 1920s Stalin, his young wife and a handful of the most powerful Politburo members and their families lived next door to each other in the Kremlin. The kids would run in and out of offices and apartments and were looked after by whoever had the time and the inclination. It was a village, a collective, brimming with enthusiasm and idealism, but it was also a time of austerity, and the country's top leaders, including Stalin himself, made no more money – didn't want to be paid any more money, I mean – than an ordinary Russian worker, even though each of these men influenced literally millions of people's lives or, more often, deaths. So at the end of the month money was tight and as food was expensive, they would borrow from each other. Five roubles here, ten roubles there, so each family could have a pot of soup for supper. We're talking about politicians who every day crushed thousands of Russians, had them beaten to a pulp before executing them in the name of revolution. Isn't that amazing?'

Christoffer Brinch didn't know what to say. Amazing wouldn't have been how he would have put it. She sensed his dissent and declared: 'The vast majority of Danes have a totally dysfunctional attitude to life and death. They take life far too seriously.'

'What do you mean?'

'I don't know … Perhaps I've grown too cynical. It's a work-related disorder, just ignore it.'

'No, do tell. I want to know.'

So she told him.

'When I was young I saw two Chinese men who were about to be executed. They had been caught smuggling drugs, and in the country they happened to be in, the punishment for that was being shot on the spot, something the two smugglers knew perfectly well. But though they had a maximum of one minute left to live, they were arguing. Their row was about food, or more precisely how to best cook hóngtáng … It's a bit tricky to translate, but it's a kind of Chinese borscht from Heilongjiang Province in the north. Each man insisted his recipe was the true one: the dish must be made from red cabbage ... not at all, it must be made from beetroot ... you must add bay leaves ... no, *never* put in bay leaves, they ruin the taste, and so on. Even when the police colonel walked behind them and released the safety catch on his pistol.

'The first man was killed with a shot to the back of his head, but his friend carried on talking, even though he was now addressing a corpse, and he didn't stop until he himself was shot ... We live, we die, it doesn't matter. "Life is precious." What rubbish! Life is cheap: bang and you're dead. And what's the big deal?'

During her monologue Irene Gallagher's face had come alive. Now it relapsed into her usual inscrutable expression. Christoffer Brinch said: 'Very few people have seen what you have.'

'Yes, I forget that sometimes. And while we're on the subject of being forgetful, I want to apologise for calling you an idiot when we first met. You're not an idiot, but that's so like me – I often push people away.'

Christoffer Brinch smiled.

'You only said that I *looked* like an idiot, but I forgive you.'

She changed the subject.

'Have you received the report we discussed last time, and have you had time to read it?'

'I've read it. But I hope you're not asking me to sling mud at some random police officer. It won't help us and the judge won't allow it anyway.'

'We're not talking about some random police officer here. I'm asking you to learn the central passages by heart. There's no more convincing weapon than a lawyer who can reel off multiple facts without needing to consult any documents. But you should use it only if you think it's relevant.'

'That seems fair. I'm happy to agree to that, but there needs to be a rational starting point or your report is useless.'

'I believe you'll get your rational starting point during the trial.'

Christoffer Brinch had his doubts, but didn't voice them. Instead he asked: 'Where did you learn to gather that kind of information on people, and how could you even know that it might prove relevant one day? I mean, you must have worked on that report long before you were arrested.'

'I can't tell you that, it would be illegal. All you can know is that I've friends in various places, but don't ask me where because I would hate to have to lie to you. However, I can tell you that I learned to gather information many years ago in a wonderful place called Fairfax County. You probably haven't heard of it.'

Christoffer Brinch took off his glasses and popped them into his jacket pocket. Without them she grew blurry to him, which was his intention. He folded his arms across his chest.

'Please don't get me wrong, I want to defend you, but I've been wondering whether you might not be better off with a lawyer with security clearance, with whom you could talk more easily. For your own sake, it's something I'd like you to consider.'

Irene Gallagher reached out and touched his arm.

'You don't want to help me? You're the only one on my side in so many ways.' She sounded nervous.

He swiftly backtracked.

'That's definitely not what I was saying. Of course I'll help you.'

She pulled back her hand and breathed a sigh of relief.

'I'm so glad to hear that, Christoffer.'

CHAPTER 46

THURSDAY 14 OCTOBER 2010, SØLLERØD

'I think we've got ourselves a couple of stalkers, Simon.'

The Countess attempted to deliver this with a light touch as if her discovery was vaguely amusing, but failed. She was standing in the living room, watching the road from the window. It was morning, but not yet light. Simonsen was having breakfast in the kitchen, so she raised her voice. 'Hello, are you there?' He was, and yes, he had seen the car in the road too.

The Countess joined him in the kitchen.

'How long has it been there, and why didn't you tell me?'

Simonsen put down his spoon. He was eating oatmeal porridge with fresh grapes and cinnamon, his favourite meal of the day.

'They've been there all night and it's pure provocation, so let's ignore them.'

'You're not going to do anything stupid, are you?'

'No, that's what I'm trying to tell you – we'll simply pretend they're not there. They're bound to get bored eventually.'

The Countess agreed, they probably would. Nevertheless, the presence of the car worried her.

'Those letters of yours have really rattled their cage, and I'm not sure it was a smart move. You may not care, but I don't like it, it's … intimidating.'

Yesterday Konrad Simonsen had summoned in writing three senior FE chiefs for interviews at Police Headquarters, making it clear that if they didn't turn up voluntarily, they would be arrested. The summons also served as a reminder that it was still the Police Force that decided whom it wanted to interview, and that only a very few people in the country were excluded from such a summons, a group that didn't include military personnel.

He didn't think he would get anything from the interviews, assuming the FE chiefs either couldn't or wouldn't want to help him, but he considered the humiliation of being subjected to such a procedure suitable payback for FE's behaviour in Store Hestehave Forest. Simonsen still felt that he owed them a response, on top of his request for information to the Justice Minister.

The Countess had sat down opposite her husband with her newspaper and her tea.

'You haven't seen my Dictaphone, by any chance? I can't find it anywhere.'

The Countess grunted an uninterested *no*. It wasn't the first time it had gone missing and it always turned up in the end.

'How odd. I swear I've looked for it everywhere, but—'

He broke off. He had remembered something that had slipped his mind this morning, although he had spent most of last night thinking about it.

'Has *Dagbladet* arrived yet? Didn't you say that it would be delivered by taxi overnight?'

He wanted to find out if *Dagbladet* had decided to publish his leaked request to the Justice Minister, and if so, how many column inches they were giving the story. He had gone to bed relatively early – he had needed to – but the Countess had stayed up late and should have been sent a copy of the newspaper.

'What do you think this is?'

It was only then that he noticed she wasn't reading her normal morning paper.

'Tell me or show me. Did they go for it?'

Dagbladet had indeed gone for it. The story featured on three pages inside the newspaper, and they had included a big picture of him. The paper was siding with the police. The two journalists who had written the article clearly did not understand why the need for military secrecy should hinder a criminal investigation into the murder of sixteen children in cold blood.

The Countess turned the pages.

'The leader also mentions the investigation, and it doesn't spare anyone's blushes. Look, Simon, at the last paragraphs.'

It's a simple question: do you want to live in a country where military organisations are free to protect killers, sabotage police investigation whenever they feel like it and wipe their arses with the Constitution? And meanwhile you're paying for it all?

If so, today is your lucky day, because that's precisely the country you live in.

If not, let the politicians know and shout it out loud because the walls of the Ministry of Justice are thick and the Justice Minister listens only to his own cronies.

Dagbladet's *view is clear. We say NO!*

What about you?

Konrad Simonsen was delighted. With its combative attitude the newspaper had added to the mounting pressure on the Justice Minister to support the Homicide Department. The Countess was more subdued.

'Don't be seduced by your own wishful thinking, Simon. *Dagbladet* has no core values. Or rather: it adopts whatever views will boost its circulation.'

The Countess got ready to go to work. Simonsen walked her to her car and waited by the gate until she had left. She hadn't asked him to, but he felt that she would appreciate it.

The man in the car across the road stayed put, which was what Simonsen had expected. He resisted the temptation to make an obscene gesture and went back inside, where he forced himself to review the Homicide Department's accounts, which – strongly encouraged by the Deputy Commissioner – he had decided to plough through. It was a task he traditionally loathed and it was best undertaken at home where he wouldn't get distracted; or rather, allow himself to get distracted in order to get away from those damned numbers.

Around lunchtime the surveillance car drove off, but it returned within the hour, with fresh passengers, both men bearded, Konrad Simonsen noticed. He wrote the time down, without quite knowing why. A little later Arne Pedersen rang with good news about Irene Gallagher. He and a handful of officers had discovered that on the day of the killings, she had visited a café on Elvindsvej opposite the Messiah Church in Charlottenlund.

She had arrived at ten o'clock in the morning, and stayed for about forty-five minutes, drinking coffee and reading a dense book about Bismarck – the battleship, not the statesman.

At one o'clock a news channel had managed to get an interview with the Justice Minister. The leaked request from the Homicide Department and *Dagbladet's* coverage of it had made the headlines across the media that morning, and pretty much everyone – opposition politicians at the more frivolous end of the political spectrum, pundits, a former intelligence chief and political commentators – agreed that the Justice Minister had no option other than to cede to the police, but Konrad Simonsen himself was starting to doubt it would happen. The Prime Minister had been cornered by a couple of journalists at Christiansborg Parliament, who demanded to know his view on *Dagbladet*'s story. He had refused to comment, which was to be expected, but had then added there was always a reason why certain information was classified. If one assumed that the Prime Minister's seemingly throwaway remark was in fact carefully planned, then it didn't bode well for the Justice Minister's willingness to co-operate with the Homicide Department.

And Simonsen's scepticism proved to be quite right. When the Justice Minister arrived at the studio for the one o'clock news, he absolutely refused to intervene in the Army's and FE's reluctance to pass on information about Irene Gallagher to the police. *There's always a reason why certain information is classified*, was the mantra he eagerly repeated. However, his refusal was couched in general terms. He didn't want to discuss leaked information until he officially received the request from senior police management. While it was only published as a leaked report in *Dagbladet*, it wasn't an official matter for him to deal with. Here, however, the Minister made a mistake because he went on to criticise, in fairly strong terms, senior police management for its careless handling of its papers when it came to the press. Overall, though, he made a good impression, Konrad Simonsen thought, and acknowledged that his gamble had backfired. He had only succeeded in stirring up a hornet's nest.

Feeling annoyed, he turned off the television and returned to his accounts. Shortly afterwards the email he had been expecting arrived: the Deputy National Police Commissioner had hit the roof when his boss, the Justice Minister, had insinuated that his office had leaked the request to *Dagbladet*. As a result he had submitted the request himself rather than wait until the National Police Commissioner returned from his Alpine holiday. Sadly it was unlikely to make any real difference now – the request would be denied. Anyone with half a brain could see that.

CHAPTER 47

Konrad Simonsen had visited Kastellet before, a few times as part of his work, but also when Anna Mia's mother and he were young and in love.

Back then they had lived nearby and their Sunday afternoon walks would often take them to the star fortress where they would enjoy the architecture and stroll down the paths on the green embankments that surrounded the five bastions. The fortification had been begun in the seventeenth century by King Christian IV and was fiercely defended against the British during the Bombardment of Copenhagen in 1807. Its jail had housed several prominent prisoners over the years, including Johann Struensee, the idealist ahead of his time who had paid with his life when he tried to promote his liberal ideas to the Danish people and grew a little too close to the Danish queen.

Konrad Simonsen parked in the car park of the Danish Resistance Museum and walked the short stretch to Kirkepladsen, a square bounded by the fortress to the north and south, to the east by Kastelkirken Church, and to the west by the Commander's House. The Defence Chief – Denmark's ultimate military leader – had until recently had his private residence and offices in the Commander's House, but since his retirement a couple of years ago the building had stood empty.

Kirkepladsen was normally a peaceful spot. Although Kastellet was Army property and was guarded by a handful of soldiers from the Royal Guards, the place looked ordered and welcoming, more like a park than a fortification. But today was an exception, Konrad Simonsen thought, as he took a look around. Order was the last word to describe the current situation. Chaos would be more appropriate.

A large number of journalists had gathered in front of the Commander's House and teams of reporters were busy with television crews. Three fire engines were parked in the middle of the square; in between them he saw the remains of a bonfire, which was not terribly disturbing in itself, but the surrounding buildings were in a conservation area, and the Fire Brigade wasn't taking any chances. Several office workers and a few military people in uniform were standing outside, most of them looking angry. More importantly, most of the windows in the Commander's House were open, and in each of them he could see two or three men, many of them young, watching the square. They were calm, unperturbed by the commotion, as if signalling to the people in the square that they had experienced being shot at, they had driven patrols without knowing when or where the next roadside bomb would explode, they had been under rocket fire: in short, that they had been to war, so no matter how anyone tried to clear the house, it didn't frighten them. If anyone fancied a fight, they were ready for one, and if not, well, that was OK too – it was all the same to them.

'Do you know how they got in?'

Konrad Simonsen turned around. An old police officer, whom he knew, was standing behind him. Simonsen shook his head. No, he didn't. The police officer explained.

'They helped each other reach the windows, broke a few panes of glass so they could open them, and then they all climbed in. Meanwhile, a dozen guardsmen were standing ten metres from them, threatening to shoot. Their rifles are loaded, and no one would have blamed them for shooting the trespassers, those are their orders. But you know what the war veterans did? Nothing! They simply ignored the guardsmen, even when they fired warning shots.

'In the end the guardsmen had only two options: give up or shoot the veterans. So they left. Except for their commander, who was screaming and shouting at them like a madman, but even he couldn't bring himself to fire his gun. The veterans ignored him as well, and eventually he grew hoarse and walked away. It takes guts to ignore a soldier with an automatic rifle that can cut you in half before you even have time to blink.'

Simonsen asked: 'Why was there a fire?'

'The veterans lit a bonfire and threw their medals onto it.'

'What do they want? Have they made any demands?'

'I thought you would know about that. I mean ... didn't you coordinate this action with them?'

The police officer was evidently well informed. It was true that Simonsen had received a call an hour ago from one of the veterans from the club, saying that someone intended to support his confrontation with the Army. But that was all he had been told.

'No, I haven't coordinated any of this. Do you know why they're here?'

'They're angry at the revelations in *Dagbladet*, but they have no specific demands.'

'You've spoken to them?'

'Yes. I went inside the house to stress that the building has great historical significance and to tell them to look after it properly.'

Konrad Simonsen wanted to know how he had gained access.

'I just went in through the front door. It was straightforward. But then again, I didn't constitute much of a threat to them. I couldn't very well throw them out all on my own, could I? They told me that they would leave of their own accord in an hour's time and I believe them. So now you know, and you're the only one I've told.'

'Why?'

'Because you're meeting with the Defence Chief, who is hopping mad, especially with you, the Chief of Copenhagen Police, that's my boss, and – I'm not kidding you – our nation's highly respected Justice Minister. That's what I've come to tell you. They're waiting for you over in Søndre Magasin, but the media doesn't know that the Minister is here, and he would prefer it to stay that way.

'As it happens, he was already here when the veterans arrived. His son-in-law, who has been fighting in Afghanistan, was being awarded a medal today, and he wanted to be here for that. But back to your question: I'm telling you because you might be able to use this information to your advantage, and because the vast majority of us regular police officers support you, and not FE. As do the veterans. And most of the media.'

'This isn't about me against the Army.'

The police officer smiled. That might not be how Konrad Simonsen saw it, but he was probably the only one. The policeman told him how when they received the call about a disturbance and veterans breaking into the very core of the military, at Kastellet no less, senior police officers had declared it a major incident. Almost one hundred officers in riot gear, equipped with tear gas and the whole kit and caboodle, were gathered in haste and blue-lighted to the scene in four vans, as were countless patrol cars. The police officer continued his account, grinning by now.

'Unfortunately, the head of operations and three of his colleagues made a mistake – you know how easily communication breakdowns occur, it happens all the time. Everyone drove as fast as they could to *Kastelsvej* rather than Kastellet. The whole lot of them are currently parked outside the Nicaraguan Embassy, and that's where they'll stay for the time being because the Justice Minister has issued fresh orders. If it's at all possible, he wants to resolve the situation without the use of force.'

<hr />

Søndre Magasin was now the home of the Army library, which contained specialist literature about the three Armed Forces. The library was open to the public, but received barely any civilian visitors. The police officer escorted Konrad Simonsen through the reading room and into a workshop behind it, used for binding and repairing books.

The police officer opened the door for Simonsen, but didn't enter himself. There were three men already inside: the Justice Minister, the Defence Chief and the Chief of Copenhagen Police. The mood was tense. You didn't have to be a psychologist to see that, Konrad Simonsen thought, as he joined the others at the small table. The welcome wasn't warm. The Defence Chief nodded stiffly, the Justice Minister's *thanks for coming* wasn't all that hearty. Only the Chief of Copenhagen Police, who clearly wanted to signal where his sympathies lay, greeted him with a cheerful *hello, Simon*. Konrad Simonsen looked at the Justice Minister, presuming he was the one who would run this meeting. The Minister outlined the situation in a frosty voice, then pointed at Simonsen.

'Are you responsible for this mess?'

Simonsen answered honestly. He had organised nothing, but he believed that others might have done so in order to help him.

'But you leaked your irritating request to the press, didn't you?'

'Yes.'

The Defence Chief's *I knew it!* triggered a vicious look from the Minister, but his only comment on the leak was a brief, nasal sound before he asked: 'Can you make them leave the Commander's House?'

Simonsen had been expecting the question and had prepared his reply.

'What's the alternative?'

'What do you think is the alternative?'

'We could let them stay there until they get hungry and leave of their own accord; after all, it's just an empty building, so there's no risk—'

Simonsen's words were deliberately chosen to provoke the Defence Chief, and he succeeded beyond even his expectations. The man furiously cut him off.

'*Just* an empty building? Are you out of your mind? You're talking about the Commander's House, do you have any idea—'

The Justice Minister interrupted him.

'Shut up!'

The Defence Chief turned red, then fell silent. The Justice Minister looked at Simonsen, who said: 'All right, I'll have a word with them. If they're prepared to let me enter, that is. However, if they leave of their own accord, they'll do so without any of them being charged or prosecuted. That gives me something to bargain with. But we have two problems. First, will your men obey their orders?'

Simonsen's question was aimed at the Chief of Copenhagen Police, but again the Defence Chief interrupted him.

'This is Army property, and I'm fed up with this discussion. If the police don't clear our building, then I'll call in some people who can. Irrespective of what the three of you think.'

These were dangerous words, and they made the Justice Minister reply: very slowly, very softly and very clearly.

'No, you won't. You'll do as I tell you to do, and you'll pay extra attention to what I tell you *not* to do.'

'I don't take my orders from you!'

'No, but I can call someone you definitely do take your orders from. That someone doesn't fancy getting mixed up in this, so I would prefer not to have to do that. As should you, because when I tell him that you don't recognise the government's right to make decisions in this situation, he'll suspend you immediately.'

The Defence Chief mumbled something about having been misunderstood. The Chief of Copenhagen Police said darkly: 'My officers won't like being told to clear that house, but they will do it, especially if they know it wasn't possible to negotiate any other solution.'

The Minister nodded a quick *very well*, then he asked Konrad Simonsen: 'You said you had two problems. What's the second?'

'If we have to use force to clear the building, it's not a great idea to have the press around. The news for the rest of this week will be nothing but violent images, you don't have to be a spin doctor to realise that. So I suggest that the Guardsmen escort all journalists from the area.'

The Defence Chief vetoed the proposal immediately.

'This will make the Army appear in the worst possible light to the media. Forget it, it's a job for the police. Besides it can wait until we know whether or not the troublemakers will leave of their own accord.'

The Chief of Copenhagen Police protested.

'No way. My people are here to clear the building if they have to, not to maintain law and order on Army property, which is clearly a Defence responsibility. That's enough!'

Konrad Simonsen thought it might prove unwise to express yourself so bluntly to a man who was the ultimate head of Denmark's Police Force, but the Justice Minister didn't seem to mind. Instead he ordered the Defence Chief: 'Clear the press from Kastellet, but no guns, they're not necessary. And you, Detective Chief Superintendent, as soon as that's done, try to get inside the building. I expect you to be successful.'

Half an hour later the four men met again. Konrad Simonsen had been inside the Commander's House and concluded that the veterans were already getting ready to leave. The broken glass from the smashed windows had been neatly swept up, wrapped in newspaper and placed in a wastepaper basket. A couple of 500-kroner notes had been left on a windowsill to cover the cost of repairs. There was no other damage.

The veterans to whom he spoke were monosyllabic about the purpose of their action, but there was great anger among them that FE was willing to protect Irene Gallagher after she had manipulated and exploited Captain Bjørn Lauritzen, who – like so many others – had never been given the help he deserved after his combat experiences. It was just as Konrad Simonsen had guessed, and after that there was nothing more to talk about, so the last ten minutes he was inside the house were spent chatting to a veteran he knew from the club in Vesterbro. They talked about chess.

Simonsen summarised his visit, inflating trivialities and casual chit-chat to major feats in the art of negotiation. The others accepted his presentation, they clearly couldn't care less. The veterans were leaving the building, that was all that mattered. The meeting was closed. The Defence Chief couldn't get away quickly enough. The Chief of Copenhagen Police, too, was soon gone. The Justice Minister said: 'You'll be coming with me. I'll give you a lift to Police Headquarters. If you came here by car, get someone to pick it up.'

They didn't speak on their way to the car park, and it was not until they had left Kastellet that the Justice Minister spoke again.

'I want you to listen to me very carefully because what I'm about to tell you isn't up for discussion. This is me being kind because you were honest with me this afternoon, but I'm not sure you'll see it that way.'

'I'm listening.'

'Your provocative request will be refused. No politician, myself included, wants to touch classified FE files, especially not if that classification implicates foreign powers.

'All right, so a few legal sticklers and experts might cry foul, but an overwhelming majority of Danes either don't care or would happily agree that in certain circumstances the Police and the Army should not have to inform the public of their activities. I'll throw you a bone, of which more later. But first: you'll withdraw your provocative summons of senior Defence chiefs, and in turn FE will stop harassing you. I'll see to that. And I won't accept any more stunts from your side that involve me. If you do it again, I'll sack you and ride out the inevitable storm, so now you know. Are we clear?'

Message received. What else could Konrad Simonsen say? He tried to change the subject.

'What about your own Ministry's pressure on my investigation, not to mention the Public Prosecutor?'

'An error for which I apologise. It won't happen again. But has it ever crossed your mind that it might be in Denmark's best interest if Irene Gallagher sods off to New Zealand or wherever the hell she decides to go? Criminals walk free all the time, you know that better than anyone, and perhaps we're all better off without her.'

Simonsen protested at this.

'It's not in the best interests of my sense of justice. Besides, she killed one of my officers. As Justice Minister you can't just let that go.'

The Minister drove down a few more streets without replying. Perhaps he needed time to digest Konrad Simonsen's words. Then he chose to ignore them and returned to the promised bone.

'I'll make sure that someone in the Army who knew of Irene Gallagher's work in Bosnia reviews her file and decides whether there's any relevant information they can pass on to you that isn't classified. It's not much, but it's all you're going to get. What do you say to that?'

'That it's not much, probably nothing at all.'

The Justice Minister smiled.

'I'm sure you're right, but at least you can tell yourself that you tried.'

CHAPTER 48

SUNDAY 17 OCTOBER 2010, PALADS CINEMA, COPENHAGEN

'When and where are you meeting him?'

The Countess pressed her lips together and shook her head. She wasn't going to say. Simonsen could scarcely believe it.

'But surely you can tell me? Don't you know who he is?'

She shook her head again, irritably this time.

'Really, Countess, we're on the same side.'

'No, we're not. I'm on the side that has sworn not to say anything to anyone, and it's a promise I intend to keep.'

Simonsen had just had the FE breakthrough he had been hoping for. The PET chief had called to tell him that he knew an FE officer who was willing to pass on information about Irene Gallagher and Bjørn Lauritzen's time in Bosnia in the mid-nineties. The PET chief could vouch for the man, but the conversation would take place on the officer's terms or not at all. Furthermore the man insisted on speaking to the Countess. She was the only one whose word he trusted.

Konrad Simonsen had handed the phone to his wife.

'Please would you at least tell me when you're meeting him?'

'Later today, now stop pestering me.'

The Palads cinema complex contained seventeen screens, and the film for which the Countess had bought a ticket was showing in one of the smaller ones. She sat down two chairs into the penultimate row. The film wouldn't start for another fifteen minutes, so she took a book from her bag and began to read. Ten minutes later she heard a voice behind her

'Don't turn around. I don't want you seeing my face.'

The Countess said softly but clearly: 'I won't turn around, you don't have to worry.'

'Are you recording this conversation?'

'No. You picked me because you trust me, and you can. I keep my promises.'

She sensed that her words reassured him because his breathing rate slowed. He told her that he was risking his job and possibly his liberty for what he was about to do, and she thanked him. Then he told her that he knew part of the truth, but not all of it, which she accepted. At last he began.

'Irene Gallagher acted as an intelligence officer for the Americans. She was a major in the US Navy while working for us—'

'You mean FE? I'm sorry for interrupting you, but it's important that we don't misunderstand each other on this point.'

'That's quite all right. Yes, FE, but she was paid by both agencies. Her job in Bosnia wasn't, as you've probably guessed by now, that of a judge advocate. It was to visit UN troops and persuade platoon commanders from the Nordic, Polish and Dutch forces to report any sightings of Serbian surface-to-air batteries.

'The Serbs used a Russian system that NATO called SA-6 Gainful. It was fairly powerful and could fire three missiles simultaneously. It was a missile from such a system that shot down an American F-16 plane in 1995. Whenever the Americans found out where those SAM batteries were located, they would usually blow them to smithereens. Mostly by firing a cruise missile at them – which they launched from the air or from the American naval fleet in the Adriatic. Other times – this was early on in the conflict – the location of the SAM batteries was merely recorded.'

'So Irene Gallagher recruited Bjørn Lauritzen?'

'Yes, and that happened on his first deployment, in 1992. Then they fell in love. They met up back home in Denmark. She became pregnant with his baby, but ended up having an abortion in November 1992.'

'You're saying that by 1995 they had known each other for three years?'

'Yes, and I don't think it was a coincidence that she was sent down to check up on him in 1995. I'm sure she fixed it, though I've no proof.'

'Her last trip is the one we're really interested in.'

'When she drove by Jeep from Tuzla and later from Little Denmark to find him, she had personal motives. It was definitely a private trip, unless she was doing something for the Americans, but I don't think so.'

The Countess thought that given how little the Homicide Department knew about Irene Gallagher and Bjørn Lauritzen in Bosnia, this was valuable information that the man was giving her, but ultimately did it really change anything?

'Thank you for the information.'

'There's more. First you need to know that any trace of Irene Gallagher's activities in the former Yugoslavia, or anywhere else for that matter, can no longer be found in any archive. If indeed they were ever documented. Her file was destroyed long ago, and as far as what happened on Bjørn Lauritzen's and Ole Nysted's last day in Bosnia, I don't believe anything was ever recorded. The information given to Copenhagen was only delivered verbally.'

The Countess understood.

'You think something major happened during Bjørn Lauritzen's and Ole Nysted's last trip?'

'I do. That's what this is really all about, but I don't know what it was. If I were to hazard a guess, I'd say that the two Danish soldiers did something bad when they drove their tank into the forest where the Serbs were murdering Muslim men and boys. Something that Denmark definitely doesn't want to come out.

'I know that they drove that tank through a brook and that there was room enough to manoeuvre it, so I reckon they executed a lot of Serbian soldiers in that forest, but I can't be sure. All I know is that they were practically snatched away from Bosnia the next day, and that Bjørn Lauritzen was sent all the way home to Nordjylland but both he and Ole Nysted were allowed to keep their field promotions, which doesn't tally with the way they were sent home. It looks like a kind of bribe, so they would keep quiet.'

'How do you know this?'

'You don't need to know that.'

'Why is FE helping Irene Gallagher? Who decided that?'

'The senior brass, which includes the boss himself, although I believe he hates Irene Gallagher's guts. But their thinking is that the best possible outcome is for her and her husband to disappear off to New Zealand, rather than her being convicted and jailed in Denmark. She knows too much, would be my guess.'

'Are you saying that FE doesn't think she'll be convicted?'

'That's right. We don't think she will, and we're probably right about that.'

'Do you know if she's guilty?'

'I think she is, but I'm not sure. I've seen so many … dirty tricks in my time, and you never can tell. Things aren't always how they appear. But one thing I do know: FE had absolutely nothing to do with the canal boat killings. We don't work like that. No one would ever think of approving such an atrocity.'

The Countess passed a card over her shoulder.

'This is my private number. Please would you contact me in a week's time? In case there are any new developments.'

No one took the card. She asked: 'Are you there?' and got no reply. She turned around.

He was gone.

CHAPTER 49

By mutual agreement between Christoffer Brinch on behalf of the defendant, the Public Prosecutor Kirsten Hansen and the Copenhagen courthouse, the trial of Irene Gallagher had been brought forward as much as was possible without the haste being deemed legally irresponsible.

All parties were interested in obtaining a quick decision. Christoffer Brinch had been aware of the indictment for less than a week when the trial started, but that didn't matter as Irene Gallagher insisted on her defence strategy being that the police had fabricated evidence against her. She didn't think it necessary to call any witnesses.

Nine serious-looking jurors, three women and six men, all of retirement age, sat to the right of the judge, a middle-aged woman notorious for her dry, controlling conduct and cool distance from anyone else in the courtroom. Trials in the Copenhagen courthouse were not exactly cosy, as a rule, but they were relatively informal in tone – except when she presided. She was known as a very active judge and would often intervene when witnesses were giving evidence, if she thought it necessary, something other judges only rarely did.

The public gallery was packed to the rafters. Half the seats were allocated to the press, some were reserved for family members of the canal boat victims, and two seats were for the police. The rest were available to the public, to anyone willing to queue for a long time.

The judge arrived, sat down and indicated that everyone else could sit too. Then she opened by declaring that this trial was likely to touch upon subjects which, due to security concerns, must not become public. On those occasions the court would sit in private and issue a reporting ban. Furthermore, she would only permit such subjects to be discussed if they had direct and obvious relevance to the case. No general background information would be permitted. Then she asked the prosecution to begin.

The Public Prosecutor read the indictment aloud, whereupon Irene Gallagher declared that she was not guilty of all charges. Kirsten Hansen then spent about an hour and a half elaborating on the charges. From the original indictment, she had dropped the charge of manslaughter of the Japanese teacher and the sixteen schoolchildren, but had retained the charge of being an accessory to the attack on Juli Denissen in the summer of 2008. This charge would later allow her to hint that the motive for the canal boat killings was to prevent the attack on the young woman being exposed. It was flimsy, but it was all she had to work with. The accused was further charged with the murder of Bjørn Lauritzen. In relation to the death of Ole Nysted, the army veteran found suffocated by carbon monoxide in his hut, it hadn't been possible for the police to prove his death wasn't a suicide, so there were no charges in that respect.

When Kirsten Hansen had finished speaking, it was the turn of Christoffer Brinch to comment on the indictment. He got up and addressed the jury.

'My client believes that all the evidence presented against her is false and was fabricated by officers from the Copenhagen Homicide Department for the purpose of having her wrongly convicted. The defence will, as the trial progresses, expose this manufactured evidence.'

He sat down. The judge asked in astonishment: 'Don't you have anything else to say?'

'No.'

'Have you explained the risk of such a defence to your client?'

'Yes, I have.'

'It seems highly unusual to the court.'

Irene Gallagher said loudly: 'I know what I'm doing.'

The judge came down on her hard.

'That's the last time you speak in my court without my permission!' She glowered at Irene Gallagher until she received a surly nod, after which the judge accepted the defence strategy with a shrug, then ordered a ten-minute recess. She was a smoker.

Klavs Arnold found Kirsten Hansen during the break. Simonsen had decided that a member of the Homicide Department would sit in on the trial, and as he himself would be called as a witness at some point and was thus banned from the public gallery until he had been on the stand, this job was mostly shared between Klavs Arnold and Arne Pedersen.

'That's a kamikaze strategy she has picked, but it can only be to our advantage. This might be easier than I feared,' commented the prosecutor.

'You've been worried about the outcome?' Klavs Arnold said.

'Not in terms of the murder of Bjørn Lauritzen, that indictment will stick, but the canal boat killings stand or fall on the video from Charlottenlund Beach. It's the only solid evidence I have. On the other hand: if Christoffer Brinch depends on discrediting all the evidence on the grounds that the Homicide Department manufactured it, we're home and dry. No Danish jury will buy that.'

Back in the courtroom Kirsten Hansen explained the death of Juli Denissen in detail. It took time. She took care not to rush her presentation. The information was complex, and she would often summarise and repeat what she had said while showing pictures and maps to the court. Christoffer Brinch objected to none of this. On the contrary, he nodded his approval of this course of events.

When she had finally finished, the judge checked her watch and decided there was time to hear the first witness before lunch. Ella von Eggert was called and escorted to the stand by a court usher. The judge advised her that she had no duty to bear witness against her sister, but if she chose to give evidence, she was under oath and could be punished for perverting the course of justice.

Ella von Eggert replied indignantly: 'I've waited a month for the truth to come out, and I look forward to telling you how the police lied to me, forced me to sign a false witness statement and made all sorts of threats. So I'm very happy to give evidence.'

'If you lie to the court, you risk up to four years' imprisonment.'

'I'm not lying, the police are lying. All of them.'

Kirsten Hansen handed Ella von Eggert her witness statement.

'Please would you read aloud the first ten lines?'

'I won't as it happens. I'm not here to read aloud. Besides, it's all a pack of lies that the police made up.'

Kirsten Hansen looked imploringly at the judge, but she merely shrugged. The court had no power to force a witness to read aloud. If the witness refused, then Kirsten Hansen would have to read the statement herself.

Irene Gallagher whispered to Christoffer Brinch, 'My sister is right, the police misrepresented her statement. Make the prosecution produce the sound recording, so we can compare the two.'

Brinch nodded. It was an excellent suggestion.

When Kirsten Hansen had finished reading out the statement, she asked Ella von Eggert: 'Is this your signature?'

'I was coerced into signing under duress, I never said those things.'

'Answer my question: is this your signature?'

'Yes, it bloody is, but it's not valid.'

The judge reminded Ella von Eggert that swearing in court was not permitted. Then it was the turn of Christoffer Brinch to cross-examine her. He asked the witness to recount in her own words what she believed had occurred when she was interviewed by the police. Ella von Eggert told the court how on Wednesday 15 September Homicide Chief Konrad Simonsen and Sergeant Nathalie von Rosen had, after they physically – and against her express wish – forced their way into her home, continued to put pressure on her to implicate her sister.

'Partly by showing me lots of dreadful pictures of those poor, dead Japanese children – it was unbearable. The police officers left eventually, but about a week later, on the twenty-fourth of September to be precise, Deputy Homicide Chief Arne Pedersen arrived. He claimed that he had drafted my witness statement on the basis of an audio recording from my first interview, and that I had to sign it. He was very unpleasant, positively menacing, and so I signed.'

She went on to explain how Pedersen had examined her car, which had just been returned to her after it had been stolen. She had been too scared to stop him, she said. Afterwards he had left.

'Was your witness statement to Homicide Chief Simonsen and Sergeant von Rosen recorded on a Dictaphone?'

'Yes, it was.'

'You're absolutely sure of that?'

'I am.'

Christoffer Brinch turned to the judge.

'The court could ask the police to produce the recording, so we can decide who is telling the truth.'

The judge considered this. Then she pointed to Klavs Arnold and told him to stand up.

'I see that you're present in court, Sergeant. Tell me, was the interview recorded?'

'Yes, it was.'

'Can the police produce the recording?'

'Of course. I'll make sure it gets here in the next half-hour.'

'You do that. Meanwhile we'll break for lunch. And you, Mrs von Eggert, don't leave this building unless you're in the company of a court usher.'

Irene Gallagher returned to her cell with her defence lawyer. A prison officer followed them at a discreet distance.

'Once the police admit that they can't find the recording, I want you to reiterate my sister's assertion that Deputy Homicide Chief Arne Pedersen had an opportunity to examine her car. I want the jury to remember that.'

Christoffer Brinch frowned.

'I thought the recording would prove that your sister was telling the truth. Isn't that what you told me?'

'Yes, and it will, indirectly.'

'And if the police produce the recording?'

'That won't happen.'

She was quite right. The Homicide Department couldn't find the sound file or, more accurately, either of the two recording devices on which it would be stored. One was a USB stick to which the original file from Konrad Simonsen's Dictaphone had been transferred. Having been used for drafting the witness report, it had since been stored in a steel cupboard which, for reasons no one could remember, was in the Countess's office. Now the USB stick was gone, and someone must have removed it. It was hard to think of any other explanation.

The other copy was on Konrad Simonsen's Dictaphone. But that had been missing for more than two weeks and when, as Klavs Arnold questioned him, he tried desperately to remember the occasion on which he'd had it last, he suddenly remembered that it was during his interview with Irene Gallagher when he had left it – turned off – on her desk.

Kirsten Hansen was embarrassed to have to inform the judge that the police couldn't find the USB stick with the sound recording, which the judge announced to the court when the trial resumed. The jury was therefore free to believe either side, but in any case should not attach too much importance to the allegations against the Homicide officers.

Christoffer Brinch was then asked to resume his cross-examination of Ella von Eggert. He asked her to describe Arne Pedersen's search of her car, something to which the Public Prosecutor didn't object. After Ella von Eggert's subsequent testimony, the judge chose to end the session for that day. She was annoyed. The entire incident had been messy and she hated mess, especially in her courtroom.

CHAPTER 50

THURSDAY 4 NOVEMBER 2010, COPENHAGEN CENTRAL CRIMINAL COURT

During subsequent sessions the Public Prosecutor managed, to some extent, to redeem herself after her poor start.

She successfully linked Irene Gallagher to Bjørn Lauritzen on several occasions, and in particular the defendant's false report of the death of Lauritzen on the Storebæltsbroen Bridge made an impression on the jurors, you could tell from their expressions. Christoffer Brinch didn't try to undermine the evidence; Irene Gallagher regarded it as unimportant and told him to let it pass without comment.

The judge also allowed the prosecution to say in very general terms that the defendant and Bjørn Lauritzen had worked together in Bosnia in the mid-1990s and thus knew each other from there. Christoffer Brinch didn't object to that either. The prosecutor then spent a long time explaining to the jury that Bjørn Lauritzen had committed the canal boat killings on Sunday 22 August, and here the evidence was so compelling that the judge subsequently advised the jury that Lauritzen's guilt must be regarded as a fact.

Again Christoffer Brinch was silent; he repeatedly declined to cross-examine witnesses or make any comment. Everyone was therefore surprised that he chose to cross-examine the forensic technician who had examined Ella von Eggert's car. The technician had just informed the court that a hair belonging to Bjørn Lauritzen had been found under a metal nut that held the passenger seat in place. Christoffer Brinch rose to make a couple of devastating counterpoints, to which Irene Gallagher had drawn his attention. He held up a document.

'According to your report, you found traces of zinc oxide in Ella von Eggert's car. Please would you tell the court, in layman's terms, what that is?'

'In the form in which we found it, a very fine white powder.'

'Where did you find it? You're welcome to check your report, if you can't remember.'

'I do remember. I found it in several places: on the dashboard, the front and the back of the sun visor, the buckle on the seat belt, the internal door handle, all of which were on the passenger side.'

'What is zinc oxide used for?'

'Many things, I would imagine, including dusting for potential fingerprints on dark surfaces. Iron dioxide, which is red, is used on light-coloured surfaces.'

'Is the interior of Ella von Eggert's car light or dark?'

'Dark.'

'Is zinc oxide a normal part of a detective's equipment?'

'Yes, it is.'

'What did you think when you discovered the substance in the places you described?'

'I thought that someone must have dusted the car for fingerprints before we got it in for examination.'

'But you didn't write this down in your report?'

'Of course not, that's not my job. But I would have told the police, if they had asked my opinion.'

'Were you asked?'

'No.'

Christoffer Brinch paused to give the jury time to digest the information. Then he displayed a photograph on the large flat-screen that had been put up in a corner of the courtroom. The picture was razor-sharp and showed a dark hair trapped around a metal nut.

'We know that the hair belongs to Bjørn Lauritzen, the defence isn't questioning that. This is about another issue, and please excuse my unscientific questioning, but does it seem likely to you a hair that had fallen from someone's head would end up as shown here?'

The forensic technician hesitated slightly before replying.

'No, not the way you're asking.'

'How do you mean?'

'I mean that a strand of hair can't just fall off and end up in that way, it obviously can't trap itself under the nut. But there could be any number of reasonable explanations for it being pushed underneath, which was how I found it.'

'So this is quite common?'

'No, it's rare, but it happens.'

'Could the hair be in this position because someone deliberately put it there?'

'Yes, absolutely.'

Christoffer Brinch asked the court usher controlling the monitor to zoom in on one end of the hair, the follicle. Then he continued: 'In your report you describe the strand of hair as follows: "an approximately eight-centimetre dark brown strand of hair with the follicle intact, torn from the scalp of a Caucasian male". Please would you explain to the court how you tell the difference between hair shed naturally and hair torn from the scalp?'

'There's a big difference, and the short version is that all hair has a growth phase and a resting phase, and it is during the resting phase that hair falls out. A strand of hair torn out, especially in the growth phase, will have a follicle and often a little bit of scalp tissue still attached.'

'So this strand of hair wasn't shed naturally, it was pulled out?'

'Yes, definitely. That's why I wrote *torn from the scalp* in my report.'

'But the police wouldn't appear to have attached much significance to that. Tell me, is there a discernible difference between a strand of hair pulled from a living person and a person who died recently – let's say, two days before?'

'No, I don't think so. But I'm not sure.'

'So this hair could have been pulled out at Bjørn Lauritzen's post-mortem, let's say, by the police representative present—'

Here the judge cut Christoffer Brinch short.

'That's enough speculation. Do you have any further questions for the witness?'

Brinch apologised. He had only one question left.

'With your considerable experience of forensic investigation, would you say that it's more likely the hair was placed deliberately where you found it, or that it ended up there in the normal course of events?'

The forensic technician was reluctant to respond, clearly uncomfortable with the question.

'That's impossible to say with any degree of certainty.'

The judge said: 'You weren't asked for certainty, but for an assessment of what you thought more likely. And I too would like to know.'

The man thought about it, pulling a face and pursing his lips. It was hard to decide whether he was summoning the courage to defy the judge or whether he was pondering his answer. At length he said: 'I think it's more likely that the hair was placed deliberately where I found it. And I should have made that clear in my report, but I hadn't realised it until now. Unfortunately!'

CHAPTER 51

It was the first time during the trial that Irene Gallagher had told Christoffer Brinch to refute a witness statement as strongly as he could, while also instructing him on exactly how to do it.

It concerned the examination of the image technician who had processed the video from Charlottenlund Beach, where Irene Gallagher had met a man who, according to the prosecution, was Bjørn Lauritzen. Christoffer Brinch promised to do what he could. Irene Gallagher asked him: 'Do you want to know whether it *was* Bjørn Lauritzen, or would you rather not?'

'Can we produce the man it was? That would clearly be our best option.'

'No, I'm afraid we can't.'

'Then I prefer to remain in ignorance.'

Irene Gallagher said hesitantly: 'Someone tricked me, that's why I met him. But I lied about it to the police and I should never have done that.'

She looked upset and for a moment he wanted to hug her, but he satisfied himself by saying: 'I'm your defence lawyer, not your prosecutor; you don't have to say any more.'

He knocked on her cell door in order to be let out.

The image technician was nervous. It was her first time giving evidence in court, and the Public Prosecutor had to put her at ease and repeat some of the questions. Twice the judge had to ask her to speak up. But although she was nervous, there could be no doubting her expertise.

She had taken several pictures posthumously of Bjørn Lauritzen, including some where his arms were positioned in the same angles as the man on the beach video. Then she had combined individual pictures, minimised, rotated and angled his body, and pasted her manipulated image onto a still picture from the video. The two pictures matched and the result looked convincing. At the same time, she was cautious in her conclusion: her work showed that the man from the video could indeed be Bjørn Lauritzen; it was certainly one possibility, but equally it could be another man of the same build.

She had also calculated the man's height based on the height of Irene Gallagher and that of a flagpole in the background. Here she was surer of herself: the unknown man's height matched that of Bjørn Lauritzen, 1.87 metres, as stated in the post-mortem report.

While she explained this to the court, an embarrassing incident occurred when her boss, Kurt Melsing, who was in the public gallery, made a series of minimising, downwards gestures in order to get the witness to express less certainty.

The judge practically exploded. She had Melsing removed immediately and threatened him with unpleasant consequences. The technician subsequently tried to modify her statement, but the judge cut her off. The court had heard her evidence, and she wasn't allowed to backtrack. The prosecutor handed over the witness to the defence for cross-examination.

Christoffer Brinch was well prepared. He started with the obvious question.

'How many other men, in your estimate, would match the image superimposed on the man in the video you've just showed the court?'

'Lots.'

'Are we talking hundreds?'

'No, many more.'

'Millions, if we include the entirety of the world's population, am I right?'

'Yes, I would think so.'

'How many Danish men are one point eight-seven metres tall?'

'I don't know.'

'One hundred thousand, according to official statistics. So the unidentified man in the video could be one of tens of thousands of men other than Bjørn Lauritzen. However, I want to know more about how you calculated the man's height. You told the court earlier that your calculation was accurate. I want to know how accurate.'

The technician explained how she had carried out no less than ten control experiments with the same mobile phone camera on the same beach, from the same distance and—

Christoffer Brinch interrupted her.

'Surely there must be some margin of error? However, as you speak with such confidence, can we then deduce that the variation in your calculations is less than nought point one per cent? You would normally describe that as a very high degree of certainty, wouldn't you?'

The woman gave this careful consideration before she replied.

'No, that variation is too small.'

'So a difference of nought point five – five times as great?'

'Yes, I would agree with that.'

'So a difference of a maximum of nought point five per cent?'

'Yes.'

'Right, let's bear that in mind. Now, I'm perfectly aware that you're not a doctor, but did you know that people are shorter in the evening than in the morning? It's because the spine compresses a little during the day, and then stretches out again at night because we lie down. For a man the height of Bjørn Lauritzen, the difference between his morning and evening height would have been about one point five centimetres.'

The technician went bright red. Christoffer Brinch continued with his cross-examination.

'According to his post-mortem report, Bjørn Lauritzen was killed in the evening. After death the spine no longer recovers, therefore we know that at the time of his death, Bjørn Lauritzen was one point eighty-seven metres tall, as you yourself have stated in your report. But it also means that coming up for twelve noon on Charlottenlund Beach, if indeed he was there, Bjørn Lauritzen would have been one point eighty-eight metres tall. And possibly a little taller, as he had allegedly been swimming for three hours by then, something which doesn't compress the spine. I don't know how good your mental arithmetic is, but are you in a position to tell the court if the unidentified man could still be Bjørn Lauritzen?'

'But we might be talking fractions of a millimetre here. I've only given his height in whole centimetres.'

'Answer my question.'

The witness tried appealing to the judge.

'Please can I be permitted to explain so I can factor in millimetres of the man's height? That's where the confusion lies, I'm
sure of it.'

Christoffer Brinch said: 'It sounds almost as if you *want* the man
to be Bjørn Lauritzen. But let me ask you again: if your own calculations and my summary of how a person's height changes during
the day are true, can the man in the video be Bjørn Lauritzen?'

The technician braced herself, then she said quietly: 'No, he can't.'

The judge almost sneered at her.

'Louder, so the jury can hear you.'

'No, he can't be Bjørn Lauritzen.'

CHAPTER 52

TUESDAY 9 NOVEMBER 2010, COPENHAGEN CENTRAL
CRIMINAL COURT

Konrad Simonsen had given evidence countless times before
and knew the court procedures in his sleep, so while the Public
Prosecutor went through the opening formalities with him, his
name, his rank and so on, he had time to concentrate on a certain
person in the public gallery who had caught the eye of the Homicide
Department.

The man was around thirty, of average height and build, with
a blond crewcut, clear blue eyes and a slightly ingenuous-looking
face. He had attended every court session so far and clearly had
a deal with the court ushers to reserve him a seat, but Simonsen
hadn't been able to work out how, only that it must be on orders
from up high. None of the courthouse's staff was willing to say any

more and, in all likelihood, that was all they knew. Klavs Arnold and Arne Pedersen wanted the man put under surveillance, but Simonsen had said no. He didn't want to waste police resources on satisfying his own most likely unfounded curiosity.

'Tell me, are you even listening to me, Mr Simonsen?' Kirsten Hansen said, snapping him out of his reverie. There was giggling in the courtroom, and even the judge smiled when she told the witness to concentrate. Simonsen apologised and received a gracious nod from the judge that told him he was forgiven, but not to let it happen again. The prosecutor repeated her question.

'The defendant, Irene Gallagher, knew Bjørn Lauritzen and Ole Nysted. Both men were war veterans living isolated lives. Please will you review for the court the evidence supporting this fact. And here I'm thinking exclusively of evidence found in Denmark.'

Kirsten Hansen's latter remark was aimed at the judge.

From now up until lunch, interrupted only by the usual ten-minute smoking break, Konrad Simonsen answered this line of questioning. By the end, no one could be in any doubt that Irene Gallagher had known the two men, making sure that her husband's shops supplied them with food, and also that she would pay them occasional, albeit rare, visits.

They finally reached the inevitable: Kirsten Hansen asked him about Bosnia and the summer of 1995. However, no sooner had she mentioned this location than the judge intervened and ordered the case to continue in private. The public gallery was cleared. The judge admonished the Public Prosecutor as she had done at the start of the trial. Kirsten Hansen accepted the rebuke; she had to, empty protests wouldn't endear her to the jury. She asked Simonsen: 'How did Bjørn Lauritzen and Ole Nysted get on in Bosnia?'

He gave details.

'Both men were sent home with indecent haste by the Army after an incident on the thirteenth of July 1995, in which the defendant, Irene Gallagher, was also involved. Please would you describe this incident to us?'

Simonsen explained what he knew, citing the Army's lack of co-operation in clarifying what had happened.

The judge looked as if she had sucked a lemon, her features sharpening, but she didn't stop him.

'Irene Gallagher worked as a judge advocate for the Danish Army, but she also held another position at the same time. What was that?'

'She was an intelligence officer and a major in the—'

The judge banged her gavel. The noise was surprisingly loud.

'That's enough of that! Do you have any direct and verifiable evidence that circumstances in Bosnia in 1995 are in any way relevant to the charges Mrs Gallagher is facing here today?'

Since Simonsen hadn't, the judge announced it was time for lunch.

Christoffer Brinch had learned by heart major parts of the report he had been given by Irene Gallagher. After lunch he had several questions about Deputy Homicide Chief Arne Pedersen, which his client wanted him to ask Konrad Simonsen. The judge gestured to indicate that the defence could begin.

'What was Deputy Homicide Chief Pedersen's relationship to the late Pauline Berg?'

Simonsen described their relationship in vague and general terms.

'But the two of them were more than just colleagues at one point, isn't that right?'

'It was. In 2006 they had had a close ... that is to say ... an intimate relationship.'

'How long did it last?'

'About a year, to my knowledge.'

'I see. In the autumn of 2007 Pauline Berg was abducted by a mentally disturbed man. At one point your department tracked down this man, but you decided not to arrest him because you feared he would refuse to tell you where he was hiding his victim. The man spent a night at a hotel in Copenhagen. I know that you and Deputy Homicide Chief Pedersen were at Police Headquarters at the time, but tell me, was Deputy Homicide Chief Pedersen involved in the search?'

'No, he wasn't.'

'Why not?'

'He was highly distressed because of what had happened to Pauline Berg.'

'And yet he did do something that night. Please would you tell the court what that was?'

Konrad Simonsen sighed, then he said: 'Arne Pedersen went to the hotel off his own bat.'

'Why?'

'To make the kidnapper tell him where Pauline was.'

'Make him how?'

'Using physical force.'

'Was he armed?'

'Yes, he had a truncheon and a Stanley knife.'

'Fortunately he was stopped in time, but is it your assessment that he would have used those weapons against the kidnapper?'

'How on earth would I know that?'

'But that was his intention, wasn't it?'

'Yes.'

'I also want to ask you if you're aware of Deputy Homicide Chief Pedersen's angry outburst on Saturday the eighteenth of September, shortly after Pauline Berg's funeral. His remarks were later reported by three different journalists in three different newspapers.'

'Yes, I am. I've spoken to Arne about it and stressed that it wasn't a very sensible thing to say.'

'*We'll get him, and that Gallagher bitch, just you wait and see. We'll nail them. I don't care how.* This is the statement that you describe as not "a very sensible thing" to say?'

'It sounds worse when it's repeated out of context.'

'*We'll nail them. I don't care how.* Don't you think that speaks for itself?'

Konrad Simonsen didn't comment on this, and Christoffer Brinch didn't push for an answer. Instead he jumped to his final topic.

'On Monday the twentieth of September, you and Deputy Homicide Chief Pedersen interviewed Irene Gallagher at her home in Næstved?'

'Yes, that's correct.'

'Were you present during the whole interview or was Deputy Homicide Chief Pedersen alone with my client at any point?'

'The latter. I received a call and went outside for a period.'

'For how long?'

'Ten minutes, maybe fifteen. I don't know exactly.'

'What was your telephone call about?'

Simonsen explained how he had been tricked into believing that his daughter had been in an accident.

'Did you try to trace the call later?'

'Yes.'

'What was the result?'

'The call would appear to have come from Police Headquarters. That's as far as we got.'

'Is it possible that someone called you for the purpose of making you leave the interview so that Deputy Homicide Chief Pedersen and Irene Gallagher were left alone?'

'Of course that's possible. As are plenty of other explanations.'

Christoffer Brinch thanked the witness. He had finished his cross-examination. The judge asked: 'You draw no conclusions?'

'Not yet, but I will do so later. The defence wanted to establish that my client and Deputy Homicide Chief Arne Pedersen were alone at some point during the interview.'

The judge accepted this, but Christoffer Brinch privately decided he was as mystified as she was. He didn't know why this was so important either but his client insisted it was.

The court was adjourned for the day.

Konrad Simonsen and Arne Pedersen, who had been sitting in the public gallery, met in the courtroom. Pedersen was upset. 'What the hell is happening, Simon?' he exclaimed. But Simonsen didn't know.

'Last week they lied about me planting evidence in her car. I wasn't even near her car. We hadn't got a warrant at that point.'

Simonsen placed a hand on his deputy's shoulder in an attempt to calm him down.

'We've been through this ten times, Arne. No one thinks that you planted evidence. And of course Ella von Eggert signed her witness statement of her own free will, we all know that.'

However, Arne Pedersen refused to let himself be placated. His voice rose.

'And then there's everything that has happened today, I can't bear it. They're destroying my reputation.'

'There's nothing we can do now except stay calm. Control yourself, Arne. You can't scream and shout here, it's not a very clever thing to do.'

His boss was right. Arne Pedersen tried to compose himself. He went on in a relatively normal tone: 'Are you driving back to Police Headquarters? I could do with someone to talk to.'

'Yes, that's fine. But first I have to—'

Konrad Simonsen broke off as a young woman stepped in between them, put her arms around Arne Pedersen and gave him a warm kiss.

It was Louise Berg.

CHAPTER 53

TUESDAY 9 NOVEMBER 2010, COPENHAGEN

Klavs Arnold waited outside Copenhagen Central Criminal Court until that day's session was finished. He had decided to take matters relating to the unknown young man in the public gallery into his own hands. He could see why his boss wouldn't allocate scarce police resources to identifying the man, but no one could prevent someone in their spare time – someone like him, say – from discreetly following the man to see where he was going. And that was exactly what Klavs Arnold was doing late this afternoon.

He had hoped that the man had a car parked nearby, whose registration he could look up – it would be the easiest way of identifying him – but the man did not appear to have one. When he left the court, Klavs followed him along the short streets to Kongens Nytorv, where his quarry took plenty of time to study any shop windows he passed. Klavs stayed about twenty metres behind his quarry and would slip into a doorway or linger at a bus stop every time the man stopped. When he reached Kongens Nytorv, he crossed the square diagonally and continued down Store Kongensgade, still at the same relaxed pace and still taking an interest in the shop windows. Then he was gone, vanished into thin air.

Klavs Arnold ran forward, stopped and looked round in every possible direction but was unable to spot him. He shrugged and thought that it had been worth a go; he could always try another time if he felt like it. But as he turned to walk back to the Court, the man appeared right in front of him, smiling. Klavs Arnold needed a moment to pull himself together, then he showed the man his warrant card.

'You're in a visitation zone, so I'm entitled to ask you for ID. Do you have some?'

The man's smile broadened, but there was nothing threatening about his attitude so Klavs Arnold smiled back. The man said: 'You bet I have.'

He produced a passport from his inside jacket pocket. It was black with white text reading: *Diplomatic Passport, United States of America.*

Klavs Arnold reached for the passport, but the man was faster and snatched it back.

'I believe there's a procedure you need to follow if you want anything else. Am I right?'

He was right.

Klavs Arnold said carefully: 'Yes, I'm sorry. I do know that. But would you mind telling me your name? Voluntarily, I mean. And may I also ask why you are taking such an interest in the trial of Irene Gallagher? We ... I mean, I've been wondering about that.'

The man shook his head regretfully.

'Not now, maybe later when we know the verdict. Then we might talk. After all, now you know where to find me.'

He laughed as he turned away.

CHAPTER 54

'Once I've been acquitted, may I invite you home for dinner to thank you for your brilliant work?'

Christoffer Brinch didn't reply to Irene Gallagher's invitation. They were eating lunch in her cell while the court was in recess. Brinch wiped his mouth.

'I don't like this. Are you absolutely sure you know what you're doing?' he said.

'Quite sure.'

'Ethically it feels wrong, I'm really not happy about it.'

'I'm not happy about what the police have done to me either, and surely I'm entitled to the best possible defence ... Or perhaps you don't agree?'

Christoffer Brinch hesitated, knowing full well that he shouldn't, so he decided to nod instead. His client smiled. He didn't return her smile, but made his excuses. He needed five minutes of fresh air and a little time to himself before going back inside the courtroom.

Outside he walked over to a small raised section of the cobblestones where the city's stocks had once stood. This was where petty criminals and prostitutes had been whipped. Suppression not justice, he thought glumly, and realised at that moment he had reached the end of his legal career.

For the first few decades it had been about money, but in recent years it had been about justice, about his personal – albeit modest – contribution to his country as a society governed by the rule of law. Now he was done. Once this trial was over he would never set foot in a courtroom again. He had been trapped in a web spun by his client, he had been manipulated and used as a pawn in a chess game he had understood far too late. All he could do now was finish off this dirty job, he had no other choice. He spat in the street, something he hadn't done since he was a child.

When the court resumed after lunch, a forensic technician gave evidence regarding the murder of Bjørn Lauritzen. He first stated the date and time of the death and continued: 'The victim was shot first in the back of his head as he sat on a box, and immediately afterwards straight through his forehead. It wasn't a powerful weapon, and there are no exit wounds, which corresponds with the two calibre five-point-six-millimetre bullets found inside the victim's head.'

The technician then meticulously went through the angles and estimated distance of the shots, which took some time. When he had finished, the Public Prosecutor asked a few minor follow-up questions. Christoffer Brinch refrained from cross-examination.

The next witness was also a forensic technician. She described to the court the discovery of a pistol in Irene Gallagher's garage during a police search. The weapon was in a plastic bag, hidden in a bucket of road grit. The pistol was a Ruger Mark I 22LR, produced by Sturm, Ruger & Co. in Connecticut, USA, and was first sold in 1948. The pistol's front sight had been filed down. Ballistic examination of the pistol and the two bullets found in the skull of Bjørn Lauritzen had subsequently proved that this was the murder weapon.

They had also found fingerprints and DNA material on the pistol: one set of fingerprints on the barrel had yet to be identified as they didn't show up on the police database. The other set of fingerprints was on the grip and these prints, as well as the DNA material, belonged to Irene Gallagher.

Then the technician explained about the plastic bag. It was a food freezer bag sold in the Fakta supermarket chain. She told them which factory produced the bag, and using molecular examination tests, she had also managed to establish that the relevant batch had been sold in the Copenhagen area. Finally she informed the court of a second set of fingerprints and a palm print found on the plastic bag that indicated the prints had been left when the previous bag on the roll had been torn off. The prints had yet to be identified, but due to their size were likely to be those of a child.

That was it, the technician was done. Christoffer Brinch prepared to cross-examine her.

'As far as the unidentified fingerprints on the pistol are concerned, is it correct to say that they're located as if the person who left them was handing the pistol to someone else? I mean, with the muzzle of the pistol pointing at him or herself?'

'Yes, that would be correct. That's exactly how they're positioned.'

'Were the fingerprints left before or after the pistol was last fired? That is, if it's possible to say anything about that.'

'That's definitely possible, and the fingerprints were left before.'

'Are there any prints on the pistol's trigger?'

'No.'

'Didn't you wonder about that?'

'Yes, a bit.'

'The fingerprints on the grip: do they include the forefinger?'

'Yes, they do.'

'Which should really be on the trigger, if you understand what I'm saying?'

'I do.'

'If we return to the unidentified fingerprints on the barrel, which suggest that the pistol was being passed to someone, do the prints on the grip thus correspond to someone taking the pistol?'

'Easily. In fact, I'd say definitely yes. At one point we compared the fingerprints on the barrel with those of Bjørn Lauritzen because we thought that he might have handed it to his killer. But there was no match.'

Christoffer Brinch thanked the technician, turned to the judge and paused for a few seconds before beginning to speak in a loud and clear voice.

'My client alleges that, as was asserted to the court by an earlier witness, when Deputy Homicide Chief Arne Pedersen was alone with Irene Gallagher during the interview in her home in Næstved, he handed her this pistol and asked her if she had seen it before.

'She took it, examined it and denied this, whereupon Deputy Homicide Chief Pedersen returned it to his briefcase. Thus it is my client's assertion that the prints on the pistol's barrel belong to Deputy Homicide Chief Pedersen, and the reason they weren't recognised by the police's own database is that Deputy Homicide

Chief Pedersen, or others colluding with him, removed his finger-prints from the database.

'My client also believes that the prints on the plastic bag in which the pistol was found belong to one of Deputy Homicide Chief Pedersen's two children. As I represent Irene Gallagher, may I respectfully ask the court to have these claims tested, and to ensure that this work is carried out by a body independent of the Copenhagen Police, and that I, or a court-appointed impartial person, be allowed to witness this process?'

There was silence in court. No one stirred. Everyone held their breath as they took in the enormity of Christoffer Brinch's words. Even the judge sat as if in a trance. Finally she pulled herself together.

'I assume you're aware that your charges are absurd?'

'I've made them on behalf of my client and they can easily be verified, which I—'

'Yes, I get that. Which leaves me no choice. This court is adjourned for three hours while I have these insane claims investigated, but we'll resume again at five o'clock – I don't want such an important undertaking left unreported overnight.'

At five o'clock precisely the court was back in session. The judge had a face like a thundercloud as she opened proceedings with an announcement. First, it had been established that Deputy Homicide Chief Arne Pedersen's fingerprints had been removed from the police fingerprint register. Secondly, Deputy Homicide Chief Arne Pedersen's fingerprints were a match with the prints found on the barrel of the pistol that had killed Bjørn Lauritzen. Thirdly, the fingerprints on the plastic bag in which the pistol was found belonged to one of Deputy Homicide Chief Arne Pedersen's twin sons – which one could not be determined, but it clearly didn't matter. The judge continued to speak, now addressing the Public Prosecutor.

'On the basis of this discovery, the court strongly suggests that all charges against Mrs Gallagher be withdrawn.'

Kirsten Hansen nodded. She had no choice in the matter, everyone knew that. The judge declared the case dismissed and told Irene Gallagher that she was free to go.

Half an hour later Christoffer Brinch shut himself in his office. Several of his staff had stayed on at work to congratulate him when he came in, but he had marched past them without a word. He took a bottle of brandy from his drinks cupboard, twisted off the cap and drank straight from the bottle. A little later, when the alcohol was starting to kick in, he snatched his beautifully framed diplomas and certificates of distinction from the wall behind his desk and smashed them against his computer screen in between swallowing mouthfuls of brandy. Afterwards, with great difficulty, he upended his bookcase. Several members of his staff rushed into his office in alarm. He screamed at them to leave and they quickly retreated.

Finally, one of the partners called his wife, saying her husband had lost the plot and she had to come to the office immediately. Mrs Brinch reacted calmly, patiently listened to the partner and then declared that if Christoffer chose to destroy his own property, it was his business, and if he drank himself senseless, it was probably because he needed to. However, she said she would be grateful if someone would drive him home or put him in a taxi when he eventually had got whatever was bugging him out of his system.

PART IV

The House in Bosnia

CHAPTER 55

'... up to three years for tampering with the evidence, in addition to being charged with the murder of Bjørn Lauritzen.'

In a flat voice the National Police Commissioner reviewed the charges and their potential consequences for Arne Pedersen. The Deputy Commissioner, who looked as if she hadn't slept the previous night, listened with a rigid, ashen face. The meeting was taking place in her office. The National Police Commissioner's secretary, a pleasant woman whom everyone at Police Headquarters liked and respected, was taking the minutes. Her eyes were moist and she would often dab them with a tissue. The Countess, who hadn't been invited to the meeting but had turned up with her husband without anyone objecting, was incandescent with rage. Her eyes were narrow, her mouth a tight line, and when she moved she did so in jerks, as if suppressed rage had short-circuited her range of movement. Only Konrad Simonsen seemed to take the situation in his stride.

The National Police Commissioner continued talking.

'I have set up a special investigative group of two experienced detectives from Aarhus Police and two from PET, who will examine the case against Pedersen.

'You need to know that he's likely to be charged and remanded in custody this afternoon, probably in isolation – don't minute this, Margrete – and I've set up another group to examine all his past cases. It's a legal catastrophe, a nightmare, I can't even begin—'

He got no further. The Countess leaned across the table and snatched away the piece of paper from which he had been reading while holding it up in front of himself almost like a shield. She scrunched it up and flicked the ball to the floor. Then she said, in a voice so filled with rage and unlike her normal tone that even her husband's jaw dropped: 'Don't think for one minute that you'll get away with this. In a few weeks, when we can prove that these ridiculous charges were fabricated, I'll personally make sure that your incompetence and disloyalty to your staff are exposed so extensively by the media that everyone will demand your departure, quicker than you can say "has-been".'

The Commissioner turned red, beads of sweat appearing around his nostrils. He stuttered, barely able to pronounce the words: 'Are you threatening me?'

'That's exactly what I'm doing. And these aren't empty threats, I can assure you.'

'For God's sake, Countess, we must be able to work something out. Something that doesn't … something we can all live with.'

The Commissioner looked around anxiously. His secretary said to the Countess: 'Do you genuinely believe you're helping matters? Because I don't.'

The Countess calmed herself down, but didn't apologise. Then, to everyone's surprise, the Deputy Commissioner stepped up. She was a woman who had recently grown into her role, in her own slightly awkward manner. One day at a time, she had secured the respect and loyalty of her staff. She said quietly to the National Police Commissioner: 'I'm happy to chair this meeting. You've already briefed me thoroughly. I should have offered to do so … perhaps even insisted on it … when we spoke earlier.'

She nodded to the secretary, indicating that she would no longer be required, then rose to her feet before anyone had time to reply and opened the door to her office. The Commissioner looked like a drowning man who had discovered a life jacket at the very last second. He started to mumble disconnected phrases – *that would be better …* *much more direct, more suitable for all ranks concerned* – and staggered towards the open door. The secretary gathered up his papers, nodded to the Deputy Commissioner and chased after her boss.

When the pair of them had left the office, the Deputy Commissioner closed the door and returned to her seat. On her way she briefly touched Konrad Simonsen on the shoulder, a gesture which, coming from anyone else, would have seemed out of place, almost condescending, but not from her. She wasn't like that, both her guests knew.

'I'm showing my hand now. If you, Simon, think that I should refuse to do what I'm about to outline for you, then tell me and I'll refuse. I'll be sacked, but so be it. I've been thinking a lot about whether to refuse the orders anyway, but I can't see how that would benefit anyone and it might even do more harm, not least to Arne. But it'll be your decision as well, not just mine.'

Simonsen and the Countess accepted her terms.

'You have two options, Simon. You can retire. Should you decide to do so, I can offer you an extremely favourable financial package. Or you can insist on staying and I'll then suspend you immediately for an indefinite period of time, but on full pay. Both of you – and really this applies to the whole Homicide Department – are banned from discussing this case with the media, and you, Simon, are banned from discussing it with anyone at all. I'm not sure if the latter ban is legally enforceable according to your union and general freedom of expression laws, but I haven't checked because we have much bigger problems. Over to you, Simon.'

Both women looked at him and concluded that he still seemed unperturbed. And indeed he replied immediately, without taking any time to consider her offer.

'I wouldn't dream of allowing myself to be pushed into retirement. And I agree: no one benefits from you being sacked.'

The Deputy Commissioner looked strangely relieved because it wasn't just her own job that had thus been saved.

'That was what I had hoped you would say. You'll get all of this in writing. Do you need me to inform you of your suspension formally?'

Konrad Simonsen made it easy for her.

'No, don't, I understand. I'll leave my warrant card on my desk before I go.'

'You're only allowed to take away personal property and, strictly speaking, I should send an officer to accompany you while you gather your things together, but I'm not going to because I don't care what you take. There, I've said it. I'll make sure that you get the keys to Simon's office, Countess, discreetly, because I presume you're not – despite all the bans – done with this case?'

The Countess replied grimly: 'You bet we're not.'

Simonsen got to his feet, but the Deputy Commissioner protested: 'Sit down, Simon.'

He did as he was told.

'I assume I'm not the only one who has been contemplating Arne's situation. I mean, of course no one believes that he was stupid enough to take a plastic bag from his own home and also leave his fingerprints on the pistol he's accused of planting to incriminate Irene Gallagher. Not even the most moronic criminal would do that, and Arne has been a police officer for more than twenty years. There's no way he would make such rookie mistakes, even if he had had malicious intent.

'Furthermore, it makes no sense that he would remove his prints from our register to avoid being identified from a fingerprint he could simply have wiped off the gun earlier. That is also the view of the investigative group. They don't believe he's guilty, but they don't know what else to believe. And neither do I. But then again, they can't pretend that Arne Pedersen's fingerprints weren't on that blasted pistol, because they were.'

She looked imploringly at Simonsen, who asked: 'Why are you speculating about matters of which you know nothing?'

The Deputy Commissioner reddened slightly. She asked almost humbly: 'Surely you don't believe that he did it?'

'No, he didn't. Anything else you want to know?'

There wasn't. On their way out, the Countess told the Deputy Commissioner, 'I'll call that wimp and apologise. After all, it's not his fault.'

Simonsen also had a parting comment.

'Make sure that Arne is put in a cell here at Police Headquarters, no matter whose arm you have to twist. And clear a section especially for him. You know that police officers in prison are rarely treated well by the other inmates.'

CHAPTER 56

FRIDAY 12 NOVEMBER 2010, SØLLERØD

The mood was sombre.

The Countess had ordered in from a restaurant, expensive food but it seemed out of place, as if there were something to celebrate, and she was wishing now that she hadn't done it. At the time it had seemed like a way to signal that she and her husband had their own life and were not easily intimidated – after all, worse things happened at sea. But the gesture had fallen flat. No one enjoyed the food, it had merely been shovelled down and not commented on. Kurt Melsing was visiting them. He had invited himself and the Countess thought it was a good idea. He was possibly the person with whom Simon worked best, despite their personalities being wildly different. Each headed a specialised department and was respected for their skills.

But during dinner and afterwards Kurt had been noticeably more subdued than he normally was, and Simon acted as if he had mentally moved to the moon. He was beyond reach of normal conversation and, when they spoke to him, needed the sentence repeated as though he had just woken up. At one point Kurt remarked on his friend's situation with ruthless honesty.

'I'm not surprised they suspended you, Simon. They had no choice. I would have done the same.'

The Countess protested. Simonsen didn't. Yes, of course they had to, but it was a minor issue, not worth getting riled by, and soon his attention had wandered away again.

As hostess the Countess tried to keep a minimum of conversation going, until she realised that she was primarily talking to herself and then she gave up. When the subsequent lengthy silence didn't seem to bother the men, she started reading a book.

At about seven o'clock someone rang the doorbell, and the Countess looked at her watch with a frown. Anna Mia and Klavs

Arnold were due, but that wasn't for another hour. She went to open the door and was startled. Standing outside was the last person she had expected to see: Christoffer Brinch, Irene Gallagher's defence lawyer.

He introduced himself politely with a small bow and apologised for turning up unannounced. However, he very much wanted to help, it was important to him.

The Countess asked suspiciously: 'Help with what?'

'With the terrible situation in which I have put Deputy Homicide Chief Arne Pedersen.'

'And how do you imagine you can help? It's a bit late for that, don't you think?'

Brinch didn't know, but there was bound to be something. The Countess didn't budge from the doorway.

'If you have come here to do penance, you can leave right now.'

'I'm not. The truth is I would have to defend the case in exactly the same way if I were to do it again. But now it's over and that makes all the difference.'

The Countess, who was perfectly aware of the conflict between his professional obligation and legal ethics, thought about it for a few seconds, then stepped aside with a brief and not very hospitable: 'All right then, in you come.'

In the living room, Christoffer Brinch repeated what he had said, then continued: 'As a defence lawyer, I'm bound by client confidentiality, of course, in relation to everything I become aware of as part of my work, and I can be sanctioned if I pass on information about a client without just cause. But I have every right to talk about a fictitious case involving a defence lawyer X, and a defendant Y, and a list of other non-existent persons.'

He proceeded to review the trial in detail and told them how Y was always several steps ahead and knew things of which the police and the Prosecutor were ignorant. Christoffer Brinch's parable was well prepared and very enlightening for the others. Even Simonsen listened closely.

Brinch concluded, 'I don't know how I can help you, but I'm an extremely good lawyer, I have an extensive network of expert witnesses and a considerable amount of legal expertise at my disposal. Besides, I'm a rich man and happy to use my own financial resources.'

No one answered this directly but it was met with a warming of the atmosphere that implied he could stay if he wanted to. The Countess enquired,

'Can I offer you anything?'

'Hmm ... I drank myself senseless last night, something I haven't done for about thirty years. Perhaps a glass of brandy – hair of the dog.'

The Countess smiled faintly, then she fetched a glass. When she passed it to him, she said: 'We have enough money, so financial assistance won't be necessary.'

Anna Mia and Klavs Arnold arrived shortly afterwards, but they were not alone. They had Anica Buch and Louise Berg in tow. Anna Mia kissed her father on his forehead, as did Louise, who claimed she owed him one. Then Anica kissed him as well, seeing as the other two had done. The four new arrivals fetched chairs and joined the circle. Anna Mia explained why she had brought two extra visitors. It was pure coincidence, or rather two *different* coincidences, because ...

The Countess stopped her by shaking her head. It didn't matter, they were here now, and as she could see – here the Countess glanced at Simon – her father didn't care why.

The three young women livened up the atmosphere and soon the conversation grew animated, with many suggestions being made about what they could do to fix the injustice towards Arne. Many different scenarios about how he could have been tricked into leaving his fingerprints were put forward, examined, rejected and reconsidered in a modified version. The Countess and Kurt Melsing eventually began to join in. Only Simonsen stayed out of it. Eventually the conversation faded away and everyone turned their attention to him.

'Dad, this is ground control. How about you wake up? What do you think we should do?' asked Anna Mia.

Konrad Simonsen shook his head and looked at each and every one of them in turn, almost as though he had only just discovered they were there. Then he said: 'I'm going to Serbia to see that house for myself and find out what happened there.'

CHAPTER 57

Arne Pedersen was put in a cell at Police Headquarters. Some prisoners were moved so he had a corridor to himself. No one objected. Apart from its protective value, this arrangement complied with the instruction in court that he spend two weeks being remanded in custody in isolation.

Neither the group that had been set up to investigate his case nor the Public Prosecutor objected. Perhaps this was a tacit admission that while no one seriously believed the charges against him were true, they had no other option given the evidence than to … well, charge him. As a result, colleagues or close friends could visit him in the custody cell whenever they wanted to. The custody officer broke every one of the normal rules for prisoners held in isolation, knowing full well that his boss wouldn't be seen anywhere near the cells; none of his superiors wanted to be dragged into the case. Besides, the Deputy Homicide Chief had given him his word that he would not abuse his privilege to influence the legalities of his case, and the custody officer wasn't going to be someone who couldn't show a little bit of common sense in the face of otherwise rigid rules. In short: he looked the other way no matter who visited or for how long they stayed, and he also overlooked time and time again the prisoner's mobile lying in plain sight on the only table in the cell.

'Do you need anything?'

Klavs Arnold had taken out his notepad, ready to take requests. Arne Pedersen said no, nothing, he had everything he needed.

'Just call, no matter what time it is. You can also call if you want to talk. Do you have a charger for your phone?'

Yes, he had a charger for his phone, and yes, he would call if necessary. Arne Pedersen sounded weary. He added: 'And please don't say that Stella can bake me a cake, because it would be the fourth cake I've been promised today.'

Stella was Klavs Arnold's wife. She was a busy woman who didn't normally bake cakes for men – they could bake their own if they wanted cake – but on this occasion Arne Pedersen's remark hit a bullseye. He saw the disappointment in his colleague's face and felt bad.

'Tell her I look forward to tasting the result of her efforts and that it's very kind of her to think about me. Now, would you please fill me in on what's going on rather than acting as my butler?'

Klavs Arnold told him what he knew about Simon and his trip abroad, which wasn't much. Even so Arne Pedersen had several questions of which the Jutlander could answer only a few. Yet his friend persisted with them, so it took some time before Klavs Arnold reached the real reason for his visit.

'Together you and I must review, moment by moment, every scenario, even the most far-fetched, where you could possibly have left your fingerprints on the barrel of that blasted pistol. And if we don't come up with something the first time round, we'll do it again, and this time we'll be even more thorough, and we'll go on and on like that until we find the answer.

'It might be today, it might be tomorrow, it might be in two weeks … it doesn't matter. What does is that we get to the truth. So let's initially focus on the timeframe from the canal boat killings until the point we discover the pistol in Irene Gallagher's garage. I have a printout of your calendar, and we'll start by getting an overall impression of the period.'

Arne Pedersen was sceptical.

'I've already thought back to every situation, of course I have, and there's no truth, as you call it, to be found anywhere.'

'Yes, there is, and we're starting now.'

'The thought that that bitch was in my home is unbearable. That she rifled through my private things – I can't stand it.'

'Yes, I'm sure that's not much fun. Now, let's get going.'

'Why did you say initially focus? I couldn't have left the prints outside the timeframe you've chosen, that's impossible.'

Klavs Arnold, who had also considered various scenarios carefully without getting anywhere, reacted sharply to this.

'And that's the last time the two of us use the word "impossible". It's a fact that your prints are on that gun, and given that it did happen, then obviously it wasn't impossible at all. So start thinking, Arne, now!'

They drafted a log listing where he had been, with whom, and what he had been doing in the forty-day period identified by Klavs. It was slow going, despite Arne's excellent memory. The Jutlander insisted on as many details as possible. Did the meeting finish at one o'clock or a quarter-past one? Arne Pedersen threw up his hands, surely it didn't matter, but apparently it did. And so they inched their way forward until they were finally done, four hours later.

'I'm going to my office now to type all this up. I'll give you a copy, which you'll review – several times if need be – and anything you remember: add it. No matter how trivial, just add it. Meanwhile, I'll check everything that can be verified independently, so we're as sure as we can be that we haven't made any mistakes.'

Arne Pedersen was exhausted. He lay down on his bed, interlaced his fingers behind his head and looked at the Jutlander before telling him, 'I once read a book about prisoners who dug a tunnel from their barracks and out under the fence that surrounded a prison camp during the war. This happened in several camps, including at Horserød, where this story took place. The point is that the man responsible for the tunnel, its architect if you like, couldn't let it go when it was finished. Instead he continued to improve it, strengthen it, add more light, align the sides so they looked nice, though by this point it already served its purpose, which was to get the prisoners out.'

Klavs frowned at him.

'You want to tunnel your way out of here?'

Arne eased out one hand and slapped it over his eyes.

'Sometimes I think you deliberately hide behind your ignorance. It was an analogy with you and your pedantic list, you moron.'

His criticism bounced off the other man. Klavs said practically, 'You can't tunnel your way out from the first floor, and where I come from, we have no use for an ana-what-do-you-call-it.'

They had played this game many times before, the pair of them. Winding each other up, pulling each other's leg. Often just to pass the time, if they were on an assignment where the hours dragged. It was odd that they had the energy for it now, Arne Pedersen thought, and without having decided whether he really wanted to involve his partner in this or not, said: 'I'm getting a divorce. My wife sent me a letter this morning – a bloody letter – she couldn't even be bothered to come here in person. Anyway, that's how it is.'

Klavs Pedersen, who had just got up to leave, sat down again.

'How do you feel about that?'

'I don't know. It's strange, but I'm nowhere near as sad as I ought to be. In fact, not at all. In some respects it's a relief. I'll miss the boys the most.'

'They won't disappear just because you don't live with their mother.'

Klavs was right, of course.

'Would you please do me a really big favour?' Arne asked him.

Klavs nodded without knowing what it was.

'Will you go see my kids tonight and tell them that I've done nothing wrong, no matter what they may have heard? I'd really appreciate that.'

Klavs gestured to the mobile on the table right next to Arne.

'Why don't you just call them yourself?'

'I'm afraid their mother will lodge a formal complaint that I have a mobile in my cell. Remember, I'm supposed to be remanded in isolation. I don't even know if she'll let you in, but it would be great if you would at least try. I mean, she's being completely unreasonable – she's acting as if this whole circus is purely to make her life miserable. But you go now, I have a book I want to finish … and … thank you, Klavs.'

Klavs dismissed this show of gratitude with a grunt. Then he glanced at his watch.

'You won't be doing any reading. You have a visitor in five minutes.'

'Who is it?'

'Someone way too cute and young for you, Arne.'

CHAPTER 58

'Go and smile at her. Everyone does the first time they see her in real life.'

Anica Buch nudged Konrad Simonsen and, when a handful of Chinese tourists were summoned by their guide at that same moment, he took up her suggestion since he wouldn't have to fight for space.

On their way out, Anica said: 'I can see why the staff get a bit fed up with her. Here we are in one of the world's biggest and most impressive museums, countless immortal works of art, and then half the visitors make a beeline to her from the entrance without bothering to look left or right. Then they spend three minutes staring before heading for the exit.'

'But it's the staff who put up the arrows to her.'

'Yes, otherwise they would spend all their time telling visitors where to go. But what did you think? Did she live up to your expectations?'

Simonsen nodded, absolutely, she was everything he had hoped for.

It was his first visit to Paris. Though he had, in his own opinion, travelled a fair amount, he had somehow never managed to visit this city. It wasn't deliberate, of course, it was just how it had panned out.

They had arrived the night before and gone directly to their small hotel in Saint-Germain-des-Prés. Everyone had wanted to go straight to bed after two busy days.

When Simonsen had announced last Friday that he would be going to Serbia, a battle had immediately erupted as to who would go with him. Everyone felt they were the obvious travelling companion with just the right skills for the trip. They appealed to Simonsen one after the other, without anyone questioning that the decision was up to him. Which he made – brutally – taking no account of the candidates' feelings.

'Kurt, because we'll need someone to carry out forensic investigation, and Anica because she speaks the language. I need no one else and it's not up for discussion, this isn't a holiday. And before you complain, remember that Arne is in prison, and we have a job to do. You other two are needed here.'

Even the Countess and Klavs Arnold had accepted this, without whingeing. Only Anna Mia spoke up and she sounded disappointed.

'So what will I be doing?'

'You can comfort me.'

It was Louise Berg who said this. Anna Mia said out loud what everyone else was thinking.

'Because you've gone and got yourself involved with a married man, who is twice your age and who'll definitely be released from prison in a couple of weeks?'

Louise laughed lightly, tossed her hair in a practised manner and said with a smile: 'No, because I'm not going to Serbia.'

Anna Mia concluded that Louise might end up being a good friend, after which she, too, accepted her father's decision.

Christoffer Brinch also disagreed, but in his own quiet and highly effective manner.

'Don't forget that you're no longer backed by a bureaucracy. Someone needs to organise hotels, train tickets, plane tickets, car hire and accommodation in the village of Ljubicevac, to mention just a few of your … logistical problems.

'Besides, you'll be travelling to Bosnia-Herzegovina and not Serbia, more precisely the Republika Srpska – yes, it's completely impossible to pronounce, unless you're Serbian – both Srebrenica and Ljubicevac lie near Bosnia-Herzegovina's western border with Serbia.'

Kurt Melsing said in a tone that suggested the mere thought of it exhausted him: 'Then there are visas.'

The lawyer corrected him. Danish nationals could travel freely around Bosnia-Herzegovina for up to ninety days, so no visa was necessary. But he recommended going by train, *so wonderfully anonymous*, from Copenhagen to Paris and then onwards from there by plane. France had, so far as he recalled, a connection to Sarajevo via Zagreb.

Konrad Simonsen was beginning to catch on.

'You're a seasoned traveller?'

Christoffer Brinch didn't answer directly, but leaned towards him.

'I'll handle all the practicalities. The three of you will have nothing to worry about. In contrast to you, I have a powerful organisation at my disposal. No one in my firm, not even the newest intern, is in any doubt that supporting you is top priority.'

Simonsen was convinced.

Thus he, Kurt Melsing and Anica Buch had left Copenhagen Central Railway Station early in the morning, and the lawyer had been true to his word. He had bought first-class train tickets and reserved a compartment, just for them. In addition, he had arranged a veritable feast of drinks and sandwiches, which beat the offerings of the train caterers by miles. More importantly, however, he had promised Kurt Melsing that anything he needed for the trip would be waiting for him in Sarajevo. It meant that the forensic scientist was spared the trouble of having to bring his own equipment, which was cumbersome and could cause problems with customs. Melsing had simply handed a list to Christoffer Brinch, who would be travelling to Sarajevo on a direct flight. They assumed that no one was watching him.

They changed trains in Hamburg and again in Cologne, where they had an early dinner – winter stew with potato dumplings – in full view of the enormous and beautiful Cologne Cathedral, which turned out to be right next to the Central Station.

During dinner the Deputy Commissioner called to tell them that Anica Buch had been assigned to special duties and would be reporting directly to her, so she was now free to go abroad. By that point, the young officer was already several hundred kilometres away from her usual place of work. Konrad Simonsen thanked the Deputy Commissioner, rang off and thought that his new member of staff couldn't be accused of trying to climb the greasy pole. She had thrown in her lot with the Homicide Department at a time when it was experiencing its greatest crisis ever. He was impressed and would bear her loyalty in mind when things eventually got back to normal.

That morning in Paris Simonsen had been woken by the noise coming though his balcony door from the street below, where greengrocers were setting up their stalls and the first car horns honked impatiently. They had breakfasted together in a café along the Seine, but afterwards Kurt had gone back to the hotel to rest. He felt unwell and worried that he was getting the flu. Anica had then selected five sights Simonsen simply had to see on his first visit to Paris. He had spent most of the day being a tourist – a tourist with his own personal guide at that.

The Louvre had been the last item on Anica's list. From there they went back to the hotel where Simonsen was hoping to catch a nap before dinner.

But it was not to be.

In her room Anica discovered that someone had left a note on the small desk by the window. It was on a sheet of white A4 paper, the kind used in a printer. The handwriting was in red capital letters and was in Cyrillic.

CHAPTER 59

TUESDAY 16 NOVEMBER 2010, SARAJEVO

Kurt Melsing studied the threatening letter for a long time. Simonsen left him alone, drawing conclusions, while he himself looked at the cloud formation below him. The plane prepared for landing in Sarajevo Airport. Eventually Kurt said angrily: 'Why didn't you show me this earlier?'

Simonsen had dreaded this question and he had no good answer. He replied honestly: 'I was scared you would want us to go home.'

Kurt narrowed his eyes and said slowly, 'This mustn't happen again, Simon. Because then I really would go back to Denmark. What the hell were you thinking?'

'I'm sorry. I made a mistake.'

'A mistake you won't make again!'

'Yes, a mistake I won't make again.'

'Right, let's forget about it. Tell me the circumstances once more, please.'

Simonsen did, although there was nothing much to tell. Anica had discovered the note on the table in her hotel room yesterday afternoon. Together they had gone downstairs to reception and shortly afterwards managed to speak to the maid who had serviced the room. She had found the letter on the floor in the hallway when she let herself in around eleven that morning to clean. She took it to be a message someone had stuck under the door and had picked it up and put it on the desk, so the guest couldn't possibly miss it.

The maid couldn't read it herself, but Anica Buch could. The words were in Serbian and announced that if the Danes didn't stay out of Bosnia, they risked a bullet to the back of their heads. Kurt nodded inappropriately as if he were endorsing this threat, and stated without a hint of fear: 'That doesn't sound very nice. What's the drawing and what does it say?'

The threat had come with a logo at the bottom to indicate the identity of the sender. A crudely drawn sketch of two words circled two-thirds of the way around a horseshoe shape. Simonsen explained, 'It's a wolf – yes, I know it looks like a duck with teeth, but the text says: *Drina Wolves.*'

Kurt interrupted him.

'Drina Wolves? I thought those thugs were eliminated ages ago.'

'You know this organisation?'

'A paramilitary group from the Balkan wars – not to be confused with the Drina Corps, which was a regular part of the Serbian Army. It was the unit primarily responsible for the Srebrenica massacre, and its commander was, as far as I recall, later convicted in The Hague. Drina Wolves, however, was a random collection of Serbian psychopaths, no military standards but a vile instrument for the abuse of civilians.

'Murder, torture, arson, terror, rapes, ethnic cleansing – they represented the whole spectrum of evil. It was usually Bosnian

Muslims who would bear the brunt, but also any Croatian families they came across. However, something here doesn't add up.'

Simonsen had worked that out too. First, there was no way that FE would ever collaborate with a bunch of butchers like the Drina Wolves. Secondly, if the organisation still existed, its leading members were busy hiding from the authorities for fear of a one-way ticket to The Hague, and it was hard to believe that the organisation was resourceful enough to discover and locate three Danes in Paris. The two men agreed on this. Simonsen summed up.

'Someone knows we're coming to Bosnia and they don't like it, that's pretty much all we can deduce. Along with something about a dog's bark being worse than its bite.'

'I agree. But what does Anica say?'

'She's scared of them – the Wolves, I mean – though she's trying to hide it. I think she may have some past experience of them, but I haven't asked her directly. Even though … I mean, she came to Denmark in 1990, and I don't know if they existed back then.'

'And yet she has come with us to Sarajevo. Because I hope you gave her the choice of going home after finding this?'

'Of course, and she thought it was too dangerous for us to continue, but if I wasn't going to go back, neither was she.'

The three Danes were all waved through customs. Likewise the passport official barely bothered checking their papers before letting them in. Konrad Simonsen wondered about this; tiny signals had set off his internal alarm. Not only had the custom officers let them into the country without checking their passports, it was as if they didn't even want to look at them. Something wasn't right.

In the arrivals hall Christoffer Brinch greeted them like long-lost friends, but then again, he was like that – ebullient – and he valued good old-fashioned courtesy, as they had learned. Kurt Melsing asked immediately about his equipment: the chemicals, microscope, a computer with a decent satellite connection. The lawyer assured him that everything was in order, but if they would please follow him, he had a hire car parked right outside.

They picked up their luggage, but had taken only a few steps when three young officers stopped them. One asked in perfect English, politely but firmly, if they would accompany him. There was no alternative. The two other officers formed a discreet rear-guard a few metres behind them, but the message was clear.

They were taken to a customs area and shown into a room where they were asked to sit down at a table. They were told to wait. The officer apologised for the inconvenience, but there were some circumstances he needed to investigate. He didn't reply to Christoffer Brinch's many questions.

Just over half an hour later the officer returned with a colleague, almost a carbon copy of himself but armed with a notepad and pen, who would appear to be there to take minutes. The officer demanded to see their passports and the details of each were care-fully copied down by the minute-taker. When that was done, the officer asked them why they had come to Bosnia-Herzegovina, and Christoffer Brinch replied on everyone's behalf.

They had come to this wonderful country for a holiday and to enjoy the beautiful landscape. The officer wanted to know how they knew one another and without skipping a beat, the lawyer invented a bridge club whose annual proceeds were spent on European breaks. This was their fourth trip. Previous visits had been to Portugal, Scotland and Corsica. The minute-taker wrote as quickly as he could. When he was finished, both officers left with a 'wait, please', and while the Danes waited they agreed that they had sailed through the interview.

Shortly afterwards a woman entered the room. She wasn't wear-ing a uniform, but from the way in which she ordered the soldier who had accompanied her to a corner, it was clear that she was used to being in charge. Then she announced that regrettably all four of them would be put on the first plane back to Paris. It departed in five hours, but she would organise food and drink for them in the meantime. She, too, spoke excellent English.

Christoffer Brinch protested indignantly. What legal grounds did she have for this deportation? As far as he was aware Bosnia-Herzegovina was a democracy with a decent legal system – she cut him off, then brought up the failed trial in Copenhagen of Irene Gallagher and the subsequent arrest of a senior police officer.

She knew that they had come to her country to find out what had happened in and around the Danish observation post in

Ljubicevac in the summer of 1995. However, fifteen minutes ago, they had all lied to the police about the real reason for their visit, which was against the law – and it was on the strength of this offence that they would be denied entry. Christoffer Brinch fell silent; the woman was right, and his legal expertise couldn't help him now. Instead he produced a fat wad of Euros from his inside pocket and held it in his hand. Perhaps they could find a way out of this situation. She shook her head, no, they couldn't, and he should put his money away, the sight of it could easily be misinterpreted. Christoffer Brinch put the money away as quickly as he had produced it.

The woman then addressed Anica Buch directly in Bosnian, her hands also doing some talking. When she had finished, Anica summed up.

'She says that Bosnia has a long and traumatic history: Nazis during the Second World War, Ustaša – the fascist Croatian terror organisation that killed tens of thousands of innocent Serbs – and finally, the Serbian Army's genocide of Muslims in 1995. They're just three vile episodes amongst many. But it's her and her people's history, and it shouldn't be told by four random foreigners, who know nothing about what they risk stirring up.'

Konrad Simonsen thought that she had a point. He also thought that their visit would be an extremely short one, and indeed it seemed that would be the case during the next ten minutes as they read through and signed their deportation papers. Then the minute-taker slipped back into the room and handed the woman a folded piece of paper, which she opened and read. Her attitude changed completely. She explained, without a hint of personal irritation, that a huge mistake would appear to have been made, and apologised profusely for detaining them unnecessarily. They were free to go.

Outside the airport an astonished Christoffer Brinch turned to Simonsen.

'What on earth was that all about?'

'Well, I wouldn't like to say. But I think that FE might have beaten us to it and asked for a favour.'

'But why were we suddenly allowed to enter the country after all, how did that happen?'

'That decision came from someone with a lot of power,' Konrad Simonsen answered. It was as close as he could get to an explanation.

CHAPTER 60

Christoffer Brinch had hired a Land Rover, and when he and his fellow travellers emerged from the airport, he found a parking ticket on the windscreen. Served him right, Konrad Simonsen thought; the lawyer had parked with the front of the car projecting over a pedestrian crossing, so people were having to walk around it.

A traffic warden – or possibly a traffic police officer, he couldn't tell – was waiting for them. He looked cross, but the plain-clothes woman who had thrown them out of the country only a few minutes earlier had accompanied them outside. She ushered the warden away and scrunched up the parking ticket. They thanked her and said goodbye. She waved after them as they drove off, which seemed completely bizarre, to put it mildly.

As Christoffer Brinch knew the way, he did the driving. Soon they had left Sarajevo behind and were heading north-east. The weather was misty and above them a pale sun struggled to break through the grey and white cloud cover. The lawyer explained: 'It's only eighty kilometres to the village as the crow flies, but the terrain becomes increasingly mountainous the further we get into the Dinaric Alps, while the roads become correspondingly poorer. The last sixteen kilometres are gravel only. Yesterday the trip took me almost three hours, but then again the weather wasn't as good as it is today, so if you assume that we'll get there by two, two-thirty, you won't be far wrong. On the plus side, it's a beautiful drive with impressive mountain scenery and autumnal colours. I bet you won't ever have seen anything quite as beautiful.'

Konrad Simonsen decided to use the time to have a nap. He had no interest in the landscape, no matter how impressive it was. Anica Buch had her own way of dealing with the length of the trip. 'If you want a break from the driving, I'm happy to take over.' She tried to make her offer sound like a helpful gesture, but the lawyer turned her down. It was nice of her, but he already knew the way. Only Kurt Melsing paid attention to the landscape. They drove past a giant billboard for Coca-Cola and some sheep in a field.

At one point Brinch handed out envelopes and satellite phones. The envelopes contained money, enough to meet their needs during their visit. He explained: 'You can forget about credit cards out in the countryside, they don't use them. The currency is called *Konvertibilna Mark*, and one of those is the equivalent of just under four Danish kroner. Your new phones will have coverage wherever you are – except when driving through mountain tunnels, then the connection goes immediately. We'll be staying in groups of two; each pair will have its own host family, who will also provide us with food. Conditions are primitive but perfectly tolerable, and your rooms are clean and tidy, in case you were wondering. There is a bathroom, but the water is rather cold.'

Anica asked: 'Who will be staying with whom? Have you decided that yet?'

The lawyer hadn't, it was up to them to decide. Kurt Melsing turned to Simonsen, who pretended not to notice him. Instead he said: 'Anica and I will take one of the houses.'

He didn't explain his decision and nobody questioned it.

Brinch said, 'Now don't be nervous, I'm not going to launch into a lecture, but in brief, Bosnia-Herzegovina comprises primarily two regions: the Federation of Bosnia and Herzegovina, which is popu-lated by Croats and Bosnian Muslims known as Bosniaks, and the Republika Srpska, dominated by Serbs. Ljubicevac is in the second region. The population is between four and five million and the official languages are Bosnian, Croatian and Serbian, which all ...'

Konrad Simonsen yawned. He should have known that to a lawyer 'in brief' was an extremely flexible concept.

In Banja Luka, about halfway to their destination, they stopped for a break. It was the second-biggest town in the country, and the administrative centre of the Republic of Srpska. They found an international hotel where they ate an excellent if somewhat bland lunch, and Brinch refuelled the car.

When they were ready to drive on, Anica managed to get behind the wheel, which speeded up the trip considerably. Not that her driving was hazardous, because it wasn't, rather the lawyer's driving had been very ... cautious, Simonsen thought, glad of the change. However, half an hour later the quality of the road deteriorated and the terrain grew so rugged that even Anica had to reduce their speed to a crawl, to avoid skidding off a cliff side or ending up in one of the countless idyllic mountain lakes they passed. Simonsen had to go back on his earlier lack of interest in the landscape.

Everyone watched in awe as new vistas, each more beautiful than the last, slowly rolled past while they were driven deeper and deeper into the mountains. An expanse of pale yellow hills merged in soft curves; the horizon was broken up by limestone colossi soaring aggressively towards the sky, some scattered with trees in their gaudy autumn foliage although most were naked and barren. Then forest took over with trees growing so close to the road that it grew dark inside the car, except when they crossed bridges spanning turbulent rivers. Whenever they entered a tunnel, and there were plenty of those, it was impossible to guess what they would find on the other side. More forest, an open limestone landscape with not a single shrub for miles around or a small cluster of grey houses with giant haystacks outside? It could be any one of these. They rarely saw any people.

They reached their destination as it was coming up to two o'clock. The village of Ljubicevac lay in a forested area at the foot of the mountains, near the border to Serbia. They were descending towards their destination from a ridge when Brinch pointed out the village to them, and they had plenty of time to study it before they arrived. A few dozen houses were huddled together with no obvious signs of planning. Some of them were made from crude bricks, others of roughly dressed stone. The roofs were often faded and made from thuja or cedarwood shingles nailed in place, but in most cases the wood had been replaced by galvanised iron sheets, which had acquired a beautiful rusted patina as the galvanising wore off. Seen from the ridge this gave the village a strangely picturesque look.

Only two-thirds of the houses had more than one storey. A fence enclosed an oval pen stretching around half the village in which a herd of pigs wandered about with their snouts to the ground. On the far side of the village was a beautiful cemetery, surrounded by a fence, whose size was disproportionate to that of the village, one of many testimonies to the Balkan wars. Another was a house missing its gable; the sooty rafters in the attic told their own terrible story.

Simonsen asked Christoffer Brinch: 'How do people here make their living?'

'Quite a few of them have a small pension, I believe. Apart from that they sell sheep and vegetables at the market in Nova Kasaba, about ten kilometres away. But don't be deceived by the size of the village. Many of the houses are empty. I don't know if it's because of the civil war or if people simply moved away.'

'Any shops?'

'One, a village store of some sort. And a meeting place where the old people sit outside at a few tables, smoking and drinking wine or playing pétanque. I had a glass of wine there myself yesterday and it was very good – brilliant in fact. And a glass cost only one Danish krone! Hang on, Anica, take a left up there. I want to show you something.'

She drove another two hundred metres after turning off the road before she was told to pull over next to an enclosed paddock where a donkey was munching the sparse grass. Brinch got out and the others followed suit. The lawyer pointed towards the donkey.

'That's where Little Denmark used to be. I had some of the locals point out the place to me yesterday.'

Konrad Simonsen looked about him. There was forest behind him and stretching up to the fence. To his left he could make out the highest village roofs, which were on about the same level and separated by an area of coarse yellow grass, apparently with no roads or paths crossing it. Below him several copses merged into the one he was standing near, and the road continued in a long curve until it disappeared into the vegetation a kilometre or two below him. Apart from the village, he could see no other houses, only a flock of sheep scattered here and there on the slopes. His eyes settled on the fence in front of him. Some boards were of relatively fresh spruce, while the rest were of splintered grey or white timber, clearly years old. He addressed Kurt.

'Once we've unpacked, we're coming back up here. We need to be absolutely sure of the location. When we are, I want us to make a map of the area – just a sketch, it doesn't have to be completely accurate. That's something you're good at, isn't it?'

'Saying I'm good at it is probably an exaggeration of my cartographic skills. But I'm willing to give it a try.'

That would do so far as Simonsen was concerned He only needed a sketch, and possibly some photographs to back it up.

Anica's and Simonsen's hosts turned out to be an elderly couple. The man was bony and tough with liver-spotted skin and clear, watery blue eyes; the woman small and chubby in a floral dress and with peeling pink polish on her nails. Both of them were around seventy. They had made the first floor of the house available to their guests and intended to sleep in the outhouse themselves, Anica explained to Simonsen as the wife talked nineteen to the dozen.

They were shown into the house, which reminded them more than anything of a 1950s Danish holiday cabin. Their hostess gestured to the staircase behind the kitchen, which took them to the first floor. While Simonsen struggled with his heavy case, Anica said: 'There's a big room and a box room. I'll take the box room. Our hostess stressed several times I must do this, though it's what I would have done anyway. Dinner is at six o'clock, it's chicken, and she asked if we would prefer to eat alone, but I said no. Is that OK?'

It was. Simonsen made it up the stairs and opened the door to his room. As Anica passed him, she asked: 'Please may I come with you to the observation post?'

Yes, that was all right with him. She thanked him, and he entered his room without replying.

The room was large and bright, dominated by a double bed, but with space for a desk, two big teak wardrobes, which had been cleared out for him, and a comfortable revolving leather chair with its back to him and facing a bookcase on which sat a small television. It was neat and tidy. A bowl of big red apples had been set out for him. He decided that it had proved to be a huge advantage that Christoffer Brinch had come with them. Apart from the incident in the airport, which wasn't the lawyer's fault, their trip here had been unproblematic.

He had barely finished the thought when the armchair revolved one hundred and eighty degrees.

In it sat a younger man – one he had seen before.

'Welcome to Bosnia, Detective Chief Superintendent. Come in and close the door behind you.'

CHAPTER 61

Arne Pedersen's living quarters had improved even further. His floor space had been doubled and now included the neighbouring cell. The custody officer also let the two doors into the corridor stay open so long as his prisoner promised only to move between cells. The neighbouring cell was a purely practical arrangement rather than any gesture towards improving his living conditions. It had been turned into an interim interview room where up to five people could sit down around the table, unless they suffered from claustrophobia.

The four experienced investigators from the group the National Police Commissioner had set up to examine the charges against Arne Pedersen had quickly reached the same conclusion as everyone else, including all the crime reporters in Denmark: namely that the Deputy Homicide Chief must have been tricked into leaving his prints on the pistol used to kill Bjørn Lauritzen. It was the only explanation that made any sense. Every other theory was absurd.

Nor did anyone dispute that the revelation that Pedersen's fingerprints were on the murder weapon had caused the trial of Irene Gallagher to collapse. Therefore she was the only person who could have benefited from the set-up. These were the findings of the group and they were supported by a highly classified conversation with FE, which had denied point-blank that they had sabotaged the trial. FE might have been involved in the destruction of evidence against their former employee, they couldn't dismiss this conjecture entirely, and yes, they had wanted Gallagher to be acquitted and then for her to go away as far as possible, but they had never tried to pin the blame for her alleged crimes on innocent people, and they were definitely not responsible for the Deputy Homicide Chief's travails.

The two PET agents in the group were sure that their military colleagues were telling the truth, and soon convinced the two police investigators of the same. What now remained to be done was to find out how Arne Pedersen's fingerprints had found their way onto the murder weapon. The group started working with Klavs Arnold on the only lead it made any sense to investigate. As a result Arne Pedersen was interviewed constantly, which explained why the neighbouring cell had been brought into use. Eventually, though, the prisoner had had enough. He invoked the Administration of Justice Act.

'The defendant has no duty to give evidence.'

'Shut up, Arne, and join us next door.'

'I want a lawyer.'

'And I want a pay rise seeing as you can't even be bothered to help yourself. Please could you get a move on? I'm picking up the kids today, preferably before five o'clock or I'm in deep trouble with the nursery school teachers.'

The Countess came to visit Arne Pedersen. She brought a late lunch for them – delicious open sandwiches that she knew he loved – as well as beer, if he fancied it, and mineral water. She hauled in a sizeable picnic basket as if they were going on a long trip. While she laid the table, she asked: 'How are you, Arne?'

'I'm terrible, they're brainwashing me. And that heavy-handed Jutlander is the worst.'

'I was referring to your divorce.'

'I don't think I've taken it on board yet. I hardly ever think about it, and I'm not just saying that because I don't want to talk about it. It's the truth. I miss my children, but I would do that even if I weren't locked up. Have you heard from Simon?'

'I'll be speaking to him tonight and I'll contact you afterwards, I promise.'

And, speak of the devil, just at that point Simonsen rang.

The Countess listened – he had cut short her initial exclamation of joy on hearing from him, saying there wasn't time for that. Arne Pedersen was on tenterhooks, but her focused expression and the six brief declarations of *yes* in a row didn't make much sense. She rounded off by assuring her husband that she understood, though she very much looked as if she didn't when he rang off.

'What did he want?' Arne asked.

'He wanted me to go to the American Embassy.'

She sounded mystified.

'Of course he does.'

'Immediately.'

'Well, don't keep them waiting. What are you going to do when you get there?'

'I don't know. Do you know the American ambassador to Denmark?'

Arne Pedersen didn't, as it happened, the Americans must have forgotten to invite him to the reception ... She interrupted him – '*No, not personally, you idiot!*' – but his name and what he looked like. He borrowed her Smartphone and soon found what she was looking for online. He was better at that sort of thing than she was.

The Ambassador turned out to be an attractive woman of about fifty. Arne Pedersen said: 'An ambassador is usually some rich man or woman who has contributed big time to the President's election coffers, and who then gets Denmark or some other small country for a couple of years in return, but I think she might be a real career diplomat, not just a rich upstart, if I remember rightly. I had just forgotten that she was a woman. Now you get out of here and find out what on earth is going on. I want to know everything, so call me!'

He practically shoved the Countess out of the cell while stressing how dreadful everything was for him and that it was crucial she should call him later.

In a distracted voice she promised to do so, and had forgotten all about him by the time she left the building.

The American Embassy in Copenhagen is normally regarded as one of the most heavily guarded locations in Denmark, but this November afternoon the Countess felt as if she were merely visiting a department store.

She parked illegally in a side street close to the Embassy, and thought if she didn't get a ticket, there was something amiss with the Copenhagen traffic wardens. She strolled to the embassy where she was met by two men who appeared to have been waiting outside for her. The first uttered her name interrogatively, and she confirmed it, after which she was allowed to bypass every single security check before being ushered into a lift, which brought her to the second floor. She was then shown down a corridor and into the Ambassador's office.

The Ambassador welcomed her almost effusively, but without it becoming embarrassing, which showed great diplomatic skill given the situation. She was offered a chair and immediately afterwards a telephone call was transferred to the Ambassador's landline on her desk. She spoke for a few minutes before passing the handset to her guest. The caller was Simonsen, who asked his wife where she was. She told him. Then he told her about a man he had met under strange circumstances. A man who claimed to be a cultural attaché at the American Embassy, a frequent visitor to the Ambassador's office and the holder of a degree in Danish language and literature, specialising in the 'Late-nineteenth-century Modern Breakthrough', from the University of California, Berkeley. Simonsen was calling to ask the Countess to verify the man's identity by asking a few questions. He passed the handset to a stranger with a friendly voice, who was ready to answer her.

She looked around the office and asked him: 'What's the picture behind the Ambassador's desk, next to the portrait of the American President?'

He answered her by quoting the opening words: *"In Congress, Fourth of July 1776. A declaration by the representatives of the United States of America, in general Congress assembled"*,' and then informed her that she was looking at one of approximately two hundred original copies of the Declaration of Independence. It was the personal property of the Ambassador and was valued at more than three million kroner.

The Countess thought that put an end to Arne Pedersen's theory the Ambassador was a career diplomat. She thanked the man on the phone and asked him to tell her something about Andreas Brandes's famous *Critique of Nineteenth-Century Poetry*, and could almost hear his smile across the phone line: he was terribly sorry, but sadly that was one of the lectures he had missed. He didn't correct her deliberate error of getting Brandes's first name and the title of the book wrong. She thanked him, and was handed back to her husband. The Countess pronounced her verdict without hesitation.

'He's associated with the embassy, but unlikely to be their cultural attaché. There's no way he ever studied nineteenth-century Danish literature.'

Then she added carefully, in order not to upset him as she knew her husband was embarrassed about his poor English: 'And you do know that John Doe isn't his real name, don't you?'

CHAPTER 62

'Now do you believe me?'

Konrad Simonsen tossed his satellite phone on the bed. Yes, he did. He had just had it confirmed that his visitor was working for the Americans in a senior capacity.

'You may be listed as your country's cultural attaché, but that's not your real job and your alleged academic expertise in Danish literature is a lie.'

The man didn't deny this, but looked rather reproachfully at Simonsen. Did he really have to bring that up?

'Nor is your name John Doe.'

The man smiled. He had the kind of eyes that invoked trust.

'No, it isn't.'

'So what is your name?'

'It's whatever you want it to be.'

Simonsen got up, overcome by a sudden revulsion against this constant secrecy. He never really knew what was going on, everyone else was always one step ahead of him, and he constantly had to guess at a truth, which – in the best-case scenario – he could only ever hope to confirm partially. He unzipped his suitcase and started angrily chucking clothes into one of the wardrobes. He was an eyewitness, he was possibly even on the front line, but he wasn't taking part as a soldier nor as a general, only as a measly little spectator and he was fed up with his role. He raised his voice:

'Tell me your name!'

'John Tyler.'

'And is that your real name?'

'No.'

Simonsen threw his empty suitcase on top of the wardrobe. Then he composed himself and pulled up a chair next to John Tyler.

'You're good at spotting people who are following you, I hear. Is that a skill you acquired while fostering cultural links? And where did you learn to speak Danish? It's pretty near perfect.'

'At Berkeley, as I told you earlier, and I've spent a lot of time in Copenhagen.'

'You seem to know a great deal about me, but I know nothing about you. I don't like that. Was it you who made sure that my fellow travellers and I were allowed into the country even though we had already been thrown out?'

'Yes.'

'How did you do that?'

'By talking to a man who spoke to another man who let you in. But aren't you much more interested in *why*?'

Simonsen ignored his question, though the man was right, of course.

'How did you know that we had been detained?'

'Because you didn't leave the airport.'

'And yet here you are in my room before I've even arrived. How is that possible?'

'I came by helicopter.'

'How did you know my destination?'

'We followed Mr Brinch yesterday, then asked around the village.'

'I could have chosen another room. You couldn't know that. And who are *we*?'

'Then I would currently be speaking to Mr Melsing; it makes no difference to us. And *we* are me and the people I work with.'

'You're telling me not to ask any questions about them?'

'Oh, you're welcome to ask.'

Outside a dog started barking, it sounded frightened. Simonsen got up and peered through the window. An old man was threatening the dog with his stick. He wore a black beret, a grey sweater and trousers. He looked strong and sinewy; perhaps he had beaten the animal in the past. It certainly looked like it. Simonsen couldn't see the dog now. He turned back and continued his awkward conversation as he tried to exert an authority he didn't feel.

'You'll tell me why you and your country are so interested in Irene Gallagher and my visit to Bosnia-Herzegovina. Afterwards

I'll tell you why I'm here, though I have a hunch that you already know. Then we'll see if there are grounds for a partnership.'

John Tyler pondered the suggestion for a while and replied slowly, as if to convince himself that what he said was the truth.

'I'll tell you about Irene Gallagher, but not in detail. You have knowledge of a location, which I don't, but it's one that I would very much like to find. Why I want to know this location you may discover later, if you find what you're looking for, and … one other thing also falls into place.'

'I thought that people like you worked closely with your Danish counterparts. Why don't you just ask them for the location of the place you say I know? I would be very surprised if they refused to help you.'

'That makes two of us. I, too, am surprised that they won't co-operate. But as far as Irene Gallagher is concerned, then …'

John Tyler told him that Irene Gallagher, as Simonsen probably already knew, had worked for several years for … *let's call it the US Army*. In connection with that she had acquired considerable knowledge about the precautions America took around the world to protect itself against international terrorism. She knew the set-up inside out, so to speak. In 2002 she had told her personal contact in … in an important American agency, that she had discovered a particularly dangerous operative in an Al-Qaeda cell in Sarajevo, who was planning to abduct a senior American civil servant.

The message had been passed on to the local CIA agent, but no steps were taken to deal with the operative, as any such intervention normally required verification from two independent sources. Shortly afterwards, however, the CIA agent received a similar tip-off from Copenhagen, which led to the capture of the operative, a twenty-year-old Bosnian university student and – this wasn't something he was proud of – the young man was subjected to extraordinary rendition for interrogation in another country, one where the authorities weren't so fussy when it came to 'enhanced interrogation methods'. Unfortunately it turned out that the operative knew nothing about Al-Qaeda. Even worse the operative didn't survive, so far as he knew.

John Tyler spoke increasingly slowly. Simonsen summarised his story.

'The boy was kidnapped, flown to a dictatorship where he was tortured and killed, all when he had nothing to tell?'

'I did say I'm not proud of it. Some years later, two of my colleagues happened to be talking, and they discovered that Irene Gallagher was the source of *both* tip-offs about the operative who had turned out to be innocent. At the same time, other alarm bells started ringing. I don't want to go into detail about that now, but an internal investigation was launched. This investigation is still ongoing. I'm a part of it.'

'What's the link between your sad tale and this place?'

'When I started looking into the matter, I discovered that the alleged operative had been summoned as a witness at the war crimes tribunal in The Hague, just before Irene Gallagher concocted the false accusations against him.'

'He was due to give evidence about things that had happened here in 1995?'

'Yes, but like I said, we'll get to that later.'

'Did Irene Gallagher know that he had been summoned?'

'Yes, she did. She also knew that we were very keen to have a word with her. A wish she definitely didn't share.'

They had reached a tentative understanding. Simonsen could see where the conversation was heading and gave himself plenty of time to consider. Outside the sun had broken through the clouds and was now casting a white beam of light through the window onto the rose-patterned wallpaper on the end wall. A shadow from the bedpost broke the beam.

'Why have you made yourself known to me? You could just have followed us and we would have led you to your supposed location.'

'Because we have mutual interests and because you would probably have noticed me.'

'You can have us thrown out of the country if we don't help you.'

'Probably, but what good would that do?'

'None, only I noticed that you haven't threatened me with it.'

'Threats make a very poor basis for a partnership.'

'What if I don't want to work with you?'

'Then I've made a mistake. I should have followed you as you suggested.'

'And how do you see me explaining this to the others?'

'It's straightforward – we used to be four, now we're five.'

Simonsen made up his mind. He stuck out his hand and they shook firmly. Then he said: 'You should have kidnapped Irene Gallagher, and not that poor young man.'

It was the first time during the conversation that John Tyler's voice revealed any emotion.

'Trust me, that option has been given serious consideration, but sadly it's not going to happen.'

CHAPTER 63

TUESDAY 16 NOVEMBER 2010, LJUBICEVAC

The donkey had moved. It was now at the farthest end of the paddock.

Otherwise nothing had changed, and Simonsen concluded that this reflected the lifestyle of the village: stagnant, sleepy, every day the same. Then he remembered the house with no gable and regretted his condescension. Given his own comfortable life and trivial problems, he really had no right to judge.

He had just arrived, along with Anica Buch. Kurt Melsing was already there. He was sitting on a folding chair with a wooden board on his lap supporting four pieces of A4 paper that he had taped together. With a soft pencil in one hand and a rubber in the other he was drawing the map Simonsen had asked him to produce. He was almost done and the result was excellent.

Christoffer Brinch turned up soon afterwards. The lawyer began by apologising for his presence in a self-effacing manner and assuring

Konrad Simonsen that he was not going to interfere. He knew he was only there to make practical arrangements, *but I'm fascinated by what you're doing, so if it's all right ...* He sounded like an overexcited little boy and it bordered on the embarrassing. Simonsen peered down the road at the American, who was making his way towards them.

'The man down there is called John Tyler. He works for the American government. I've had a long conversation with him from which I have learned that he shares our interest in Irene Gallagher, so from now on we'll be working with him. He speaks Danish and has more information than we do, so he could prove very useful. You need to know that he's a little shy when it comes to talking about himself, so please don't ask too many questions.'

Kurt Melsing asked: 'And you're quite sure that Mr Tyler is who he says he is?'

Simonsen assured him that he was, which was good enough for Kurt. But not for Anica Buch, who sounded surprisingly angry.

'Does he speak Serbian?'

Simonsen didn't know, but she could always ask him. His new young colleague didn't seem to welcome any competition. She was a rough diamond whose edges he needed to smooth, but time would probably see to that.

John Tyler shook hands and smiled as he introduced himself to them and they to him. Then he took a small step back and assumed a waiting position as if to indicate that he wasn't here to pull rank or show off to an already established group.

Simonsen told the American about Little Denmark and how their first task was to establish that it had definitely been located where they were currently standing. Kurt, who had resumed working on his map, said without looking up: 'This is the place, Simon. But I'm sure you'll want to check for yourself.'

Simonsen took a rolled-up picture from his inside pocket and smoothed it out. It was of the observation post in the spring of 1995.

The photograph showed the end wall of the observation post, which was roughly three metres tall. It was constructed from black, khaki and white sandbags, the walls were approximately one metre thick, and the roof flat and layered. The first layer was a row of solid branches, followed by three layers of sandbags, then more branches, this time laid at an angle across the first ones before it was topped with another three layers of sandbags. A soldier was proudly standing in front of it. He wore a camouflage uniform with the Danish flag on his shoulder, and a blue UN beret. Right behind the building the barrels of two Leopard tanks protruded, potent and menacing. In the background, which was somewhat blurred, an M-shaped formation of white rock soared into the air. Four slopes of reddish-brown alpine scree rolled down the rocks and all the way out of the picture to the left.

Kurt pointed to a roughly hewn slab of granite, sunk into the ground at the edge of the road a few metres behind Simonsen.

'If you squat down over there, you'll see that the view is exactly the same. You have at least two unique markers in the background: the limestone massif, of course, but also the contours of the land-scape. I've noticed a few other things, if you're still not convinced.'

Simonsen was impressed: Kurt had only seen the photograph once before, and that was several weeks ago. Then again he was famous for his photographic memory.

Christoffer Brinch and Anica Buch followed Simonsen to the milestone. All three of them squatted down and compared the view to the photograph while John Tyler, without having been asked, acted as the soldier in the picture so the dimensions could be estab-lished. There was no doubt: this was where Little Denmark had once stood. When he had rejoined Kurt, Simonsen asked: 'What were the other things you mentioned?'

'Do you still have doubts?'

'No, but I would like to know.'

Kurt hastily finished the last corner of his map, then he got up and showed the others an area where the ground had been disturbed. He explained that sandbags were filled with soil if no sand was available, and there wasn't any here. Soil and sand offered very simi-lar protection against bullets. Then he produced some metal pieces from his pocket.

'And I found these bits. Your soldiers did a good job clearing up after themselves, I must say, but these had been tossed in the grass at the edge of the forest. There are many more of them, I only took a few.'

'They're from cans, aren't they?' said Anica.

Kurt replied: 'They are indeed ring pulls, and they are made from aluminium.'

In connection with their investigation the Homicide Department had questioned fourteen former soldiers who had been with Bjørn Lauritzen in Bosnia. Simonsen had read all the witness statements thoroughly several times; by now he almost knew them by heart. One of the veterans had told him how they used to play poker at Little Denmark to pass the time. Unfortunately, a couple of soldiers had lost big, which had soured the mood, so Bjørn Lauritzen had banned them from gambling with money. Instead they used ring pulls from cans and for a time they had worn their chips in a string around their neck as evidence of their skill at card games.

Simonsen wondered why, when back home in Copenhagen, Kurt would stammer and mumble incomprehensibly. He could be a real trial to talk to. Here on this trip, however, he spoke freely and fluently.

Simonsen spent the next ten minutes exploring the landscape with the binoculars he had brought along. He had managed to get exactly the same brand as the pair Bjørn Lauritzen had owned fifteen years earlier. In particular Simonsen was looking for the farmhouse, which he knew had been situated approximately one to one and a half kilometres down the slope at the end of the road, at the start of the forest. But it was gone now. Nevertheless he took his time, ignoring the fact the others were waiting for him. When he was done, he handed the binoculars to Kurt, who declined them, and nor did any of the others want to borrow them, so he took the home-made map and used it to indicate his plan.

'We're going down there tomorrow, we'll take the car as Kurt will probably need to bring a lot of equipment. Let's say we'll leave at nine. But there's another matter that might also be worth looking into. Bjørn Lauritzen and Ole Nysted allegedly drove a tank all the way down there, up through the forest and reappeared behind where we are now, after which they joined their mates from the observation group. A little later everyone retreated to Tuzla. In the forest Lauritzen and Nysted picked up a handful of refugees, who were sitting on the tank when they returned to Little Denmark. Later, it seems all three tanks carried refugees to Tuzla. But that might be an unrelated story. In any case, in order to get through the forest, the tank had to drive along some sort of waterway. And the reason I'm so vague about this is that several witnesses each describe it differently: as a brook, a river, a stream, a watercourse, an almost dried up riverbed. I don't know which is correct, but I would like to find out.'

Kurt said, 'Shouldn't we wait until tomorrow? It'll be dark in an hour, Simon. Perhaps Anica should start by asking the locals if there is a watercourse of some kind in the forest; they're bound to know.'

'I would like to make the most of the rest of the daylight. If you look at the landscape and compare it to witness accounts, the watercourse has to be behind us, so we might as well walk over and check, seeing that we're here. And then we can possibly return another day.'

John Tyler and Kurt walked with Simonsen. Anica was sent back to the village to find some locals to talk to, as Kurt had suggested, and Brinch went with her. He didn't fancy exploring an unfamiliar forest: a summary when they returned was good enough for him.

The three men made good progress along the path, which joined the road a few hundred metres before the old observation post and led into the forest. Simonsen seized the opportunity to ask a personal question of his old friend.

'How can it be, Kurt, that you speak … yes, I'm being frank now … completely normally here, while back home you're often inarticulate?'

Kurt shook his head.

'I don't know. It has been like that for me ever since I was a child. At school no one could understand me, and they sent me off for all sorts of tests. At some point they even medicated me, but I never had any problems in the playground. Only in class. Now I've accepted that it's just the way I am, and that I'll probably never know why. Nor does it matter. What difference would it make?'

Konrad Simonsen thanked him for his honest answer. Tyler told them about a woman he knew who was the same, except that she stuttered.

The path ended without them finding any watercourse. They hesitated in front of the forest; it was quite dense. Tyler checked his watch.

'We have twenty-five minutes of light left, that's ten minutes in, ten minutes out and a five-minute margin. What do you say? It's your call.'

The two older men said ten minutes was fine and that they preferred John Tyler to lead the way and keep an eye on the time as he seemed best equipped for it. They walked slowly through the trees: Hungarian and Caucasian oak, Balkan beech often smothered by aggressive climbers that reached all the way up to the crown and, on the slopes where the limestone was exposed, gnarled pine trees growing like trolls, knotted and warty, but tough survivors in this hostile environment.

Everywhere the forest floor was covered by wet, rotted leaves that could prove treacherous when the ground underneath was hard. Simonsen slipped twice with no serious consequences, tersely rejecting the helping hands trying to get him back on his feet.

They had walked less than one hundred metres before a broad watercourse blocked their path. It wound like a serpent through the forest, its banks wide and pretty much merged with the vegetation. The water – yellow from the many fallen leaves – flowed relatively quickly down the ridge towards the south. A heron was perched on a rock in a river bend, half-hidden by a bay tree, exploring the water below it.

Konrad Simon concluded, 'They could have driven a tank through the river, especially in the summer when the water level is lower than it is now. And they would have been able to get through the forest and onto the path we've just followed. Many of the trees would have been young then, and the tank could easily flatten any that got in its way. It's too late today, but it would be good if a younger man would volunteer tomorrow to walk along the bank to where the road ends. Perhaps he could start an hour earlier than the rest of us.'

John Tyler replied with a grin: 'Then you need to explain to the younger man exactly why you want him to walk along your watercourse, because he doesn't quite understand yet.'

Simonsen promised to give him further directions now that he had been noble enough to volunteer, but said that would have to wait until they were back on the road. The going was easier there.

Kurt said darkly, 'So this is where those bastards got away with mass murder. It must have been truly revolting. But why on earth Lauritzen would be driving his tank around in here is beyond my imagination. If he wanted to rescue some of the victims, he would be better off out on the tundra where the Serbian Army unit firing shells at the refugees was in his line of fire. He must have known that.'

Konrad Simonsen had another theory. He had a horrible suspicion that the soldiers in the tank had a more selfish reason for driving down the river, but he didn't want to share it with anyone yet. When they were back by the road, he loaned his binoculars to John Tyler and told him, 'Bjørn Lauritzen and his junior drove along the river from where we just were to where the road ends and the forest begins. But they drove in the opposite direction. Back then there was a farmhouse there, it's gone now, but that's where we need to look around tomorrow morning.'

Tyler lowered the binoculars.

'There was a house there?'

Konrad Simonsen nodded.

The American had grown pale. 'Holy shit.'

CHAPTER 64

TUESDAY 16 NOVEMBER 2010, POLICE HEADQUARTERS

Arne Pedersen was a disappointed man. The Countess had forgotten him.

He complained to Klavs Arnold: their agreement could not be clearer – she had promised, not just once but several times, that she would definitely call him when she was done at the Embassy to let him know what had happened. But she hadn't called, she had forgotten all about him.

Klavs Arnold's sympathy was lukewarm. He knew nothing about an embassy visit and nor did he care, he had enough on his plate as it was. His wife had sent him off straight after dinner. She would put the kids to bed and clear up, he didn't have to worry about that, his job was to help poor unjustly incarcerated Arne Pedersen. Last night poor unjustly incarcerated Arne Pedersen had been the subject of an extended prime-time news programme about how dreadful it was for him to lose his job and be brutally separated from his loving family all because of a situation where anyone with half a brain could see that he had been framed.

This was followed by a short interview with his wife and the twins – 'It's hard to fall asleep at night when they've put Daddy in prison' – after which a law professor portentously reviewed just some of the many flaws and shortcomings with which the Administration of Justice Act, in his learned opinion, was riddled. The feature had sent Arne Pedersen's popularity rating soaring, not least among the female half of the country's population, and that included Stella Arnold.

Klavs said: 'She'll probably call later. Meanwhile, let us go over the top three possibilities again. I've a theory, which might just prove to be the solution.'

'But she promised to ring me straightaway, not later.'

The Jutlander ignored this and pulled out a slim file from the considerable pile of papers he had brought with him, now lying on the table between them. He opened it on the first page.

Klavs Arnold and the four officers from the investigative group had worked hard and meticulously. Based on the list of Pedersen's activities in the period spanning 22 August to 29 September, they had, after extensive discussion, selected eight episodes that they thought most likely to have put their colleague in a situation where he could have been tricked into leaving his fingerprint on the small Ruger pistol.

Out of the eight incidents they had identified three as highly likely: during Irene Gallagher's interview in her home on 20 September, and during the two conversations Arne Pedersen had had with the now late Ole Nysted on 13 and 17 September respectively, when on the first visit Arne Pedersen had become drunk, and on the second the veteran had bitten him.

Arne suggested: 'Please could we start with your theory?'

He knew only too well how mentally exhausting it was to go over the same sequence of events yet again. It was tempting to go down the path he had already travelled, using the same words and phrases, parroting them without thinking afresh. But if he did that, his story would be a waste of everyone's time because it would be nothing but a copy of the last time he told it.

Klavs explained his theory.

'It's highly likely that Irene Gallagher broke into your home, though we don't know when, as well as Pauline's flat, which she probably did on the morning of the twenty-second of August, before she picked Bjørn Lauritzen up at Charlottenlund Beach and drove him back to his home in the forest. Now let's presume that she *didn't* break into your home at a time when she knew there *wouldn't* be anyone there, but on the evening of the thirteenth of September when she had learned from Ole Nysted that you were extremely drunk. She could have taken your hand and pressed it around the barrel without you waking up.'

The two men discussed the proposal for about fifteen minutes, but neither of them really warmed to it, not even Klavs Arnold. Viewed through Irene Gallagher's eyes it was risky, and there were too many unknown factors for her to have a realistic expectation of getting what she had come for. They let the proposal die a death and began the hard part.

Together they went through the top three possibilities again for the fifth time, but this time Klavs had new information. He had brought along a selection of photographs the forensic technicians had taken inside the hut while Ole Nysted was lying dead from carbon monoxide poisoning on his sofa. The death had been treated as suspicious, so the technicians had been careful to record everything and the images were sharp.

Most were of the body of the deceased, but the technicians had also photographed his hut, and Klavs had selected these interior shots in the hope that they would stimulate Arne's already excellent memory. It wasn't a bad idea. Arne did actually remember a few more details once he looked at the pictures; during his first visit he had picked up an ashtray from the floor after accidentally knocking it off the coffee table when he and Ole Nysted were drinking, and on his second visit he had left the door open while he went to fetch firewood, not just to make it easier when he came back with the logs, but also to get some fresh air into the hut.

Although they had little value, Klavs Arnold praised him for these minor new observations.

'Perhaps we should take a look at that hut tomorrow. Everything inside it is untouched since Nysted's death; it's still a crime scene. If you recount your story when we're inside the hut, you'll probably remember more.'

'I'm sure you haven't forgotten I'm on remand. The custody officers have already been more than fair, and I don't want to push my luck.'

'You won't have to. The investigative group is simply taking you off for an important review of a crime scene. We can do this officially, and I would like nothing more than to drag you around Denmark in handcuffs.'

Arne said nothing to this. Something else had caught his attention. He pointed to a picture of the dead veteran.

'His injured foot mended remarkably quickly. Look, his bandage is gone. Five days earlier, when I visited him on the seventeenth, he could hardly walk.'

'My God, you're right. None of us thought about that. I don't have the post-mortem report here but I'll get it immediately.'

Klavs Arnold had already stood up. They both felt a sudden tingling excitement. This was new. This was a place they hadn't been before.

Klavs Arnold had had a sneak preview of the report while he rushed back to Arne Pedersen's extra cell and was practically shouting as he entered.

'Nothing ... there's nothing here about an injury to his foot! He tricked you.'

They read the four pages of the post-mortem report closely, but it was true. There was absolutely no way that Ole Nysted had cut his foot with an axe five days prior to his death. The next question was obvious, and Klavs asked it.

'Why would he want to do that?'

But no matter how many theories they came up with – and Arne Pedersen was now re-energised, newly enthusiastic about the undertaking – they could think of only two occasions where the fake injury had played a part in what had unfolded: the first was when Arne Pedersen had gone outside to get firewood, and the second was when, at his host's request, he had fetched a bottle of whisky from a cupboard. Those were the only two instances, so they had to go over them again. Arne started with the firewood.

'I'm sitting on the sofa to his left, then he asks if I would please fetch some logs … Bloody hell, that's it! I'm an idiot. I should have worked this out ages ago. That's why she filed down the front sight – it all fits, as do the young couple in the forest – everything makes sense now!'

In his excitement Arne had leaped up so quickly that he knocked over his chair. At that moment his mobile rang. He looked at it suspiciously, now wasn't a good time for calls, but answered it nevertheless. It was the Countess. Klavs Arnold tried with all his might to practise his normally well-developed patience. Dear God, it was only a matter of minutes before he would know the answer, and what did a few minutes matter in the greater scheme of things? But he couldn't help thinking that if his friend dropped dead right now – after all, such things have been known to happen – then Klavs would never know how Arne Pedersen's fingerprint had ended up on the pistol. It was a frightening thought.

CHAPTER 65

WEDNESDAY 17 NOVEMBER 2010, LJUBICEVAC

The sound of a gunshot jolted Konrad Simonsen from his sleep. He sat up in bed, wondering if the bang had been a part of his dream. Once he had collected himself, he fumbled for the alarm clock he had put by the headboard. The clock face glowed when he picked it up, and he could see the time: almost two-thirty in the morning. He got out of bed and turned on the light, but to no avail. He knew electricity in Ljubicevac was unreliable; power cuts were common, especially at night. Brinch had already warned them of this during yesterday's drive from Sarajevo, without anyone paying much attention.

By the faint light from the alarm clock, he found his clothes and managed to pull on his trousers, shoes and jacket, giving up on his shirt and socks. There was a knock on the door, and he unlocked and opened it. It was Anica, as he had expected. He couldn't see her, only make out her outline. She asked anxiously: 'That was a gunshot, wasn't it?'

'I think so.'

'It was right outside, wasn't it?'

'It might have been. I'll check.'

Her agitation spilled over into panic. She didn't want to be alone, she was coming with him, they would walk down together, she didn't want to be alone under any circumstances, he mustn't leave her. He felt her grab his arm and assured her calmly that he wouldn't leave her, they would go downstairs together, of course they would. He was quite sure that she had nothing to worry about, they were perfectly safe indoors. He freed himself, put on his coat and realised that his eyes had now adapted to the darkness, which was no longer quite so dense.

Outside the pale moon lightened the darkness on the side of the street where the Land Rover was parked. Simonsen could make out two figures standing next to it. A couple of dogs nearby started howling, protesting pitifully that something in the night wasn't as it should be. Soon afterwards Simonsen's hostess appeared in the street. She was carrying a child whom he hadn't seen before. The child clung to her and buried its head in the crook of her neck. Simonsen and Anica walked towards their car, but stopped when the beam of a strong torch swung around the corner. The beam bounced up and down, then the person wielding it joined them. It was Kurt Melsing.

'What happened, Simon? There was a shot.'

They walked up to the car where by now four old men had gathered. They grinned, pointed and chattered to one another in their own language. The windscreen of the car was gone except for a rim of glass shards all around the rubber seal. Kurt pushed the old men aside and shone his torch through the hole to assess the damage to the car.

'Sawn-off shotgun ... with that spread there's no doubt about it. A single shot from a distance of three to four metres, I would think. They're lead pellets, banned in Denmark for environmental reasons since 1996. My guess is three-point-five millimetres, size three. There's no damage to the car except for the windscreen, and we can easily drive it once we've cleared out the glass and the pellets.'

Anica asked: 'Who would do such a thing? I don't like this.'

Both men played the situation down. After all, no real harm had been done. Perhaps she could ask the spectators if any of them knew what had happened. She did, but to no avail.

They stayed by the car for another fifteen minutes, as did the locals who had turned up. There was no practical reason for doing so, it was more a feeling that they needed to be with other people while digesting the incident. Simonsen started to get cold. It was a chilly night, probably close to freezing.

'That's enough for now, isn't it? After all, we're not going to learn anything else tonight,' he said.

Kurt handed Simonsen his torch. His phone had a torch function so he could get back to his own room without any difficulties. Simonsen wondered if his mobile had a similar facility. He must find that out at some point.

He and Anica returned to their rooms. In the passage he handed her the torch, but as he was about to leave her, she said: 'Simon.'

She had never called him that before, and it sounded wrong coming from her, pushy even, possibly because she was so young or possibly because they hadn't known each other for very long. Nevertheless he responded with an obliging: 'Yes?'

'I know this sounds foolish, but please would you come with me to my room to see if anyone is there? When I left, I didn't have time to lock the door behind me and … Oh, I know it sounds silly, but please would you?'

Of course he would, it was no trouble.

Simonsen pointed the torch slowly and systematically into each corner, twice, and at her request also under the bed. 'There's no one here, Anica, you're safe to go to sleep.' Still she hesitated. She said she could see that he was right, but she was still scared. He offered to stay a little longer, which was when he spotted the note as he happened to point the torch at her bed.

'What is it, Simon?' she cried. 'They've been here, haven't they? They've been in my room!' She pressed herself against the wall and whimpered something in Serbian.

The paper was the same as in Paris, an ordinary sheet of printer A4. The handwriting was also the same, red Cyrillic capitals, but the wolf drawing had been executed a little more skilfully than the last time. The message was pinned to her pillow with a cheap souvenir dagger, the handle gilded and shaped like a dragon. It had been pushed through the paper and into the pillow.

He took the dagger and put it in his coat pocket. With the message folded around the torch in one hand and Anica's hand in the other, he pulled her towards his room. In his suitcase he found a hip flask of rum, which he opened, pouring some into the cap. After two shots, she began to relax.

'You take my bed and try to get some sleep. I'll sit in the chair. I'm not going anywhere. We'll read the letter tomorrow,' he told her.

She protested vehemently. She had already read some of it, she had to read the rest. Had to! Didn't he understand? He relented and handed her the message, while pointing the torch at the ceiling so she could read by the glow it cast. She sat stony-faced for a long time, as if she couldn't decipher the letters, then she started to cry softly. He wondered if he should sit down next to her and hold her, but decided against it.

'Please translate it for me. I, too, want to know what it says.'

She tried, but it took time and to begin with her words came haltingly. The first part read: *Muslim sow, before we are done …* She struggled with the next sentence. There was no direct Danish translation, but the meaning was … very bad, in a sexual way. She started crying again, but in between two sobs, translated: *Muslim sow, before we are done with your arse, you will beg us to kill you.*

When she had finally stopped crying, she said firmly: 'We have to go home first thing tomorrow morning.'

He dismissed this. 'Let's wait and see.'

She protested, almost angrily: 'Don't you understand? They're going to rape me, torture me to death.'

'I know it doesn't sound good, but I don't think it'll come to that. Try and calm down, get some rest.'

He turned off the torch. After a while he could hear that her breathing had grown heavy and more regular. He made himself comfortable in the chair so that he, too, could sleep when suddenly she said: 'You can lie on the bed if you want.'

Simonsen made no reply. Instead he faked a few snores, as if he had fallen asleep.

CHAPTER 66

Louise laughed, and Arne laughed too. Her laughter was infectious, and he liked laughing with her. It felt wonderful.

They were sitting on the bed in his cell, leaning against the wall, their feet pulled up underneath them as they watched *Toy Story 3* on Louise's Mac. Louise had downloaded it properly, not streamed it illegally from the Internet. She made a point of stressing her honesty; she didn't want to break any laws when she was with him, or at least not yet. She had also bought fizzy drinks in huge paper cups with straws, and even bigger tubs of popcorn. *As if we were in a real cinema.* She kissed him and he ate his popcorn. The drink, however, he only sipped. He couldn't stand the oversweet taste. It was just past twelve noon, and Louise wasn't due at work until six. Arne thought that being held in isolation had its upside, so he forced down a mouthful of drink and dulled the taste with a handful of popcorn.

They were halfway through the film when the custody officer knocked and announced that his lordship had other visitors and that it was preferable he entertained them in the adjacent suite. Shortly afterwards Klavs and the two PET men from the National Police Commissioner's investigative group arrived. They could barely fit into the cell. One PET man said to Louise: 'I'm afraid we'll have to interrupt your movie, we need Arne. But I'm sure you'll be allowed to wait in here. He'll only be an hour, possibly less.'

Louise Berg wasn't used to being bossed about by men. She rose, sized up the PET man from head to foot, exhaled, pulled a face and stuck her nose in the air.

'No, thank you, I won't be sitting in a cell on my own. And I'm sure your conversation can wait until we've finished watching our film.'

The PET man looked imploringly at Arne, who laughed. Now what?

Klavs Arnold took over. He had once worked as a bouncer at a nightclub and was well versed in female moods: from huffy to coquettish via challenging, oh, so vulnerable, argumentative, self-righteous and many more. The common denominator was that he didn't put up with any of them. He knew how to handle his colleague's young girlfriend, so he grabbed her by the elbow, turned her to face the door and marched her outside with his hand on her back and a firm grip on her shoulder.

'Off you go, Louise – we'll see you later.'

She accepted the situation, partly because she liked Klavs Arnold, and partly because she knew she couldn't expect to win every battle. Life wasn't like that.

'Get your hands off me, you orc! I'm perfectly capable of walking on my own. You owe me a movie. And get my Mac, I need it.'

One of the officers from the investigative group had rigged up a projector, which he controlled from his laptop. He aimed the lens directly at the cell wall and the arrangement worked reasonably well. Klavs had been appointed speaker and would be presenting the first set of results. He had been given the best seat at the table and was looking straight at the pictures projected onto the wall. The Jutlander began by saying that everyone had worked overtime, especially Forensic Services, and that some of the results were still at the preliminary stage. It was definitely just a matter of time before they were confirmed, but at least Arne had been warned if, against all expectations, problems arose later. Then Klavs asked for his first picture, which showed Ole Nysted's kitchen cupboard with its orange curtains.

'This is how you saw the hut veteran's—'

Arne cut him off.

'Please don't call him that. His name was Ole Nysted.'

'That's how you referred to him before.'

'Yes, and I'm trying hard not to.'

Klavs conceded that it was a fair point, then he tried again.

'This was how you saw Ole Nysted's kitchen cupboard the first time you visited him. Or rather, you didn't see it, because the curtain was drawn shut. Which is also how it looks today, as you'll see shortly.'

He described the cupboard: it was an old teak bookcase which had been painted, then screwed directly into the wooden wall of the hut. The bookcase was divided down the middle and had three shelves on each side. A curtain rail had been attached to the top for the two orange curtains, but the rod was approximately twenty centimetres longer than the cupboard on both sides, and in order to fit it, battens had been screwed into each side of the bookcase. Here Arne interrupted.

'Please would you get to the point?'

The prisoner, however, was ignored. Klavs continued his presentation.

'The battens become important later on. The curtains were probably put up to protect the contents of the bookcase from the smoky stove, not to make it look nice. Next picture.'

This showed a much-enlarged screw hole.

'The holes tell us that someone – and that person is likely to have been Irene Gallagher – fitted two cupboard doors behind the curtains in such a way that when she later removed them, she would leave only a few insignificant screw holes.'

One of the PET men insisted on taking over at this point. He, too, was getting fed up with the level of detail.

'Technical explanations and all the evidence backing it up will be available in our report. The bottom line is that the handle on one cupboard door, the one that wouldn't open, wasn't really a handle at all, but the barrel of a gun. Only you couldn't see that from the front because the design of the handle was one where you had to reach through a hole in the cupboard door.'

Klavs took over again. He explained, somewhat superfluously, that some of their conclusions were based on Arne's own witness statement, but as it was supported by the technical evidence, the investigative group had accepted his explanation.

'In addition to your statement, we have four other pieces of either technical or strong circumstantial evidence that Irene Gallagher attached two doors to that cupboard specifically in order to incriminate you, before removing them later.

'The first piece of evidence is the size of the pistol. Its relative rarity and small calibre now make sense because Gallagher needed a barrel that was round and not too wide. A Ruger Mark I 22LR is particularly suitable, and she also filed off the front sight to have more of the barrel's length to work with when it needed to double up as a cupboard door handle. More importantly, however, is that under an electron microscope we discovered two pressure marks on the barrel, which indicate metal brackets having been used to fix the pistol to the inside of the cupboard door.'

The PET officer took over, again without having been asked. He was clearly an impatient man, something that suited Arne just fine.

'The two other pieces of evidence are very technical, and you can read about them later. Finally we have the young man and his married Roma girlfriend who on the fourteenth of September photographed Irene Gallagher in Lorup Forest with her toolbox and two grey boards under her arm. The date fits perfectly, as do the boards when you estimate their size from the photographs and compare them to the measurements of the kitchen cupboard doors.

Though Forensic Services have pointed out there is a margin for error of one point four per cent in their calculations.'

'But was Irene Gallagher capable of building a cupboard door like that? It doesn't sound straightforward.' Arne put the question to the PET officer so as not to trigger another lengthy explanation from Klavs Arnold but it was the Jutlander who replied.

'Definitely. When she was young, she helped out at her grandfather's carpentry business, remember. And she wasn't building an altarpiece. On the contrary, the more home-made the cupboard looked, the better.'

One of the PET officers had brought four bottles of beer with him. He opened them all and the men toasted the excellent result.

Afterwards one of the investigating officers cautiously ventured that he had a tiny favour to ask of the two Homicide men, and please don't misunderstand, but ...

It was a very long run-up to what turned out to be a simple request.

'Would you mind if we present this as something that the four of us in the investigative group discovered? I don't want to take credit for your work, I hope you know that, but it looks better if the solution comes from us, rather than you. Later, in six months, say, we promise to leak the truth to our colleagues.'

Neither Arne Pedersen nor Klavs Arnold minded; in fact they thought it sounded very sensible as this way there could be no suspicion of a fix by the man under investigation and his Homicide colleagues. One of the PET officers drained his beer and ended the visit by addressing Arne.

'I'll talk to the Police Prosecutor and ask him to drop the charges against you. You can expect to be released in an hour at the most. But I'm happy to take responsibility if you want to go to your office right now and wait there. Just don't leave Police Headquarters.'

But Arne Pedersen declined. He didn't have a bed in his office and all this talking had made him sleepy, so he thought he would make the most of his last few minutes in prison and have a nap.

CHAPTER 67

It took some time to clear out the shards of glass and pellets from the Land Rover.

As they did, they talked about everything but the shooting. Simonsen had dismissed it as a childish prank, and as Anica Buch, Kurt Melsing and Christoffer Brinch all played along with that, there was really nothing more to say on the matter. Last night's threatening letter to Anica was also ignored. Just another prank, nothing to worry about, they had more important things to do. The Homicide Chief emphasised his words by slamming his hand on the roof of the car. He had taken a break from tidying the glass. His lower back was aching, and it was time for someone else to take over. Someone like Anica. She was great at picking things up. As the youngest and thus most flexible member of the team, she had a special responsibility to help out, the men had told her in unison. Her night-time demand that they all return to Denmark had been forgotten.

When they were done, they got in the car, but initially drove only as far as the location of the former Little Denmark. There was something Simonsen wanted to examine there, but he didn't tell them what it was. He got out while the others stayed in the car, and they watched him spend a long time gazing across the landscape, first without his binoculars, then with. After what seemed like forever he took out his satellite phone and made a quick call, and then he returned to the car.

Anica asked with interest as she started the engine: 'What did you learn and who were you talking to?'

But the Homicide Chief deflected the question.

'Something here doesn't add up,' he announced.

That was all he said, and she didn't ask again.

Anica followed the road down the ridge to where there had once been a farmhouse. It was the same journey undertaken by

Bjørn Lauritzen and Ole Nysted in their Leopard tank and Irene Gallagher in her Jeep fifteen years ago. The weather was cool and grey like yesterday, but there was no sign of rain and the wind had dropped.

'This is as far as we can go.'

The hard surface ended and the forest lay ahead. They got out and looked around at an area the size of six football pitches, Kurt estimated, spanning both sides of the road. It was bordered by the forest to the east and north, to the south by a stream. To the west it gradually merged with the mountain tundra, which stretched further down the ridge, grey-brown grass interrupted here and there by a stunted bush. The area they would be examining was lusher: stinging nettles, grass, dock, sorrel, low shrubs, herbaceous perennials with withered flowers and oak saplings. In spring there would probably be an abundance of flowers, Simonsen thought, annoyed that he hadn't worn his wellies, given that the Countess had ordered him to pack them. They were back in his room. How irritating.

John Tyler joined them. They hadn't noticed him until now, but he had been waiting for them at the treeline. He had followed the watercourse as they had agreed the night before, and could confirm that it would be possible to drive along it in a tank, especially in July when the water level would have dropped considerably. He looked bright-eyed, and Konrad Simonsen thought enviously that he had probably slept in a five-star hotel in Sarajevo and commuted back to them by helicopter. The Americans knew how to look after their own. He pulled Tyler to one side and updated him quickly on last night's events. The young man nodded, but made no comment.

Kurt assumed responsibility for the search; crime-scene investigation was his profession, so it was only natural. He explained to the others that the area they would be searching was extensive and the level of vegetation meant it would take time, but it was important to move slowly, not rush. Their first step should be finding themselves a good stick to use in the search.

Then they were each allocated a section of terrain along with a whistle and a pile of marker flags – red pennants attached to fifty-centimetre aluminium poles with a sharp end.

Kurt Melsing said, 'There was a house here once, so initially we're looking for foundations – not bricks or rubble or anything else. You can mark any bricks you find if they look interesting, but we're looking for the actual foundations. Whistle only if you find those.

'If you run out of flags, go back to the car for more, I have plenty, but before you do so, leave two flags to indicate how far you've got. You must always put your second-last and last flag next to one another, even if it's just temporarily. Don't touch anything you find: mark it, but leave it alone. That's important. And I stress again: take plenty of time. Better to be too slow than too fast.'

They walked towards the forest to look for sticks, but had gone only a few steps when Christoffer Brinch stopped, exclaimed and pointed to a cluster of stinging nettles.

The skull lay on its side. It was marbled brown and the crown and forehead were covered in moss. Grass had grown up through one eye socket and the jaw was hanging open in a grotesque grin. Several of the chalk-white teeth were missing.

Everyone fell silent. When Kurt Melsing took one of Christoffer Brinch's marker flags and stuck it into the ground a few centimetres from the skull before walking on, everyone followed him, all of them now more serious or pensive than before, as if they had finally realised what they were dealing with. Fifty metres further on, just before they reached the forest itself, John Tyler put down the second flag. Simonsen, who wasn't far behind him, walked past without looking at his discovery.

The whistle sounded about thirty minutes later. It was Kurt who blew it. The others walked up to him and saw that he had found what they were looking for: red and black brick foundations, a quarter to half a metre tall, uneven, as if the rest of the house had been snapped off by a giant hand. Kurt was taking pictures as everyone arrived. He stopped and said: 'There used to be a house here, as you can see. It would have had a floor space of about one hundred and fifty square metres, and there would have been a cobbled farmyard, which is what we're standing on now, and one or possibly more wooden buildings over there. I presume a barn, maybe a stable as well. Tell me, which of you has found bricks – large or small, it doesn't matter?'

Only Christoffer Brinch and Konrad Simonsen raised their hands. They had been searching further away from the foundations than the others. The lawyer said: 'I marked them to begin with, then I stopped. There are just too many.'

Kurt Melsing nodded. That sounded about right. He took a packet of cotton-wool buds and a roll of small plastic bags from the pocket of his anorak. He bent down and rubbed the cotton-wool bud against the side of a brick, after which he tore a plastic bag off the roll and carefully dropped the cotton-wool bud inside it. Then he repeated the process with a fresh cotton-wool bud and another brick.

Anica asked: 'What are you doing?'

Kurt looked up. He was just preparing his third cotton-wool bud.

'I'm pretty sure that this farmhouse was hit by an explosion, which demolished it. However, I'll test for traces of explosives to be quite sure. If I'm very lucky, I can determine the type of explosive used while I'm out here, otherwise it'll have to wait until we get back.'

Tyler said: 'That won't be necessary. The explosive is PBXN-7 or PBXN-107. It's a mixture of fourteen per cent polyacrylate and eighty-six per cent RDX. The latter is best known in Europe under the name T4.'

All eyes turned to the American. Christoffer Brinch asked: 'Serbian bombers?'

'No, three Tomahawk cruise missiles fired from the Adriatic Sea off the Bosnian coast from the *USS Utah* on Thursday the thirteenth of July 1995. The first was launched at thirteen-oh-two, the next two at thirty-second intervals.'

There was silence. The technical description, the blunt logistics, none of it really squared with the many flags they had just stuck into the ground. And yet they were two ways of describing the same event. They needed time to take it all in.

Above their heads a bird chastised them. They didn't notice, nor did they react to the first dense drops of rain. Eventually Kurt said: 'It's just a shower. We'll wait in the car until it passes.'

Inside the car Simonsen said, and it was part statement, part question:

'So the house was blown up.'

'Yes, I'm afraid so,' Tyler confirmed.

'Why?'

'I don't know yet.'

'When will you?'

'Soon. When we've checked something.'

Once the rain had ended, Tyler said: 'Walk to the edge of the area, maybe further, possibly even into the forest, and see if you can find any remains ... parts of a car, a mudguard, anything metal, seats, tyres ... any major objects. They're likely to be metal.'

'Why are we looking for cars out here?' Anica asked the American, but it was Simonsen who replied.

'We're not, or not just that. We're looking for a portable surface-to-air missile system.'

John Tyler corrected him.

'Not just one, but seven. She reported seven.'

'Was that what you were looking for inside the forest when we arrived?'

'Yes.'

'Did you find any traces?'

'No.'

They had completed their search an hour later, and it had proved just as fruitless as Tyler's original examination. Simonsen said to the American:

'She tricked you.'

He grimaced.

'Yes, she did. She called the commander of the aircraft carrier group directly. She had served under him as a legal counsellor, and he trusted her implicitly. Seven SAM batteries in one place: it was a massive coup. A cruise missile isn't something you just launch, they cost an arm and a leg for a start. The big ones – the ones that were used here – cost two million dollars each.'

'Didn't you save the coordinates she gave you?'

'That's not how it happened. She had a satellite phone ... one of the very first ones used in the field incidentally. She put it down on the ground, the first missile locked onto its signal, and the next two missiles simply tracked the first. So, yes, we had coordinates. Or rather, we could read her coordinates and they were transferred to a reconnaissance unit, which photographed the area the next day, as is standard procedure.

'But no one ever looked at the pictures or, if they did, they never noticed the absence of any remains of surface-to-air missile systems. Today those pictures and coordinates are in an archive somewhere, but we have a lot of that material and we also have millions of pictures, and finding just a few is, if not impossible, then extremely demanding in terms of manpower, which makes it prohibitively expensive even given the seriousness of the Irene Gallagher case. And I can tell you that Washington is taking this extremely seriously.'

'So no one at the time wondered about the seven batteries?'

'In fact, several people did. It seemed bizarre the Serbs would hide all of them in the same location. They had never done so before, for obvious reasons. But no one ever took a proper look at the case. Until now.'

'So what you need is to find out why Irene Gallagher called for the cruise missiles to attack this area?'

'Yes, and I have a feeling you can tell me.'

'So do I, but it's better that we wait until Kurt comes back, because I believe he has something he would like to show us.'

They both looked over at Kurt Melsing. He was walking from flag to flag with his camera.

When he was done, he showed Tyler and Simonsen three locations, which he had marked with flags during his trip with the camera. Anica and Brinch had no desire to take a closer look at his findings, so they continued their search in an area that had yet to be examined. Putting a flag in the ground next to bones was one thing, but studying human remains in detail they could do without.

The first discovery Kurt showed the other two consisted of two bones, the top halves of a fibula and a tibia, both clean with no tissue remaining. At the bottom of both bones they could see irregular, angled fractures. He slipped on a pair of plastic gloves, carefully picked up the bones, raised them and explained: 'These bones were crushed thirty centimetres from the heel *before* the explosion. An explosion would never cause this kind of fracture.'

Konrad Simonsen asked: 'Do the other two locations you've marked show the same thing?'

'Yes. One is a foot in a crushed boot, the other a femur with a crushed kneecap. There have been animals here since the incident, of course, and the bones are scattered across a wide area. Some might have been taken into the forest, but … it's clear that Bjørn Lauritzen drove the tank over the men's legs after tying them up and making them lie down in the courtyard.'

Simonsen added: 'And that fits with the screaming Ole Nysted couldn't cope with. It wasn't the screams from the women in the house, if indeed any of them were still inside. No, it was the screaming *men* who haunted him when he came home. And that explains why Bjørn Lauritzen drove the tank up and down the watercourse …'

Kurt completed his sentence.

'He was washing blood and flesh off the caterpillar tracks.'

Kurt nodded.

The two men took turns explaining the incident to Tyler, who wasn't familiar with the veteran's witness statement. Afterwards the American concluded: 'Irene Gallagher ensured in an efficient but utterly murderous way that any evidence of her lover's crime disappeared, as did any witnesses.'

'Yes, but she also made sure that Denmark didn't end up in an extremely awkward position, that part needs telling too. Neither the Danish public nor the Serbian Army would have looked kindly on Bjørn Lauritzen's and Ole Nysted's actions, to put it mildly. There would have been an outcry in Denmark, and the Serbs would probably have taken revenge on our soldiers abroad.'

'So why did Irene Gallagher even report it to Copenhagen?'

'She had to. Bjørn Lauritzen and Ole Nysted had to leave Bosnia immediately, that much was obvious. Once home they probably signed a confidentiality agreement, and both were paid off in the form of active-service wage supplements long after they were back in Denmark.

'They were also allowed to keep their field promotions to Captain and First Lieutenant respectively. So they didn't tell anyone. Why would they? And the handful of senior FE and Army officers who did know had not just one, but several, good reasons to keep this a secret even fifteen years later.'

Kurt summarised Konrad Simonsen's conclusions.

'The Danish public isn't used to Danish soldiers deployed abroad committing one war crime, let alone two. Support for our presence in Afghanistan would have collapsed if this had come out. Not to mention the career prospects of certain leading members of our Armed Forces. From FE's point of view there's still every reason to keep this a secret.'

Simonsen asked: 'What do we do now? Do we carry on searching the area?'

Tyler said, 'No, we'll stop now, and I'll make sure that trained personnel arrive tomorrow to help us.'

The three men walked slowly towards the Land Rover. There were still unanswered questions; Irene Gallagher's and Bjørn Lauritzen's motive for the canal boat killing, for one.

It didn't seem plausible that she would commit four new murders purely to prevent the truth about a double massacre coming out. Knowing the truth was one thing – and it was possible that Pauline Berg had uncovered the truth, at least they would assume so – it was quite another to convince anyone else without much tangible evidence. At most, Pauline Berg was a problem for the Army in general, not for Irene Gallagher and Bjørn Lauritzen personally. Something was wrong.

Simonsen dismissed Tyler's suggestions.

'You can't attribute motive to Bjørn Lauritzen in any meaningful sense of the word. After he came back to Denmark, he imploded. His respect for his own life and those of others had been erased by his experiences here. He's not the first veteran to whom this has happened. Habituated to violence, he would probably kill anyone Irene Gallagher told him to kill. He needed no other reason.'

'And her motive?'

'Was completely different, much more down-to-earth and personal, I think.'

John Tyler hit the nail on the head with his response.

'Bjørn Lauritzen and Ole Nysted knew nothing about the cruise missiles! They were in a tank in the forest a few kilometres away, and if they even heard the explosions when they were playing their Town Hall bells at maximum volume, they wouldn't have known where they had come from or what had caused them. And no one told them later … That would have been an extremely dangerous thing to divulge, so no one ever did.'

Simonsen said: 'Exactly. Bjørn Lauritzen had no idea that his lover murdered the very women he was trying to save and I'm sure Irene Gallagher was keen for it to stay that way. But one piece of the puzzle is missing: something that meant so much to Bjørn Lauritzen that not even Irene Gallagher could get round it.'

Simonsen was interrupted when Christoffer Brinch came racing towards them, the expression on his face clearly showing that something was wrong.

'What's happened? Why are you running?' asked Simonsen.

The lawyer was in poor physical shape. He struggled to catch his breath and gulp: 'Anica is missing.'

CHAPTER 68

THURSDAY 18 NOVEMBER 2010, THE HOUSE IN BOSNIA

When John Tyler had promised additional help yesterday, he hadn't been exaggerating. The area around the ruined farmhouse, which had been left to nature for years, was now buzzing with human activity.

Konrad Simonsen surveyed the scene and thought that this was one advantage of being a superpower: if you wanted something done, you always had the resources. Four enormous tents had been erected diagonally opposite him, where the road ended, and a dozen men were currently working on putting up a fifth and a sixth. Six Portakabins had also arrived and now made up a small village at the opposite end of the area. Lavatories, shower rooms and offices were also up and running.

At the scene itself at least twelve forensic scientists and their assistants were working, and they had priority access to the area. Everyone else could walk only on the paths they had cleared. These were marked with acid-yellow plastic strips tied to metal posts hammered into the ground. These paths criss-crossed. Some were wide enough for two big diggers to pass; others were narrow and only allowed people to walk single-file.

Whenever the forensic scientists found human remains and had documented and photographed them, they were placed in a body bag and moved to one of the two big tents where dozens of tables ensured forensic pathologists could work on DNA analysis, gender and age determination. The transport of body bags took priority. Even the biggest trucks or diggers would stop when they passed, and the drivers would turn off their engines and remove their caps.

Everything was extremely well organised, from the group of local police officers standing further up the road and keeping out people without a valid errand, to the two young men who permanently circled the area offering bottles of cold water to anyone who wanted one.

Kurt was standing next to Simonsen as they watched the scene unfold in front of their eyes. Surplus to requirements, they had nothing else to do.

Kurt said, 'All of this in less than thirty hours – that's seriously impressive. They have also replaced our windscreen with an original, not some rubbish copy. It was flown in from Beograd and two mechanics fixed it in ten minutes. I'm sure they're sappers, but when I ask any of them where they are from, they just smile and shake their heads, if they don't turn their back on me and leave. And none of them is in uniform.'

Simonsen pointed to the ruin where a team of soldiers was busy with pneumatic drills, diggers and trucks to take away the bricks.

'They're removing the entirety of the foundations, not a stone will be left behind. Have you also noticed that before they open up a new path, it's carefully checked and any remains of the house are secured? They're very thorough.'

'All evidence must be removed, is that it?'

'Yes, I think so.'

'I visited one of the mortuaries. Their work is extremely professional, no doubt about it. I was free to walk around, but they wouldn't let me take pictures. They remove any objects that could identify the men – not the women, only the men. Primarily their clothes and shoes. They burn everything round the back. You can see the smoke rising behind the last tent. By the way, take a look at what I managed to smuggle out.'

He showed Konrad Simonsen a genuine Drina Wolves badge. It was round and depicted a black, howling, red-eyed wolf.

'What are you going to do with that?'

'Nothing, it's just a souvenir. While we're on the subject, any news of Anica?'

'No, not yet, but I spent half an hour this morning reassuring Christoffer. He's still very worried. Perhaps you should have a word with him as well? You have such a calming effect on people.

'Anyway, why don't we go to the mess for lunch before we talk to John? It'll take us fifteen minutes at least to walk through this maze. Perhaps we should walk around instead, it might be faster.'

But no, they wouldn't be doing that, Kurt explained. Outside was a restricted area with signs and friendly but firm guards, so walking around – rather than through – was not an option.

They sat down at a table in Portakabin IV with a cup of freshly brewed coffee, the best they had had for days. Simonsen, Kurt and Christoffer Brinch sat on one side, John Tyler on the other. Simonsen opened the conversation, and he went straight for the American's jugular.

'You're destroying evidence. Would you tell us what's going on here?'

Tyler didn't try to dodge the question.

'We're building a holiday park. A scenic haven for Croatian, Serbian and Bosnian children with playgrounds, a football pitch, tennis courts, an obstacle course and, of course, dormitories, kitchen, dining halls and so on.

'It's a present from my country to Bosnia-Herzegovina and the Republika Srpska. If you want to be pompous, you could call it a small acknowledgement by us to the Serbs of the democracy they've managed to introduce in recent years, both here and on the other side of the border. And as far as destruction of evidence is concerned, you're right of course – that's the real purpose of this enterprise, but very few people know that.'

Kurt snarled: 'You bastard!'

The American didn't bat an eyelid. He explained bluntly that it wasn't in US interests that the events that had taken place here became public knowledge. And he was sure it wasn't in Denmark's interests either.

'OK, moment of truth. Let's pretend it's our decision: do you think it would benefit your country if this became public? It's a simple question, so spare me your deliberations. Yes or no?'

It took a few seconds before the three Danes realised that he was waiting for an answer from every single one of them. They mulled it over. Simonsen's no was the first to be uttered, then Kurt Melsing's. He sounded bitter about it, but he still said no. At length Christoffer Brinch said: 'All things considered, sadly, also a no.'

It was to Tyler's credit that he didn't gloat. Instead he was ready to listen and be helpful, if he could be, within the framework they had now all agreed upon. Christoffer Brinch was the first to voice his unhappiness.

'It's intolerable that Irene Gallagher goes free. It disgusts me to my very core. Now there's no evidence against her here either, and she'll never be convicted for her misdeeds in Denmark. In a month she'll be in Wellington soaking up the sun, despite having God knows how many lives on her conscience.'

John Tyler clearly agreed. For a moment he turned pale with rage and this was unlikely to be just for show, Simonsen thought. And indeed the American struggled to articulate his response, but the truth was, yes, she would go free.

He told them the USA would love nothing more than to have her extradited, but it would never make the request as it didn't have a snowball's chance in hell of that being granted by a Danish court, for the simple reason that in the USA Gallagher would be tried by a military tribunal under the US Navy code, which would be held in private. So the bottom line was that she would never serve the life sentence she would otherwise undoubtedly have been given.

Kurt asked, 'Aren't you scared that at some point she might talk to the press?'

Tyler shook his head.

'Not at all. And we're not worried that you might either. We've already discussed it. The story alone isn't strong enough. Unless you have irrefutable evidence to back it up, no newspaper or TV channel would ever dream of running it. But apart from that, it's clear that Denmark, or more specifically people in the Danish military, would like Irene Gallagher to go as far away as possible. It's not just about what happened here fifteen years ago, it's also about the scandalous trial she was put through. Besides I'm guessing that people in Copenhagen don't feel too good that they hid the truth from us for so many years. That knowledge was probably her get-out-of-jail card, so to speak.'

'Tell me what you're going to do with the bodies?'

'We'll try to identify the women, but we'll claim that they were the victims of a Serbian mortar attack. The men will be given an anonymous funeral in a Christian cemetery, that's all. And I'm afraid that's not up for discussion.'

It was Konrad Simonsen's turn to speak. He started tentatively, by acknowledging that he wouldn't be returning home with any evidence. Not that it mattered, he understood that now, seeing as he would never be able to go public with the story.

'But I'm somewhat annoyed about it. In the next few weeks I and other people will have to … process it, shall we say? And that's where I would really like to have something official up my sleeve, something the other side is desperate not to—'

John Tyler grinned as he interrupted. He had got the message.

'When are you going home?'

'Tomorrow we were thinking.'

'All right, I'll make sure to give you a nice little file with the most exquisite evidence for all of this. But I warn you – it'll blow up in your face if you make it public. It's just to help you bluff, that's all.'

Somewhat surprisingly it was Christoffer Brinch who made a helpful suggestion.

'Nor would it do any harm if our great ally hinted through unofficial channels that, having cleaned up our mess in Bosnia, Washington expects Denmark to make sure her dirty laundry is never aired in public. Something along those lines, but expressed in more diplomatic language.'

John Tyler liked the idea. It would undoubtedly put pressure on … on some of the people who would be involved in 'processing' the matter. Such a request was entirely appropriate. He promised to discuss it with one of his superiors and they would have to see where it led.

Konrad Simonsen had one last item to raise. He had already discussed it with the other two men and asked for their support if he should get a chance to raise the matter. It was important, he claimed.

'The young Muslim man who was kidnapped in Sarajevo as a result of Irene Gallagher's false charges and flown to a torture chamber somewhere where – in your words – the authorities aren't so fussy when it comes to enhanced interrogation techniques. Is it possible that the young man might have been a woman, and might her name have been Jelena Khrobic?'

The question hit John Tyler like a punch to the stomach, it was clear to them all. He made no attempt to hide it but avoided Simonsen's gaze by staring at the ceiling while he fought his own internal struggle.

They allowed him to suffer for a few seconds, then Christoffer Brinch said in a low voice: 'Young man, just now you asked us a very simple yet very difficult question, which we really had to dig deep in order to answer honestly. Now it's your turn. The USA that kidnaps and tortures people by proxy, using extraordinary rendition, is that the USA you represent?'

Tyler took a deep breath. Then he said in a steady voice: 'No, that's not the USA I represent. And, yes, her name was Jelena Khrobic.'

CHAPTER 69

The Countess took no joy in the work she was doing. It was never pleasant to investigate your colleagues, she thought, and it felt even worse when a suspicion against someone was confirmed. Yesterday morning when she was on her way to work, Simon had called her about something that had long troubled him.

It was about the Muslim women in the farmhouse – she knew the house he meant, didn't she? According to the *Dnevni Avaz* newspaper article, these women had all been heading for Tuzla on the 13 July 1995, where they would be safe from the Serbs. It was reported in the newspaper article that Anica had translated and presented at the meeting in Simonsen's office about a month ago … but to his way of thinking something here didn't add up.

When he had told his wife his doubts, she too was troubled. As was Klavs Arnold when she explained the problem to him.

'Why didn't any of the Danish soldiers who were stationed at Little Denmark tell us about the women? There was only one road from the farmhouse where they had been abused out to the rest of the world, and that road ran straight past the Danish observation post.'

Klavs Arnold tried coming up with a sensible explanation.

'At that point the soldiers had been ordered into the two remaining tanks, after Bjørn Lauritzen had driven off in the third. The engines were running and ready to go when their captain returned. He came back an hour later, as far as we know. But the point I'm making is: how much can you see from the inside of a tank? Not one of the soldiers ever mentioned that the house in the valley below them was blown to smithereens, for instance.'

The Countess shot down his argument.

'I admit there are substantial variations in the witness statements. Some mention Serbian guns and mortars, others just gun salvos from the forest, and a few talk about air attacks. But fifteen to twenty women don't walk past two tanks in broad daylight on a three-metre-wide road without *someone* seeing them. And why didn't the women ask the soldiers for protection? After all, that was why they were there.'

Now this could be the result of collective amnesia among the soldiers when they were questioned, a known phenomenon both the Homicide officers had experienced before, but neither of them really believed that was the case here. They agreed to ring all the witnesses who could be contacted by phone and ask them about the women. Two hours later they had reached an unequivocal conclusion: there had been no women on the road at that point.

Shortly after that Simonsen rang back with fresh information – something that rendered their recent efforts redundant, but confirmed what they had discovered. The house had been destroyed by three American cruise missiles and all the women inside had been killed.

Klavs Arnold said: 'That raises some interesting questions about Anica's newspaper article.'

The Countess was already looking at the young woman's report, but found that only the translation of the newspaper article was attached rather than the original article itself. The Countess said: 'That'll be hard to track down. Any ideas?'

The Jutlander said yes. It was Malte Borup who had run Anica's slideshow when she presented her research to the investigators. Perhaps ... the Countess was already on her way to his office. Ten minutes later she returned with a printout.

'This is the article or rather a screenshot of it, and I've asked Malte to take a close look at it. Now we need to find an interpreter: Serbian, Croat, I don't care, but it must be possible to get one quickly. Please would you deal with it, Klavs? I have a lunch appointment in town, but I'll be back before two.'

———

The interpreter was a young woman and they had to explain her task twice before she understood. Even then she was still confused because she repeated:

'You want me to tell you if the newspaper text matches the Danish text?'

The Countess confirmed, yes, that was all they wanted.

The interpreter said: 'The newspaper article is about binmen striking in Mostar with the name Jelena Khrobic inserted in three places where it makes no sense. The photo caption says that rubbish is piling up in the streets of Mostar, but ... well, you can both see that for yourselves.'

Klavs Arnold thanked her.

All that had happened yesterday. Today's assignment for the Countess and Klavs Arnold was to work out what exactly had happened to Jelena Khrobic, given that she didn't bleed to death on 13 July 1995 south of Cerska after being hit by Serbian gunfire.

They had gone to see Malte Borup the moment he turned up for work. He apologised when he saw them.

'I'm sorry, but I didn't have time to examine the newspaper article until last night. I had promised to pick up Emil early, he was poorly and ... anyway, that's how it is. However, the image has been manipulated, and not even particularly professionally. If you take a closer look, you can easily see where it's been done.'

Klavs Arnold stopped him, it was no longer relevant, but they would like to know more about Anica Buch. After all, Malte shared an office with her and they had questions he might be able to answer. The Countess began: 'Did Anica tell you anything about how she tracked down Jelena Khrobic?'

Malte answered, 'Can you both stop pacing back and forth, please? I don't know which one of you I'm supposed to be talking to. If you want me to help you, then just say so.'

The Countess looked at Klavs and smiled. Then she said: 'Anica tricked us, as you have probably worked out by now. She went to great lengths to concoct false information about Jelena Khrobic. What we don't understand is why she didn't just tell us that she couldn't find anything on the girl? It would have been much simpler. Did she tell you how she was getting on with her investigation? People usually do when they're in the same office.'

Malte confirmed that Anica had told him about her progress, important or not, every day, and that there had been times when he thought she really could unearth the missing girl's fate.

The Countess was satisfied. It was the answer she had been expecting.

'Can you remember the last thing Anica told you about her research before she mentioned the newspaper article?'

'Not exactly, after all I had my own work to do. But I think it was when she learned the girl's name and where she had gone to school. I remember her showing me a school photo.'

'Can you look at our computers without knowing our passwords?' Klavs asked him.

'I would never do that. Simon would hit the roof.'

'But you could, if you wanted to?'

'Not without a password, that's impossible.'

'Can you work out the password?'

'You mustn't do that, it's not allowed.'

Klavs took a deep breath and phrased his question differently.

'Let me try this another way: how long will it take you to give us access to Anica Buch's computer?'

'Ten minutes. If you order me to, that is. And if Simon knows that you accept full responsibility.'

The Countess looked at the files on Anica's computer, while Klavs Arnold examined a pile of papers on her desk. The Jutlander was the first to get a result. He held up a piece of paper with two handwritten notes: Bx204Glo and Bx231Glo.

When the police found people who had gone missing, they didn't file a report unless a crime had taken place. The exception to this rule was patients who had gone missing from psychiatric hospitals. They were registered with a Bx report as it was known, for the simple reason that absconding patients often went missing repeatedly and they often went back to the same familiar places. By checking the Bx register, officers would therefore have a good idea of where to find them.

Klavs Arnold said: 'And this piece of paper was right behind a printout of her alternative translation. Worth looking at those two reports, don't you think?'

The reports were from Vestegnens Police Force, both with the same subject matter, but written on different dates. On 17 April 2007 a missing patient, Jelena Khrobic, had been found by police in Glostrup Shopping Centre; on 2 August 2007 exactly the same thing had occurred, including the location where she was found. In both instances the woman, who was completely harmless but couldn't cope independently, had been driven back to the Psychiatric Unit at Glostrup Hospital.

The Countess called a professor on the hospital's senior management team. She knew that he took a pragmatic approach to working with the police. If he believed that it was in his patient's best interest, he would release information which, strictly speaking, should be kept confidential. If not, he would release nothing, no matter how many persuasive arguments the police could come up with.

The Countess was put through after barely waiting and told the professor about Jelena Khrobic and the reason for her interest. He listened without interrupting, then asked for the chance to think it over. It was difficult to decide if his patient would benefit from speaking to the police, and he would need to check that first. He promised to get back to the Countess as quickly as possible. And that was what happened, although it wasn't the professor himself who made the call. A woman rang to tell the Countess that she should contact the Centre for Torture Victims at Gentofte Hospital, and that the Centre was expecting her call.

CHAPTER 70

THURSDAY 18 NOVEMBER 2010, LJUBICEVAC

The Land Rover was packed. Christoffer Brinch was behind the wheel, and Kurt Melsing was in the back, with his shoes off and his feet up on the seat. Simonsen was standing outside the car, next to Tyler. The American had a parcel in his hand.

'How long will you be staying here? And are you coming to Denmark afterwards to continue your ... cultural work?' Simonsen asked him.

'I'll stay here until the human remains have been processed, which could be two days or it could be ten, it's impossible to say. And yes, I'll be returning to Denmark, but I'm hoping for a few days back home first.'

He handed the parcel to Konrad Simonsen. It contained everything he would need and Tyler had also enclosed a Danish translation, just in case. His bosses had welcomed Christoffer Brinch's excellent suggestion of a word in the right ear in Copenhagen, and the matter was already in hand.

Tyler shook hands with the two men in the car. It had been a pleasure, he said, and looked as if he meant it. He turned to Simonsen.

'Right, then, I'll be off before this gets embarrassing. And I know it's none of my business, but you're kind of soft-hearted. I would have just driven off and left her.'

'When I was young I made a very big mistake, but no one ever found out. If they had, my life would have taken a very different turn,' Simonsen replied enigmatically.

The American laughed.

'I don't believe that for one moment! You Danes can't help giving people second chances. You'd probably have been given one as well. But goodbye, Simon, I hope we'll meet again.'

'Goodbye, John, I hope so too.'

Simonsen held out his hand, but received a hug instead. It felt odd, he wasn't from that generation.

When the American had left, Simonsen walked down the street and stopped outside a deserted house. Then he shouted: 'Are you coming with us or do you intend to spend the winter here?'

He waited ten seconds. When there was no reply, he called out again.

'We'll wait one minute, then we'll unload your bags.'

Anica Buch emerged from the house. Her face was a frozen mask and she stared at the ground, avoiding all eye contact. Simonsen opened the car door for her and Kurt swung his legs across to make room for her. Without turning his head, Christoffer Brinch said dryly, 'If I were your lawyer, Anica, I would advise you to say silent the entire way to Copenhagen airport.'

CHAPTER 71

FRIDAY 19 NOVEMBER 2010, THE CENTRE FOR TORTURE
VICTIMS, GENTOFTE HOSPITAL

'Are you the woman they call the Countess?'

She confirmed it and suppressed a natural urge to ask him how he knew; it was better to let the man speak at his own pace. She was in the staff canteen at Gentofte Hospital at a table some distance from the others, as if it had been put there specifically to facilitate a private conversation. The man opposite her was a consultant psychiatrist at the Centre for Torture Victims, and you certainly couldn't call him handsome. He was small and pear-shaped, spoke in a grating tone as if spitting out his words. His face was pallid and bloated and his straggly, gelled hair flopped over his forehead almost as far as his eyebrows. Yet despite his appearance there was something about him that invoked trust. It was hard to pinpoint what, but it came across after only a short acquaintance.

'It's odd. I have no less than five rooms furnished deliberately so that visitors will feel comfortable there, and yet I bring my guests to the canteen whenever I can. Tell me, what do you know about this centre?' he asked.

The Countess didn't know very much. The consultant summarised its history and then said: 'So you want to talk to one of my former patients, Jelena Khrobic? I'm surprised. When I heard that you were from the Homicide Department, I thought you had called for completely different reasons.

'Anyway, the procedure is as follows: first you explain to me why you want to talk to Jelena and what you want to talk to her about. On the strength of that, I'll decide whether it's a good idea. If I think it is, I'll contact her and then it's up to her whether or not she wants to meet you. This may seem very restrictive but, trust me, this procedure isn't designed purely to be a nuisance, it's there to protect my patient. Would you like some more coffee? They do very good pastries as well.'

He fetched more coffee and some pastries. The Countess told him the story of Bjørn Lauritzen, Ole Nysted and Irene Gallagher, in Bosnia in 1995 and in Copenhagen in 2010. She left out the part about the Serbian soldiers whose legs were crushed, and the three cruise missiles the US Navy had launched from the Adriatic Sea.

The consultant said: 'I know about the incident in Bosnia, at least as Jelena experienced it. But she can tell you about that herself, if you speak to her. Ole Nysted came here twice and spoke to Jelena as one of the steps in her recovery.

'Both times I picked him up and returned him to his home in the forest. It was kind of him to come, especially since he himself suffered badly from PTSD. Jelena also wanted to talk to Irene Gallagher, but she refused to visit. More than anything Jelena wanted to meet up with Bjørn Lauritzen, she felt very close to him, but I couldn't track him down.'

The Countess said: 'May I ask you some questions? I have quite a few.'

'You'll have to wait. There are two conditions you need to be aware of and that you must promise to respect, if you are to speak to Jelena.'

The Countess nodded. She was ready to listen.

'Jelena is, in many ways, one of my success stories. She has been the victim of terrible atrocities, more gruesome than any human being can imagine, and her mind broke completely as a result. Today, however, she lives an almost normal life.

'She's all right and I think she's happy. This is very rare for my patients, and it's primarily because Jelena is one of the strongest human beings I've ever met. Nevertheless, she suffers from certain after-effects. One of them is that she has gaps in her life and you mustn't talk to her about them, because no one knows what will happen if … It doesn't matter – just don't talk about them.'

The psychiatrist explained how in 2003 Jelena Khrobic was kidnapped and flown from Sarajevo to Minsk in Belarus. Here she was tortured for months until she had a mental breakdown. Three years later she was found chained to a bed in a psychiatric institution in Kiev in the Ukraine, more than four hundred kilometres from Minsk, and no one – not even Jelena herself – knew how she had ended up there. She was discovered purely by accident by four Danish doctors. They had gone to Kiev as part of a Danish aid project for Ukrainian psychiatry, which wasn't very up-to-date due to its lack of resources.

Jelena heard the doctors speaking Danish to one another and had spontaneously recited two lines from a Danish nursery rhyme. The staff said those were the first words they had ever heard her say.

At that point no one knew who she was, but the doctors made sure she came to Denmark, where she was admitted to the Psychiatric Unit at Glostrup Hospital. Very slowly she began to improve and her memory partially returned. In the spring of 2007 she had become his patient on a treatment programme which concluded successfully in the summer of 2008.

For some strange reason – no one knew why – Jelena Khrobic's memory from August 1995 until her kidnapping in 2003 was gone, or almost gone. It seemed likely that she would have been at school or in education of some sort during the period in question, and that she had also worked as a waitress at one point, but that was pretty much all she could remember.

The psychiatrist concluded: 'Normally it's the trauma my patients forget or can't talk about, but with Jelena it's the opposite. The times she has forgotten have been relatively calm and normal for her, I think, or they were compared to the other things she has suffered. I've never experienced that before, but I've read about similar cases so she's not completely unique.'

He paused, finished his coffee and looked at the Countess as if waiting for a sign from her that he could continue. She smiled to prompt him, and he carried on talking.

'The other thing you need to respect is that today Jelena lives a very simple life. She has a husband and a child and another on the way. They're all she cares about, she shuts out the rest of the world. She never watches television, reads newspapers or listens to the radio. As a result, she knows nothing about the canal boat killings, the deaths of Bjørn Lauritzen and Ole Nysted or the trial of Irene Gallagher, and you'll do nothing to change that. Her family, her vegetable garden and her piano playing are her life, and she's happy with that.

'Besides she has made up her mind that the world is a good place. She has forgiven those who hurt her and decided that the three Danes she met in Bosnia in 1995 all helped her and that they're her friends. But it goes deeper than that. If anything ... how do I put this ... *negative* happens to her, another person behaving badly ... she'll immediately turn it into something good. You may say that her world is forever rose-tinted, and I would like that to continue even if it means we have to tell her a few little white lies from time to time. It's how she survives, so you've no choice but to accept it. I made exactly the same demands of Pauline.'

It wasn't until the Countess's mouth dropped open, surprise written across her face, that she realised he had done it on purpose, detonating Pauline Berg's name like a bomb.

His smile was not without charm.

'Sorry, I couldn't resist that.'

She said: 'I hope you have plenty of time.'

He did and began to explain his remark. Pauline Berg had contacted him last autumn for exactly the same reason as the Countess, namely to talk to Jelena Khrobic. To begin with, however, the consultant had turned her down.

'Pauline Berg was mentally unstable, and I didn't think her being with Jelena was a good idea. The first time we met, we discussed it – well, argued about it is probably more accurate.'

Pauline had stormed out, angry and resentful. But she had returned a few weeks later, and they had agreed that she would have several conversations with him – not for Jelena's sake but for her own.

The Countess interjected: 'You treated Pauline?'

'No, I wouldn't call it treatment; we just talked four or five times in October and November last year. Sometimes it doesn't take much before someone starts to feel better, but an actual treatment plan – no, that wasn't an option. Although her experiences during her abduction were traumatic, I was already dealing with a long queue of people whose suffering had been far greater. In a perfect world with no limit on resources, I would have taken her on as my patient, but as you know, that's not how the real world works.'

The Countess soon realised that the consultant knew everything about the Homicide Department and about Pauline's obsession with the Juli-non-case, which had ultimately turned out to be a case after all – and a case that had triggered several other incidents.

'How did Pauline find you and Jelena Khrobic? Do you know?'

'Yes, indeed I do. It happened initially by chance.'

A year ago Pauline had been contacted by a woman, an ex-girlfriend of Jonas Ziegler, the shop assistant and former forester, who was Pauline's only real lead in her investigation into the death of Juli Denissen, but also a lead who didn't want to talk to her. The girlfriend, however, had now been dumped for someone else, was mad at her ex and wanted to harm him as much as possible. She did so by revealing to Pauline what he had said in confidence when he and his girlfriend were still together.

When Juli Denissen was attacked by Bjørn Lauritzen on Melby Common, Jonas Ziegler had heard her scream. Hidden behind a dune, he had watched what happened to her. He had recognised her attacker, a man he had met before in the forest, a hermit who, at times, would stay in the old munitions depot a few kilometres further up the coast.

Three days later, Jonas Ziegler had plucked up his courage and gone to see the man in the bunker, only to discover he happened to have a visitor. Ziegler hadn't threatened or blackmailed them with his knowledge, but the upshot was that the woman offered him a better-paid job as a shop assistant in Tune, in return for him keeping his mouth shut about what he had seen on the Common three days earlier. Later, Ziegler discovered that the woman's name was Irene Gallagher and that her husband owned the chain of shops where he was now working.

The consultant explained: 'That was the breakthrough for Pauline, the first she had had. She went to the bunker where Bjørn Lauritzen lived, but he wasn't there anymore. She did, however, find a picture on the wall, a page torn from a Norwegian Army magazine, of Bjørn Lauritzen arriving in Tuzla in the summer of 1995 in his tank with eight Muslim refugees riding on the outside. It listed Lauritzen's name and rank, though he himself didn't feature in the picture as he was inside, driving the tank. The article went on to describe a young Danish-Bosnian girl, Jelena Khrobic, who had been rescued from the hell of war. Pauline took the picture with her.'

The psychiatrist then spoke about how Pauline's next step was to research online Danish soldiers in Bosnia, and here she found the second soldier in the tank, Ole Nysted. In contrast to Bjørn Lauritzen, Ole Nysted was easy to track down. He had a fixed address, no matter how primitive his hut.

'Pauline visited him three times before last Christmas, until Irene Gallagher heard about it and banned him from seeing her. He confirmed the ban himself the last time Pauline visited him, but by then he had already told her about his conversations with Jelena Khrobic here at the centre. However, Ole Nysted didn't know where Bjørn Lauritzen lived, which of course was Pauline's all-consuming interest.'

'I won't deny that what you've told me is incredibly important,' the Countess said, 'so why on earth didn't you contact us long ago as a witness?'

'But I did – three times, would you believe, until I got fed up. The Homicide Chief himself promised to call me back when he had time, but he never did.'

The Countess didn't comment on that, though she had a pretty good idea of what could have gone wrong. It might also explain why they had never heard from Jonas Ziegler's ex-girlfriend either.

'And eventually Pauline was given permission to meet Jelena Khrobic?'

'At first only with me present, but as it turned out, the two of them got on really well. Pauline was exceptionally good at being careful with Jelena, she was empathetic and cautious. Later they met in private, quite often, I think, but I don't know exactly how frequently.'

'Do you have any idea why Pauline never told anyone in the Homicide Department about her breakthrough, as you so accurately describe it?'

'Yes, I can be absolutely sure about that because she told me so herself: no one had taken her seriously for years, so she was going to solve the case herself and hand you Bjørn Lauritzen on a plate. Just so you know, I tried to get her to change her mind and involve you, but to no avail. She wanted to go it alone. But that's where we leave it for now, don't you think?'

'If you say so. I still have a lot of questions, especially if I don't get to meet Jelena.'

The consultant got up and they carried their trays to the stand.

'You're welcome to contact me again. I'll think things through and get back to you. Is there anything you want to say before you leave?'

'Yes, one thing: what exactly did Pauline want from Jelena Khrobic?'

'Well, they had a shared interest although with different motives.'

'Finding Bjørn Lauritzen?'

'Precisely.'

CHAPTER 72

SATURDAY 20 NOVEMBER 2010, OUTER COPENHAGEN

The flat was vacant. It was located between Rødovre and Brøndbyøster stations in a quiet area with a floor space of one hundred and ten square metres, comprising a living room, two bedrooms, a kitchen, a bathroom and a hallway, in a modern two-storey apartment block.

'What do you think? Wouldn't it be great for us?'

Arne Pedersen broke away from the window where he was watching a mother carefully push her baby on the swing on a playground.

'It's really nice, it's perfect.'

'It's no more money than Pauline's flat because hers is closer to the city centre and a bit bigger, but I think this one would be better for us. We'll only have to pay for the legal paperwork, and according to the bank that won't be a problem because the mortgage is cheaper, so it'll soon pay for itself. Also there are two of us now, though I know that you'll be paying maintenance to your children, possibly more than the minimum in order that they can stay in their home. I understand that and I respect it.'

Arne appreciated the way Louise viewed things, but she was wrong.

'Their mother is an accountant and makes at least three times what I do. They can easily afford to stay where they are.'

'You never told me your kids were posh.'

She was teasing him and he knew it, but even so he was on tenterhooks. The twins were due to arrive soon, and it was vital that Louise got on well with them. Children of that age could be impossible to please, however hard you tried.

'So what do you say? Shall we buy it?'

He was speechless. A thousand thoughts rushed through his mind, and he didn't understand why he didn't just utter the little word *yes*, which was all it would take – and which was what he truly wanted to say. She grew serious as if she could read his mind, and stroked his cheek.

'Just kidding. Take all the time you need, Arne. You don't have to give me an answer now, you can think about it. But if you want to, please tell me what's on your mind, so we can talk about it.'

What could he say? That sometimes he feared in, say, a month's time he would be just another in the long line of her lovers, and would curse himself for having been stupid enough to think that he could be a permanent part of a carefree young woman's life.

'I know that I mustn't say it, but—'

She put her hand over his mouth. Not again. Yes, he was ancient and, yes, she understood it wasn't something he could just ignore, but she didn't have the energy to listen to it now. Another time, but not today.

'You and me, it's right. I can feel it and it's getting stronger and stronger, if you know what I mean, so I have no doubts at all,' she told him.

'Yes!'

'Pardon?'

'I'm saying yes, let's move in together and see what happens.'

She smiled sweetly as, partly in earnest, partly in jest, she started counting on her fingers: seat up when you pee, we share the house-work, don't you dare be unfaithful to me, and at some point I want two children. Then she checked her watch.

'They'll be here in twenty minutes. You have just enough time to tell me about Anica, as you promised. She seemed really nice, but I gather it was just a front.'

They sat down on the floor with their backs against the wall, and Arne told her everything. Anica Buch had left a threatening letter in her own room in Paris – warning them against going to Bosnia. She had written it herself, but made it look as if it was from a horrible militia organisation. That organisation, however, hadn't been active for fifteen years and furthermore it never oper-ated outside Bosnia, so Simonsen had been very sceptical about Anica from then on.

Arne continued: 'Not to mention the fact the supposedly aggres-sive handwriting was in nice, red girly capitals. She repeated her trick in Bosnia, this time using a dreadful souvenir dagger from Paris as a prop, with some additional unpleasant words saying she would be raped and murdered, no less. She also paid a man in the village to shoot the windscreen out of their hire car in the middle of the night.'

'But why? Was FE running her?'

'Yes, I'm sure they were, but they were way too smart to meet her. She only spoke to a voice on a telephone a few times. I don't think for a moment that they believed she would make any real difference, her job was just to get Simon and the others to go home.'

'Why did she do it?'

'Ambition ... greed. She believed the rumours that she could expect a brilliant career in intelligence if she helped them. It was hopelessly naive. But she got herself in deeper and deeper, and eventually could see no other way out than to leave. So she hid out for twenty-four hours in an abandoned house, with no water or food, until Simon called to her that it was time for them to go home. And then out she came with her tail between her legs.'

'What's going to happen to her now?'

'I don't know. That's Simon's decision.'

'Does he decide everything for you?'

'Well, he decides whatever he wants to decide.'

'He can be scary, but he's also ... someone you respect, in a good way. Pauline felt the same way about him. He was the only one who would pull her up when she crossed the line, and afterwards she valued that. Do you think he'll give Anica a second chance?'

Arne thought it depended on what else she might have got up to. There was something about a sound file that needed examining, among other things.

'But she has the potential to be a very talented investigator, you can't take that away from her,' he conceded.

The twins arrived and the ten minutes their parents had agreed would be long enough for a first meeting with Louise quickly turned into an hour. She took over as soon as the boys got there and in a way that didn't seem in the least bossy or affected. First she introduced them to their new room, saying that, yes, they would have to share because she and their dad couldn't afford a bigger place, it was just the way it was. But she would leave her computer in there, so they could play games on it. She had a thirty-six-inch monitor and a super-fast, multi-core processor, but if they wanted to play the really great games, they would have to invest in a new video card. She would pay half, and they would have to split the difference between them. It was a serious matter and they negotiated while Arne Pedersen listened in happily: 'Then you'd better get yourself a paper round, mate. After all, you're ten years old, aren't you?' And later: 'Tough, that's just the way it is.'

Afterwards they played their own version of squash in the living room. She had brought four small rackets and a bouncy rubber ball in her bag. Everyone was desperate to win, and the competition was fierce. Louise trash-talked the kids as best she could to get the psychological upper hand: *losers, losers, I can't believe how bad you are*, and they gave as good as they got, calling her a *basic bitch* – God knows where they had learned that – and *loser Louise*. It was a draw by the time Arne sent the ball through the living-room window, shards of glass exploding outwards. The boys and Louise agreed: he would have to buy the flat now.

Arne was on top of the world when his boys finally went home and he made no attempt to hide it.

Louise told him, 'I've always been good with kids, especially boys. Right, let's have a shower, I'm sweating like a pig. And then I want you, for the first time in our new home.'

'And what about practicalities such as a towel?'

'It's in my bag, now come on.'

Afterwards they sat like they had before on the floor with their backs against the wall, still naked. He looked at her.

'You're so beautiful.'

She pinched his belly.

'Thank you, fatso.'

A little later she said: 'God, I feel good now. I knew it!'

'Knew what?'

'That if I didn't tell anyone all the stuff Pauline told me about Bosnia, about those poor militia soldiers and the cruise missiles, about Irene Gallagher, Jelena Khrobic and Bjørn Lauritzen – by the way, did you know that his nickname was The Crazy Pole? – but anyway, if I kept my mouth shut about all of it and kept trusting that you police officers would find out the truth eventually, something good would also happen to me, something really wonderful. I've felt that ever since Pauline died. It's like that with me sometimes and I'm hardly ever wrong.'

She kissed him for a long time and he returned her kisses. Afterwards he sat lost in his own thoughts for a while before saying quietly: 'Louise, what did you just say?'

CHAPTER 73

Her parents had been saving for years and she and her big brother had been looking forward to it for just as long.

It would be Jelena Khrobic's first visit abroad, with the exception of a school trip to Flensburg in Germany, which turned out to look just like Randers and where it had rained the whole time. The morning the family left the sun was shining brightly and Randers High Street was being decorated for that evening's street party. The image of four big men in blue council uniforms with their beer guts and confident movements as they carried white flagpoles from the truck to the holes in the street, where they erected them in unison, burned itself on her mind, and she would often remember it in the eleven years that would pass before she came home again. For her it became an image of Denmark itself.

They went by coach, it was cheaper. Hamburg, Berlin, Prague, Vienna, Zagreb, Tuzla – a string of exciting cities, foreign landscapes, languages she didn't understand, different food. She took it all in and couldn't wait to tell her friends back home in Denmark. From Tuzla they drove to Bratunac, their final destination, where her grandparents lived. Along the way they passed many soldiers, and her parents started to worry. In Denmark they had discussed at length whether the trip was safe, but other Bosnians had visited their homeland despite the unrest, and they reported that if you didn't get involved or court trouble, there was no danger. Besides once they got to the village, they would be safe. Her parents were born and bred there, they had gone to school with both Serbs and Croats, and they still had many friends among both communities. Nothing bad would happen in Bratunac.

They had brought presents for her grandparents, trinkets that were warmly received, and her grandmother took Jelena to the market. There would be a wedding in a week, one of her cousins was getting married, and the women were busy with the preparations. Jelena

Khrobic helped them. Then, one night, war came to Bratunac: two Muslim families were burned to death in their homes. The next day another of her cousins and a handful of other young men caught a Serbian teacher. They hung him from a window while his wife and daughters screamed and pleaded with them to spare his life. The wedding was cancelled, hatred exploded, everyone was terrified.

Jelena Khrobic paused. She reached into the pram and adjusted the duvet around her daughter, who was asleep with her dummy hanging half out of her mouth. She removed the dummy and put it in her pocket. The Countess took the opportunity to get her bearings. They were walking along Bistrup Hegn, an area north of Copenhagen, which she knew very well, although she hadn't been here for years. She glanced furtively at Jelena Khrobic as if it would be wrong to stare at her directly.

She was a petite woman, with slim hips and shoulders, small breasts and quick movements, which reminded the Countess of a bird pecking at seeds. Her nose was big and slightly curved, as is often seen in women from the Balkans, her eyes were deep-set and dark, her features fine. Her long black hair had been put up in a messy bun with a silver hair clip. Her voice was bright and a little mournful, as though she were explaining why she was late for a meeting with a girlfriend.

They had escaped to Srebrenica. *Sigurna zona, slobodna zona, tampon zonaalle* – the country inside the country, the safe zones, everyone was talking about the safe zones, and Srebrenica was a safe zone. There the UN would guarantee their safety, the Dutch soldiers would protect them. Two days later the Serbian Army took control of the city. She, her brother and parents were herded into a factory hall along with dozens of other Muslim families. Shortly afterwards the soldiers came for her brother and father. She never saw them again. She and her mother slept in the factory hall, huddled together on the hard concrete floor. The girl was hungry, but didn't want to ask about food. Or about her father or brother because what could her mother say or do?

The next morning a handful of men arrived and selected some of the women, fifteen or twenty of them, who were loaded onto two trucks. She and her mother went in one of them. The men were unkempt, their uniforms casually cobbled together, some didn't even have one and they were even more terrifying than the soldiers from the day before. They drove for an hour until they reached an empty farmhouse by a forest where more men of the same kind were waiting.

She was thrown on a table and the men took turns raping her. Other men restrained her mother, who was screaming and struggling. Afterwards it was her mother's turn and when they were done with her, they killed her. The man who murdered her mother was a blacksmith. He had strong hands with bony fingers, gnarled from years of hard graft, and he strangled her with his bare hands just to show his friends that he could. The other men laughed, the blacksmith was always such a joker, then they attacked the rest of the women, and when they got bored with raping them, they started on them with their knives.

Bjørn Lauritzen had kicked in the door so hard that one hinge broke and it had dangled from the other. His tank was parked outside, a formidable reason not to fight back, and the men took fright. They had tried hiding the women in a back room and throwing a blanket over the worst of the blood, but they didn't have time to conceal everything before he burst among them in the living room. He roared like thunder for their *leader, boss, who?* Ten sets of fingers pointed at a middle-aged man, a chef from the Hotel Royal in Srebrenica, a family man with four children, a regular and pious churchgoer.

Bjørn Lauritzen gutted him and threw his intestines on the floor in front of him. If there had been even a spark of rebellion among the men, it had been extinguished now. He led them all out into the farmyard, beat up the youngest and sent him packing into the forest, then tied up the rest and let them sit on the cobblestones against the house wall with their eyes blinded with gravel.

Jelena Khrobic continued: 'He went into the house and spoke to the women several times, but they wouldn't come out, they were scared of him. It was stupid of them, but they didn't know any better. I stayed mostly in the farmyard. I didn't want to be in the living room because my mother was lying there.'

'Did you speak to Bjørn Lauritzen?'

'Yes, a little. He didn't say much, just a few words, but he found some underwear for me in the house, I don't know how, and he carried me behind the house, so I could wash myself. Walking hurt me, but he promised me that it would get better. Then he made a final attempt to get the other women to come outside, but they still wouldn't.'

On leaving the house, the tank turned around and drove across the men's legs at speed. It happened quickly, taking only a few seconds, after which the tank crawled down a short slope and disappeared into the forest. A little later the sound of the Copenhagen Town Hall bells tolled ominously in between the trees. The men in the farmyard were screaming, insane cries of pain as they rolled around as much as they could when all tied together. Shortly afterwards, Irene Gallagher pulled up in front of the farmhouse in her Jeep. The car had a Danish flag and Jelena Khrobic spoke Danish to her. She asked if the men were going to die and if someone was coming to help the women inside the house.

'Irene Gallagher called for an ambulance and told me it would arrive shortly. I was to go inside the house and wait, then everything would be OK again. She gave me her necklace. First she put it in the palm of my hand, but then she tied it around my neck. I lost it later on a plane, but it was sent to me in a parcel when I was ill in Glostrup Hospital. I don't know who sent it to me, but I always wear it now.'

She proudly showed the Countess the necklace – a gilded chain with a stylised silver butterfly pendant – then picked up her daughter. The baby had woken up. They found a bench and Jelena Khrobic breastfed her as she talked.

She had gone inside the house as she had been told and through the window she saw Irene Gallagher reverse the Jeep and drive off, only she'd forgotten her mobile phone. Jelena Khrobic had gone outside and shouted for her to stop, but the Jeep was already far away by then. Even so Jelena Khrobic had continued to follow it, slowly because she was in such pain. She didn't know why, only that she wanted to get away, away from the men and their unbearable screams, away from the terrible house – she hobbled along in the sunshine. Ten minutes later, the Serbs destroyed the house.

She saw their missiles fly across the treetops, one after the other, and thought that it was good that her mother was already dead. When she had been walking for some time, she reached a house made from sandbags and where there were Danish soldiers. Here she was given water and some white pills, which the soldiers insisted that she swallow. Later Bjørn Lauritzen arrived and all the soldiers and several refugees drove to Tuzla. For some of the journey she had sat inside the tank with Bjørn Lauritzen. He had kissed her on the head, called her a little princess and tried not to show her that he was crying.

The Countess asked: 'Did you tell him that the house had been bombed?'

'No, I lied to him. He didn't deserve to hear what had happened. I said that the women had walked towards Tuzla, which was where we were going. Many people walked there that day, but I was lucky, I got a lift. That's what I kept thinking in the next few weeks, that I was lucky, that I shouldn't complain. I had Bjørn and Ole and Irene, many people didn't have anyone, and if you went walking in the forest, you would always see young girls like me, who had hanged themselves with their scarves. You would come across them hanging there in the middle of all the green, but I didn't want to hang myself. I couldn't do that when they had done so much to save me.'

Jelena sat her daughter up in the pram with the duvet and pillows around her back and sides for support. She looked for the dummy. The Countess pointed to her pocket, and she smiled, sucked the dummy clean and popped it into the child's mouth. Then they continued along the pavement and Jelena picked up her story.

She had been kidnapped in an open street in Sarajevo. Two men had stepped up either side of her and dragged her into a car that had pulled up at the kerb out of nowhere. It happened so quickly she barely had time to think before the car was back on the road. A handkerchief was forced into her mouth and a black fabric bag was pulled over her head, after which they pushed her into the gap between the front seat and the back.

In a flat – she didn't know where it was – she was questioned all night by three Americans. About people she didn't know and events she had never heard about. In the early hours of the next morning, she refused to answer any more questions. The three men discussed her fate as if she weren't even present. The two younger ones weren't keen to take the next step, mainly because their captive was a woman, though that wasn't a rational argument. The oldest American was the most persuasive. Five weeks earlier, four US Marines had been killed in the town of Jbala, south of Baghdad. One of the victims was the man's younger brother, and the suicide bomber had been a woman so he didn't have a shred of sympathy for a little Arabic terrorist bitch who thought she could get away by denying everything. His arguments swayed the other two. On the morning of 4 January 2003, she was put on a special plane in Sarajevo Airport. The plane was a Gulfstream III jet, the number on the tail was N829MG. It was known as the Torture Jet.

She was interrogated immediately upon her arrival in Belarus. The questions she had been asked in vain in Sarajevo were now repeated in Minsk. Four men were present. They spoke English, Arabic, Russian and Belarusian, but only poor Bosnian, and she struggled to understand them. Then they beat her up, though that didn't improve her language skills. A German-speaking interrogation leader was summoned, and more beatings followed. She screamed and cried, they laughed and carried on. For two hours she was alternately beaten and interrogated. Eventually they stripped her naked and sexually assaulted her with their truncheons: the latter merely for fun. Then they threw her into a cell on a concrete floor, and there she spent many hours, shivering with cold, listening to the screams of her wretched fellow prisoners, in shock, unable to comprehend what had happened to her.

She was dragged off for another interrogation, this time with a Serbian-speaking leader, a small, friendly man with a neat moustache and icy eyes. She confessed to everything, signed anything they put in front of her and sobbed when she couldn't provide sensible answers to his many questions. She was suspended by her wrists, doused in water and electrodes were attached to her body. The pain exploded in her and sent her beyond hell, while her body jerked like a badly operated puppet on a string. She pleaded and begged with him to stop, made up pathetic stories to satisfy him. But it bought her only a short reprieve before her lies were quickly exposed. The nice man shook his head regretfully and increased the voltage. At one point her body gave up. She passed out, and they dragged her back to her cell.

This went on for weeks until the interrogation where her mind broke and she became incapable of communicating. A doctor was summoned. He examined her and threw up his hands while shaking his head: she was mentally gone, her torturers could save themselves the trouble, they were wasting their time.

The Countess forced herself to look at Jelena.

She exuded a childish joy, an artless gratitude to be walking here pushing her daughter in a rusty, second-hand pram. It was simple, it was enough. At the same time she recounted, precisely and in graphic detail, the incomprehensible horrors she had seen and experienced, evil without limits, and the Countess felt ashamed to be listening to it. It was difficult to reconcile the contrasting experiences as happening on the same planet.

The Countess looked away and found support in the road, an ordinary Danish residential road, reality and normality right in her field of vision, with its concrete slabs, kerbstones, tarmac, and look, a freshly painted red fire hydrant … It was just like when she was little and would hide her face behind a pillow when there was something scary on the television.

Jelena Khrobic told her how she had recovered at the Psychiatric Unit at Glostrup Hospital where many kind people had helped her. It had taken time, but it had happened. Then she got married and her surname changed from Khrobic to Sørensen. She had given birth to a daughter, soon she would have another child, and she was making plans for them all. If her children turned out to be bright and she could afford it, they could study, get an education, she hoped for that, and perhaps one day she would be able to work so they would have a bit more money. Her husband was often tired and she wanted to help him, it would be nice to be able to do that. She continued:

'I'm sure it'll happen soon. Perhaps next year, yes, next year I'll find a job.'

The Countess was convinced that she would.

'I bought you a present from Pauline.'

She had prepared a story about Pauline Berg having got married and moved far away to a place from where she couldn't write or make phone calls, but she was happy and sent Jelena her best wishes. The story made no sense at all, but Jelena Sørensen swallowed it whole. She was pleased for Pauline, her friend deserved a good life, it was nice to know that she was happy.

'Perhaps she'll come visit me one day.'

'Yes, perhaps.'

'I'll look forward to that.'

They sat down on another bench. Jelena Sørensen couldn't wait to open her present. She unwrapped it and was overjoyed. It was a magnificent Duplo Lego set for her daughter to play with when she was a little older, and an expensive bottle of purple Chanel nail polish for herself. How very nice of Pauline, especially since Jelena knew that her friend never had any money. She took off her necklace and gave it to the Countess.

'Please would you give this to Pauline? I'm sure you'll see her at some point.'

The Countess promised to do so. Then she steeled herself, she still had a few more questions.

'Jelena, did you ever tell Pauline about the Serbian missiles?'

'Yes, and the next time we met, we looked at pictures on her computer, and there we found them.'

'Did you also tell her that Irene Gallagher had forgotten her mobile phone when she drove away from the house?'

'I can hear that you know Pauline well. Yes, I did, and she was very interested in that. Pauline wants to understand everything, she's so clever.'

That left only one question for the Countess to ask.

'And you and Pauline want to find Bjørn Lauritzen?'

'Yes, we really do. He lives near Præstø, but we don't know exactly where. Pauline spoke to some people who know where everyone is if they own a mobile.'

'Does Bjørn Lauritzen have a mobile?'

'No, I don't think so, but Irene does, so when she calls him ... No, that doesn't make any sense. I don't really know. I think perhaps

Pauline could see where Irene was going in her car ... I think that was how it was.'

'So what did you do?'

'I called Irene and asked her if she would please give me Bjørn's address, but she said Bjørn was very busy.'

'When was that? Do you remember?'

'Yes, that's easy. It was the twentieth of July, the day before my husband's birthday.'

'So did you give up then?'

'No, Pauline spoke to her as well, but they had a row.'

'About what?'

'Pauline shouted that we would find Bjørn eventually, and that Irene could just wait. But I know why that is.'

'Why is that?'

'It's just because they don't know each other yet.'

CHAPTER 74

WEDNESDAY 24 NOVEMBER 2010, MINISTRY OF FINANCE

On Monday morning Konrad Simonsen had received a call from the National Police Commissioner who, somewhat overjoyed and clearly nervous, told his suspended Homicide Chief that he had good news.

According to the Commissioner's best and most competent assessment, the chances were high that Simonsen could return to work very soon, but a few things needed clarifying first and so he had been summoned to a meeting later that afternoon at the Commissioner's office with him and some representatives from the Ministry of Justice.

Konrad Simonsen had announced frostily that he would let them know when he was willing to meet and whom he wished to be present. The Commissioner had panicked and protested, he couldn't possibly convey that to the Justice Minister. Simonsen suggested that he should get his secretary to do it instead and had hung up.

Fifteen minutes later he had a call from an irate civil servant at the Ministry of Justice who wanted to know who on earth Konrad Simonsen thought he was. Simonsen shouted back that he was someone who didn't have time for a meeting right now. He was busy preparing for a press briefing on evidence he had uncovered in Bosnia. Then he slammed down the phone.

Another hour went by and he was starting to think that the Danish Central Administration really was losing its grip. Then the Permanent Secretary from the Ministry of Justice, no less, called him. He was smarmy, asking in saccharine tones how things were and when they could meet. Simonsen stuck to his guns: twice now he had given a simple and straightforward message to the country's most senior lawyers and yet people still didn't seem to understand. So he was going to make a third attempt and he would say it very slowly this time, seeing as it was so difficult to comprehend. He would tell them when and where he wanted to meet and who could be present. On this occasion he didn't hang up, he merely laid down the phone and smiled as *Detective Chief Superintendent* and *hello, are you there, DCS Simonsen* continued to be emitted from the handset for a remarkably long time.

After his rudeness he was left in peace for twenty-four hours, then Helmer Hammer paid him an unannounced visit. Hammer was in high spirits. Konrad Simonsen had put a bomb under all of Central Administration, not to mention the Ministry of Defence, which was dreading having to add another scandal to an already long list. In short, he had upset a lot of powerful people and made many more nervous, and he, Helmer Hammer, was pleading with him on bended knee, appealing to him for the sake of their friendship, to please be allowed to chair the meeting about which everyone was talking, but which – Hammer knew this perfectly well – had yet to be arranged. Please, he simply had to be there.

Konrad Simonsen walked right into the trap. He promised Hammer that he could indeed be the chairman, should one be needed. But he had forgotten that Hammer had handed in his resignation and would be leaving his position shortly. This left barely one working week in which to hold the meeting, which, excluding the weekend and days when Hammer was already busy, left them with very few options.

Hammer said: 'Right, let's make it tomorrow at one o'clock at the Ministry of Finance.'

He wanted to try to limit the number of participants to the absolute minimum. Was there anyone Konrad Simonsen wanted to invite? There were, at least three people and possibly four, he replied, if he could persuade the fourth person. So it would be Simonsen himself, the Countess and one or two special advisers.

'Why the Ministry of Finance?' he enquired.

Helmer Hammer grinned as he explained.

Konrad Simonsen had been discussed at the very heart of power. The government's powerful Coordination Committee had spent almost fifteen minutes debating the matter off the record, and the Prime Minister had told the Finance Minister – the government's strongman – that the matter must buried once and for all, and sooner rather than later. Those were his exact words, Helmer Hammer knew that with absolute certainty because he had taken the minutes himself, except that no one had minuted this point on the agenda as it wasn't even a point, but had in fact specifically been assigned as any other business because …

Here Konrad Simonsen had pressed his hands over his ears and refused to listen to any more.

The table had been laid with elegant silver coffee pots, delicious biscuits from artisan bakers – no cheap supermarket rubbish here – and the coffee was strong and served in genuine china cups with saucers and spoons that all bore the logo of the Ministry of Finance, who clearly didn't stoop to using mass-produced mugs, plastic or paper cups. As he sat down at the large, Finnish-designed conference table, Konrad Simonsen concluded that the Ministry's employees were clearly more dishonest than the rest of the population – why else put logos on both saucers and spoons? But he kept this observation to himself. He had promised the Countess he would be a good boy.

There would be ten people around the table. In addition to Simonsen and the Countess and their two special guests, the Ministry of Justice was represented by the Minister himself, who bravely, but typically for him, had turned up without any civil servants while the Ministry of Defence was represented by the Defence Chief and the head of FE, both in uniform, and its Permanent Secretary. There was also Helmer Hammer, and the Finance Minister was expected but had yet to appear.

The Defence Minister was conspicuous by his absence, but this was because the Finance Minister would rather he didn't attend. The Defence Minister was known to be a loose cannon – and would not be an asset in a situation that was messy enough as it was. The Finance Minister had therefore ordered the Defence Minister to be present, whereupon the Defence Minister had refused point-blank and was staying away in a fit of pique.

The participants drank coffee and waited for their host. The mood was unusually glum; only Helmer Hammer at the end of the table seemed on form, as was the Justice Minister, which was his natural state, almost regardless of what he was doing.

The Finance Minister arrived, greeted everyone with a wave, apologised for being late without explaining why and nodded to Helmer Hammer to open the meeting. Hammer began with a few perfectly phrased and uncontroversial pleasantries whereupon he handed over to the Countess. To most people's surprise, she continued in the same vein: in recent weeks the Homicide Department had been made aware of a series of events so disturbing in nature that it had no other option but to convene this unconventional meeting, to receive advice from on high on how to handle the information in question. She continued like this for a few minutes, after which she changed tack completely.

Her voice sharpened as she recounted events in Bosnia in 1995. She described how these had interfered with the police investigation into the canal boat killings. When this was done, she addressed the FE chief directly and produced one strongly convincing document after another to support her allegations. Original American surveillance photographs of Bosnia dated from 14 July 1995; a list of names of murdered Muslim women and another with the names of murdered Serbian militia soldiers; a printout of Irene Gallagher's communications with the American aircraft carrier, the *USS Theodore Roosevelt*, on 13 July 1995, when she requested that they should launch cruise missiles at the coordinates provided; a handful of photographs of broken bone as well as an eyewitness account from a woman who had witnessed the whole event, a witness to whom she would return.

She concluded: 'There is much more to come. Later I'll review the main points of the Homicide Department's report into how FE systematically sabotaged our investigation for the purpose of having Colonel Irene Gallagher acquitted, which, as you all know, they successfully achieved, but let's pause here for now.'

The Finance Minister looked at the Defence Chief and said coolly:

'I think this requires a response.'

But the Justice Minister was quicker.

'If this leads to any demand that Irene Gallagher be tried again, then forget it. Quite simply, that's not within our power, and our legal advisers say – I've just been told this again today – that no fresh charges will be brought against her.'

The Countess declared with a dark expression that she agreed, that she already knew and had accepted this, no matter how hard it was to stomach.

Then it was the turn of the FE chief, and he was ice cold. He strongly rejected any accusations that FE would deliberately sabotage court cases or murder investigations. Furthermore he didn't care for frivolous accusations against Irene Gallagher; the woman had just been acquitted and, to the best of his knowledge, this was because she was innocent. But perhaps the Homicide Department was advocating kangaroo courts, and convicting people on the strength of rumours and conjecture?

'The Homicide Department, completely outside its remit, has wasted taxpayers' money on unearthing material that – whether or not it is true – cannot be used in evidence. Such material is irrelevant in this case because it's classified. If it were published, which seems to be your thinly veiled threat, it would compromise national security. And I won't hesitate to point out that certain … foreign powers … have made clear in advance their attitude to the events in question becoming public knowledge. If this were to happen, it would go down very badly.'

He addressed the Countess directly, as she had earlier addressed him.

'Any attempt to publish your material, be it in the newspapers, television or on the Internet, will be met by an immediate court order.'

The Countess smiled broadly at him, then she nodded to the young woman by her side, who had yet to speak. She now leaned forward and studied the FE chief closely before beginning to speak calmly in Swedish.

'I'm Alva Axelsson from *Dagens Nyheter*. And my editor-in-chief has asked me to tell you that she doesn't give a damn about Danish court orders.'

She tried to say *court order* in Danish. Her Swedish accent was too strong, which made the words sound amusing, but no one around the table doubted how serious she was. The FE chief fell silent.

The Finance Minister said forbiddingly, 'What do you want, Detective Chief Superintendent? Because I'm guessing that if you really want to, you can persuade our Swedish friend to think twice.'

But Konrad Simonsen merely shook his head as though he found it inconvenient to be addressed, so it was the Countess who replied for him.

'To begin with, we want you to listen to what happened to a young woman called Jelena Khrobic.'

This was the psychiatrist's cue. He rose, positioned himself just behind Helmer Hammer and quietly told them the story of Jelena Khrobic, including the details of her treatment in Minsk in 2003. It was difficult to hear it all, and frankly unpleasant. Afterwards, there was complete silence until Helmer Hammer addressed the Countess.

'I presume that you have some wishes – financial, administrative, human resources – and now is the time to discuss them.'

The Defence Chief straightened up in his chair.

'What do you mean, human resources?'

The National Police Commissioner added: 'I only followed orders. That can't possibly be wrong.'

Helmer Hammer explained to them that, in his experience, there were two things that became easily expendable whenever top politicians were in trouble: one was money, the other was civil servants. They could spend the former and sack the latter. He carried on in the same light vein.

'Besides, it's always healthy to stir the pot every now and then, let a few heads or five roll … It keeps everyone else on their toes, so to speak.'

Here the Finance Minister interrupted him.

'I haven't got time for this nonsense, Helmer. Some other time, yes, but not now. Countess?'

She thought that he must have been well briefed for this meeting, given that he knew her nickname. She started on her list of demands, pretty much without anyone objecting.

Compensation to Jelena Khrobic. The Countess suggested ten thousand tax-free kroner per month for the rest of her life, plus a generous trust to fund her children's education. She was sure that FE could come up with a clever and convincing story about why Jelena Khrobic would be getting the money. After all, they were so imaginative. The Finance Minister didn't even blink, *Granted. Go on.*

Furthermore, the Countess suggested that Denmark should take responsibility for running the holiday park, which the USA had given … The Finance Minister interrupted her here and said he would look on that favourably.

She asked suspiciously: 'Look at favourably?'

Helmer Hammer translated, it meant yes, and so she continued.

Konrad Simonsen would obviously be reinstated with immediate effect, but given the stress he had been subjected to, she felt that another three weeks of holiday seemed only fair. All eyes turned to the National Police Commissioner, who cringed. He didn't like it. After he had agonised over the request for a while the Justice Minister went over his head with a *yes, of course, and for you too.*

The Countess thanked him and continued speaking

'We would also like your permission to ... work with PET, shall we say, on a specific matter, which I would prefer not to discuss here. But what I mean is: get their help with a few things.'

The Justice Minister laughed.

'You're already getting our help. I'm not completely ignorant of what happens behind the scenes, but fine, now I'm making it official. Can we do anything else for you?'

The FE chief pointed rudely at Simonsen and the Countess, and asked suspiciously: 'How can we be sure that you won't publish your—'

He got no further before the Finance Minister vented his suppressed rage.

'*We?* Tell me, have you lost your mind? There's no *we* as far as you're concerned. You do your job, and you leave the big questions to me and the Justice Minister. I've never heard such arrogance, it's getting worse and worse ...'

The FE chief turned bright red, but controlled his anger, even when the Justice Minister explained for his benefit: 'We trust the Homicide Department because we have no other choice.'

The meeting was over, there was nothing more to discuss. Helmer Hammer asked the Countess – out of courtesy – if she had anything to add. She shook her head, but passed the question respectfully to her husband, to give him the opportunity to respond.

Simonsen had said very little during the meeting. The Countess had been the voice of the Homicide Department and when she had tried to involve him, he had deflected her request with a curt *yes, that's fine,* or similar. It was a habit he had acquired in recent years. His gaze would grow distant, and she was starting to doubt whether he was fully aware of what was going on around him. It certainly didn't seem like it when he sat like this, staring blindly into space, as if he could see something far away, something that nobody else could. Usually the Countess would leave him to his own devices until he snapped out of it, but it made her uncomfortable, especially in situations like this when other people were present.

The participants had started gathering up their papers, when Simonsen suddenly began speaking.

He talked about visiting the veterans on Vesterbro, and the terrible state they were in. Their forgotten lives, the repeated failures of the authorities, how injustice and unfairness were the norm rather than the exception for them, the price of war, a price that Denmark wasn't willing to pay. The others listened only out of politeness and it began to get embarrassing. What was the point of this sentimental tosh, given they had already reached agreement? Simonsen carried on regardless. He had a vision.

'Imagine if it furthered your Army or Ministry of Defence career if you volunteered in various ex-servicemen's organisations or helped individual veterans. And also the reverse: that it would harm your career prospects if you didn't. Imagine if senior management led by example. That would be wonderful and there are so many ways to help ex-servicemen's clubs.'

Here Simonsen reeled off many examples: they were always short of people in the kitchen; every day they needed dozens of things, which the clubs had to go cap in hand to get, everything from lavatory paper to chalk for the pool table; help with filling in forms and applications for physical or mental health support for veterans; there was outreach work, for which there was rarely time, and many, many other important things; odd jobs, little things, yes, but when added together they formed a huge void in the assistance offered to ex-servicemen.

Nevertheless, these things weren't the real issue, which was that such massive and personal – he repeated the word *personal* – support from the Army would mean that the veterans wouldn't be forgotten as they were now in the political process when money was being allocated.

It really had become embarrassing. What could they say? The Defence Chief muttered half-heartedly that it sounded like an excellent idea, as did the FE chief – yawning as he said it – and even the Permanent Secretary nodded vaguely, *definitely, definitely, an interesting thought, fine and caring.*

Out of the blue, Simonsen struck. He wasn't dithering in the slightest, when he practically shouted at them: 'I'm delighted that's what you think. By the way, tell me – how many hours of therapy does it take to pay for one armoured personnel carrier, just roughly?'

The Defence Chief shook his head.

'Who knows?'

'Well, not you clearly. So tell me instead, which is more expensive: a machine gun or a prosthetic leg, if both are of the finest, most up-to-date design?'

Again the Finance Minister turned out to be the quickest on the uptake. He said tentatively: 'Now that might be an idea. An offer to military personnel to participate in a voluntary befriending programme for ex-servicemen … voluntary, as in *do it*. Maybe the project isn't so foolish after all, but it must be focused. Besides, I'm sure the idea would go down well with the population in general, which would be no bad thing. Perhaps we should suggest the forming of a small committee at the next government meeting?'

The latter was addressed to the Justice Minister, who had no objections. Konrad Simonsen pointed to the Finance Minister.

'Don't bury it, give me a timetable that you'll personally vouch for. Remember that setting a good example goes all the way up to the top, no exceptions! And more importantly, no more fine speeches. We've heard enough of those. Volunteer in the kitchen, cook the dinner and then help clear up afterwards.'

Helmer Hammer said: 'Watch it, Simon. You're in danger of overreaching yourself.'

The Finance Minister, however, accepted the demand.

'Give us eight months, these things take time. We need the backing of the Opposition or it won't be sustainable. Besides, it must be undertaken in partnership with senior military management and the relevant trade unions or it'll be just window dressing.

'But when we have an actual proposal, I'll invite you to a meeting where we can discuss it. I won't give you a formal right to object, let alone the right to veto, but I'll keep my promise, and if you don't like the result, you can always yell at me later.'

EPILOGUE

WEDNESDAY I DECEMBER 2010, PACIFIC OCEAN
19°40's 169°04'w

The man was now groaning at regular intervals. He would let out agonised short cries as though trying not to trouble the other passengers, but was nevertheless in so much pain that he could no longer control himself.

The Countess checked her watch. She had set it to local time when they took off from Vancouver. Now it was coming up to four o'clock for the second time on this trip. The next fifteen minutes were the ones she had been looking forward to and had spent ten days planning with PET.

She took a sip from a water bottle and saw to her satisfaction that the woman sitting next to her in the middle seat had taken off her sleep mask and was closely following events at the front of the plane. Irene Gallagher had been asleep for most of the journey so she and the Countess hadn't spoken, merely nodded politely to one another on the few occasions when practical necessity required it, such as three hours earlier when Irene Gallagher had got up to go to the lavatory. Now the Countess turned to her.

'Good morning.'

Irene Gallagher looked confused.

'You're Danish?'

The Countess confirmed this, born and bred, then she said: 'I've read that in the trenches during the First World War, soldiers would use quinine to simulate illness. It made them look as if they were at death's door, even though there was nothing wrong with them.

Today we have other and better methods. I don't know what our friend consumed, but he certainly looked nigh unto death when the cabin crew last checked up on him. Pity you missed that. You were asleep.'

'Who the hell are you?'

'I'm someone who has literally travelled halfway around the world to watch what's about to happen. And, frankly, I'm as excited as a child at Christmas. Now pay attention. Our sick friend has practised, he's really very good, but then again, he did train at Dramaten in Stockholm. His name is Oskar Svensson, by the way.'

The man's moaning increased; the intervals between the onslaughts of pain seemed to be growing shorter. Most of the other passengers were now awake and anxiously following events. It was dark outside, daybreak was still some hours away.

'We were rather baffled by your choice of flight connections: Copenhagen–London, London–Montréal, Montréal–Vancouver and finally Vancouver–Auckland. It's something of a detour when you could just have gone Copenhagen–London–Sydney–Wellington. But I think we've solved the riddle: by taking this route you made sure you were travelling exclusively over Danish, British or Canadian territory or airspace – three countries with a legal system that wouldn't extradite you to the USA without concrete evidence of serious crime. Any other route would be risky for you. You're a careful woman who takes everything into consideration, I must say. Or pretty much everything.'

Irene Gallagher said nothing. She merely glowered at the Countess, but she was visibly nervous. The Countess carried on.

'The truth is that you were never scared of the CIA or FE or your dirty tricks in Bosnia in 1995 being made public; you were only scared of Bjørn Lauritzen, or rather that he would find out what you did to those poor women in that house in Ljubicevac in Bosnia, because if he did he would definitely kill you, regardless of your friendship or your old love affair, even if it meant his chasing you to the ends of the earth.

'And that's why Pauline Berg and Jelena Khrobic proved to be a lethal combination. Individually they weren't a threat to you. As long as she was alone, Pauline would never, even if she eventually found Bjørn Lauritzen, be able to convince him that you were behind the launch of three cruise missiles. Nor was Jelena Khrobic a problem on her own. She believed the missiles were Serbian, it was her chosen truth, and besides, she thought you were her friend.

'So, like I said: on their own they weren't a problem, but together – now that was a whole other ball-game. Together they would be able to convince Bjørn Lauritzen of the truth, which would be a big problem for you. A problem you couldn't solve simply by killing Lauritzen, because Jonas Ziegler and Pauline Berg would then put two and two together and realise what you had done. That wasn't a risk you could afford to take, so you made Ziegler arrange a meeting with Pauline, who chose the canal boat trip. It was something she often did, it was her way of relaxing. We know the rest.'

Irene Gallagher hissed: 'Curiosity killed the cat.'

The Countess let out a forced laugh and said, 'If you're referring to Pauline's death and are saying it to intimidate me, then it won't work. But speaking of curiosity: if there had been not four, but *twenty-four* adults in that canal boat, was Bjørn Lauritzen supposed to kill them all?'

'The other passengers and the crew were meant to jump overboard, but they didn't, the idiots. They paid the price for that.'

The sick man let out his first proper scream. Shortly afterwards the captain made an announcement asking for any doctors among the passengers to come forward. A small man in his sixties rushed up the aisle to the front of the plane. As he passed the Countess, she remarked to Irene Gallagher:

'Now that was a stroke of luck. And he's a real doctor too. His name is Allen Stirling and he heads the Renal Surgery Unit at the Queen Elizabeth Hospital in Birmingham, so he's more than competent to diagnose the acute appendicitis from which our excellent Swedish actor is suffering. It's a dangerous business, a ruptured appendix; without surgery it will leak into the abdominal cavity and the patient might die, which I'm sure is what Mr Stirling is explaining to the captain as we speak.'

'You evil bitch, I'll kill you!'

The Countess was unperturbed.

'I don't think so. Close combat was never your strong point, whereas I used to be rather good at it. Besides, I brought along the young man sitting on your other side. Just in case, as they say.'

Irene Gallagher turned her head. Her fellow passenger in the window seat, a well-proportioned young man, had also woken up. He looked at her coldly without saying anything.

The captain made another announcement over the public address system. In ten minutes the plane would make an emergency stop in Pago Pago Airport as a passenger had been taken ill. It would mean an hour's delay to their estimated arrival time at Auckland.

The Countess placed her hand on Irene Gallagher's forearm, and gloated when she furiously shrugged it off.

'Now you're frantically wondering: Pago Pago, where is that? And I'll tell you shortly, but first I have something for you.'

She took a piece of jewellery from her pocket, a necklace, and laid it in Irene Gallagher's lap.

'This is yours, I believe. It's rather tasteless, in my opinion. But back to Pago Pago. It's the capital of Samoa, or rather, the capital of *American* Samoa, but you've probably already guessed that. So in five minutes' time you'll be under American jurisdiction, and I've a strong suspicion the authorities would like a word with you, seeing as you've dropped in.'

Irene Gallagher had started to shake. The muscle above her right eye was twitching. The Countess consoled her:

'Don't be like that. You live, you die, you win some, you lose some, you go on holiday – that's what I'm about to do – you spend the rest of your life in jail – that's what'll happen to you – it's swings and roundabouts for all of us. But you have to take the rough with the smooth, don't you? I know from Christoffer Brinch that's your philosophy.

'By the way, he sends you his warmest regards, as do the Copenhagen Homicide Department.'

The Countess spent a long time watching Irene Gallagher as two tall marines frogmarched her across the runway towards the car park at the end of the airport terminal. It was still dark, but the area was well lit. Then the Countess turned her attention to her husband. Konrad Simonsen had been flown from Copenhagen by a special plane belonging to the US Navy and had landed only fifteen minutes earlier. She kissed him and reproached him for not wearing a coat. It was a cold night.

Simon asked: 'How was your trip?'

'The first sixteen hours were dull, the last ten minutes were great. Is my luggage here yet? And where do I collect it?'

John Tyler, who was standing on the other side of Simonsen, told her that her luggage had been unloaded, but that she should forget all about practical matters for the next two weeks. She and her husband were guests of the American government, which meant they should think only of enjoying themselves.

'This is a beautiful island,' he continued. 'Wait until it gets light – the tourist brochures aren't lying, it really is a small tropical paradise.

'We'll drive to the east coast – it's only ten kilometres – where Deirdre is waiting with breakfast. We'll have grilled lobster for lunch. You'll have your own house, of course, it's a few hundred metres from ours, and I assume you would like to unpack and maybe have a nap after breakfast, but that's entirely up to you.'

He led them towards the area into which the soldiers had disappeared with Irene Gallagher. The Countess asked curiously: 'There's a Deirdre Tyler?'

His *yes* was almost *no*. There was a small detail they just needed to sort out first.

His words were mostly aimed at the Countess, but Simonsen paid close attention. A detail, excellent, he was good at those.

'And about the name Tyler, not to mention John ... I can't totally vouch for either of them,' the American admitted.

NOTE ON THE AUTHORS

Lotte and Søren Hammer are siblings from Denmark. Younger sister Lotte worked as a nurse after finishing her training in 1977 and her brother Søren was a trained teacher and a lecturer at the Copenhagen University College of Engineering. After Søren moved into the house where Lotte lived with her family in 2004, they began writing crime novels together. To date, they have written five books in this series: *The Hanging, The Girl in the Ice, The Vanished, The Lake* and *The Night Ferry.*

NOTE ON THE TRANSLATOR

Charlotte Barslund translates Scandinavian novels and plays.

Recent novels translated: *The Lake* by Lotte & Søren Hammer, *A House in Norway* by Vigdis Hjorth, *The Owl Always Hunts at Night* and *I'm Travelling Alone* by Samuel Bjork, *Fatal Crossing* by Lone Theils, the *Wildwitch* series by Lene Kaaberbøl, *A Fairy Tale* by Jonas T. Bengtsson, *The Son* by Jo Nesbo, *The Arc of the Swallow* and *The Dinosaur Feather* by Sissel-Jo Gazan, *Retribution*, *Trophy* and *When the Dead Awaken* by Steffen Jacobsen, *Machine* and *The Brummstein* by Peter Adolphsen, and *Pierced*, *Burned* and *Scarred* by Thomas Enger.